The New Jedi Order series boldly ventures into uncharted Star Wars territory, bringing an element of dark tragedy and suspense into the adventures of Luke Skywalker, Han Solo, Leia Organa Solo, and the other legendary figures of that galaxy far, far away. Now veteran Star Wars author Kathy Tyers continues the epic struggle between good and evil as the New Republic, led by the battered but still unbroken Jedi, braces for the next onslaught of its merciless alien foe. . . .

By Kathy Tyers

FIREBIRD
FUSION FIRE
CRYSTAL WITNESS
SHIVERING WORLD
STAR WARS: THE TRUCE AT BAKURA
ONE MIND'S EYE
CROWN OF FIRE

STAR WARS

THE NEW JEDI ORDER

BALANCE POINT

KATHY TYERS

A Del Rey® Book

THE BALLANTINE PUBLISHING GROUP • NEW YORK

A Del Rey® Book
Published by The Ballantine Publishing Group

www.starwars.com
www.starwarskids.com
www.randomhouse.com/delrey/

ISBN 0-345-42858-7

Manufactured in the United States of America

First Edition: July 2001

10 9 8 7 6 5 4 3 2 1

Thank you!

To George Lucas first, of course.

Then to Martha Millard, Scott Bach, Shelly Shapiro, Sue Rostoni, Allan Kausch, and Lucy Autrey Wilson for professional guidance; to all of the *Star Wars* authors who keep expanding this universe, especially James Luceno, Michael Stackpole, R. A. Salvatore, Timothy Zahn, Aaron Allston, Troy Denning, Dan Wallace, and Bill Smith; to Robert Flaherty, Cheryl Petersen, and Matthew Tyers for specialized assistance; and to Mark Tyers, who kept me upright when it would've been easy to collapse.

STAR WARS: THE NOVELS

— What Happened When?

10–0 YEARS BEFORE
STAR WARS: A New Hope

THE HAN SOLO TRILOGY:
The Paradise Snare
The Hutt Gambit
Rebel Dawn

APPROX. 5–2 YRS. BEFORE
STAR WARS: A New Hope

THE ADVENTURES OF LANDO CALRISSIAN:
Lando Calrissian and the Mindharp of Sharu
Lando Calrissian and the Flamewind of Oseon
Lando Calrissian and the Starcave of ThonBoka

THE HAN SOLO ADVENTURES:
Han Solo at Stars' End
Han Solo's Revenge
Han Solo and the Lost Legacy

STAR WARS
Episode IV:
A New Hope

0–3 YEARS AFTER
STAR WARS: A New Hope

Tales from the Mos Eisley Cantina
Splinter of the Mind's Eye

8 YEARS AFTER
STAR WARS: A New Hope

The Courtship of Princess Leia

9 YEARS AFTER
STAR WARS: A New Hope

X-Wing Isard's Revenge
THE THRAWN TRILOGY:
Heir to the Empire
Dark Force Rising
The Last Command

11 YEARS AFTER
STAR WARS: A New Hope

THE JEDI ACADEMY TRILOGY:
Jedi Search
Dark Apprentice
Champions of the Force
I, Jedi

12–13 YEARS AFTER
STAR WARS: A New Hope

Children of the Jedi
Darksaber
Planet of Twilight
X-Wing: Starfighters of Adumar

19 YEARS AFTER
STAR WARS: A New Hope

THE HAND OF THRAWN DUOLOGY:
Specter of the Past
Vision of the Future

22 YEARS AFTER
STAR WARS: A New Hope

JUNIOR JEDI KNIGHTS:
The Golden Globe
Lyric's World
Promises
Anakin's Quest
Vader's Fortress
Kenobi's Blade

23–24 YEARS AFTER
STAR WARS: A New Hope

YOUNG JEDI KNIGHTS:
Heirs of the Force
Shadow Academy
The Lost Ones
Lightsabers
The Darkest Knight
Jedi Under Siege
Shards of Alderaan
Diversity Alliance
Delusions of Grandeur
Jedi Bounty
The Emperor's Plague
Return to Ord Mantell
Trouble on Cloud City
Crisis at Crystal Reef

25–30 YEARS AFTER
STAR WARS: A New Hope

THE NEW JEDI ORDER:
Vector Prime
Dark Tide I: Onslaught
Dark Tide II: Ruin
Agents of Chaos I:
Hero's Trial
Agents of Chaos II:
Jedi Eclipse
Balance Point

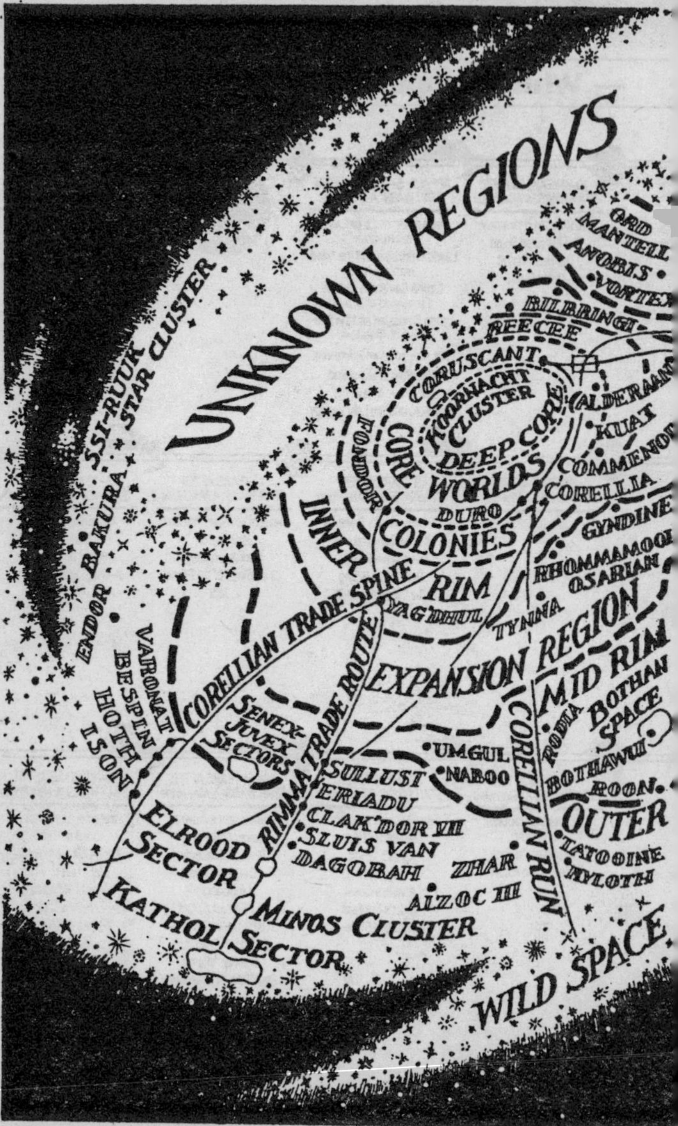
UNKNOWN REGIONS
SSI-RUUK STAR CLUSTER
BAKURA
ENDOR
VAIRONAT
BESPIN
HOTH
ISON
ORD MANTELL
ANOBIS
BILBRINGI
REECEE
CORUSCANT
KOORNACHT CLUSTER
DEEP CORE
FONDOR
CORE
WORLDS
KUAT
CORELLIA
GYNDINE
DURO
INNER
COLONIES
RIM
YAG'DHUL
OSARIAN
TYNNA
CORELLIAN TRADE SPINE
EXPANSION REGION
MID RIM
RODIA
BOTHAN SPACE
BOTHAWUI
SENEX-JUVEX SECTORS
RIMMA TRADE ROUTE
UMGUL
NABOO
SULLUST
ERIADU
CLAK'DOR VII
SLUIS VAN
DAGOBAH
ZHAR
AIZOC III
CORELLIAN RUN
ROON
OUTER
TATOOINE
RYLOTH
ELROOD SECTOR
KATHOL SECTOR
MINOS CLUSTER
WILD SPACE

UNKNOWN REGIONS
NIRAUAN
ORD
MANTEL
VORTE
BILBRINGI
CORUSCANT
KOORNACHT CLUSTER
DEEP CORE
CORE WORLDS
FONDOR
KUAT
COMMENO
CORELLIA
DURO
COLONIES
GYNDINE
INNER
RIM
TYNNA
EXPANSION REGION
MID RIM
BOTHAN
SPACE
BOTHAWUI
OUTER
CORELLIAN TRADE SPINE
RIMMA TRADE ROUTE
CORELLIAN RUN
SULLUST
NABOO
SSI-RUUK STAR CLUSTER
BAKURA
ENDOR
BESPIN
HOTH
ELROOD SECTOR
DAGOBAH
MINOS CLUSTER
KATHOL SECTOR
WILD SPACE

DRAMATIS PERSONAE

Anakin Solo; Jedi Knight (male human)
C-3PO; protocol droid
Darez Wuht; admiral (male Duros)
Droma; spacer (male Ryn)
Han Solo; captain, *Millennium Falcon* (male human)
Jacen Solo; Jedi Knight (male human)
Jaina Solo; Jedi Knight (female human)
Leia Organa Solo; New Republic ambassador (female human)
Luke Skywalker; Jedi Master (male human)
Mara Jade Skywalker; Jedi Master (female human)
Mezza; refugee (female Ryn)
Nom Anor; executor (male Yuuzhan Vong)
R2-D2; astromech droid
Randa Besadii Diori; refugee (male Hutt)
Romany; refugee (male Ryn)
Tsavong Lah; warmaster (male Yuuzhan Vong)
Viqi Shesh; senator (female human)

They appeared without warning from beyond the edge of galactic space: a warrior race called the Yuuzhan Vong, armed with surprise, treachery, and a bizarre organic technology that proved a match—too often more than a match—for the New Republic and its allies. Even the Jedi, under the leadership of Luke Skywalker, found themselves thrown on the defensive, deprived of their greatest strength. For somehow, inexplicably, the Yuuzhan Vong seemed to be utterly devoid of the Force.

The first strike caught the New Republic unawares, as it struggled to deal with rebellion sown by Yuuzhan Vong spy Nom Anor and his agents. With the New Republic force thus occupied, the alien advance fleet launched their first assault, which destroyed several worlds and killed countless beings—among them the Wookiee Chewbacca, loyal friend and partner to Han Solo.

During a brave attempt to contact and make peace with the enemy, Senator Elegos A'Kla was murdered by Yuuzhan Vong commander Shedao Shai, who delivered the body to Elegos's close friend, Jedi Corran Horn. Horn then challenged Shai to a duel—the prize being the planet Ithor. Horn bested Shai, but the Yuuzan Vong destroyed Ithor nonetheless.

The New Republic government unraveled a little more with each setback. Soon the Jedi Knights splintered under the strain. Chafing under what some perceived as Luke's excessive caution, a renegade group of Jedi under the leadership of Kyp Durron advocated using every available resource to defeat the Yuuzhan Vong—including unbridled aggression, which could lead only to the dark side. The philosophical dispute drove a wedge between the Solo brothers, Jacen and Anakin, while sister Jaina focused instead on her new role as a pilot with the elite Rogue Squadron.

Consumed with guilt for failing to save Chewbacca, Han Solo turned away from his family, seeking expiation in action—and foiled a Yuuzhan Vong plot to eliminate the Jedi. Han returned with what seemed to be an antidote to the debilitating illness Mara Jade Skywalker endured. But not even that victory could erase the loss of his dearest friend—or mend his marriage to Leia.

Leia, too, was beset with guilt. By disregarding a vision of the future, Leia feared she had condemned the Hapan fleet to ruin at Fondor. A pitched battle at the shipyards was shattered by a weapon of uncontrollable destructive power fired from Centerpoint Station—a weapon armed by her younger son, Anakin.

Now, as the Yuuzhan Vong tighten their noose and press inward toward Coruscant and victory, Luke and Mara, Han and Leia and their children, as well as the New Republic itself, must find the balance they have lost—before there is nothing left to lose.

PROLOGUE

Lieutenant Jaina Solo rolled her X-wing fighter up on its port S-foil and shoved her throttle forward. A seed-shaped Yuuzhan Vong coralskipper had been harrying her wingmate. As it went evasive, a minuscule black hole appeared just off its tail and gulped down every splinter of laser energy Jaina poured into it.

She matched her X-wing's speed to the skip's and pursued. There'd been dozens of battles since Colonel Gavin Darklighter invited her to join Rogue Squadron. Her pride hadn't faded, but the thrill sure had. Too many midnight scrambles. Too much death, too little sleep.

But I'm in Rogue Squadron, she reflected, feathering her throttle, *not because of who my parents are, and not because the Force is strong in my family.*

But based on her own piloting skills. Besides, Rogue Squadron ought to include at least one Jedi Knight.

The skip she was chasing swooped toward the Bothan Assault Cruiser *Champion. Champ* was flying cover for another refugee convoy. Kalarba's industrialized moon, Hosk, already wobbled in its orbit. The situation was hauntingly similar to Sernpidal's last hours, almost ten months ago. There would be even greater losses, here—to the Kalarbans. But to Jaina, like her dad, Sernpidal had been a tragedy that might never be matched.

Vaping these skips wouldn't bring back Chewbacca,

but it helped deaden Jaina's bitter memories. Keeping one finger on her stutter trigger, she showered the coralskipper with crimson laser splinters. Multiple bursts of low-power energy tired and distracted the skip's energy-sucking dovin basals. As the colonel once put it, "Tickle its teeth, then ram a fist down its throat."

Her sensor showed the vortex draw back slightly, a little closer to the enemy ship that projected it. On her primary screen, a Chiss clawcraft swooped in from behind. "Covering you, Rogue Eleven."

Now! Jaina tightened her index finger on the main firing control, loosing a solid burst from all four of her lasers. The skip's tiny, projected gravity well bent her laser blast, but she'd shot high to compensate. The anomaly sent two of her shots wild. It focused the other two exactly where she wanted them, painting the crystal-paneled cockpit with flaming sheets of light.

We've got the tactics to beat them in an even fight, now. But it's never even. They keep killing us and keep coming. Their ships even heal themselves! The Yuuzhan Vong had converted whole worlds into coralskipper nurseries and blasted one of the New Republic's biggest military shipyards, at Fondor. Surviving major yards—Kuat, Mon Calamari, Bilbringi—had gone to full alert, with carrier groups deployed to defend them.

Crystal shards and hot gravel blasted off the coral-skipper, propelling it into a slow spiral out of the fire zone. The Yuuzhan Vong pilot didn't eject. They all died with their ships—by choice, it seemed.

And *still* they kept coming, while New Republic pilots were pulled home to defend their own systems.

"You're clear, Ten," Jaina exclaimed.

"Thanks, Sticks."

"Anytime." Jaina pulled to starboard and spotted a catastrophe in the making. "Rogues, more skips coming in at 349 mark 18. They're headed for *Champ*'s drive nacelles."

"Copy that." Major Alinn Varth, commander of Jaina's flight, put an edge on her voice. "Time to make coral dust. Eleven, Twelve. On me."

Jaina double-clicked her comm to acknowledge the order, then pushed her throttle forward. She inverted her X-wing, following Rogue Nine over *Champion*'s ventral surface, so close and so low she could almost count rectennae and rivets.

Brevet Admiral Glie'oleg Kru, a Twi'lek, commanded *Champion*. Since Fondor, Jaina heard about a newly made captain or admiral at almost every engagement. Other worlds recently lost—Gyndine, Bimmiel, and Tynna. Here at Kalarba, Jaina's intelligence briefer had speculated that the aliens were trying to cut the Corellian Run, a vital hyperspace route to the Rim. Druckenwell and Rodia had just gone to full alert.

Another convoy of Kalarban ships, including dozens fleeing the ruin of Hosk Station, had just jumped. Despite all efforts to find and destroy a huge dovin basal the Yuuzhan Vong had obviously dropped on Kalarba, Hosk was losing altitude with each orbit. Its Hyrotii Zebra fighters were long gone, all ten of its turbolasers disabled. Enemy vessels that showed on her screen as many-legged creatures pursued the metal-sheathed moon, gobbling up shuttles that lagged behind the convoy. Hosk's polar cluster of towers was already skewed more than thirty degrees from its normal orientation. Soon Kalarba would be another dead world, useless even to the Yuuzhan Vong.

Jaina rounded *Champion*'s starboard fighter docking bays into a blazing free-for-all. Three coralskippers jumped her, flinging brilliant plasma bolts. Her pulse pounded as she went evasive, juking in all directions without thinking, keeping her right middle finger tight on the secondary trigger.

"Sparky," she ordered her astromech droid, "I need one hundred percent shields at thirteen meters."

Letters flashed on her heads-up display as the R5 unit, her companion ever since joining Rogue Squadron, complied just in time. Static buzzed in her headset. A dovin basal grabbed for her shields.

Another new skip vectored low and to port. Jaina feathered her etheric rudder and shoved the stick over, chasing while stars spun. *Just that much closer, Vong. Just that much closer . . .*

Her torp brackets went red with a lock-on. Triumphant, she squeezed off a proton torpedo. As it rode blue flame toward the alien fighter, she held course, squeezing off more scarlet splinters, distracting the dovin basal—

"Eleven," a voice cried in her ear. "Break starboard!"

Hutt slime! Jaina goosed her throttle and broke, pitching against her flight harness. The X-wing shuddered. "I'm hit," she cried. Adrenaline made her clench the controls. She eyed her primary board. "Still got shields, though." She feathered stick and rudder, bringing the X-wing about. "And maneuvering."

But now she was mad. Coralskippers, designated scarlet on her heads-up display, swarmed *Champion* and its defenders. But one, swooping back toward *Champion*, had to be the skip that just put scorch marks on her S-foils.

She rammed her throttle forward.

Now she saw the big enemy ship astern of *Champion*. Just smaller than a Star Destroyer, its configuration reminded her of some weird marine creature. Its thickest arm pointed forward, probably command and control. Two thinner arms stuck out dorsally, two ventrally.

From the ventral arms, blinding plasma was already pouring out at *Champion*.

Two flights of New Republic E-wings swooped in to hit the new arrival. Staying hot on her skip's tail, Jaina squeezed her stutter trigger.

"Rogues." The colonel's cry caught her off guard. "Somebody just sucked *Champ*'s shields. Get clear!"

What had they done, brought in another big one just out of Jaina's line of sight? She wrenched her stick and punched for full speed.

She was passing *Champion*'s port nacelle when light broke through from deep inside. Slowly, with an eerie, fatal beauty, a seam opened on *Champ*'s glossy side.

"Sticks," a voice shouted in her ear. "Eleven, get clear!"

"Full power, Sparky!" Jaina called. "Go—"

The blast flung her against her instrument panel. Rudder pedals seemed to crush up through her legs. Her cockpit's sides buckled, then vanished. A siren shrieked in her ears, blaring in rhythm with a synthesized voice.

"Ejection. Ejection."

She flailed down into the Force, grasping desperately. Almost . . .

A white explosion of pain washed awareness away.

CHAPTER ONE

Jacen Solo stood with his father outside the mud-block refugee hut they were sharing on Duro. Jacen's brown coveralls had accumulated a layer of grit and dust, and his wavy, dark brown hair fell over his ears, not quite long enough to pull back into a tail. Under a translucent gray dome, tension wrapped around him like a Zharan glass-snake—invisible, but so palpable through the Force that he could almost feel its coils constrict.

Something was about to happen. He could feel it coming when he listened through the Force. Something vital, but . . .

What?

A Ryn female—velvet-furred with a spiked mane, her tail and forearm bristles graying with age—stood talking to Jacen's dad, Han Solo.

"Those are our caravan ships," she bellowed, waving her hands. "Ours." She snorted, and the breath *whonk*ed through four holes in her chitinous beak.

Han swung around, narrowly missing Jacen with his left arm. "And right at this moment, we can't afford to take them offworld to run systems checks. You've been in a restricted area, Mezza."

Splashes of red-orange fur highlighted Mezza's soft

taupe coat. Her blue tail tip trembled, a gesture Jacen had learned to interpret as impatience.

"Of course we've been in the ship lot," she snapped. "There's never been a security fence Ryn couldn't get inside, and those are our caravan ships. Ours." She tapped her threadbare vest, which covered an ample chest. "And don't tell me to *trust* you, Captain. We do. It's SELCORE we don't trust. SELCORE, and the people up there." She waved her arm skyward.

Han's mouth twitched, and seventeen-year-old Jacen could almost feel him trying not to laugh. Jacen's dad could sympathize with refugees making unofficial reconnaissances, especially on board their own ships. But Han was in charge now. Instead of showing his amusement, he was supposed to enforce SELCORE regulations—publicly, at least, for the sake of a few juvenile offenders. He and Mezza would undoubtedly settle the real issues later, in private.

So Han plunged back into the argument.

Jacen watched the show, trying to pick up one more piece of the puzzle he felt in every cell of his being. Trained as a Jedi and unusually perceptive, he could tell that the Force was about to move. To shift.

This time, he didn't dare miss the clues.

His right cheekbone twinged. He touched it self-consciously, then swept his hair back from his face. It needed cutting, but no one here cared what he looked like. His legs were still growing, his shoulders broadening. He felt like an awkward hybrid of trained Jedi and barely grown boy.

He leaned against his hut's outer wall and stared out over his new home. The dome had been engineered by SELCORE, the New Republic Senate Select Committee for Refugees, to hold a thousand settlers. Naturally, twelve hundred had been squeezed in. Besides these outcast

Ryn, there were several hundred desperate humans, delicate Vors, Vuvrians with their enormous round heads—and one young Hutt.

And the relentless Yuuzhan Vong kept sweeping across the galaxy, destroying whole worlds, enslaving or sacrificing planetary populations. Lush Ithor, lawless Ord Mantell, and Obroa-skai with its fabulous libraries—all had fallen to the merciless invaders. Hutt space and the Mid Rim worlds along the Corellian Run were under attack. If the Yuuzhan Vong could be stopped, the New Republic hadn't figured out how.

Han Solo stood with his left hand on his hip, arguing with Mezza, who led the larger of two Ryn clan remnants, but keeping one eye on the transgressors, a group of youths about Jacen's age, with fading juvenile stripes on their cheeks. The Ryn clans occupied one of Settlement Thirty-two's three wedge-shaped arrays of blue-roofed huts. The synthplas dome arched overhead, as gray as the polluted mists that swirled outside.

Jacen had been blessed—or cursed—with a sensitivity that he once hid behind labored jokes, and he did find it easy to see both sides of almost any argument. Part of his job here was to help his dad negotiate. Han tended to cut to solutions, instead of listening to both parties' points of view. Han had chased the Ryn over half the New Republic, trying to gather his new friend Droma's invasion-scattered clanmates. As world after world closed its doors to refugees, the Ryn had been beggared, duped, and betrayed. They'd taken terrible losses. They needed a sponsor.

So a reluctant Han Solo registered with the burgeoning Select Committee for Refugees. "Just long enough to settle them someplace." That was how he explained it to Jacen, anyway.

Jacen had fled here from Coruscant. Two months ago,

the New Republic had called him and his brother Anakin to Centerpoint Station, the massive hyperspace repulsor and gravity lens in the Corellian system. There'd been hope that Anakin, who had activated Centerpoint once before, could enable it again. Military advisers had hoped to lure the Yuuzhan Vong into attacking Corellia, and they meant to use Centerpoint as an interdiction field, to trap the enemy inside Corellian space—and then wipe them out. Even Uncle Luke hoped the station might be used only in its shielding capacity, not as a weapon.

The New Republic might never recover from the catastrophe that followed.

Jacen could see stress in his dad's lined face and his labored stride, and in the gray growing into his hair. Even after all these years of hobnobbing with bureaucrats and tolerating his wife's protocol droid, patience clearly wasn't his strong suit.

Standing on the dust-beaten lane outside the Solos' hut, Mezza's opposing clan leader twisted his own tail between strong hands. The fur on Romany's forearms, and the tip of his tail, stood out like bleached bristles.

"So *your* clan," Han said, pointing at Romany, "thinks *your* clan"—pointing now at Mezza—"is likely to hijack our transport ships and strand everybody else here on Duro? Is that it?"

Someone at the back of Romany's group shouted, "I wouldn't put it past them, Solo."

Another Ryn stepped forward. "We were better off in the Corporate Sector, dancing for credits and telling fortunes. At least there we had our own ships. We could hide our children from poisoned air. And even more poisonous . . . words."

Han stuck his hands into his dusty coverall pockets and caught Jacen's glance. Jacen could almost look him in the eye nowadays.

"Any suggestions?" Han muttered.

"They're just venting their frustrations now," Jacen observed.

He glanced up. The gray synthplas dome over their heads had been imported in accordion folds and unfurled over three arched metal struts. The refugees were reinforcing it with webs of native rock fiber, roughly half the colony working double shifts to strengthen the dome and their prefab huts. The other half labored outside, at a pit-mine "reservoir" and water purification site assigned by SELCORE.

Abruptly Han flung up an arm and shouted, "Hey!"

Jacen spun around in time to see one young male Ryn somersault out of Romany's group and crouch for fisticuffs. Two from Mezza's group body-blocked him with surprising grace. Within seconds, Han was wading into an out-and-out melee that looked too graceful to actually endanger anyone. Ryn were natural gymnasts. They swung their opponents by their bristled tails, hooting through their beaks like a flock of astromech droids. They almost seemed to be dancing, playing, releasing their tensions. Jacen opened his mouth to say, *Don't stop them. They need to cut loose.*

At that moment, he collapsed, his chest flashing with fire as if he'd been torn open. His legs burned so fiercely he could almost feel hot shrapnel. The pain blasted down his legs, then into his ears.

Jaina?

Joined through the Force even before they were born, he and Jaina had always been able to tell when the other was hurt or afraid. But for him to sense her over the distances that lay between them now, she must've been terribly—

The pain winked off.

"Jaina!" he whispered, appalled. "No!"

He stretched out toward her, trying to find her again. Barely aware of fuzzy shapes clustering around him and a Ryn voice hooting for a medical droid, he felt as if he were shrinking—falling backwards into a vacuum. He tried focusing deep inside and outside himself, to grab on to the Force and punch out—or slip into a healing trance. Could he take Jaina with him, if he did? Uncle Luke had taught him a dozen focusing techniques, back at the academy, and since then.

Jacen.

A voice seemed to echo in his mind, but it wasn't Jaina's. It was deep, male—vaguely like his uncle's.

Making an effort, Jacen imagined his uncle's face, trying to focus on that echo. An enormous white vortex seemed to spin around him. It pulled at him, drawing him toward its dazzling center.

What was going on?

Then he saw his uncle, robed in pure white, half turned away. Luke Skywalker held his shimmering lightsaber in a diagonal stance, hands at hip level, point high.

Jaina! Jacen shouted the words in his mind. *Uncle Luke, Jaina's been hurt!*

Then he saw what held his uncle's attention. In the dim distance, but clearly in focus, a second form straightened and darkened. Tall, humanoid, powerfully built, it had a face and chest covered with sinuous scars and tattoos. Its hips and legs were encased in rust-brown armor. Claws protruded from its heels and knuckles, and an ebony cloak flowed from its shoulders. The alien held a coal-black, snake-headed amphistaff across its body, mirroring the angle of Luke's lightsaber, pitting poisonous darkness against verdant light.

Utterly confused, Jacen stretched out through the Force. First he sensed the figure in white as a respected uncle—then abruptly as a powerful depth, blazing in the

Force like a star gone nova. But across this slowly spinning disk, where Jacen's inner vision presented a Yuuzhan Vong warrior, his Force sense picked up nothing at all. Through the Force, all Yuuzhan Vong did seem utterly lifeless, like the technology they vilified.

The alien swung its amphistaff. The Jedi Master's lightsaber blazed, swept down, and blocked the swing, brightening until it washed out almost everything else in this vision. The Yuuzhan Vong's amphistaff seemed darker than any absence of light, a darkness that seemed alive but promised death.

The broad, spinning disk on which they both stood finally slowed. It focused into billions of stars. Jacen picked out the familiar map of known space.

Luke dropped into a fighting stance, poised near the galaxy's center, the Deep Core. He raised his lightsaber and held it high, near his right shoulder, pointing inward. From three points of darkness, beyond the Rim, tattooed assailants advanced.

More of them? Jacen realized this was a vision, not a battle unfolding in front of him, with little to do with his twin sister.

Or maybe everything to do with her! Did these new invaders symbolize other invasion forces, more worldships—besides the ones that were already beating back everything the New Republic could throw at them? Reaching out to Jaina, maybe he had tapped the Force itself—or maybe it broke through to him.

The galaxy seemed to teeter, poised between light and darkness. Luke stood close to the center, counterweighing the dark invaders.

But as their numbers increased, the balance tipped.

Uncle Luke, Jacen shouted. *What should I do?*

Luke turned away from the advancing Yuuzhan Vong. Looking to Jacen with somber intensity, he tossed his lightsaber. It flew in a low, humming arc, trailing pale green sparks onto the galactic plane.

Eyeing the advancing horde, Jacen felt another enemy try to seize him: anger, from deep in his heart. Fear and fury focused his strength. If he could, he would utterly destroy the Yuuzhan Vong and all they stood for! He opened a hand, stretched out his arm . . .

And missed.

The Jedi weapon sailed past him. As anger released him, fear took a tighter hold. Jacen flailed, leapt, tried stretching out with the Force. Luke's lightsaber sailed on, shrinking and dimming with distance.

Now the galaxy tipped more quickly. A dark, deadly tempest gathered around the alien warriors. Disarmed, Luke stretched out both hands. First he, then his enemies, swelled to impossible sizes. Instead of human and alien figures, now Jacen saw light and darkness as entirely separate forces. Even the light terrified him in its grandeur and majesty. The galaxy seemed poised to plunge toward evil, but Jacen couldn't help staring at the fearful light, spellbound, burning his retinas.

A Jedi knows no fear . . . He'd heard that a thousand times, but this sensation was no cowardly urge to run. This was awe, it was reverence—a passionate longing to draw nearer. To serve the light and transmit its grandeur.

But compared to the forces battling around him, he was only a tiny point. Helpless and unarmed, besides— because of one moment's dark anger. Had that misstep doomed him? Not just him, but the galaxy?

A voice like Luke's, but deeper, shook the heavens. *Jacen,* it boomed. *Stand firm.*

The horizon tilted farther. Jacen lunged forward, determined to lend his small weight to Luke's side, to the light.

He misstepped. He flailed for Luke's hand, but missed

again. And again, his weight fell slightly—by centimeters—toward the dark enemies.

Luke seized his hand and held tightly. *Hang on, Jacen!* The slope steepened under their feet. Stars extinguished. The Yuuzhan Vong warriors scrambled forward. Whole star clusters winked out, a dark cascade under clawed enemy feet.

Plainly, the strength of a hundred-odd Jedi couldn't keep the galaxy from falling to this menace. One misstep—at one critical moment, by one pivotal person—could doom everyone they'd sworn to protect. No military force could stop this invasion, because it was a spiritual battle. And if one pivotal person fell to the dark side—or even used the ravishing, terrifying power of light in a wrong way—then this time, everything they knew might slide into stifling darkness.

Is that it? he cried toward the infinite distance.

Again, Jacen perceived the words in a voice that was utterly familiar but too deep to be Luke's. *Stand firm, Jacen.*

One of the Yuuzhan Vong leapt toward him. Jacen gasped and flung out both arms—

And grabbed a flimsy bedsheet. He lay on his back, on a cot under a corrugated blue synthplas roof. The room was bigger than a refugee shelter. It had to be the medical end of the dome's hardened control shed.

"Junior," another familiar voice drawled. "Hey, there. Glad you could join us."

Jacen looked up into his father's wry half smile. Worry lines crowded Han's eyes. Behind him, the Ryn named Droma clutched and twisted his soft red and blue cap, and his long mustachios drooped. In recent months, Droma had become his dad's . . . what? His friend, his assistant? Certainly not a partner or copilot, but a real presence.

The settlement's most valuable droid, a 2-1B medical unit that Han pirated no-one-knew-where, lingered on Jacen's other side, retracting a flexible breath mask.

"What happened?" Han looked befuddled. "Hit your head on the way down? Skinny, here—"

Droma pointed at the droid and finished Han's sentence. "—wants to dump you into the bacta tank." Ryn were shrewd observers, perceptive enough to lock into other people's thought patterns and finish their sentences.

Han swung toward his friend. "Listen, bristle-face. When I want to say something, *I'll* say it—"

"Jaina," Jacen managed. The back of his skull throbbed in rhythm with his pulse. Evidently he *had* hit it as he fell. He almost opened his mouth to describe what he'd seen, but he hesitated. Han was already confused by Jacen's emotional paralysis, and the way he'd begged out of the other Jedis' rescue and fact-finding missions. As hard as Jacen had tried to pull back from Jedi concerns, the Force wouldn't leave him alone. It was his heritage, his destiny.

And if the fate of billions rested on a balance point so narrow that one misstep could doom everyone, did he dare even mention his vision until his own path seemed clear? He'd almost gotten himself enslaved once, following a vision into danger. The Yuuzhan Vong had gone so far as to plant one of their deadly coral seeds against his cheekbone. Maybe this time, he'd been given a private warning to steer clear of some dangerous course. Would he know it when it opened up in front of him?

This vision hadn't eased his confusion at all.

"What?" his father demanded. "What about Jaina?"

Jacen squeezed his eyes shut, refusing to trivialize the Force by using it to ease a headache. *What is it,* he begged the unseen Force, *that you want me to do?*

Or would he cause the next galactic catastrophe by trying to prevent it?

"We've got to contact Rogue Squadron," Jacen blurted. "I think she's been hurt."

CHAPTER TWO

At the control shed's other end, a shapely young Ryn female sat near the middle of a wall of mostly dark displays, cradling a child in her lap. The colony's resident Hutt—Randa Besadii Diori—lay snoozing along the near wall. His long tan-colored tail twitched.

"Piani." Han Solo stepped into the main room right behind Jacen. "We need a line out."

The smile faded below Piani's chitinous beak. Ryn were such sensitive body-language readers that she was probably closing in on what had them worried. "Out-system?" she asked.

"Yes," Jacen said. "Can you raise the relay repeater? We need to get a message to my sister, with Rogue Squadron."

Piani eased her sleeping child away from her shoulder, then laid him in a padded cargo crate on the floor.

"I'll try," she promised. "But you know Admiral Dizzlewit. Sit down, have a bedjie."

She motioned toward a sideboard, where several small, dark fungi steamed beside a hefty pot of caf. Bedjies were easy to raise—seed a shallow tank with spores, wait a week, and come back with a net. They were becoming standard refugee fare.

Jacen wasn't even slightly hungry, but Han grasped one between thumb and forefinger and nibbled. Steamed, unspiced bedjies were unspeakably bland, but the Ryn matriarchs had taken to hoarding their herbs.

"Solo!" Randa awoke from his nap. He rolled over and ponderously pulled his upper body into the air. "Why are you here?"

Jacen had tried to get along with Randa. Raised as a spice merchant, sent by the Hutts to run slaves for the Yuuzhan Vong, Randa had defected at Fondor—supposedly.

"Getting a message out," Jacen said numbly. *A Jedi knows no fear*, he'd been taught. *Fear is of the dark side.*

Fear for himself, he could thrust aside. But for Jaina? He couldn't help being afraid for his sister. They were linked at an uncanny depth.

Still young, relatively light, and lithe enough to move under his own power, Randa slithered closer.

"What are *you* doing here?" Han demanded.

Randa puffed out his sloping chest. "I told you. With my parent Borga defending Nal Hutta with only half the clans' support—and pregnant with my sibling, at that—where am I? Stranded, as shipless as one of these idiot Vors. I am willing to stand communication watch day and night. That way, I will hear any news from home and free up your workers for—"

"We'll talk about it," Han interrupted. "Piani, what—"

Scowling, the Ryn whirled her chair away from her set. "I can't even get through to Dizzlewit. He left orders. 'No civilian use of relay without authorization,' " she mocked. "So I applied for authorization." She shook her long, sleek mane of hair. "I can notify you as soon as I get it."

Han glared. He and the Duros Admiral Darez Wuht had ended up crosswise twice before his first week on Duro ran out. Admiral Wuht hadn't even tried to pretend he felt hospitable toward refugees.

It'd been hoped that the Yuuzhan Vong wouldn't be interested in a planet that was nearly dead. SELCORE, searching the Core region for a place to locate millions of war refugees, had struck a deal with the Duros High House, one of the few remaining local governments that still seemed willing to accept refugees at all. Displaced people could help reclaim its surface, bring abandoned manufacturing plants back on-line, and take over the food-synthesis plants that still fed Duros in their orbital cities. Duros who had worked groundside could go home. Refugees with military experience, it had been argued, might even help defend Duro's vital trading hubs, including one of the New Republic's top ten remaining shipyards.

Except that the refugees weren't volunteering for military service in anything like the numbers Wuht anticipated.

Commanding the orbital cities' overlapping planetary shields, four squadrons of fighters, and the Mon Cal cruiser *Poesy*, Admiral Wuht provided the refugees some cover, even as the orbital cities retooled for military production. With the Fondor shipyards lost and all the other main military shipyards such obvious targets, the New Republic was hastily decentralizing military production.

Unfortunately, most of the New Republic's other warships in this area had been redeployed to Bothawui, or out the Corellian Run. Jacen had heard that the Adumari had attempted a flanking attack on Yuuzhan Vong positions up near Bilbringi. He hoped it was true.

Jacen eyed Piani's comm board. "How's the cable to Gateway? Could we get them to send out a signal faster?"

Thanks to SELCORE's official presence at that nearby settlement, Gateway reportedly had a dependable uplink, even an outlink. Insulated fiber cables connected the two domes, but Duro's only surviving fauna—mutant fefze beetles—found fiber cables perfectly tasty. Duro's corrosive atmosphere was too murky for line-of-sight transmitting or satellite bouncing.

Predictably, Piani shook her head. "Gateway's scheduled to send out a cable rider in two days."

Gateway was bigger, just older, and much better established than this settlement. *Better organized,* Jacen guessed, not that he meant to criticize his dad. Han was giving Settlement Thirty-two his all. Thirty-two maintained a pipeline that provided Gateway with water, which was reclaimed from an ancient numbered pit mine. Gateway maintained the communication cable and supplemented Thirty-two's food production.

Han thrust his hands into his pockets and eyed Jacen, raising one eyebrow. "You're not chasing mynocks with a flitterfly net?"

"I hope I am." Jacen fingered hair back behind his ears. "I didn't want to get you worried—"

"We're at war. Everybody's worried."

The moment passed without either of them mentioning Chewbacca, and Jacen drew a shallow breath of relief. These days, nearly everyone had suffered at least one loss. Piani's mate hadn't reached Gyndine's capital city in time to catch an evac ship. He was likely dead, or worse. They all had to carry on.

"What can I do to help?" Randa slithered closer.

"Nothing," Han snapped. He turned to Jacen. "Tell me if it's important. If you need this checked, I'll see what we can raise on the *Falcon.*" He gestured toward the dome's main entry.

A caravan's worth of ragtag ships had been hauled from the landing crater by mammoth cross-terrain crawlers—equipment courtesy of SELCORE, designated for reclamation work—and parked under tarps, protected from corrosive fallout. The security guards had just turned Mezza's young clanmates out of that area.

Jacen's worry for Jaina struggled with his administrative concerns as his dad's assistant—for about three seconds. "Yes," he said, glancing guiltily at Piani, who belonged to Mezza's clan and wasn't much older than the offenders. "It's important."

"Right." Han pointed at Randa. "You stay here. Let me know what you hear out of Nal Hutta."

"Depend on me, Captain." Randa plucked a bedjie off Piani's hot plate and dropped it whole into his mouth.

Twelve minutes later, Jacen perched on the *Millennium Falcon*'s high-backed copilot's seat. Han whacked a bulkhead, not in the joking way Jacen had seen him do it so many times, but angrily.

"Hey," Han growled, "fossil. Gimme generator, and I don't mean tomorrow."

And in its inimitable way, the *Falcon* produced a glimmering array of lights.

Han dropped into his own seat and flicked three switches. "Give her a minute to come up."

"Right," Jacen assured him. *I know* was what he wanted to say, but he understood. Han had recovered enough from Chewie's death to have the *Falcon* modified—including better air scrubbers for ferrying refugees, and a nonreflective black exterior that Chewie would've howled over—but he'd never installed a standard copilot's chair. Just being on board the beloved hunk of junk made Jacen slightly nervous.

Jacen eyed a wire bundle that hung from a half-opened bulkhead. Han and Droma came out here now and again. *Tinkering*, Han called it. *Therapy*, Droma whispered.

They waited in silence. The weeks when Han's grief had overwhelmed them all drifted up into Jacen's memory.

He'd happened into a cantina when Han had gone looking for oblivion. And on a worse night, he'd heard Han scald Leia, using words that never should've been spoken and could hardly be forgiven. Jacen had never mentioned that night to his mom. She probably hoped Jacen had forgotten.

Jacen doubted his dad remembered even saying them. He hoped his mother could somehow forget.

Pain wasn't always a bad thing, though. Jacen almost wished Jaina's pain would blast back into his awareness. At least that would mean she was alive.

They might find out in a few minutes.

A cascading rhythm of beeps rang in the cockpit as the repeater frequency came alive. Han slapped a tile on the bulkhead. "Solo here, in the *Millennium Falcon*. Call is for Coruscant, New Republic military. I want Colonel Darklighter's office."

Then they waited again.

"Jacen," Han said softly. "What's scared you off from using the Force? Two years ago, you were as gung ho as Anakin. I haven't seen you levitate anything since you got here."

Jacen gripped the arms of Chewbacca's chair. "It's complicated." His dad wasn't criticizing. He just didn't understand. He'd already said he was glad for Jacen's help, but now that Jacen had bailed out of the larger fight, he was falling farther and farther behind his Jedi siblings.

"Try me." Han's eyes bored into Jacen.

Jacen had told him what happened at Centerpoint. The powerful hyperspace repulsor and gravity lens had responded to Anakin's touch, all right. It reactivated just as before.

And at that moment, the Yuuzhan Vong fleet—the one

that the New Republic had hoped to lure to Corellia—appeared out of hyperspace at Fondor instead.

Han's cousin Thrackan Sal-Solo insisted that the mighty shield should be used as an offensive weapon. He tried to bully Anakin into firing at the Yuuzhan Vong across the vast distance between systems.

Jacen begged Anakin not to take the shot. Firing that weapon would have been the ultimate aggression.

Anakin yielded to Jacen. For one moment, the brothers shared a true moral victory.

Then Thrackan seized the controls. He blasted the Yuuzhan Vong battle group and decimated the noble flotilla that Hapes had sent to the New Republic's aid, thanks to Leia Organa Solo's diplomatic efforts. The Yuuzhan Vong retreated, the surviving Hapans fled home, and now, Thrackan Sal-Solo was being hailed as a hero.

"I could've fired Centerpoint without hitting the Hapans," Anakin had insisted. Jacen had resisted believing him for almost a week. Then the self-doubts caught him. Maybe Anakin could've done it all. Destroyed the aliens, spared the Hapans, saved Fondor.

When *did* aggressive defense become the aggression that was forbidden to Jedi?

Keeping only his lightsaber, Jacen found passage from Coruscant to Duro. If he couldn't fight alongside Uncle Luke and the others, maybe he could at least help his father manage refugees.

Now, surely, he was on the right path. "I only know that you can't fight darkness with darkness." That didn't explain anything. He tried again. "So maybe a Jedi shouldn't fight violence with violence, either. Sometimes, I even think that the more you *fight* evil, the more you empower it."

Han Solo opened his mouth to protest.

"It's different for us," Jacen insisted. "If we use the

Force aggressively, that can lead to the dark side. But where does strong action become aggression? The line keeps blurring—"

The console beeped, rescuing him. "Rogue Squadron," a tenor voice rang in the cockpit, "Colonel Darklighter's office. Captain Solo, is that you? We were just trying to raise you."

Jacen's heart plunged through his stomach.

"Yeah, it's me," his father growled. "We're checking on Jaina."

"Good timing," the voice answered. "This is Major Harthis, by the way. Jaina's X-wing has been destroyed in a firefight. She had to go EV. A fellow pilot brought her in."

"Injured?"

"Legs, chest. Bacta ought to take care of it."

Han grunted as Jacen exhaled in relief.

"Her pressure suit held, but she was close to an attack cruiser, one of ours, when the drive blew. She got a massive mag-field exposure."

Jacen's blood turned icy. "Will she recover?"

Han echoed his question into the pickup.

The voice hesitated. "Tentatively, yes. We'll update you as soon as we know. We're also trying to raise her mother. Is Leia with you?"

"Isn't she back on Coruscant?"

"No, Captain. SELCORE administration seems to have lost her."

"*Lost* her?" Han echoed sarcastically. "Sorry. I can't help with that."

Jacen flicked the console's edge. "I could stay out here," he offered. "I'll try to find her."

Han's eyes focused on something in the distance. "Sure," he said. The pain in his voice reminded Jacen that things were not well between his parents. "You do that."

Leia Organa Solo glanced into a dark corner, where her young bodyguard Basbakhan stood like a darker shadow. She hadn't taken on a planetwide project since . . . was it Basbakhan's homeworld, Honoghr?

She sat at the head of a long synthwood table. Surrounded by bickering scientists, she would've liked to cradle her head in both hands, plug her ears, and demand that they stop acting like children.

Duro did that to people.

Conditions here were appalling. Still, with Borsk Fey'lya clinging to power on Coruscant, this was one way she could shore up the New Republic, protect the Jedis' reputation, and wear herself out so thoroughly that every night she dropped onto her cot too exhausted to worry about her own scattered family. Over the past year, she'd been bounced from system to system, caught up in on-again, off-again administrative and diplomatic work, wherever the New Republic's Advisory Council pretended not to send her.

Even if she was starting to feel like a nonperson, this Duro project might be the most significant job she ever took on. To remake a world in these terrible times would be an enormous victory.

Her reconstructive meteorologist clenched a fist on the tabletop. "Look," the scientist growled, glaring at the huge, furry Talz sitting opposite her. "There were excellent reasons for setting our domes on the dry side of these ranges. The worst toxins fall with the rains. Any settlement placed on a wet side, like our partner Thirty-two, will be utterly unsuitable for spiro-grass rangeland, but ideal for water reclamation. If we try to alter our wind patterns, we'll set up an environmental catastrophe."

"Would anyone even notice a catastrophe?" The Talz sat with his large, lower pair of eyes shut, his small upper pair blinking slowly. "Rangeland needs more water than you seem to think. With all due respect . . ." He nodded up the table to Leia. "Not only here, but in other areas, we cannot depend on mined groundwater. It's saturated with soluble toxins and costly to pump."

"While we're here—" A Ho'Din plant-development specialist rested his off-green forearms on the tabletop. His long legs almost didn't fit under the conference table. "I would like to petition for Sector Four of the reclaimed marshlands. I have several promising vegetative species under development—"

"I apologize for interrupting my esteemed colleague," the cereals specialist put in. "But Sector Four was promised to the grains project—"

"And where's Cree'Ar?" The meteorologist, Sidris Kolb, spoke Leia's mind. So far, Dr. Dassid Cree'Ar had missed every one of these weekly meetings.

Not that I blame him, Leia thought wryly, watching the Ho'Din pass her datapad back to her personal aide, Abbela Oldsong. At each meeting, they downloaded their current research into Leia's administrative files. Cree'Ar, a plant geneticist, sent his reports via his own datapad.

Leia had known many truly eccentric people, whose brilliance showed not only in their results, but in odd personal habits—Zakarisz Ghent, the slicer-turned-intelligence expert, came to mind. Fired by her vision of creating a haven for refugees who'd lost everything but their lives, and could yet lose even that, Leia had agreed to work as a liaison between this bickering gang of researchers and SELCORE back on Coruscant. The researchers were happier alone in their labs, or surrounded by a few subservient techs.

She didn't put her name on that weekly report. She

was sick of dealing with Coruscant's new breed of bureaucrats and their veiled condescension. They could find her if they tried hard enough.

Leia couldn't fault Cree'Ar's techs for their devotion. His most recent breakthrough, cooperating with the distinguished microbiologist Dr. Williwalt, had been a bacterial sludge capable of topfermenting tanks of toxic, pollution-laden water pumped out of the swamps. It digested the leavings of Imperial war factories, leaving rich organic sediment and a gaseous factor they could collect and use for fuel.

Under Cree'Ar's supervision, refugees were pouring local-made duracrete into SELCORE-imported forms, dividing sectors of the toxic marsh that Gateway dome surmounted. They'd created six miniature ecosystems, cleansed six half-klick squares of marshland, added tons of cleansed soil-building material, and created Duro's first arable croplands since the Duros left the surface.

No wonder Cree'Ar didn't take time off for staff meetings. He probably was as tired of bureaucracy as Leia was herself. She had wrung a hefty SELCORE budget out of the New Republic's Advisory Council as her payment for traveling to the Hapes Cluster and begging for the Hapans' military aid—her own contribution to the Centerpoint disaster.

Mustn't think about that. It wasn't her fault. Wasn't even Thrackan's, really. No one had intended to see the Hapan fleet wiped out.

It all came down to communication. It bothered her that the paired settlements could barely keep the cables intact. How could she supervise a planetary reclamation project, a symbol of rebirth amidst all this death and loss, when no other settlement reported to her scientists on a regular basis?

Her cereals man turned to the elderly microbiologist.

"What we really need," he suggested, "is a strain of microbes that will digest particulates out of the air. Then we could take down the domes and move out onto the surface."

"That's true," Leia said dryly. "Until we scatter, we're sitting flinks for Yuuzhan Vong sharpshooters."

The cereals man's bushy eyebrows shot up.

How like a scientist, she reflected, so involved in his own project that he'd forgotten the galaxy staring over his shoulder.

Abbela Oldsong finally finished taking Leia's datapad around. Adjusting her pale-blue shoulder wrap, she handed the datapad to Leia, who eyed the readout, then saved new information before returning it. As usual, Cree'Ar's file was longest. All this would go into her weekly burst for SELCORE. She nodded to her aide, who hurried out with the datapad.

"Thank you for taking time out of your busy schedules. Remember," Leia added somberly, "anything we do at cross-purposes not only slows our effort but wastes the resources SELCORE is willing to send." Gateway and Thirty-two were already at odds, co-opting each others' shipments whenever they could. "I'll see what I can do," she promised her rangeland manager, "about getting you a freighter load of those inorganics."

"Thank you." Aj Koenes, the Talz, opened one large eye to glare at meteorologist Kolb.

Leia emerged from the research building, which was an elegant prefab shipped in by SELCORE. Her own office, due south in the cylindrical admin complex, would take a good stiff walk to reach. She wanted to move and think. Basbakhan followed at a distance, happiest when she ignored him. That way, he could keep his mind on his sworn obligation to protect her. She strode down

Main Street, as they'd taken to calling it, swinging both arms.

Gateway had been erected on the ruins of Tayana, an ancient Duros mining city. Under the new refugee huts, two upturned rock layers came together, one relatively soft and one exceptionally dense. Leia hoped to convert the old hard-rock mines into shelters, in case of breaches in the dome or other emergencies. SELCORE had sent two mammoth stone-chewing machines, and she'd been promised a state-of-the-art mining laser.

If she paused and stood still, she could hear the big chewers underfoot.

Chewers.

Chewie.

Leia's chest ached every time she thought of the beloved Wookiee. She strode on, frowning. She couldn't flinch every time something reminded her of his name. Naturally, it'd taken a falling moon to kill the big Wook. Duro had no moon, only twenty orbital cities.

On her left, an open-sided barn housed her major construction machinery, used for outside projects and new housing.

Housing! She'd been warned to expect an influx of Falleen and Rodians.

Not at Gateway, she hoped. That combination would be explosive. Refugee settlements were springing up all around the planet's equator. They nestled like baby Vors under the protective orbital cities, sheltered by their planetary shields.

A new neighborhood lay beyond the construction barn, a few duracrete-block buildings made from her engineers' experimental concoctions—local cement, mixed with marsh grass that'd been steeped in an antitoxin brew and then heat-dried. Beyond that, a hydroponics complex gave off the unsubtle odor of organic fertilizer.

She entered the admin complex by its north door, then plodded up a flight of stairs that circled an interior light-well. A U2C1 housekeeping droid hummed softly, its hoselike arms sweeping back and forth, rattling with the pebbles that constantly fell out of local duracrete. Two stories tall, plus a basement, this building had been constructed on-site by SELCORE before the big ships left.

Was that only nine weeks ago? Leia opened the door of the sparsely furnished room that served her as office and quarters. Near the north-facing window—which overlooked the research building, construction shed, and a patchwork of refugee families' straggly garden plots— she'd placed the massive SELCORE desk. A stranger had offered a pair of heirloom wall sconces. "I don't want to burn down our tent," she'd explained, so Leia agreed to keep them until that family took permanent housing in the new apartments Leia hoped to build, the projected Bail Organa complex.

Along the left wall were her cot and a cooking unit. The refresher was down the hall.

Something smelled odd. C-3PO stood beside the focus cooker.

His head swiveled. "Good evening, Mistress Leia. I am sorry, this would have been more savory an hour ago—"

"Not your problem, Threepio." She sank down at the table. "I'll eat now, before it gets any worse."

Whatever it was—probably soypro cutlets, beside a pile of local greens that had been overcooked to a slimy gel—probably had been tasty once. She made appreciative noises for C-3PO's sake. His culinary programming wasn't at fault. Her meeting had gone long.

He took up his usual position at the routing board, assigning incoming supplies and checking duty lists. He would spend the night working there.

"May I wonder, Mistress Leia . . ."

She chewed a rubbery bite. "Go ahead, Threepio."

"If you would permit me to make a personal inquiry . . ." He trailed off again. Leia thought she knew what was coming.

"Is it possible," he said, "that Captain Solo will be permanently absent from our . . . operation? I had rather thought he might appear, or at least communicate, by this time."

The soypro stuck in her throat. "The last time he called in, he didn't know exactly where he was going."

She eyed the protocol droid's gleaming finish. Was that a touch of corrosion on his left shoulder? She'd sent him outside the dome several times, grateful for an assistant who didn't need to breathe. Duro-stink wasn't toxic to most species, but the atmosphere had gotten significantly worse over the last few decades, and now working outside without rebreathers was nearly impossible. Masking up had become habit for most of them.

"Why do you ask? Han hasn't exactly been respectful to you, over the years."

C-3PO let his arms hang at his sides. "Recently, I was given a reason to take some pride in our ongoing relationship. I was surprised to learn that on Ruan, he was greeted as something of a hero by my cyborg counterparts."

"Say that again, Threepio?" She rocked forward. Han, a droid hero? "Where did you hear that?"

"After we returned to Coruscant." C-3PO reached out expansively with one arm. "There was a HoloNet story you might have missed, since you were somewhat preoccupied. On Ruan, several thousand droids held a peaceful demonstration against the Salliche Ag establishment, which had meant to deactivate them—"

"I remember that," she broke in. "Vaguely." Something about droids being warehoused, so that if the Yuuzhan Vong arrived, they might be presented as a peace offering. Obviously, Ruan didn't intend to resist the invaders.

"In the subtext," he said, "I found additional references to someone that the droids had called a 'long-awaited one,' the 'only flesh and blood' who would be able to help them. As it turned out, Captain Solo did save them from imminent destruction. In our recent flurry of activity, I neglected to mention—"

"Good heavens," Leia said softly. "Whatever was he thinking?" She'd love to rub his nose in *that* little tale.

Actually, she'd love to rub his nose against hers. It'd been so long.

Did his long silence mean that an enemy had found him? But he had Droma's help, now. He'd made it plain that he didn't want hers.

If he was dead, and their last words had been scornful taunts, she would regret it for the rest of her life. She was almost tempted to stretch out with the Force, looking for him.

No. He could be on the other side of the Mid Rim by now. If she reached out and felt nothing, she would fear the worst. She finished her meal in silence, then assembled her dishes for C-3PO to recycle.

"Whatever happens, I'll take care of you," she promised. "I need you."

Then she frowned at the datapad beside her elbow. Before she could turn in tonight, she had to check on the secondary rock-chewer crew. She needed to make sure Abbela sent off her weekly burst to the main Duros orbital city, Bburru, and then renewed their request for better satellite data. Then there was Gateway's still-nonfunctional bakery. Its staff had requested a shipment of salt and sucrose, anticipating a cereal crop. Ruan had sent this year's surplus burrmillet seeds as a goodwill gesture—and then slammed the door on accepting any more refugees.

Also, SELCORE still hadn't delivered that mining laser.

No wonder she hadn't had time to go looking for Han. She would've given everything to see him, the way he'd been before tragedy tore them apart. He'd matured so much from the scoundrel she'd come to love, although he'd never lost the glimmer in his eyes, or the quirk to his lips—till he lost Chewie. Suddenly, he was Han with the itchy trigger finger again. Han with the low-life friends. *Scoundrel* she could tolerate, even enjoy. All right, she admitted to herself: *Scoundrel* she'd adored. Over the years, he'd learned to drop the defenses that first turned him into a scoundrel. He'd learned to let her glimpse his real idealism. He needed warmth in return.

Over the years, slowly, she'd learned to give it. She loved both sides of him, the knight-errant and the scoundrel—but this time, she must wait until he came to her. She couldn't baby a full-grown man.

At least he'd been involved in the Ryn rescue episode. Unlike Han, she tried to stay current on HoloNet news. His ongoing involvement with the Ryn seemed like a sign of recovery.

Four hours later, she let down her long coil of hair and tumbled onto her cot. *What am I doing here?* flitted through her mind. Living with only a protocol droid for company—Basbakhan and Olmahk slept in the stairwell—made her feel as if she'd forgotten something critically important, day after day. It really was fortunate she was too tired to worry ... much too tired ... to worry too much, anyway ... about him ... or the children ...

Her last thought was, *I really should reach out through the Force for them. How many days has it been?* ...

CHAPTER THREE

The war vessel *Sunulok*, under way for decades, showed its age in a thousand small ways.

Luminescent colonies of lichen and bacteria grew at intervals near its passengers' head level. Many of those colonies flickered, and some had dulled or dimmed. Communication nodes, where tiny nondedicated villips stood on protrusions of fiery red-orange phong coral, had turned as gray as ash.

Striding down one of its coral-lined arteries, Tsavong Lah ignored those marks of age and death. A living cape clung to his shoulders by its needle-clawed gripping fingers. Rust-colored scales hung like armor plates from his breastbone and shoulder blades. Each larval armor scale had been seeded against bone while a priestly choir sang atonal incantations on his behalf, renewing his pledges of devotion to Yun-Yammka, god of war. Over half a year, the plates had grown slowly, stretching his tendons, tugging his joints to new angles. Then the priests had declared Tsavong Lah's painful transformation to warmaster complete.

Tsavong Lah embraced pain. Suffering honored his gods, who had created the universe by sacrificing parts of themselves.

Two sentries stood ahead. Their claw joints were immature and deadly sharp, their tattooed insignia far from complete. Outside his communication center, they snapped their fists to opposite shoulders. Tsavong raised one hand, receiving their homage and signaling his door. The organic door valve thickened at its edges, then dilated.

A striking young attendant, black honor bars burned across her pale cheeks, sat at her station. Seef sprang up and saluted. As she did, her seat extended pseudopodia and propelled itself sideways.

"Warmaster," she said reverently. "I roused the master villip in your privacy chamber, and I commanded the executor to present himself."

She strode to the far bulkhead. This part of *Sunulok* had grown an array of geometrically staggered coral blastulas where dozens of smaller villips lay quiescent.

Tsavong Lah strode past them, into the largest blastula of all. He waited until the cubicle's sphincter closed, then frowned at the leathery ball isolated on a display stand. Budded like yeast from master villips and nurtured in on-board nurseries, or raised in berrylike galls that parasitized certain swamp plants, the mollusklike genus enabled instantaneous, long-distance communication.

The villip mirrored the disgraced executor's face, sparely fleshed, with the crooked nose of multiple breaks showing great devotion—and maybe more vanity than was appropriate. In place of his left eye, he'd inserted a venom-spitting plaeryin bol.

Few of Nom Anor's contacts had ever suspected his true identity, not even his succession of duped human servants. His long-term mission included finding and neutralizing their people's most dangerous enemies. Ironically, after his major assignment at Rhommamool, a few residents of the New Republic honored him as a fallen hero—slain, they thought, in a war he had actually incited.

Yun-Harla, the Trickster goddess, seemed to smile on Nom Anor.

"Warmaster." The villip gave a good imitation of Nom Anor's voice. Its bass undertones suggested deference and submission.

"How many have they added to your herd?" Tsavong asked.

"Six thousand four hundred since we spoke. Many came from Fondor. Another dome is under construction."

"Abominable, but temporary. Be careful not to tip your hand." Tsavong's fringed lips, slit many times in devotion to Yun-Yammka, curled in a smile. Fondor had resisted one of his supreme commanders, Nas Choka, less than a klekket ago—two months by the infidels' calendar. In the process of destroying its ghastly mechanized shipyards, Choka had taken only a few hundred captives.

Then a torrent of starfire wiped out half of Choka's flotilla and three-fourths of the enemy's own ships. Tsavong's tacticians still were trying to decide whether that had been a deliberate sacrifice on the enemy's part. The infidels' usual urge to preserve life had been their greatest weakness, their most heinous spiritual perfidy. Were they learning? Had they discovered that sacrifice was the key to victory?

According to spies, the torrent originated in the system the infidels called Corellia, at a monstrous mechanical installation they named Centerpoint. Until Tsavong Lah's strategists could explain the weapon's hideous power, they advised him to find a Coreward staging point that lay behind multiple gravity wells from Centerpoint's direct line of fire.

By happy coincidence, the disgraced executor had been sent to just such a world.

"Watch for worthy ones," Tsavong reminded him.

"With better sacrifices, we might be cleansing the inner worlds now."

Nom Anor ducked his head. "And Jedi," he promised, pronouncing the difficult word well. He'd lived among these people for years. "Difficult to catch, but some seem worthy."

Tsavong Lah nodded and touched the ridge crest of Nom Anor's villip. The face faded and smoothed out. The villip retracted, sucking itself back through its mouth hole.

On his distant world, Nom Anor would be putting his new masquer back on—not an ooglith, but a newly bred type that imitated a nonhuman species. Anor's human contact, on the enemy's capital world, had agreed to deliver shiploads of captives to his current system.

As soon as Tsavong arrived there, he would have the glad task of sorting the worthy from the unworthy. A reverent mass sacrifice might convince mighty Yun-Yammka to let Tsavong reach the Galactic Core, where fertile gardens—tended by fecund slave races—were promised by the supreme overlord.

Six thousand more infidels would enhance the sacrifice, bringing him that much closer to the world he truly wanted to offer his gods.

Coruscant.

CHAPTER FOUR

Mara Jade Skywalker had been a wide-eyed child when Emperor Palpatine brought her to Coruscant. She'd survived Palpatine's training one hour and one day at a time. Now, everyone tended to think of Coruscant as ground zero again—this time, as the Yuuzhan Vong's ultimate objective.

Meanwhile, her husband was training another apprentice—obviously assuming there would be peace and justice to defend in the future. She wondered, though, if it was hope or just habit that kept them all sticking to business.

She stared over folded hands at her younger nephew. Seated next to Luke, wearing a light-brown tunic under his Jedi robe, dark-haired Anakin Solo had a saturnine intensity, a Corellian surname, and his father's wry lift to one eyebrow. Still, his blue eyes simmered with the eagerness to save the galaxy—alone, if necessary—and that was pure Skywalker.

Recently returned from Yavin 4, Luke had formed a habit of gathering several Jedi every few days in some secluded but public place. All Jedi had fallen under public scrutiny in recent months. Ithor was lost, despite Corran Horn's sacrificial effort. Renegade battle squadrons led by young Jedi Knights dived in and out of three major invasion fronts, blatantly disregarding military strategy.

Almost as damaging, the intelligence her former boss Talon Karrde recently helped the Jedi gather—concerning the Yuuzhan Vong's imminent attack on Corellia—proved false.

If the Jedi couldn't work together, they would be vaped separately, or tumble one by one to the dark side.

Seven Jedi had circled their chairs deep in central Coruscant's governmental district this morning, a few meters from a balcony overlooking a bustling mezzanine. A fountain bubbled nearby, looking and sounding like something out of the Empire's glory days . . .

The days when she'd been the Emperor's Hand. She carried around plenty of regret from those days, things she wished she'd never seen or done. But she'd made her peace. She'd given up the one thing dearest to her, her ship, *Jade's Fire*. In its place, she'd received . . . well . . . Enough.

Again she eyed Luke and Anakin. Whenever she saw those two together, she glimpsed two outward reflections of the same inner strength. They had the same compact build, though Anakin hadn't finished fleshing out—and those matching poke-mark clefts in their chins—but most telling of all, those terminally earnest attitudes.

Colonel Kenth Hamner, a strikingly tall human Jedi with a long, aristocratic face, served the New Republic's military as a strategist. He shook his head and said, "With Fondor's shipyards gone and the hyperspace routes mined, we're pulling in from the Inner Rim, even the Colonies. Rodia is in serious danger. Thank the Force, Anakin brought Centerpoint back up—"

Anakin leaned forward, gripping his hands as he interjected, "As long as we don't lose Corellia. Thrackan's likely to expel all the Drall and Selonians, declare Corellia a human-only zone, and lock out the rest of us, if we let him."

Mara knew Anakin well, so she could imagine the thoughts he didn't speak: *Because I didn't fire Centerpoint when I could have. Now Thrackan's a hero, no matter how many bystanders he killed* ... With Governor-general Marcha kicked out of office, Thrackan and the Centerpoint Party were making a strong bid for power at Corellia.

Kenth Hamner shook his head. "Don't blame yourself, Anakin. A Jedi must keep his power under control. We have to hesitate and consider the consequences. You couldn't hurry to fire Centerpoint, and you did well. Maybe Centerpoint will be the Core's last defense, if we can get it repaired. From there, we could defend the shipyards at Kuat and protect Coruscant."

"True," Luke told Hamner. A new wave of yorik coral warships had hit the Corellian Run, near Rodia. Anakin's sister, Jaina—Mara's apprentice—had deployed with Rogue Squadron toward that front, and with so many Yuuzhan Vong between them, it was difficult to sense her through the Force. Yuuzhan Vong somehow damped it down.

Bothawui, though—between the embattled Hutts and threatened Rodia—clearly was endangered. The last time Mara had heard of Kyp Durron, he'd parked Kyp's Dozen near Bothawui, spoiling for a fight and expecting it right there.

Mara had just about had it with Kyp Durron. She noted, though, the way Kenth Hamner deferred to Anakin. Anakin *had* saved her life on Dantooine, where Yuuzhan Vong warriors chased them for days while her mysterious disease slowly sapped her strength. Since the fall of Dubrillion, since the retreat at Dantooine—and especially since Centerpoint—strangers saluted barely-sixteen-year-old Anakin in Coruscant's Grand Corridor. Vendors of exotic delicacies offered him samples, and supple Twi'lek women twitched their long lekku when he passed.

Luke also wore a Jedi robe today, almost the shade of Tatooine sand. So did Cilghal, the Mon Calamari healer, who sat bowing her massive head over salmon-shaded, webbed hands. She'd brought along her new apprentice, quiet little Tekli. Tekli, a Chadra-Fan with marginal Force talent, seemed perpetually wide-eyed. Her large, fan-shaped ears swiveled whenever an atmospheric craft passed their balcony.

These days were growing long for the healers. Cilghal had confided that they were seeing stress illnesses like never before. The fearful strain of watching an invasion displace and kill so many peoples was like watching a disease eat away at a helpless friend—

Mara caught a glint of blue from Luke's direction. She intercepted his concerned glance and choked off the dismal thought. Her disease, like a protean cancer, had undergone constant random mutations, making it uncontrollable. It should have been fatal.

For three months, she'd been in remission. The tears of an alien creature, Vergere—briefly in custody, with a Yuuzhan Vong agent—had restored her strength. She hesitated to call herself cured, though. *Just as Luke hesitates to call this group a council—because it isn't. For the moment, I feel good. That's enough.*

So she eyed him right back, admiring the signs of maturity. He'd lost that half-ripe farmboy look years ago. Around his intense blue eyes, he'd gathered a network of smile lines—and furrows of concern over the bridge of his nose. Here and there, especially near his temples, he'd sprouted a few gray hairs. Altogether distinguished, she decided.

Ever since that hour in Nirauan's caves, when deadly danger forced them to fight so closely, reaching so deep into the Force that each saw the world through the other's mind, she and Luke had moments when they seemed to fight, think, even to breathe as one person. Utterly different on the surface, their strengths balanced perfectly. Destiny had been kind to Mara Jade, the former Emperor's Hand—and she didn't need the Force to see that their union made Luke Skywalker a happy man.

So naturally, the risk of her suffering a relapse worried him desperately. They still had so many dreams to chase.

Luke flushed.

Then conduct your meeting, Skywalker, she thought at him, amused by his embarrassment. *Quit worrying about me.*

Though their Force link rarely let them communicate in actual words, he clearly caught the message. He turned to Kenth Hamner and said, "Daye Azur-Jamin on Nal Hutta hasn't reported for almost a week. I asked his son Tam to head out that way—carefully—and see if he could get any leading through the siege force's shadow." As at Kalarba, the enemy's massed presence near Nal Hutta seemed to damp down the Force.

"Daye's a good man," Cilghal said softly. "Lowbacca and Tinian got out of Hutt space, didn't they?"

Luke nodded. "They just reported in from Kashyyyk. No sign of enemy activity there."

"At least the Yuuzhan Vong aren't messing with Wookiees at home," Ulaha Kore said lightly. Ulaha was a delicate young Bith, with musical talents that admitted her to any number of intelligence-rich social occasions. Ulaha looked careworn, her posture so slumped that Mara barely could see her large eyes under her protruding, hairless head.

Her comment provoked nervous laughter around the circle, which showed Mara how desperate for levity even the Jedi were getting.

"Nothing out of Bilbringi?" Hamner asked. "Mon Calamari?"

Luke let the colonel steer the conversation to the New Republic's remaining military strongholds. "Nothing unusual at Bilbringi," he answered. "Tenel Ka and Jovan Drark have stationed themselves in public places, looking for dead spots in the Force that could be Yuuzhan Vong in masquers. The same from Markre Medjev, finishing up his research on Bothawui," he said, shooting Mara a rueful glance. With Borsk Fey'lya clinging to power as chief of state, the reduced Fifth Fleet was back in Bothan space, useless to the Core. "And our supply and information lines to Mon Cal are still cut."

They'd been cut for months. The other Jedi sat silently for almost a minute, reflecting on the reports. Luke's eyes fell half-shut.

Mara laced her long fingers, hoping he wasn't trying to get a spin on the future. If the future beat him over the head and demanded to be seen, that was fine. Pushing for it was another matter.

The fountain burbled, a free-form Mon Calamari construct with irregular surfaces. Its top bowl rotated, sending sheets of water down its sides. Mara appreciated its sonic cover. Luke, though, still seemed fascinated by water that didn't have to be forced down from the sky by moisture vaporators. He called these meetings randomly, at different places, but he often chose spots near running water. Maybe he was starting to notice the shapes and patterns of his life, starting the subtle transition from young adulthood toward a hopefully wiser age.

She pursed her lips, frustrated to catch herself thinking that way. She was healthy again. She liked maturity. She respected strength.

But youth had privileges, hopes she still hadn't fulfilled, and maybe never would. She'd seized Vergere's elixir because her instincts said it would work. She had no instinctive leading on when, if ever, she might safely conceive a child.

On the far side of the circle, little Tekli cleared her throat. Fur trembled on her large round ears.

As Luke's eyes opened, Mara felt hers widen a trace. The Chadra-Fan apprentice had never spoken up during a meeting.

"I debated whether to even report this," she began, her voice a musical whisper.

Anakin's lips twisted sardonically. Mara made a mental note to speak with him about his attitude toward the marginally gifted—if Luke didn't do it, first.

"Go on." Cilghal gave an assuring wave with one webbed hand.

Tekli glanced at her mentor, then continued. "Two days ago, I was down near Dometown, in a new strip called JoKo's Alley. Looking for a friend," she added hastily, as if embarrassed to admit she'd been prowling such a riotous area of Coruscant's understory.

"Yes?" Luke gave Tekli a sober, attentive stare. Overseeing the Jedi academy had taught him patience. *They keep learning,* he'd told Mara, *as long as someone encourages them.*

"I heard someone talking in a tapcaf, about—"

"Which one?" Anakin demanded.

Luke extended a hand, palm down. "Wait, Anakin. Go on, Tekli."

She raised her head and stroked her long whiskers. "It was the Leafy Green, actually. Two Rodians were talking about one of the employees, and how if that was a human, he'd eat his . . . I couldn't hear the next words, but we've all heard about ooglith masquers, and how the

Yuuzhan Vong can pass as human. Maybe it's just general jumpiness, Master Skywalker, but it would be easy for . . . for one of your more gifted Jedi to check out."

"Do you want to go back?" Luke asked gently.

Tekli shook her head. "I'm no fighter, sir."

Mara caught a side glance from Anakin. He raised one dark eyebrow at her. She pursed her lips.

Luke glanced toward her, then Anakin. "That's all right, Tekli. I just had two capable volunteers. The Jedi will always be strongest," he added, "when everyone uses their full talents. Whatever you're given to do, do it with all your ability."

Tekli's broad nose twitched with pleasure.

"You're sure you feel up to this?" Luke demanded.

Mara walked beside him down the open-air mezzanine. Along one grand edifice, a gardener droid clung to the trunk of a singing fig tree, pruning away last year's erratic growth.

Luke's cloak billowed behind him, drawing stares. The stares bothered her, after so many years as a shadow agent—and she never wore Jedi robes unless she absolutely had to.

"Of course I'm up to it. I haven't felt so obnoxiously healthy since . . ." She trailed off. "Well, in a while."

"Or I can send someone else with you."

Mara laughed. "Anakin's fine."

She'd asked for a few minutes alone with her husband, so their nephew followed at a polite distance. Without even stretching out through the Force, she felt Anakin's alert mental state. He took his sentry role as seriously as he took everything else.

"He feels terrible about Centerpoint," she added. "That's a load, on top of blaming himself for Chewie's death. He's doing better with that, but he's carrying some serious baggage."

Luke knew it, of course. Luke caught people's feelings just as quickly as she got leadings from her instincts.

"He feels even worse about listening to Jacen," Luke pointed out. "That rift between them worries me."

"*Jacen* worries me," Mara countered. He hadn't left Coruscant in a good frame of mind, and they hadn't heard from him in two months.

They crossed a side passage. A chill breeze, probably from some ventilation system set for Talz comfort, made her shiver. Luke almost opened his mouth to speak, then shut it firmly, raising one eyebrow—a plea for understanding. He'd almost slipped and asked *again* if she was all right. He was pushing his limit for the day.

Don't hover, husband. Again, she thought words at him, but she softened the rebuke with a wink.

His lips twitched. He almost smiled. They'd had this exchange, what . . . a hundred times? It had become one of the myriad comforting rituals of their marriage, almost seven years that had tempered her bitterness with his unwavering devotion.

She glanced back. Anakin followed silently, step-scuffing along with his knee-high brown boots, the way he often did when trying to look relaxed and casual. Three young human women and a sinuous Falleen, probably low-ranking government employees, stopped walking—almost in step—and watched him pass.

With those dark good looks, Anakin definitely had crowd appeal. Coruscant needed a vital young hero. Anakin seemed to attract those who wanted Jedi vigilantes—Kyp Durron's faction—as well as those who still approved of the more traditional Jedi stance of power under extreme discipline. Kyp had courted Anakin hard, between his squadron's engagements.

Mara compressed her lips. She was almost as worried for Anakin as for his despondent brother. Anakin would surely be tempted. Precociously talented, he couldn't claim Luke's virtuous, hardworking upbringing. She'd seen Luke's memories, his deepest regrets and his most secret griefs. She knew how closely the dark had pursued him.

As it would chase Anakin, who was raised by an exsmuggler who loved to bend rules, a loving but often absent mother, her talented aide, and a protocol droid—and at the Jedi academy, in the shadow of two siblings. If Anakin didn't fall to the dark side, then having resisted temptation could leave him even stronger—maybe the most powerful Jedi of his generation.

"About that Yuuzhan Vong agent," she murmured, "if Tekli really spotted one. I want to take him alive. We could get more out of one live prisoner than one more corpse." The xenobiologists did have a few hard-won cadavers, preserved on various worlds. "Such as—what effect trank darts might have on their chemistry."

"It's not ethical to experiment on prisoners." Luke's eyes barely narrowed.

"How are we—"

"It would also be good to know if they can be stunned," he interrupted her in midobjection.

"Point."

Their living armor seemed to turn blaster bolts, but could a lower-energy stun pulse get through? Even if it only disabled the living vonduun crab, that might immobilize a warrior inside.

Running that little experiment, and certainly not on a prisoner, would mean getting closer than anyone but a Jedi would dare try to get.

And Luke hadn't demanded to take the mission. He'd

also just brought her around to his point of view without challenging her, she realized.

Mara touched his arm, and he closed his hand on hers. Their deep bond had suffered during the dark days when she thought she was dying. She'd pulled back into herself, even from Luke.

What a relief, to be able to reengage in their relationship. *Their* marriage ought to be challenge enough to last anyone's lifetime—with or without small dreams to follow them.

The dinner crowd had started to slacken as Mara led Anakin off the repulsor train into JoKo's Alley. She strolled to an overlook, planted both hands on the railing, and stared down.

Far below, layers of lights faded into the dangerous undercity. A hawk-bat swooped, picking granite slugs or some other urban wildlife off duracrete walls. A brilliant yellow turbolift cube raced an orange module up the wall across from her, returning visitors to Coruscant's more populous upper levels.

This district lay far enough down that she couldn't see the high-speed air travel lanes when she looked up, past the edge of military-controlled Dometown. Only local traffic zipped along at this level. A patrol unit hovered, its pod lights blinking a slow blue pulse.

"Quiet evening, so far." Anakin eased up alongside her, turning half away.

Satisfied with her reconnaissance, Mara put the chasm behind her and stared into the crowd. Hesitantly, she opened herself—just a bit—to the Force. Bubbles of emotional noise burst here and there, mostly from people near Anakin's age. An older Quarren couple walked past quickly, heads down, shoulder to shoulder. She saw tension in their twitching facial tentacles. The taller individual kept glancing away from his partner. They kept a broad personal space around themselves.

Carrying something a little too valuable tonight, she concluded.

In the other direction swaggered two human males, one rather loose-limbed, his face glowing with the effects of several mugs of lum. She caught a few words as they passed. ". . . over to the Peace Brigade. That way, if the Vong get this far . . ."

The voice faded, leaving Mara frowning. Coruscant, long a coal bed of intrigue, was turning into a fear-driven focus cooker. Peace Brigaders, humans who had decided to collaborate with the Yuuzhan Vong, did not wear their clasped-hand insignia openly, but she guessed that time was coming.

She slipped one hand inside her long black vest. Beneath the pocketed credcards and her comlink, she wore a loosely hooded burnt-orange flight suit, and her blaster and lightsaber—the one Luke had given her. Long habit made her carry her shoulders at just the right angle to drape her clothing over her armament. Anakin's tunic and loose pants did the trick well enough. He had one odd bulge at the belt, probably a Sabrashi fear stick, but a casual passerby would take them for a woman escorting her son on an evening out.

Son. Again she frowned. With every month that hurried past, driven by the invasion or paced by concerns about the fate of the Jedi, the urge to hold her own child tugged harder—and looked less plausible. Every month, she and Luke resolutely turned away.

Sometimes—according to Cilghal, Oolos, and the other healers—the bizarre disease that plagued her had killed its victims by breaking down the proteins that surrounded cell nuclei. Sometimes, she'd even felt that starting in, seemingly nibbling her bones or other specific organs. An illness that attacked cellular integrity could destroy an unborn child, or alter its cell structure to produce . . . to produce what? she wondered. If she ever had a child, would it even be human?

No, she would content herself with a gifted niece-apprentice and two talented nephews. She and Luke also sponsored—visited, when they could—a thirteen-year-old Bakuran orphan, Malinza Thanas. Malinza's father had died of a lingering ailment, and her mother was killed at another Centerpoint crisis years ago. Luke still felt deeply responsible for the girl, adopted by a well-placed Bakuran family. At distant Bakura, at least Malinza seemed safe from the Yuuzhan Vong.

Thinking of Bakura made Mara imagine how the defeated Ssi-ruuk might have dealt with the Yuuzhan Vong. *Did* these new invaders, evidently dead to the Force, have life energies that could have been drained off to power Ssi-ruuvi technology?

That would be the ultimate humiliation . . .

Anakin eyed a transparent kiosk. At eye level, it showed a three-dimensional, animated holo of five levels in this area.

"Looks like the Leafy Green is two corridors north," he said. "Want to catch another train?"

"We'll walk," Mara answered. "Stay sharp."

She felt him hang back, on her left, as she melted into the flow of passersby. It was a good, defensible two-person formation, with master on point.

Mara turned her head slightly. "Tonight's lesson," she told Anakin. "It's a review." Anakin would never learn skulduggery from her husband, who stuck out in a crowd like a Sunesi preacher.

"Hm." Anakin eyed a trail of moving lights, set like a slidewalk to draw pedestrians into a new restaurant.

"Evaluate constantly," she said. "The more information you collect before shove comes to shake, the more choices you'll have, and the fewer ways your enemy might surprise you."

He held his hands folded in front of him, thumbs pressed together. "I know that." They passed a door that belched out weird odors and a gaseous red mist.

"What about last week, on the simulators?" she demanded. "And while you're thinking about that, lose the Jedi pose."

His arms dropped to his sides. "Flying against you? I never had a chance."

"You attack too early. It's your pattern. Knowing your weakness is the first step toward conquering it." *And I know what you're thinking, Anakin Solo. You think I'm losing my edge.*

Mara altered course as three slightly drunken young Twi'leks lurched their way up the promenade. Anakin maintained his position, well out of their path.

He was a fast learner. His entire generation of Jedi was having to grow up quickly.

Of course, there hadn't been much peace in the galaxy during *her* adolescence either.

More moving lights arched overhead, setting eerie glimmers in clothing, hair, fur, and exposed skin. The crowd pressed tighter in the pedestrian corridor. Here and there she spotted billowy sheets of yellow fungus, developed by a Ho'Din scientist to help oxygenate dark areas of the undercity.

About half a klick farther along, the overhead lights became a tumble of arrow-shaped green leaves. She glanced through a broad doorway. The lights inside weren't as dim as many they'd passed. Across the passage was a garish skin-art studio.

"Well," she murmured, "Tekli's friend has good taste."

She pushed into the Leafy Green. Anakin kept his right elbow near her left.

The tapcaf was built around a central column. As Mara's eyes adjusted, she saw that the column had been carved and shaded to look like a living tree trunk. Above, it parted into dozens of seeming branches. Leaves fluttered in an artificial breeze.

Quite an assassin's loft, in her professional opinion—especially at center, where the branches looked strongest.

"Good evening, gentle friends. A table?"

Mara glanced down at a young Drall, maybe an early emigrant from Corellia. "Yes," she said. "Something near the door." She glanced up, considering that loft at the trunk's center. "And close to the outside wall," where she could keep an eye on the entire establishment.

"Follow, please."

The Drall led them along a soft, springy surface and paused beside a booth built to human dimensions. Mara took the seat facing the entry, leaving Anakin to watch deeper inside the establishment. Her forearm sank into the tabletop, which seemed to be covered with feathery moss. The carpet looked like fallen leaves. She hoped the food was hygienic.

"Something for you, gentles, to begin?" Their server offered the traditional hospitality, meanwhile keying holographic menus to appear over the tabletop.

"Elba water," she answered.

Anakin nodded. "Two."

The husky young Drall's furry back receded along the fallen leaves.

An artificial spring bubbled around the tree's base, humidifying the air. Mara made a mental note to tell Luke about the place. Surreptitiously eyeing other patrons, she saw nothing more hazardous than a young Dug couple arguing over dessert. She and Anakin selected options in the usual way, by flicking the heads-up menu's live spots. Then she turned sideways and leaned against the booth's inner wall.

"See anything?" she asked.

"Not worth mentioning." His eyes kept moving, though. *Good, Anakin.* "If I really hated technology, this is one place on Coruscant where I might feel half comfortable."

"True enough."

There wasn't a service droid in sight. That fact alone was almost enough to make her suspect the manager-owner. Over the long run, droids were significantly cheaper and more reliable than most hired help.

As their server returned with elba water and two covered warmer-plates, a family of Whiphids left noisily, the father humphing around his tusks. Mara spotted another attendant, walking somewhat hunched, carrying a tray out of what looked like a cavernous kitchen. He set down the tray and started gathering used serviceware off a leafy table.

That had to be the one Tekli spotted. He held himself crookedly. He could've been badly injured, but . . .

"That one," Anakin whispered.

"Check him through the Force."

She pressed farther back in the booth, narrowing the angle between Anakin and the human-looking attendant so she could see them both without moving her head. Anakin narrowed his blue eyes, leaning forward enough that a strand of hair fell across his forehead. He frowned.

"You look like the champion of the galaxy," she whispered a warning.

He compressed his lips, irked.

Then he straightened several centimeters.

Mara slid a hand under her vest, getting a grip on her lightsaber. "Nothing?" she murmured.

"Nothing."

Mara stretched out and double-checked Anakin's pronouncement. The alleged human did feel like a shadow—a dead spot, an emptiness.

Anakin was already rising from the table.

"No," Mara said sharply. "Not in the middle of a restaurant full of bystanders."

"What do we do?" he demanded. "He's going to get away."

"Hardly. He's working a shift. We finish our dinner." Mara leaned against the mossy tabletop. "And before we move in, we see if he's got reinforcements in the kitchen."

CHAPTER FIVE

Randa lumbered into the Solos' sleeping shelter. Han was out at the reservoir today, tinkering with something at the pumping station. Jacen had come back for a spare comlink.

Randa barely could fit into the open space between cots, but he tried.

"Bad enough," he fumed, twitching the end of his tail away from the pile of belongings at the foot of Jacen's cot, "that I cannot rush to my homeworld's aid. But now, to be told I must subsist on the same ration allotment as one of the Ryn . . ." He drew up as tall as he could, puffing out his midsection. "Is my body type even remotely similar to those small, furred pests? My metabolism requires—"

"Not the same allotment." Jacen slipped the comlink into a pocket and sat down on his cot, resting his back gingerly against the wall. Some of these buildings had been collapsed by rambunctious Ryn children. "The same percent of standard nutritional ration. If your metabolism is measured at three times a Ryn's, you'll be issued—"

"Not enough. I will waste, shrivel, atrophy. Already I am small for my age." In the light of the shelter's open door, Jacen saw Randa's sunburstlike irises enlarge, narrowing the pupils to slits.

"Was there news from Nal Hutta, Randa? Have you heard, is your parent in danger?"

Bull's-eye. Randa's four-fingered hands opened and closed in frustration. "I have heard nothing," he rumbled, "from my exalted parent."

"I'm sorry," Jacen attempted. "We—"

"The New Republic will not defend Nal Hutta," Randa thundered. "It is sacrificing our world, just as it sacrificed Tynna and Gyndine. We were triaged. They are pulling their forces back toward Coruscant." The mighty tail twitched again. "And those precious shipyards at Bilbringi."

"Bothawui's going to be threatened soon, too," Jacen said flatly. Randa naturally expressed his concern as fear, which easily led to aggression. "We're all in danger, Randa. The fleets are spread so thin—"

"Then why aren't you out fighting, Jedi?" Randa clenched one stubby hand. "I watched a skillful Jedi kill a yammosk. You have talents beyond anything you are able to use here. Your family has done great things."

"I have my own issues, Randa." Jacen shook his head, suspicious of Randa's flattery. He might not know Hutt sincerity if he heard it, but as for his family having done great things . . . well, Randa surely knew who strangled Jabba.

Randa wriggled closer to the shelter's single window, on the opposite wall from the door. "If we could get to Coruscant, you and I could strike a blow that would make the Yuuzhan Vong regret ever coming to this galaxy. My clan has resources on a dozen worlds. We could afford to equip our own squadron, but sadly, fighters are not built for my people."

Jacen tried to imagine a full-grown Hutt in an X-wing. The canopy wouldn't even close!

He had loved flying an X-wing, though. That ship made him feel nimble, powerful, almost invincible.

"I hear you are an exceedingly good pilot." Randa narrowed his huge black eyes and cleared his throat.

"My sister's better." *Jaina!* Three days had passed, and Rogue Squadron still hadn't gotten through with a prognosis. "So is my brother," Jacen admitted, granting Anakin the honor he earned at Lando's Folly, on the asteroid training run—and at the battle for Dubrillion.

"But your honored siblings are not here. Destiny brought us together, Jedi Solo. I could make your name even greater than it already is."

Jacen stretched his arms, cracking his knuckles. His name? At the moment, his name might as well be *bantha fodder* with the Jedi and the New Republic military.

"I will find a way to leave Duro and rush to Nal Hutta's aid, if all I can do is arrive too late and crash a ship in the middle of the invaders' celebratory banquet. Or I shall locate Kyp Durron and throw my support behind his squadron, carrying the battle to the enemy." The Hutt slithered toward the door.

"Randa," Jacen soothed, "we do need your help. Here."

"Oh?" Randa paused. "Tell me, young Solo. What can I do besides stir hydroponics vats? Besides tend the water pumps, and—"

Jacen's comlink beeped. "Hold on," he said, raising one hand in entreaty. "Randa, don't go." He yanked the comlink off his utility belt. "Jacen Solo," he said.

"This is Piani at Communications," a tinny voice announced. "We've finally got that message. You'd better get down here."

Stunned, Jacen flicked his comlink to another channel. "Dad, did you get that?"

The elder Solo's voice sounded fuzzy. Even from short

distances, low-power communications were iffy in Duro's weird atmosphere. "On my way," Han said.

The same contact person as before greeted Jacen over the voice-only link. "Her vision will clear up without medical intervention, over time. She's out of action for several weeks at the inside, though."

Han burst through the control shed's door. "Vision? What was that?"

"The exposure clouded her corneas, Captain," Major Harthis repeated. "It's reversible, but it'll metabolize very slowly." The voice hesitated. "In someone older, we might have implanted artificial eyes, or a Traxes ultrasound enhancer. But she's young, and a Jedi can heal herself pretty well." Longer pause, this time. "We're, uh, also up against some wartime shortages."

Han shook his head. "That's all right. If those eyes will heal, you leave them right where they are."

"That was our feeling. We can't tie up military personnel to nursemaid her, so we're furloughing her to family." The officious voice finally softened. "We'd, ah, like to send her to you on Duro, Captain. That'll save us the trouble of hunting down her mother."

Mara got up from the mossy table. "Stay here," she murmured. Their suspect had vanished into the Leafy Green's kitchen.

Anakin scowled at her half-finished gornt steak. "Be careful."

Wonder of wonders, the boy wasn't going to insist on following her. She'd pull off this reconnoiter alone more easily. "If I'm not back when you've finished your scrimpi, come looking."

Anakin stabbed a slice and sawed off a long, thin bite. The kitchen entry wasn't far from the refresher, and she spotted an empty table nearby. She'd already counted the Leafy Green's sentient staff and checked each one through the Force. Only their suspect seemed absent.

Now, for the kitchen personnel—in case he had reinforcements, or maybe a boss.

She walked purposefully to the empty table, then sat with her face in the shade of her hood. When all the servers—especially the one under suspicion—were off on their rounds, she slipped to the kitchen door. She palmed the opening panel as the servers had done. The door swung aside.

No one challenged her. Keeping one hand near her blaster, which was already set for stun, she eased left along a wall, away from the noisiest area. She found a station where a line of small, four-armed droids, the first mechanicals she'd seen inside the Leafy Green, were laying garnishes on trays. Programmed to react only to food configurations, they ignored her.

She heard four distinctly living presences clattering at other stations, a large sentient staff. The owner was definitely trying to project a pastoral setting. It was a place where a Yuuzhan Vong might choose to establish a cover ID.

She reached down inside herself and then listened through the Force.

Sentient One, near a cooking surface, came through loud and clear—and sweaty. There was Sentient Two, talking near One's shoulder. Number Three scurried toward the back of the establishment. Sliding silently along behind a bank of cooking machinery, Mara tracked her. Through the Force, she wasn't Yuuzhan Vong either, and when Three departed, Mara located a back door. The fourth noisemaker also cast a shadow in the Force—not a pleasant shadow, but not Yuuzhan Vong.

Behind her, the door slid open. She straightened and

pulled her vest closer. Footsteps hustled toward her. She lowered her head and stalked toward the entry.

"I'm sorry, ma'am, but you can't . . . ma'am? Ma'am!"

She jerked up her head. "*Plevay isobabble*," she exclaimed hotly. "*Dekarra do-jui!*"

A human server stood with her forehead scrunched up in bewilderment.

Mara ad-libbed again, this time pantomiming an urgency she didn't feel.

The server spread her hands and smiled, then beckoned. She led Mara out through the door into the dining area, then pointed toward the refresher.

Mara seized her hands, nodding quickly. "*Jeeaph wentz*," she exclaimed, still improvising. Then she hustled up the hall. In the ladies' refresher, she pushed one wisp of red-gold hair back under her hood, waved the water on and off several times, counted ten, then emerged and hurried back to her table. Anakin was sopping up the last of his glockaw sauce with a final bite of scrimpi.

"Just in time," he muttered.

Mara slid in. "He's the only one, as far as I can tell. One of the cooks has a bad feel to him, though. We'll grab when our quarry's on his way home."

Anakin shrugged. "You're in charge."

She made a wry face, thinking, *For the moment, Solo. In about five years, you'll probably be giving the orders.* "You're set for stun, aren't you?"

He nodded curtly.

Spotting a target who didn't show up in the Force would take a little extra attention. Mara posted Anakin at the Green's back door, and she loitered in the busy skin-art parlor across the pedestrian corridor. When the early night shift ended and late workers came on duty, she caught movement out the corner of her eye as her pale, hunched target slipped into the flow of passersby.

"Thanks," she told the attendant, who'd rolled her hookah toward the viewbubble while Mara superimposed abstract samples on her bared shoulder. "Not today, I guess."

"No body contact," the attendant called after her. "Entirely laser done."

Mara was already out the door, straightening her flight suit's neckline and hood. She located Anakin through the Force and nudged him to get moving. At the same time, she double-checked their quarry. He still wasn't there, except to her eyes.

Mara, who was tall enough to see over half the beings between them, followed the server. Now and then, she caught a clear glimpse. He held his head straight forward, looking right or left only when necessary.

"Got him in sight?" She heard Anakin at her left elbow.

"Straight ahead, easing left."

"Where? . . . There," Anakin exclaimed. "He's not wearing armor, just the masquer."

"As far as I can see. They still might not stun easily."

"We'll find out," Anakin said. "I'll get off to one side."

He edged away. Mara kept pace with the pedestrian flow while Anakin drifted left. The restaurant server reached a station where repulsor trains departed the Dometown area. Mara pushed closer, watching more attentively, flowing parallel to her target until he'd chosen a loading platform. Then she pushed through the gate behind a family of armored Psadans. She slipped one of her false IDs through the reader, then settled in to wait, keeping her head down. Out of the corner of her eye, she saw Anakin pass the gate. Not long ago, he would've waved a hand over the reader. She was glad when he used a false ID. The more he learned to operate without using the Force, the better attuned he could stay to its flow and others' movements. He would learn his own capabilities, too. In this respect, Jacen's . . . retreat, for lack of a better word . . . seemed good and honorable.

Sometimes she imagined Jacen forty years in the future, either teaching at the academy or ensconced on his own little world, like Yoda. If he survived.

The next repulsor train swept out of its approach tunnel, emerged on the side of the city-canyon, and braked silently. Mara pushed in with the rest of the crowd. By now, she'd counted and cataloged them by species, sex, and threat level. More intriguing than her fellow passengers was the fact that this run would take them right back where they started, toward the governmental zone.

The train traveled smoothly, its minimal noise covered by conversations inside the thirty-passenger compartment. Her target pushed out through standing riders as they approached Embassies Row and the main SEL-CORE office. Mara caught Anakin's glance and cut her eyes toward the door. He nodded, then followed the server.

Mara let the pod reach one more station before getting off and doubling back. She caught Anakin's sense like a shout through the Force.

The quarry was moving more quickly now, up a lane Mara knew to be lower-income housing for embassies' staffers. She hustled closer, listening for any warning from her finely honed danger sense.

The server finally turned around. Mara kept walking straight, but Anakin stopped and looked aside a little too innocently.

The target ducked down a narrow side passage. Anakin sprinted after him.

Shaking her head in frustration, Mara broke into a run. For all of Anakin's potential, he had the subtlety of a Hutt in a Mon Cal meditation pool.

He's barely sixteen, she reminded herself. *Still plenty young enough to be trigger-poppy.* At least he'd quit trying to wring vengeance for Chewie out of every suspected Yuuzhan Vong in the galaxy.

The cul-de-sac was a high gray corridor that wormed into one of Coruscant's complex edifices. A few windows, none with ledges, opened overhead. Yellowish light standards hung from the third story. The stranger hunched close to a doorway, bending toward an access panel.

Anakin sprinted forward, drew his blaster, and fired. Flickers of blue energy connected with the bent form.

The server whirled, raising one arm.

Evidently that's not close enough! Not even the ooglith masquer seemed affected, so far as Mara could tell. Her lightsaber cleared her vest as she came on.

A black shape slithered down out of the server's sleeve. With his free hand, he flung something toward Anakin. Whatever it was, it screeched as it flew.

Anakin ignited his lightsaber one-handed and lit the cul-de-sac a pale, eerie rose-purple.

Mara couldn't spare Anakin any more attention. Her danger sense was tingling. The server seized his limp black staff at both ends. It stiffened in his grasp, liquid eyes glittering, reflecting Mara's blue blade. She swept her lightsaber low, hoping to hobble the enemy agent.

He brought up the amphistaff, blocking her swing, then tried to force the locked weapons higher. Mara gave ground for an instant, shifted direction, and swung again. At the corner of her vision, Anakin swung at a small, black flying object. It swooped at his face, clawing for his eyes.

She disengaged, sidestepped, and aimed a stroke at the amphistaff's head. *Get with it, Solo! Stun him!* Until she defanged this amphistaff, she couldn't spare one hand to grab her blaster, and Anakin's was in his left hand.

The amphistaff went limp and almost fell out of her opponent's grasp. In the same instant, he abandoned his hunched posture. His face and torso stretched like something out of a bizarre nightmare.

Mara refused to be distracted. She tried another low cut, this time opening one seam of his pants near the knee. White fluid spattered on stone. She'd cut the masquer. In that moment, the amphistaff straightened again, surprising her with a stream of venom. It splashed on the exposed back of her left hand. Her quarry laughed and swung high, going for her throat. She ducked.

Her hand stung. She and Cilghal had developed a biotoxin drill, and she called scavenging white cells, now laden with the mysterious essence of Vergere's tears, to her left hand.

Evidently convinced he'd killed her, the warrior reached for a pouch at his belt. Mara straightened and swung one-handed, aiming for the pouch. Again, that tingling at the back of her mind came just in time. She backstepped swiftly as the alien flung down the pouch. Something splashed out of it near her feet. It reached up pseudopodia, grabbing for her feet.

You again! Scowling, she vaulted the sticky blorash jelly. She tossed her lightsaber to her stiffening left hand and reached inside her vest for her blaster.

Anakin was closing in from behind, out of the enemy's line of vision. His lightsaber dispatched the swooping attack creature. Then he pulled his other weapon from his belt. Not a smooth-sided fear stick at all, it almost looked like a Stokhli spray stick, but it was smaller and shorter.

Mara left her blaster holstered, reached across to cross hands on her lightsaber, and swept in again. The warrior swung his amphistaff once more.

Maybe the staff creature's ability to heal itself made it almost impervious. She swung hard and fast, aiming directly into the snake head's crest, while ducking aside. Half of the head flew off, hitting the nearest stone wall with a satisfying crunch. The amphistaff went limp.

Yes!

At that moment, Anakin fired. A blast of pale-blue webbing shot hissing out of his weapon.

Mired by gooey residue, the Yuuzhan Vong managed to fling two more razor-edged living disks. One circled Mara's head, diving and spinning. The other went for Anakin. She dispatched hers as the warrior fell, struggling against the web's stun charge. Finally, she drew her blaster. It whined as she fired off a stronger stun burst from practically on top of her target.

Even that didn't quiet him. Evidently they couldn't be stunned—at all. She closed down her lightsaber, got a good grip, and whacked his temple.

He collapsed.

Anakin sprinted close. "Let me unmask it," he exclaimed.

Mara stepped back, still gripping her lightsaber, and let youthful determination take over. She opened and closed her left hand cautiously. It still tingled, but it hadn't lost sensation.

The warrior's face seemed to be bleeding white where she whacked it. Cautiously, Anakin fingered a faint line along the creature's nose. The skin started rippling, as if something was moving under its surface—then peeled back from the motionless face, taking the wounded spot along with it. The living ooglith masquer shrank into the throat of the Yuuzhan Vong's restaurant uniform, making slurping noises as it pulled free of its carrier's pores.

Underneath, the alien was pale-skinned, with little flesh on its face. Bluish sacs hung under both eyes, with one upper cheek burned almost through, leaving a scar that showed bone. Tattoos like concentric energy bursts crossed its forehead. The exposed cheekbone showed a network of healed, jagged fractures.

The masquer created a rolling bulge as it shrank toward the warrior's legs. The Stokhli web finally trapped it near its owner's knees.

"Good idea, the Stokhli stick," Mara murmured.

Anakin stuck it in his belt. "New model, short range. Almost concealable."

"Surprised me," she admitted. It bothered her that he'd found one before she'd even heard of it. As he beamed, she pulled out her comlink. "Enforcement? Mara here. We've got our infiltrator."

CHAPTER SIX

With the captured Yuuzhan Vong laid out on an examining table and the wounded masquer contained inside a transparisteel tank, Mara folded her arms and rested against a wall. New Republic Intelligence would take over from here, but she lingered. Anakin hadn't gone far, either.

Exobiologist Dr. Joi Eicroth had pulled back her fair hair into a tail. She spread an array of tools and drug ampules on a tray near the table, then stood, shaking her head. "We know only enough about their physiology," she said, "to know that we don't know enough."

Mara pushed away from her wall. "At least we found out that a stun burst won't bring them down, no matter how close we get."

"I doubt," Eicroth said, "that many people will want to get that close."

The Yuuzhan Vong had been draped with a poncho after medics confirmed she was female. Tufts of black hair grew here and there on her skull, and half her body was tattooed with concentric designs like the ones on her forehead. Eicroth pointed out a focal point that looked vaguely like a living creature. Claws protruded from her knuckles. The exobiologist had anchored restraint bands over her forearms and across her legs and torso.

Cilghal stood with Mara. She'd examined Mara's

hand, taking skin and blood samples for the other medics. Then she tried to revive the Yuuzhan Vong. Neither inhalants nor mild shocks worked. By invitation, she, too, lingered.

Belindi Kalenda of NRI—recently demoted to Lieutenant Colonel, over the misinformation flap—strode into the room, and Eicroth straightened. Lieutenant Colonel Kalenda was small and dark-skinned, and she wore her tightly curled hair in a bunch at the nape of her neck.

She got a good look and frowned. "I'm impressed," she said. Tricked by the alleged Yuuzhan Vong defector, then again by their feint at Corellia, at least Kalenda hadn't been drummed out of the service. "I wouldn't have thought it was possible to get one of these alive." She shot one more glance at Dr. Eicroth. "You're recording? We can't waste this."

"If we get anything," Mara said. She'd faced enough of these aliens to expect a fresh surprise every time.

Above the table hung a full-body scanner. This time, there'd be body-fluid analyses, readings of organ functions, maybe even a map of the body's microelectric fields. A chem readout might hint at what drugs could affect them. Personally, Mara would appreciate information on their nervous systems—especially what might bring them down, besides whacking their temples.

She stared at the alien warrior, half wishing they might've spoken woman to woman, instead of as predator and prey, captor and prisoner. Mara knew what it felt like to slowly realize she'd been raised by the wrong side.

The Yuuzhan Vong warrior stirred. Mara stepped closer. Kalenda eyed the overhead readouts.

The warrior's eyes opened. She recoiled from the machinery above her, working her face violently.

Mara stretched out a hand. "We don't want to harm you," she insisted. "I know you know Basic. I saw you at work in the Leafy Green. Let us help you. We'll send you back to your people, if—"

The prisoner interrupted, shrieking out a long, unintelligible speech, maybe to her gods. As she did, her body arched, fighting the bonds. Dr. Eicroth edged back. Anakin stepped closer, one hand on his lightsaber.

From the warrior's right hand, a claw stretched to four times its sessile length. It slashed the steelfab forearm bond as if it were flimsiplast. Then with one arm freed, the warrior balled a fist.

Anakin ignited his blade with a *snap-hiss*.

"No!" Mara shouted.

Without hesitating, the warrior slashed her claw across her own throat. Black blood spurted. Cilghal sprang forward, pressing a wad of synthflesh to the wound with one broad, webbed hand while reaching aside for fluid packs. Another aide restrained the prisoner's free hand. A surgical droid that Cilghal had parked out of the prisoner's sight rolled close and went to work.

Mara exhaled, hoping the readouts would provide some usable information. She'd gotten a bit of data herself—even more respect for those fighting claws. She would make sure that information went out in Dr. Eicroth's report.

An hour later, as midnight passed, she sat at a light table rerunning that report and Cilghal's medical scans. The prisoner had managed to bleed to death, and Mara sent Anakin home in his skimmer. Luke stood at her shoulder, tracing with one finger the lines of multiple skull breaks. Mara watched him sidelong, trying to read his reaction. His face had been savaged years ago by a wampa ice creature. Would these people accept bacta treatment, since the only technology it required was a tank to contain the organisms?

Probably not. They wore their scars proudly.

"The claws are creatures, too," she observed out loud. It was late enough that she no longer cared she was rambling. "Parasites, embedded deep into bone. That's got to hurt."

"They cherish pain," Luke murmured.

Mara shook her head. Loosed from her hood, red-gold hair flopped over her shoulders. "This wasn't worth what we risked for it."

"You took one Yuuzhan Vong operative out of commission," Luke pointed out. "And found a way to kill the amphistaffs."

"Not enough."

"Mara," he exclaimed, and she heard the exasperation in his voice. "Just having you on your feet is almost a miracle. Can't you be thankful for small accomplishments?"

Trim from years of lightsaber drills and self-imposed gymnastic training, he'd picked up a scar or two himself, and his right hand was only a re-creation. His exquisite empathy gave both hands a powerful sensuality, though.

"You know me better than that," she muttered, turning back to the scans. "Look at the nervous system. The microelectric fields are fully redundant. If they like to suffer, they're built for it."

"That must be why they can't be stunned."

"One point for you."

Half smiling, he leaned closer to the readout. "She didn't have as many bone breaks or scars as the one they scanned on Bimmiel."

"That isn't hard to figure out. They give low-ranking

youngsters undercover work to prove themselves."
Mara fought back a yawn.

Luke stared pointedly at the Yuuzhan Vong female.

"Thanks," Mara said dryly, "but you don't have to
pretend not to notice. I have a good reason to be tired.
Let's get some sleep."

Luke had parked a skimmer on the rooftop pad. He
slipped in first, claiming the pilot's seat. Mara let him.
From the Intelligence complex, it was a short hop—
mostly open-air—back to their part of the Imperial Palace. Mara stared over a solid line of wing- and taillights.

"Reminiscing?" Luke asked.

She pulled her vest closer, hoping her sudden shiver
was due to the evening chill. Several times, close prox-
imity with the Yuuzhan Vong had seemed to spark re-
lapses of her illness.

"Hardly," she said.

He'd learned to respect her silences, and the times
when she simply didn't care to explain. She kept quiet as
he slipped the skimmer into a parking slot as smoothly as
any other pilot with fighter status. He'd retested, kept up
his hours, and was still legally qualified to fly almost anything the New Republic could scramble against the Yuuzhan Vong, short of a Mon Cal battleship.

Count on Skywalker to do everything legal and
square.

The corridors in their part of the palace were lined in
exotic woods, sculpted with intricate swirls to deaden the
echoes of feet hustling up Wayland marble tiles. Mara
hung back, keeping both hands in her vest pockets, and
let Luke open the door. It was plainer than most, but a
good meter taller than either of them.

She sent the door shut and dropped her long vest over
a service droid. From her left, a greeting tootled from

the data/recharge station. Luke greeted his mechanical friend with an equally friendly chirrup. "Hi, Artoo."

Their suite was small but elegant, and she liked living in a central location. Ahead, down three steps, a transparisteel vista window looked out over Coruscant. The spires of a new construct stuck up between Mara and the moonset.

She yawned. Leaning against a wall, she stared out at the large moon, watching as it crept lower, seeming to grow larger and duller as it slipped into city haze. Even a simple moonset looked ominous nowadays. If the enemy remade Coruscant, as they'd done to Belkadan, what color would these moonsets turn?

Warm arms slipped around her from behind. "Bed?" Luke murmured against her ear.

She closed her hands over his. "In a minute."

"What's wrong?"

"Nothing." That was her knee-jerk reaction, and Luke knew it. For some silly reason, he still asked. "I feel almost obnoxiously well."

"You're . . . uneasy, though," he said. "And, no, I didn't use the Force to see it. I just know you."

"Well done," she muttered, not in a mood to smart-mouth him. "It's not for myself. Look out there. How many thousands of homes do we see? How safe are they, really?"

His chin rested on her shoulder. He didn't answer, but his arms tightened on her waist.

"All over the Rim, they've lost homes. Whole worlds. Closer in, they're not thinking about anything but how to survive. What kind of life is that?"

She meant it as a rhetorical question, and he didn't answer. *You've learned, Skywalker!* she thought wryly. Since he didn't argue, she had to press on. "We're Jedi.

We protect life. That's worthwhile, but it has nothing to do with the kind of life they live."

"We can't make choices for them. How long have you been telling me that?"

"Years. And I'm still right. But people who live in constant terror and grief—how much better are they, really, than the slaves sprouting coral all over their bodies?"

He simply tightened his arms around her middle, so again, she had to answer herself. "Better, of course," she admitted. "They aren't in agony. But don't you ever wonder . . . or maybe you can tell me . . . what is the effect on the Force of all this violence and desperation? The threat of invasion brings out fear and anger. The dark side gets stronger. What counters it?"

"Little hopes," Luke answered. "Little joys."

Mara stared at the shrinking moon. "It's like our situation," she admitted, "but it's everywhere."

He raised one hand to stroke her shoulder.

Her head drooped. "Just preserving those who are alive feels like a dead end. But what choice do we have?"

"Only to go on serving, with every day we still have life in us." Luke's voice was softer than the dying moonlight. "To defend people who can't defend themselves. To die for them, if we must. Like Chewie did."

Mara leaned back against his chest. "I outlived the Empire," she muttered. "The loss of my livelihood—a man I loved and served. I could outlive the New Republic. I love stability and ease . . . and you, incidentally."

His hand tightened.

"But simply . . . staying alive isn't everything. Don't you see? We're only trying . . . to prevent the subtraction of life."

"You've added to mine, Mara," he said softly, dryly. "Come get some rest."

CHAPTER SEVEN

Crowded around a tracking screen in the hardened control shed, Jacen, Han, and the Ryn Piani watched a small blip grow on the tracking screen, while Randa sulked in a corner and Droma stared out the view-bubble. A tickling sensation finally thrust itself into the back of Jacen's mind.

"It's Jaina," he confirmed.

Han crossed his arms, frowning. "How is she?"

Jacen examined the feeling. "Mad," he concluded.

One of Thirty-two's snakelike cofferdams was extended to the med runner. Jacen and Han stood at the foot of its landing ramp as the hatch opened. First off was a Mon Cal pilot, wearing the tri-circle insignia of the New Republic medical service. She had long, feminine webbed hands. "Captain Solo?"

Han stepped forward. "You've got my girl, I hope." His voice echoed oddly inside the cofferdam.

"Her attendant's helping her forward. Sign here, please." The pilot thrust out a datapad.

"Nope," Han said. "Not till I see her."

Watching over his father's shoulder, Jacen spotted a dark gray coverall, dark hair chopped surprisingly short, and his sister's face, half covered by some kind of mask.

Jaina batted away her droid-attendant's extended

limb. "I can walk down a ramp. Hi, Dad. Hello, Jacen. Thanks for coming to pick up the pieces."

She walked down, limping slightly. Han embraced her, rocking from foot to foot. Then Jacen slipped his arms around her shoulders. Until he knew more about her injuries, he didn't want to squeeze.

"I'm not a skeleton leaf," she growled, tightening her grip. Her fingers dug into his triceps.

"Here are your instructions." The medical droid presented Han with a second datapad.

Jaina turned away. Two curved, darkened lenses hung from a soft headband, with several connectors alongside. Jacen hoped the meds hadn't had to implant anything under her scalp to make the thing work.

"You can see well enough to recognize us," he said. "That's not bad."

"I can tell you apart through the Force. What I see is shadows and darker shadows. It's getting better." She shut her mouth firmly, but only for a moment. "I can already make out shapes on a threat board. Sending me here was a waste of fuel—unless you've heard something I haven't." She folded her arms and glared at Jacen. "Am I terminal or something, and they just haven't told me?"

"No," Jacen exclaimed. He couldn't resist stretching out through the Force. His sister's presence pulsed red-hot—an ember, not a flame. "No, you're healing well. They just didn't want to risk you in combat. Or risk that you'd endanger someone else," he added, trying to push her anger away. Standing beside her made him edgy, almost as if the ground were vibrating.

"Not you, too." Jaina pulled off her mask and pushed her face closer to his. Her eyes did look cloudy, the pupils faintly gray.

Finished with the medical team, their dad clapped an

arm around her shoulder. "Come inside, sweetie. I'll get you settled before I head back to the pumping station."

They found her a cot in a hut with an elderly Ryn woman, whose husband had died on the *Jubilee Wheel* over Ord Mantell, and who was glad for company. As Han hurried off, Jaina grudgingly let Jacen stow her belongings under the shelter's second cot. She turned her head toward the small window.

"I can see fine, if there's enough light."

"That's a problem in Thirty-two," Jacen admitted. "The cloud cover doesn't let much in." And these SEL-CORE shelters had just one door and one window. "A little light gets in through the roof panels," he added, gesturing upward.

These huts were suited only for domed environments. One good storm would blow off the roofs, then wash the mortar out from between mud bricks that reinforced the synthplas walls.

"How long did it take to get used to the stink?"

Jacen's face warmed. He glanced at the older woman seated on the other bunk. Jaina wasn't just smelling Duro's atmosphere. The Ryn had this odor . . .

"That's partly me," the Ryn said bluntly.

"Less than a day." Jacen got the words out quickly. "And, Clarani, you know it's not you in particular. Your people just have a different body chemistry."

Jaina shook her head slowly. "Sorry," she muttered. "You're generous to take me in. The last thing you need is an ungrateful kid in your house."

"Don't worry." Clarani gestured left and right, taking in the door they'd left open for light—and the small window, with its primitive shelf-row storage. "I'm tired of sleeping alone."

When Jaina raised a hand to adjust her mask, Jacen spotted a tremor. She really had been through it.

"So bring me up to speed," he said casually. "What have the Rogues been up to, and who fried your X-wing?"

"I did. That's the worst of it."

"You?"

She sighed. "I was chasing a skip. At Kalarba," she added.

"Yes, they told us. I guess Druckenwell's gone, too?" That had been a major Imperial manufacturing center.

"And Falleen. They've reached Rodia. It's the heavy end of the hammer, pounding and pounding."

"Unbelievable," Jacen muttered, wondering if the Falleen had fought to the last drop of green blood or else used their infamous pheromones to buy a measure of freedom.

Jaina didn't offer details, and this wasn't the time to press. "I stayed a little too close to a cruiser that was under attack," she said. "When it blew, I . . . caught some radiation. I should be fine in a couple of weeks," she insisted. "No permanent damage."

"Good."

In return, Jacen gave her a fast explanation of Thirty-two's water purification project, the ancient pit mine that had filled with toxic groundwater, the settlement's nominal partnership with Gateway beyond low, blasted hills, and their supply problems. CorDuro Shipping, contracted by SELCORE to deliver supplies to the refugee domes, had missed two shipments this month and been late with the other eleven.

"There's plenty of work here," he added. "Mechanical stuff. Your specialty."

She snorted. "Save it for somebody who doesn't know how to vape skips, Jacen. They're taking this galaxy away from us. The forces need every decent pilot we can get. That's where you ought to be. Even Dad."

She sounded disturbingly like Randa—anxious, angry. Again he thought of his vision, and the potential repercussions of one step in the wrong direction.

"Instead of stuck here, taking care of helpless folks?" Clarani put in. "Think again, young woman. Who were you fighting to save? You're not out there playing death-tag for fun and excitement."

"True." To Jacen's surprise, Jaina's voice sank. "And I worry . . . a little . . . that when I get back in an X-wing, I'll punk out."

"Not you," Jacen said.

"It's different now." She laced her fingers on the lap of her dark gray coverall. "Did they tell you I lost Sparky?"

"No." Jacen turned toward the Ryn woman. "Sparky was her personal droid. She's had him—"

"A while," Jaina said. "Long enough to start depending on him. I know they're just mechanical, but . . . he was great." Her shoulders slumped.

Jacen shook his head.

"Never having owned a droid," the Ryn woman said, "I might not seem sympathetic. But we'll all lose more than we already have, before all this is over."

"You ended up EV?" Jacen asked.

Jaina nodded.

He compressed his lips. Losing a fighter around you and going extravehicular did terrible things to the comforting illusions that kept fighter pilots rushing into those cockpits. At the back of their minds, it was always the other guy who got shot up—the one who just wasn't as quick, or as good in a clinch shot, or as sharp-eyed. He stared at Jaina's mask.

"Want dinner?" he asked. "Part of the stink is what we'll eat tonight."

Jaina shook her head. "My day cycle just shifted. It's almost midnight where I've been. I just want to sleep.

"Do me a favor," she added, looking straight at him. Jacen felt her emotions shift subtly. "I want to spend the night in a healing trance. Give me a push. I can't get as deep as I want, without you."

He hesitated.

"I know," she said. He had the sense that her stare, such as it was, didn't waver. "The whole galaxy knows you've been trying not to use the Force. This is me, your sister. I need to get well."

"You're right." Embarrassed, he shoved his reluctance aside. "I'll help. But you need to know that it's gotten worse."

"Why?" she demanded. When she tilted her head up and frowned, she looked almost exactly like their mom.

"I saw . . . this vision." He described it for her.

She listened, nodding—but she asked again for his help. He couldn't refuse. Soon she lay in a deep healing subsleep, her chest rising and falling so slowly that a stranger might have worried that she wasn't breathing.

But when he looked with his spirit, he saw that her legs, right side, and left hand were all targets of an intense effort. Around and through her eyes, energy flowed with particular intensity. Bacta, that miraculous microscopic healer, had done such a good job on her tissue injuries that she wouldn't have any visible scars. She wouldn't limp much longer, either.

I'd be a good healer, he complained to himself, but he knew the answer to that. Just because he was skilled in an area, that didn't make it the call on his life. People who told him he was lucky to be so broadly "gifted" didn't have to make his decisions.

The next morning, he spotted her ambling up the alley, trailing one hand along the rough wall of the nearest hut.

He grabbed her other hand and guided her to a mess area. Ryn of all ages congregated around five females with site-built cooking pots. Jaina sniffed the air.

Jacen touched her elbow and guided her to a place in line. "Looks like—" He glanced into the nearest pot. "Mm, breakfast phraig." He lowered his voice and muttered in Jaina's ear, "SELCORE must've gotten a contract for some planet's entire phraig harvest . . ." He trailed off as the nearby cook spotted them.

"The Rogue pilot," she exclaimed.

Up and down the serving line, Ryn heads turned. Two leather-winged Vors stared down pointed faces. A family of humans set their trays aside and applauded.

Jaina's lips twisted.

"You to the front of the line, missy," the cook said. "Maybe we can't do anything for your wingmates, but you tell them—when you get back—that Camarata said thank you."

When Jaina tried to protest, Jacen elbowed her. "These refugees can only give you a touch of special treatment. It's all they have. Let them honor Rogue Squadron, if you don't want it for yourself."

He guided her to the front of the line, steadied her bowl while one of the women ladled a dipper full of pale-brown steamed grains, mixed with a few bits of dried fruit. Then he got himself a bowlful and grabbed two mugs of imitation caf.

They took a seat on a long slab of duracrete. Jaina gripped her spoon halfway up the handle and got a bite into her mouth.

"Bland," she said, "but not bad. I'm sorry I was lousy company last night."

"This can't be real easy for you."

"Always understanding everybody else's viewpoint, that's my little brother."

He smiled wryly. For about two years, she had been taller.

She shook her head, then turned aside, so he saw the reflection of a Ryn family on her faceplate. "I hate this," she said. "I'm the older sister. The ace pilot. Did you know, I almost got as many kills in the last three weeks as the squadron's top ten percenters? Do you realize what that means to me?"

"Yes. You're one of the hottest pilots there ever was."

"I'm scared to lose that, Jacen."

"Of course. But I read your diagnosis pad last night. You really are expected to get better. Fast."

"Then why did they send me here?" Her voice dropped to a whisper.

"I told you last night. The med facilities are bursting."

"Yeah," she said. "And do you know they haven't been able to raise Mom?"

"I don't understand that."

"Well, they didn't try real long and hard. But I hope nothing happened to her."

"We'd know if . . ." Jacen trailed off.

"So where is she?"

He shrugged. "Working refugees. She could be here on Duro, and we'd never know it. We can't keep the comm cables up, the murk's too thick for line-of-sight, and we haven't gotten a good antenna from SELCORE yet."

Jaina finished her breakfast and patted the duracrete, looking for her mug.

As Jacen shoved it toward her hand, he spotted motion at the edge of his field of vision. An immense, tan-colored blob of motion.

"Uh-oh," he murmured.

"What?" Her head whipped around.

"Randa," he said quickly, "our resident Hutt. Wants

revenge on the Yuuzhan Vong. He'll try to get you into his own plans for combat. He's been working on me."

"Tell him I can't."

"You tell him," Jacen said. "Here he comes."

CHAPTER EIGHT

Two days later, Jacen adjusted his breath mask and leaned against Thirty-two's duracrete main gate, waiting for the CorDuro supply shuttle. The gray dome faded toward a foggy height. SELCORE couldn't afford to equip its refugees with costly enviro-suits, only cheap chem suits and cumbersome rebreathers like Jacen's. There were times when he'd gladly blast off again.

Randa's offer rose back to his mind, but he rejected it. If he turned to aggression, that would betray everything he'd promised to stand for, not to mention his vision.

But couldn't he fight without using the Force?

On his right, the sealed end of a retracted, tube-shaped cofferdam lay along one edge of a blasted-out crater. That tube could be run out to mate with a freighter's cargo hatch. Thirty-two had been promised a load of chemical fertilizers for its hydroponics operation. Without them, the new crop of foodstuffs would wither in the tanks.

Still, it didn't take a Jedi Master to realize this freighter wasn't coming. Frowning, Jacen slipped into the wide gate, a modified airlock. He paused to let air currents whisk most of the crud off of his clothes, sloshed his boots in a settling tub, then paced up the dome's edge to the control shed.

"It isn't coming," a deep voice rumbled.

Randa had positioned his belly in front of the control board. Two older humans sat cross-legged on the floor, playing a tile game. Beyond them, the viewbubble looked out on the landing zone's blast crater.

"Any word out of Nal Hutta?" Jacen asked gently.

"The Glorious Jewel," Randa fumed, "is under remote bombardment. Missiles are bursting in her atmosphere. They are causing no damage my people's sensors can pick up from remote stations, but we know what the enemy did to Ithor."

Jacen frowned. "Did your people evacuate?"

"Many of my kajidic had already left for Gamorr and Tatooine. Rodia, too." Randa's broad slash of a mouth pulled aside. "But now Rodia's under attack."

Jacen shook his head.

"Noble news out of Kubindi, though. Tragic, but noble."

"Oh?" Jacen leaned one arm against the comm board. News from outsystem was getting rare enough to tolerate listening to Randa relay it.

"Word is out that Kyp's Dozen—"

Jacen clenched a hand at that name, but he didn't interrupt.

"—held off a Yuuzhan Vong attack force long enough that the Kubaz got every spaceworthy ship offplanet. You cannot call that anything less than heroic."

Grandstanding came to mind, but Jacen held his peace. "I thought he was over at Bothawui."

"Exactly. Anticipating their attack, he made the long trek—"

"Listen, Randa." Jacen frowned. "I just don't admire Kyp the way you do." *And Kyp has no patience with Hutts*—but Jacen didn't say that. "He killed millions."

Randa waved a stubby arm. "Long ago. He was young—"

"Well, I'm young now. And I don't approve."

"Tragic," Randa said softly. "The way the Jedi are dividing. Supposedly, Jedi protect others. I see none of that from you, Jedi Solo. Take Wurth Skidder. He was a warrior." He recited the story again: Skidder's bravery on board the Yuuzhan Vong clustership; Skidder's attempt to communicate with the hideous yammosk war coordinator; Skidder dying in bitter agony, sending the rescue crew off without him. Randa had vowed to avenge himself on the Yuuzhan Vong, honoring Wurth Skidder.

Jacen wondered what the young Hutt really wanted.

"As far as I can see," Randa concluded, "Durron is the only Jedi who truly is carrying the fight to the Yuuzhan Vong."

"That's only half true," Jacen said carefully. "The Jedi based on Coruscant are working just as hard as Kyp, without calling attention to themselves. No fanfares, no tricks flying into battle—"

Randa spat toward a bucket he'd placed in the room's darkest corner. The tile-game players startled, then returned to their game.

"How long," he rumbled, "will Coruscant hold out if the Yuuzhan Vong attack?"

"That's the last place the fleets would let them take." But Jacen had wondered the same thing. That really would be the end—and Uncle Luke had stood near Coruscant in his vision. "Listen, Randa. Master Skywalker is right—we have to be cautious about using the Force. We have to resist anger, hate, and aggression. Those will tempt us into an evil that's just as dangerous as the Yuuzhan Vong."

Randa grumbled in Huttese.

"It's right for us to gather intelligence," Jacen pressed. "To protect and advise others. To heal their hurts. That's the force of good, Randa. Kyp's people . . . maybe they haven't slipped over to the dark side, but they're sliding."

Randa clenched his tiny hands and puffed up to his full size. "Spare me your dark side and light side. If you're a Jedi, act like a Jedi, or get out of the way and let other Jedi do what this war requires . . . to protect others!"

"I'm working on that," Jacen insisted.

Abruptly, Randa turned conciliatory. "Of course you are," he soothed, but not before Jacen made one more mental note about Randa Besadii Diori's flattery: It could turn ugly in an instant. The Hutt was a spice merchant, a manipulator. "Here is my vision," Randa said. "My fantasies have matured, and you could find glory helping me fulfill them."

Jacen rolled his eyes. "Go ahead."

Randa moistened his lips with his fat, wedge-shaped tongue. "I see myself," he said, "as a pirate chieftain, wreaking havoc on the Yuuzhan Vong . . . with Kyp Durron as my example."

Jacen wondered how Kyp would react to a Hutt using him as an example.

"Who better to head my squadron than a Jedi? And fate has delivered a Jedi to me, one who has withdrawn from their normal operations. You see, Jacen, all I need is to somehow get an influence over you, then convince you to do what I want."

Surprisingly frank, for a Hutt. "There isn't a single ship here at Thirty-two that would suit your purposes."

"No," the Hutt admitted. "But over at Gateway, there are faster vessels. Ours for the taking."

"No, Randa. I won't steal, I don't want to be a pirate, and I don't believe in your vision. I'm sorry. Now, I need a GOCU line."

Sighing heavily, Randa slid away from the main comm board. Jacen settled in at the ground-orbit comm unit, drumming his fingers on its edge while he waited for his call to go through. He wondered if Randa might resort to intimidation, once it grew obvious that flattery wouldn't produce what he wanted.

Jacen's first call raised the Duros military, as usual. The Duro Defense Force was a nervous bunch these days. Admiral Wuht's comm team was on the job this morning. Negotiating the usual runaround took most of Jacen's next hour. Randa thrust his huge head through the door three times, demanding progress reports.

"Waiting for Admiral Dizzlewit," Jacen murmured each time.

Finally, Jacen talked himself far enough down the line to reach a shipping clerk who seemed willing to check records. Yes, the shuttle in question had arrived at Bburru City. CorDuro Shipping had taken charge of the transfer. A CorDuro pilot had taken off with it, bound for Urrdorf City—the smallest Duros orbital city.

Stolen! "I know these routing checks are inconvenient for you," Jacen said tightly. "You've done an incredible job, getting me this much. Many thanks."

He cut the connection and flicked his comlink. "Dad?"

After several seconds, he got an answer. "Find it, Junior?"

"The Duros diverted it." Randa's monstrous head poked through the door again. Jacen pushed his chair aside and beckoned the Hutt forward, still explaining. "Dad, I think this would justify spending the fuel to go up and talk to them." Han had taken Thirty-two's outdated I-7 Howlrunner shuttle up to Bburru twice that first week, talking to Admiral Wuht.

"No," Han said firmly. "They don't want to talk. We'll think of something. Borrow supplies from Gateway, maybe."

Jacen knew exactly what his dad meant when he said "borrow."

An unexpected transmission called Tsavong Lah away from *Sunulok*'s villip choir. In that chamber, signal villips fashioned optical fields that showed long arcs of space, sent by villips positioned for relay. Images from Nal Hutta showed the seeding of microbes that would re-shape the scum-ridden, pestilent planet—and its ghastly moon, covered with technological monstrosities—back into something fertile and lovely. Some of the organisms, bred by master shapers, would digest Nar Shaddaa's metal and transparisteel into dust that would settle into lower strata. Other microbes would break down both worlds' duracrete into sand for new soil. Still other bac-teria would attack organic matter, including the Hutts' bloated corpses, to enrich that soil. Buried under natural terrain, the world and its moon would live again.

There was also the matter of Mujmai Iinan, a lieu-tenant who had proposed taking Kubindi with half the usual number of coralskippers. Disgraced by the sub-stantial evacuation of Kubindi, Iinan waited in a medita-tion chamber. In less than an hour, the gods would receive him.

Tsavong Lah was not pleased to be called away, but the executor's report was worth hearing. Seated in the coral-lined privacy chamber, he glared at the villip's ren-dition of Nom Anor's dumbfounded face. "Not one *Jeedai*, but three?"

Nom Anor's eyes widened even farther. It was unusual

for a warmaster to repeat information. "Yes, Warmaster. Three have been spotted now."

The warmaster drew up to his formidable height, squaring his spiked shoulders. "Not by you."

"By my agents. I scrupulously avoid their presence."

"Their names," Tsavong ordered, relaxing.

"Leia Organa Solo remains supervisor of this dome. My assistants alert me whenever she approaches the laboratory."

"Your assistants approach worthiness."

"I wish I could convey your compliments."

"When Duro is liberated, you may offer them yourself."

The villip showed Nom Anor's head nod in gratitude. "You honor us all. The other two Jedi came to my attention only this morning. My agents on Bburru have monitored a number of outsystem calls from Settlement Thirty-two. They finally identified a passenger who arrived by medical evacuation ship as Organa Solo's daughter, Jaina. CorDuro Shipping reports dealing with another, at Thirty-two—Jaina's brother, the cowardly Jedi who went missing from Coruscant—"

Perplexed, Tsavong Lah interrupted, "Is this family in blood feud? Avoiding one another, to prevent embarrassment?"

"I find no evidence of either. It seems possible, though almost unbelievable—even for this godless race—that the offspring have no idea of the mother's location, nor she of theirs. The coward's name—"

"Name me no coward. He is not worthy to be known."

"Then may I offer a suggestion?"

Tsavong Lah nodded.

"I have developed a new organism."

Tsavong Lah frowned. Nom Anor fancied himself a shaper, dabbling in others' sanctified specialties.

"When we need to break down these abominable domes and let in living atmosphere," Anor continued, "it should be useful. Meanwhile, I would like to test it in the two younger Jedis' dome. *Bruk tukken nom canbintu.*" He quoted the adage: to weaken the hinges of the enemy's fort.

"Why not your own?" It would be an honorable self-immolation.

"*Belek tiu,* Warmaster." Nom Anor apologized, and the warmaster let him continue. "This research complex serves our long-term purposes, and Jedi Organa Solo helps other workers make maximum use of resources. For that reason, this dome's destruction should be delayed."

Tsavong Lah could not fault the executor's reasoning. "Only so long as she remains ignorant of your presence. Somehow, these *Jeedai* recognize us through ooglith masquers. I have little faith that your new gablith masquer would deceive her." Jedi magic worked without sacrifices to the Yuuzhan Vong gods, which made it almost as abominable as the infidels' technology. "The priests," he added dryly, "change their minds daily, whether the portents identify these *Jeedai* as abominations too evil to even sacrifice, or worthy enough to offer individually. But do not encounter her in person."

"I serve you with my life and death," Nom Anor answered.

Tsavong Lah touched his villip. Nom Anor's face faded, shrank, and was sucked back into the villip's interior.

Tsavong Lah sat for another minute, stroking his frayed lip with a finger claw. Destroying Duro's ship-crafting facility would deny his enemies warships and matériel. Cutting their trade routes again would wreak economic havoc.

And at Duro, he would make an example that the galaxy's surviving inhabitants would not dare to ignore.

CHAPTER NINE

Mara sat with Luke at a long briefing table, in a sequestered room protected by sonic containment fields. At the table's head, Ayddar Nylykerka—chief of Fleet Intelligence—stood beside a three-dimensional galactic map that gleamed over the table's modulasers. Most of its star field shone faintly blue, but a substantial slice starting near Belkadan had been reprogrammed to shine red, those systems that had been taken by the Yuuzhan Vong.

Nylykerka swept his laser pointer through that sector. "As you see, our hyperspace probes are returning limited information. Kalarba, Druckenwell, and Falleen are lost. Even if we could retain Rodia," he said, glancing at Rodian Councilor Narik, "the Corellian Run is cut." He swept his pointer through that hyperspace lane. "Our scouts report having found several more points seeded with dovin basal interdiction mines."

Councilor Narik's ears swiveled toward Chief of State Fey'lya. "Once again, a Mid Rim world is sacrificed in the name of protecting the Core ... or Bothawui," Narik said angrily.

Mara frowned. The Bothan chief of state had managed to keep the remains of the Fifth Fleet deployed at home, but he looked twitchy. Defensive. Ripples danced almost constantly across his furred face.

"With such grave damage to Fondor, we are equally concerned with protecting Kuat Drive Yards," Councilor Triebakk of Kashyyyk said through his translator droid. He gestured toward the Advisory Council's newest member, Senator Viqi Shesh of Kuat, who nodded acknowledgment.

"Centerpoint Station," Fyor Rodan of Commenor said, "is ideally positioned to defend Kuat. But what is Centerpoint's current status? Can we count on Corellia?"

Chelch Dravvad shifted in his seat, looking uncomfortable. Mara didn't envy him. Corellia had been used as a trap, a target to tempt the Yuuzhan Vong into Centerpoint's range. Now the Corellians had back-blading in mind.

"My report isn't good," Dravvad answered. "After Centerpoint was fired toward Fondor, there was some kind of interior malfunction, probably due to Sal-Solo's mishandling. That information must not reach the Yuuzhan Vong, though. As long as they consider Centerpoint operational, it provides a deterrent for this entire region."

Mara sensed uneasiness around the table. Several heads nodded somberly.

Fey'lya crossed his arms over his tunic. "And now Corellia threatens to act alone, making the Centerpoint weapon its rallying point." He glanced aside at Councilor Dravvad.

"Without Fondor's shipyards," the Corellian said, "New Republic forces could not have used Centerpoint as planned anyway. The HIMS devices, which would've allowed our forces to maneuver in and out of the interdiction field, were built there."

Admiral Sien Sovv, the Sullustan fulcrum of the New Republic Defense Force, had been threatened with a senatorial vote of no confidence after the Centerpoint catastrophe. He'd barely survived. "Chief Nylykerka," he asked, "what news from Kubindi?"

The burly Tammarian shook his head. "Our only communication has come courtesy of Jedi Kyp Durron. I'm sure you've seen that on HoloNet."

Sovv's jowls quivered with distaste. "Who hasn't? I suppose Jedi Corran Horn has returned to his usual heroics as well, by now," he suggested, turning to Luke.

Sitting next to Mara, Luke shook his head. "Corran is still in seclusion on Corellia." *Lying low,* Mara knew, after the Ithor catastrophe.

Sovv sniffed loudly.

Cal Omas, formerly of Alderaan, said, "I find it interesting that the enemy took Kubindi without harassing either Fwillsving or Kessel."

"The biology people," Nylykerka said, "believe that the Kubaz's history of genetically engineering insect species made that world's resources appeal to the Yuuzhan Vong."

"And the disinformation campaign?" Fey'lya turned to a tall, slender woman standing behind Chief Nylykerka.

Mara knew Major Hallis Saper by sight. The former documentarian, now employed by NRI, opened her hands. "We know the Yuuzhan Vong are superstitious. Unfortunately, until we can get a better sense of what they consider good and bad portents, there's little we can do to convince them they're seeing bad ones."

Admiral Sovv slowly shook his head. "Thank you, Major Saper. We will inform you as information becomes available."

Fey'lya raised the room lights to a slightly brighter level, and Nylykerka deactivated his map as Major Saper left the chamber.

Borsk Fey'lya cleared his throat, making a braying noise. "Councilor Pwoe?" He indicated the tentacle-faced Quarren seated across from him. "You requested a place on the agenda."

Councilor Pwoe lowered his head, resting his facial tentacles against his chest. "Master Skywalker," he said, "I am glad that the topic of Jedi Horn and Jedi Durron was raised. Unless you can exercise a greater measure of control over the Jedi, you must prepare for a new round of persecution."

Luke raised his head but didn't speak.

"Your nephews," Pwoe continued, "allowed Sal-Solo to fire the Centerpoint weapon. True?"

"Yes," Luke said. Mara glared at the aging Squid Head. "At the New Republic's request," Luke reminded the council.

"We are disturbed," Pwoe said. "Jedi and other vigilante groups are becoming increasingly active. Justice must be meted out under the rule of law, not by petty tyrants in X-wing fighters."

Mara eyed Fyor Rodan, who'd made no secret of his opposition to forming any new Jedi council.

Rodan stirred. "There was a time," he said, "when the presence of twenty Jedi on Coruscant might have seemed like a guarantee of our safety. Now, it seems that you head an order of twenty vigilantes and eighty do-nothings."

"Master Skywalker, apologies," Cal Omas said. "But you see how controversial the Jedi have become."

Rodan narrowed his dark eyes. "*Master* Skywalker," he said, managing to make that title sound demeaning, "it is increasingly obvious that the Jedi choose to help some peoples, but not others. Why?"

Luke shook his head, and Mara felt his mood turn deadly sober. "Jedi are responsible to the Force, not to me. I've tried to coordinate them. I've tried," he added, shooting another side glance toward Councilor Rodan, "to reestablish some semblance of organization. But there are people who feel that if we were better organized, we'd be a danger to the New Republic."

"Can you blame them?" Rodan asked. "We are determined to keep the Jedi and their quaint philosophy separate from this government."

"To the extent of refusing to sanction us, Councilor? Of threatening persecution?"

Chief of State Fey'lya's cream-colored fur rippled again. "Your agents misinformed us concerning the dangers to Corellia and Fondor. That failure contributed gravely to the Centerpoint catastrophe."

"The Yuuzhan Vong planted misinformation by altering the Hutts' shipping patterns," Luke answered. "We won't be fooled next time. And we won't be able to observe Hutt smuggling behavior anytime soon."

Point, Mara observed. The Hutts were mired in the fight of their lives.

Fey'lya sat stroking his beard.

"When peace and justice are threatened," Luke said, "our mandate to rescue becomes a mandate to defend whole worlds. It's true that some Jedi have used that mandate to rationalize extreme behavior. Despite what some of you think, I've done my best to correct them. Their freedom to make choices means they are free to make *wrong* ones."

Commodore Brand, silent until now, spoke up at last. "Hear, hear."

"It's never easy to use power," Luke said, shaking his head and giving Rodan a long look. "You've all dealt with that problem, and with the ethics of spending other beings' lives in battle."

"That is why governments have high councils," Rodan said. "To check powerful individuals."

Mara finally heard some tension in Luke's voice as he said, "And *this* body, Councilor Rodan, certainly has chosen to defend some systems at the expense of others."

Rodan, of Commenor, glowered.

Luke rested one elbow on the table. "Some Jedi have stepped back from using the Force almost entirely, for fear of misusing it. My nephew Jacen, for one."

Mara happened to be looking at Viqi Shesh at that moment. The Kuati senator raised one manicured eyebrow.

"The Jedi are scattered," Luke went on. "They're my commitment. We're all answerable to you—"

"Is that so?" Narik of Rodia muttered.

Luke turned to the Rodian. "Yes," he said, "it is. For as long as this body represents peace and justice."

Mara clapped a lid on her urge to give Narik a saccharine smile.

Narik clasped his hands over the table. "My homeworld is about to suffer the most terrible depredations—"

"And mine," Luke said, "is probably next."

True enough. Tatooine was just Rimward from Rodia. Narik's green hide darkened. "That is not my concern."

"All worlds are my concern," Luke said.

In a lounge on one of Coruscant's floating docks, Mara sank into a cushioned repulsor chair and blew out a breath. This divisiveness could bring down the New Republic, without requiring the Yuuzhan Vong to bring in a single ship.

At one edge of the floating dock, a local shuttle pulled away. Mara's eye caught movement on the lounge's far side. A tall female with short, wheat-blond hair walked toward them. Mara opened herself to the Force—and before she could reach toward the woman, she felt something primitive but alive, clinging to her body near her hip-hugging belt. She brushed at it with one hand.

"Tresina Lobi," Luke murmured to Mara.

Mara had met the woman, the first of her people—the Chevs—to show Force talent. Tresina had a charming knack for melting into mixed crowds.

"Were you expecting her?" Mara asked.

She brushed her stomach again. Granite slugs often sloughed off walls, and maybe a small one had rolled down under her long vest. She held back her disgust, trying not to distract Luke. Granite slugs were Hutt-ugly but harmless.

Luke raised an eyebrow. "For the last few minutes, anyway."

The Chev woman halted about two meters from him. "Master Skywalker, and Mara." Her voice was low and musical. "Forgive me for coming with urgent business."

"That's never a problem," Luke said graciously. "Sit down, Tresina. Get your breath." Again he glanced at Mara.

Mara shook her head. *It's nothing,* she thought at him. She eyed the Chev woman.

"I'm all right," Tresina said. Despite the woman's Jedi discipline, Mara remembered her as someone who usually smiled—but not today. "I just got back from Duro," she said. "I went out with my apprentice, Thrynni Vae."

Mara nodded. In the last year, Luke had assigned Jedi listening teams to most major systems and some critical minor ones. She crossed her hands over her vest, just below her belt line, and pressed gently. She felt nothing through the vest—no lump, no defensive wriggle.

That was not good.

"Thrynni and I have been keeping watch on several

Duros shipping concerns," Tresina said. "The situation there has been quietly getting . . . complicated."

"In what way?" Mara asked. This couldn't be her disease, flaring up again. It couldn't . . .

"Well, I hardly know where to start." Tresina shook her head. "The Duros High House wasn't at all thrilled by SELCORE's reclamation proposal. Evidently their shipping concerns bought out a few representatives, and then SELCORE carried the vote."

"Why would the shipping concerns do that?" Luke asked.

Meanwhile, Mara ran a fast physical inventory. She did feel oddly tired, infinitesimally wearier than listening to pompous councilors ought to make her. She'd never been able to sense the disease itself through the Force, but she did feel an odd thickening of her own cells, below the pit of her stomach.

It had attacked her reproductive system before. *Not this time,* she vowed. Back at their rooms, she still had a few precious drops of Vergere's tears.

Luke frowned. Again Mara shook her head slightly, then stared at Tresina.

The Chev woman's wheat-blond hair caught a gleam of the sunset light. "Thrynni and I thought we had a lead," she said. "SELCORE's contractor for outsystem goods, CorDuro Shipping, has been intercepting shipments. They're letting out tapcaf talk that they're reselling to other refugee groups, but there are quieter rumors of goods being stockpiled in another orbital city."

"Interesting ruse," Mara said, determined to concentrate. *You stick to business, too, Skywalker!*

"Then Thrynni heard a mechanic claim he'd been working on one city's drive and steering unit. They've multiplied its drive power by factors of several hundred."

"They want to be able to take it out of orbit," Mara concluded. "They could retreat, if the Yuuzhan Vong attacked the refugees down on the planet." *Including Han, Jacen, and Leia.* And now Jaina, according to a flagged medical report sent directly to Luke. "What are Duro's defenses like?"

"There's a Mon Cal light cruiser, *Poesy*. Fighter complement of E-wings and B-wings, and some local police craft they call Dagger-Ds, divided among *Poesy* and some of the cities." Tresina finally sat down. "Thrynni and I were collecting information in the capital city, the one the Duros call Bburru. We traced some of the intercepted goods from one shipyard arm to another, where it left for another habitat—Urrdorf, the one that's supposedly being modified."

"And?" Mara prompted gently.

Tresina's hands had tightened on the arms of her chair.

"Eleven days before I left Bburru," Tresina answered, "Thrynni vanished."

Luke didn't look pleased when Mara left him with Tresina at NRI, nor when she claimed she needed to do something back at the suite, but he didn't argue. He didn't need to. She knew he'd get there as quickly as possible.

As she entered, R2-D2 rolled away from his post at the local-data feed in the kitchen and whistled a query.

"No, thanks, Artoo. I don't need you at the moment."

He wheeled around and retreated.

Mara took a chair with her back to the broad window, sank down, and withdrew deep into herself. Before she used the last of Vergere's miraculous healing dose, she'd better know what she was up against. She was determined to do whatever she could, on her own. She and

Cilghal had experimented with self-examination techniques, the only possible way to deal with a disease that
continually mutated.

Focusing the Force finely, she confirmed that the odd
sense focused deep in her uterus, on one side. It was a
thickening of cells, almost like a tumor, multiplying more
quickly than her normal cells. She probed deeper, for
their cellular essence. Shifting her grip on the Force, she
poised to destroy their blood flow.

Then she sensed something weirdly familiar. Besides the
tumorlike echo of her own cellular essence—completely
familiar, after fighting her disease for this long—she sensed
another human life-signature.

It was Luke's.

By all the star dragons ever spawned, that could mean
only one thing.

Mara's eyes flew open. Her arms and legs stiffened.
Pregnant? This couldn't have happened! She'd taken all
precautions. Her bizarre disease had transformed mole-
cules and cells and attacked discrete organs. It could be
death or disfigurement—or some other, unimaginable
horror—to an unborn child. She clenched a fist. What
could she do? There were medical options—

Like a garu-bear defending her cub, she attacked that
thought instantly. She would let no medical aide harm
her child—

Again her own thoughts caught her up. Her child?

Did she carry her posterity or her death inside her?

The tall front door slid open. Luke plunged through,
and before he even got close she felt his mind trying to
grab her, protect her.

"What's wrong?" he demanded. "Mara, what is it?"

"Do you always think you have to rush in and save
someone?" she asked, making a vain stab at sounding
wry and superior. But her voice shook.

Luke dropped to his knees beside her chair. He seized her hand. "Mara, what is it? The disease?"

She took his hand. She laid it over her abdomen. "Feel this," she said softly. "Use the Force, and tell me what has happened."

He arched his eyebrows and frowned up at her.

"Don't argue," she said. "Just do it. I want an unbiased second opinion."

She watched his eyes. They narrowed, and the line of his eyebrows softened. He was preparing to comfort her, to do whatever he must.

Then his eyes widened, sending a sudden blue flash up at her face.

"This wasn't my idea." Mara swallowed on a dry throat. "It's already in terrible danger. The disease could attack it—cause mutations—"

"Mara," he interrupted. He seized her hand. "Mara, anything could kill any one of us, today, tomorrow. The Yuuzhan Vong could pull down one of Coruscant's moons, or we could fall out a window."

She nodded silently, struck once again by Luke's unwavering faith in goodness and his hope in the light. He shifted his hand slightly, shaking his head in plain disbelief.

"Life is risk," he murmured. "I don't feel anything . . . dangerous about this."

"Not yet," Mara whispered. "But this wasn't supposed to happen."

"I know," he said. His hand shifted again. His eyes fell shut. She felt his desperate concern.

Softening a little, Mara laid her free hand over his, on her stomach. Finally, she dared to envision actually holding a child, looking into a face that was part Luke and part Mara—just as her niece and nephews were part

Leia and part Han, but completely themselves. She'd pictured it many times, as an abstraction.

Then she pictured the monster her disease could make of a defenseless cluster of cells.

Defenseless? Not so long as I've got custody! Something deep inside her mind was shrieking, terrorized. Something else was dancing wildly, utterly and joyously abandoning itself to hope, to joy, to a new and total commitment.

Luke spoke softly. "Maybe Vergere's medicine made you vulnerable to the Force, as an agent of life."

She straightened her shoulders. "You want this. You're glad," she accused him.

"Until this moment," her husband said, "I had no idea how badly I did want it. I was prepared to be stoic, and give up hope—"

"For my sake?"

He raised his chin, and she felt a wordless caress.

She twisted her mouth sideways. "For two people who know each other so well, somehow we missed something."

"No," he said. "Something just changed. In me, maybe. Maybe you. Maybe in the Force itself. All I know is . . . this is the right risk to take. And that," he concluded, shaking his head, "makes me happy." He looked up again, wearing a foolish grin she hadn't seen in months. "It could make me very happy, actually—"

Mara balled her fists. "Listen, Skywalker. Nobody finds out about this. Nobody."

Still kneeling beside her chair, he slid his hands around her waist. "I agree, Mara, with one exception. You should have at least one good medic. They—"

"No. Even Cilghal really couldn't help me fight this disease. If she couldn't help me, she couldn't protect our child. That's going to be my job."

"Other things could go wrong—"

She silenced him with a glare.

He frowned, then nodded solemnly.

"And you can get *that* out of your mind, too," she snapped. "I am not going to lie down and keep watch on my symptoms, waiting for something to go wrong."

She marveled, though, at how suddenly and how completely she wanted to protect this child that didn't even vaguely resemble a child yet. Maybe, her conscience whispered, this sudden protectiveness was like the way Luke felt about her—a love so fierce and uncontrolled that sometimes it threatened the beloved's independence.

Maybe there was no such thing as real independence. Not with contentment.

This child, though, could already be under the influence of Yuuzhan Vong biotechnology. It—no, a child was not an *it*—he could die before he ever saw daylight. He could deform in a thousand deadly ways. He could . . .

"Are you all right?" Luke's hands caressed her shoulders. "Mara, we should at least have Cilghal do a few basic tests."

"No," she muttered. "No one, Luke. Not Leia, not the Solo kids."

"Just how do you expect to keep this from Anakin?" he demanded.

She laughed shortly. "The last thing a boy his age even considers is an old woman getting pregnant. Keep a lid on your feelings, and he won't suspect."

"He does expect me to be concerned for you—"

"Then I'm sure you won't disappoint."

Luke exhaled slowly, and she felt some of the tension leave him. "You're right," he said. "There are people who would pin hopes on this child that maybe they shouldn't have. He—or she . . . can you tell?"

Mara fell into the Force again, absorbing everything it would tell her. She had extraordinary powers to communicate with certain people. She'd been able to sense Palpatine from anywhere in the galaxy. So far, though, this sense was utterly primitive. Caressing the life-signature, she felt again those faint echoes—of her own savor in the Force, and Luke's.

A new thought distracted her. Her mind worked backwards, counting days, wondering . . . when?

She half smiled and answered Luke's question. "No. I can't tell. But I don't want to say *it*."

"Then, for now . . . *she?*"

"He," Mara said firmly, though she honestly couldn't tell. Then she finished the sentence he'd interrupted with his own question. "If he survives, he could be truly great—or greatly evil. Or," she added grimly, "greatly damaged, by this disease. I won't let that happen, Luke. I swear."

"This is my child, too." He seized her other hand. "Mara, you're going to have to make an allowance for that. If I get protective, please don't take it personally."

"You'd better not," she growled.

Then she folded around Luke, embracing his shoulders. He struggled up off his knees, then pulled her to her feet. His arms tightened around her back and her waist. His lips pressed hard against her mouth, his breath tasted sweet and musky, and at the back of her mind, she could feel him rejoicing.

Some hours later, Mara sat staring out the transparisteel window, watching traffic lights flow across the skyline. Flaming auroral veils framed the traffic lights.

She'd wrenched her thoughts back to Duro—and Centerpoint Station, nonfunctional again. She had the sensation that a pattern was emerging. Give her an hour or two, and she'd find it.

If she could concentrate.

"Do you think Leia is on top of this shipping problem?" she asked.

Luke's voice spoke out of the darkness, from the floor beside her deep chair. "By now, she's probably either solved it or sent Han to fix it. They've got to be in close contact."

"But you'd like to ship over to Duro and check it out."

"Stay out of my mind, Jade."

Without even trying, she sensed his glee at having turned her customary rebuke back on her.

"I'd rather go myself than send somebody else into danger," he said, "and I should talk with Jacen. I'll take Anakin, if you don't m—"

Mara glared into the darkness.

"Mm. You do mind." Almost hidden by shadow, he ran a hand over his hair. "Mara, I don't want to put you in danger right now. I—"

"Who's got the better danger sense?" Mara touched a control, admitting more of the city's night light through the window and illuminating her husband's concerned face.

Luke uncrossed his legs and leaned forward. "You can't deliberately risk that child." The intensity in his eyes reminded her of the worst days of her illness, and his despondency.

"Do you think," she answered, "that I ever—ever—deliberately risk myself? Grab some reality, Skywalker. If the Yuuzhan Vong get near Coruscant, I'm on the evac ship—in fact, I'm driving. But this isn't even close to that danger level."

His lips firmed. She could almost feel him preparing to outflank her—to bury her objections under patriarchal affection, or pull rank. Mara cherished her farmboy's sincerity, but she refused to be sheltered.

She wondered if arguing was simpler for women who *couldn't* tell what their husbands would say next.

"My instincts are shifting," she admitted, diverting his thrust before he could make it. "I've been running an inventory. I can already feel new hormones starting to kick in. I'm getting protective, too, Luke. Already."

He leaned away from her, looking so wide-eyed hopeful that she hated to burst his bubble.

"But in me," she explained, " 'protective' is active. I'm going with you. In fact, maybe I should take Anakin and head out," she suggested. "Then you could stay in touch with the Advisory Council. When they start using words like *persecution*, we have to pay attention."

He arched his eyebrows. He didn't want to be left behind, either! "We have Thrynni Vae missing, and four of our family in an area that's fallen under suspicion."

"What about the Advisory Council?"

"Kenth Hamner is an excellent strategist. He can handle an advisory role."

"The admirals like having you around," she said, pushing him just for the fun of it.

As if he'd caught a flicker of that thought—or more likely her amusement—he slumped back down in his chair. "Don't do that," he pleaded.

Mara laughed. "It'll be good to get away from this place. I think we should take Anakin, too."

"What do you think Tresina and Thrynni stumbled into?"

"That," she said, "is what we'd better find out."

CHAPTER TEN

Randa Besadii Diori stared hard at the Ryn who had been assigned to keep watch on the communications board—and him. The creature seemed to be asleep.

Silently, Randa activated a private frequency. Clicking the transmission switch did not activate his kajidic's repeater network, because one of the Duros' orbital cities was in the way.

He resolved to be patient.

With Jacen Solo self-righteously determined to do nothing, Randa had turned to the sister. Jaina was the more experienced pilot at any rate. Randa had been, he believed, more than polite—and solicitous. He'd praised her for her constant efforts to heal herself and regain her fighting trim. He'd hinted that he could get her back into action before Rogue Squadron could send another med runner, taking her back out to battle.

Today's news out of Nal Hutta had been ghastly: unknown and unknowable creatures released in droves, his relatives lying slain in their palaces. Randa must find some other way to use self-righteous young Jacen, so obviously a son of his Hutt-killing mother—and he would. The Yuuzhan Vong had trained Randa in prisoner transport.

He clicked the transmitter again. This time, a soft series of tones answered.

Splendid! He leaned close to the transmitter. "This is Randa," he said softly, keeping one eye on the sleeping Ryn guard. "Who is on watch?"

He heard static for a long time. Then, "Randa, where are you?"

His parent's voice! "I am well," he told her, "and on Duro. I have only moments. I might be able to buy our people some concessions from the Yuuzhan Vong." On board the clustership, he'd seen that they were desperate to get Jedi in custody, for study. "There are two young Jedi here. I might be able to deliver one. If they would be interested, have them contact me at the settlement they call Thirty-two. It's near a large open-pit mine that's been made into a reservoir."

"Well done, Randa," Borga said. "Something with which to bargain—we have too little of that. The invaders do not seem to indulge themselves with any of our trade goods. We are trying to win rights to Tatooine as a safe world. I will do what I can."

The moment Randa signed off, he wondered if he'd done the right thing. Selling Jacen might be a mistake. Jacen still might join him, if Jaina led the way.

Well, he could always claim the young human escaped. With two options open—his fantasies of a strike team, and the chance of buying his people a haven—one or the other would surely turn for his benefit. Maybe both.

He turned his head slightly.

The ineffectual Ryn guard slept on.

Keeping peace on a team of research scientists, who were competing for limited resources, was starting to remind Leia of trying to feed two-year-old, Force-strong twins from the same plate. Only her hopes for a reborn world and a refugee haven kept her going.

One woman pounded Leia's makeshift conference

table. "Our best hope," she said, scowling, "is to develop that 'master net.' Without a self-perpetuating web of interdependent organisms, everything we do will either undo itself in less than a generation or else overbreed without natural controls. We can—"

"Overbreed?" Dr. Plee, the Ho'Din, folded his long, pale-green arms over his lab coat. "At the moment, unless they do overbreed, how in Kessel are we going to make any headway? They've given us a planet, and it's a planet we've got to get under control . . . and he's no help at all."

Overbreed? The Yuuzhan Vong had to breed like crazy, Leia reflected. Otherwise, how could they throw away so many warriors' lives?

Then she frowned at the single vacant chair. Once again, Dassid Cree'Ar had begged off by comlink. Once, she hadn't minded it. Three times, she disliked it. But this made five meetings out of five. No wonder Cree'ar's fellow workers resented him.

"He's reactive," the meteorologist said. "He responds to crises only if we point them out."

The microbiologist raised a finger. "But he has solved every one of them. We've kept him so busy fixing our problems that he hasn't had time to do anything original lately."

"So put *him* to work on your master web," Dr. Plee growled. "Get this world seeded and clean it up, so we can take down these domes. I'm not claustrophobic, but—"

"The Sith you're not." Aj Koenes, the big Talz, nudged him with a powerful-looking furry arm. "I've seen your—"

Leia pushed wearily to her feet. "Does anyone else have a progress report?"

Sidris Kolb stood. "Cloud seeding is off to a shaky start, but—"

"Shaky?" demanded Cawa, a Quarren who had missed the previous meeting. "I asked you to delay that another six weeks. I've barely made headway with existing surface water. The last rainfall samples we took had six hundred parts per million of—"

And they were off again.

This time, Leia let them run. Sadly, everyone's project seemed to threaten everyone else's. Interlinked as they were, they ought to support each other. She *would* find a way to make them cooperate, or else she'd send them all home and start over with a fresh crew. Duro was too important to lose to their bickering.

Not many hours later, another emergency called Leia to the supply depot, where she released her frustration on a hapless shipping clerk.

"What do you mean, the rest of it isn't coming until next week? We need that allotment. The new hydroponics will stall without soluble potash, or whatever it is. Blast those Duros!"

The supply clerk, to his credit, sat there and took it until she paused for breath.

"Sorry," Leia muttered. "Not your fault. We're all getting a little short in the fuse, and I am glad to get that mining laser. Can you open a line to Bburru?"

Ten minutes later, she was getting another runaround on the ground-orbit comm unit. "Listen," she said, gritting her teeth to keep from shouting. "I want that stuff here, where it belongs. I've got the biggest population onworld."

"Sorry, ma'am," the voice on the other end said. "Cor-Duro took that shipment to Settlement Thirty-two for their water treatment plant, with an allowance for next month. They do supply you with—"

"Next month?" Incredulous, Leia glared at the GOCU. "They think we can stockpile? Who is this guy?"

The shipping clerk shook his head. "He seemed to feel that since the water purification benefits your people even more than his own, you wouldn't mind. Do you want to send a message?"

"I'm too busy to waste the effort. Contact SELCORE and see if we can get a duplicate shipment." *And a new administrator for Settlement Thirty-two*, she would've added, if she'd thought it would do any good. Maybe SELCORE could draft Lando and Tendra.

Down a stone tunnel between Gateway's laboratory building and the toxic marshes, Nom Anor had set up an underground office. Leia Organa Solo's people had dug out the long tunnel; he'd created a side passage, using small organisms that fed on soft rock. As they bloated and died, he disposed of them by the thousands, deep in the marshes. There they decomposed, their gut bacteria working the "miracles" that delighted Organa Solo's people.

He marched through his outer chamber, fingering the disengagement spot on his gablith masquer. Pore by pore, it pulled out of his body. He gritted his teeth. Unlike Warmaster Tsavong Lah and the rest of them, he did not believe that his pain fed the gods. He claimed to serve Yun-Harla, the Trickster—and if she did exist, she probably loved the deception—but Nom Anor served only himself, and his chance of promotion. He had told the warmaster the truth, by one definition. Leia Organa Solo was not true Jedi, and her daughter still was not proven—but if Tsavong Lah thought of them that way, he would be all the more impressed when Nom Anor destroyed them.

As soon as Thirty-two collapsed, Organa Solo would probably put him to work analyzing the catastrophe. He wished he didn't have to avoid her. He would love to see her face when they brought word that her children had been caught in the disaster.

He shook off the semisolid mass of masquer around his ankles, then stretched languorously, relishing the sensation of free, living air on his own skin. He had an hour to spare. To relax.

He plucked one of his tiny pets off the wall and hefted it one-handed. It didn't feel quite fully grown, which made it perfect for another purpose. Stretching up, he pressed its wriggling cilia deep into a ceiling crack. He'd weakened several sections of ceiling this way, then stationed other kinds of creatures down in the fracture zones. On his command, they could inflate themselves like woodcutters' wedges, bringing down long or deep stretches of ceiling.

It was simply one more precaution.

Jacen crouched at the edge of a hut, scraping wormlike creatures off the underside of its synthplas eaves.

"They could be edible," Mezza cautioned, gripping her hips to make a bunch of culottes fabric on each side. One of her people had found these creatures less than an hour ago. "Maybe we could raise them? Extra protein for the phraig stew?"

Jacen tried not to gag as he sealed his sample sack. "It's a thought. But feel this spot on the eaves. There's a pit." He ran a hand along the area where he'd scraped off the wriggling, finger-length creatures. "They're actually eating synthplas."

"Then carry them in something other than that skimpy little sack."

Jacen wasn't going to take them far. "Have your people watch for more." He looked down the narrow lane. "This spot is close to the off-loading area. They probably came in on a supply ship."

At Hydroponics Two, Jacen found Romany, the other clan leader—who'd been a biologist—working alongside Han and Jaina.

"Not my specialty," Romany insisted when Jacen presented the wriggling sample sack. One of the worm-like creatures seized a pinch of synthplas and started chewing.

Han glowered. Jaina put down a hydrospanner and adjusted her goggle-mask.

Jacen flicked the creature off the synthplas. "Maybe not, Romany, but you're the best authority we have, without sending over to Gateway. I didn't want to do that."

"Ri-ight." Romany ran long fingers through his bushy mane. "They'd quarantine us. And if the Duros heard about this, they might not send any more ships. We were mighty glad to get that extra shipment." He and Han exchanged a knowing look.

Jacen's mind bounced back to the Duros. "I wonder if one of the CorDuro ships brought in the egg pod these"—he shook the little sack—"hatched from." Each gray worm had nine segments and twice that many legs, with massive black eyes and mouthparts that were all out of proportion to the rest of their bodies.

Jaina shook her head.

"Can't see them?" Han asked gently.

She blinked. "I am getting better. The blurs have edges."

"Here we are," the Ryn said, eyeing the creatures, "huddled under a synthplas dome."

"Great," Han said. "Just great."

Jacen pulled his cloak around him a little tighter. "Romany, you and Mezza could organize the children into hunt teams. We've got a little sucrose set aside for treats. We could pay them by the worm."

"Hey, Droma," Han shouted over the top of a hydroponics vat. "I don't suppose you people eat little wiggly bugs."

A white-maned head appeared over the transparent lid. "With the right spices," Droma said with grave dignity, "almost anything is edible. And—"

"Randa would probably love them." This time, Jacen finished Droma's sentence.

Then he looked aside. Han stared at Jaina, arching his eyebrows, his eyes soft and sad.

Jacen glanced from his father to his sister, comparing profiles. People generally claimed she resembled a young Leia, but below her bobbed hair, her forehead and cheeks really did have the same angles as Han's. Jacen abruptly pitied any man who wounded Jaina's heart with less than a galaxy between himself and her father.

As Jaina hiked off with Romany to look for Mezza, Jacen asked his dad, "Do you think all this is going to take the edge off her fighting ability?"

"If she doesn't want it to, it won't." Han shifted his weight, frowning. "She's too much like her mother."

Jacen looked up sharply, hearing a depth of loneliness that Han never expressed openly.

"You're right," he told Han, not wanting to say too much. He hustled after Jaina, though.

He caught up at Mezza's hut. "I think it's time we went looking for Mom," he told his twin.

*   *   *

Lenya, this morning's comm operator, stared at the transceiver with her oblique eyes wide. Even Randa seemed flabbergasted. Jaina had found Admiral Dizzle-wit's soft spot: He had some sympathy for injured military personnel. Jaina had been given immediate access to the outsystem relay.

"SELCORE." A human male wearing a high blue collar and short cape appeared on the relay screen, amid the usual cloud of blurred snowflakes. Deep-space relays went down or out of repair every day, blasted by the Yuuzhan Vong or sideswiped by space debris, but nobody dared to go out and fix them. They'd lost commercial HoloNet broadcasts completely. "How shall I direct your call?"

Jaina sat up a little straighter, and Jacen pulled his hand off her shoulder.

"We're looking for Ambassador Organa Solo," Jaina said.

"Do you have official business?"

Not again, Jacen groaned to himself. One more runaround.

"Yes," Jaina said. "We're calling in from a SELCORE locale."

"Not bad, on the spur of the moment," Jacen muttered while the screen blanked.

"You're not the only one who can make the truth sound impressive."

"Get the news from Nal Hutta," Randa urged.

Gamely, they stayed on-line while bureaucratic underlings shuffled them back and forth. Then a long-faced, elegant woman appeared, her black hair pulled back severely to show exquisite ears.

"Jedi Solo," she said smoothly. "And—what a pleasant surprise, *two* Jedi Solos. How may I assist you?"

Jacen bent toward Jaina's ear, but she'd already identified the voice. "Senator Shesh," Jaina said, "we need to contact Mother. I've been furloughed out, injured. The last we heard anything specific, she was on Coruscant. Can your office trace her?"

"I'm sure we can," the senator said. "It is splendid to see you together, and looking so well." There was something false in her tone, though. Jacen leaned toward the image—

Randa pushed forward, into his way. "Senator," he gushed, "please! You must send additional troops to—"

"I'm sorry." Senator Shesh tilted her head. "We mustn't hold this line open for nonessential communications. I'll have my staff return your call."

"Wait!" Jacen stretched forward, over Jaina's shoulder. "This connection took us an hour to—"

The senator's image dissolved into a network of fine diagonal lines.

Jaina gargled a cry of frustration. "Randa! I'm the one who got the call through. I'm the one who deserved to talk to her. You ruined it!"

Randa undulated backwards, away from the console. Tempted to insist that SELCORE would surely call back, Jacen pressed his lips shut. The callback might take days, or weeks, or it might not come.

"Speaking of worms," he said, and he couldn't resist glancing at Randa as the Hutt left the shed. "Senator Shesh rubs me wrong."

Jaina frowned. "But she's been named to the Advisory Council. She's practically the head of SELCORE."

"I know," Jacen said, "and SELCORE isn't exactly keeping its commitments. Think about the way she was standing, too. And that falseness in her tone of voice . . . The way she held herself, and that strange little smile.

They reminded me of the holovids I've seen of another senator."

Jaina twisted the mask in her lap. "I hate guessing games."

"Palpatine, pre-Empire," he explained. "When he was on his way up, and he didn't care who or what he destroyed to get there."

Jaina frowned. "And she's the one," she said, "who delivers what we need to survive."

"She's also the one," Jacen said, "who put us here. Who decided Duro was safe."

"I don't like where you're taking this, Jacen."

"Neither do I," he said softly. "Not at all."

CHAPTER ELEVEN

Tsavong Lah stroked the villip in his privacy chamber. His agents had recently delivered a newly budded subordinate villip to their contact on Coruscant. This first time, his contact might need a few moments to realize she was being called. On future occasions, his agents would deliver appropriate discipline if she delayed.

She must have been eager. In only one minute, the villip softened and everted on its stand. Bumps formed on its pale surface. An aristocratic nose emerged first, then a dominating chin, high forehead, strong cheekbones, a firm stern mouth. He'd studied the human species enough to recognize the flare of her nostrils and the widening of her eyes as signs of distaste. For the villip itself, maybe—in her diplomatic work, she would have dealt with many species and their methods. She controlled her reaction quickly.

"Senator Shesh," he said, forming words in her language as prompted by the tizowyrm he'd slipped into his ear. He enjoyed seeing her eyes and nostrils twitch again, as her villip spoke his words. "I will receive your report."

The villip rotated slightly forward. She must have inclined her head, a sign of respect. "Warmaster Lah, thank you for responding to my offer to open negotiations."

"I will receive your report," he repeated. She was young in his ways. He must make some allowances.

Her eyes widened slightly. "We are withdrawing from Kubindi," she said, "and from Rodia. We wish to live at peace with your people."

Peace, as the tizowyrm translated her tongue, meant willing and appropriate submission. "Excellent," he said. "We accept your peace."

"In turn," she said, "we would like some assurance that your invasion is nearly complete. Surely you can provide your people with homes and sustenance now. Leave us the worlds that remain. We must learn to live alongside each other. In . . . peace."

His eyes narrowed, and he wondered if the tizowyrm had translated something incorrectly. Peace flowed from a submissive underling to a conqueror, never in both directions.

"Our ultimate need," he said, "is the system you have prepared. For that, receive thanks." From Duro, he could neutralize the famous Drive Yards in her home system of Kuat, as well as the monstrous weapon at Corellia— but she had been told nothing about these plans. "You have assured me you will set agents to work sabotaging Centerpoint."

The villip inclined itself again. "As soon as it can be done. Thanks also for your gift of the ooglith masquers. I enjoy traveling unrecognized. I might hope," she added in a lighter voice, "that the masking and unmasking process becomes less uncomfortable over time."

He saw no reason to coddle her. The sharp sensation of each pseudopod piercing a pore was a vital part of the masquers' function. "No," he said.

Her left eye twitched. She hadn't yet accepted the discipline of pain.

"You are to be praised," he told her, "for helping bring about a lasting *peace* for your people. Your role will be widely honored, among us and your own folk."

"But not until peace comes." She raised her weirdly mobile eyebrows. "Promise me that."

Was she learning humility, or was she simply afraid of how her exaltation would come about? She had every reason to fear. He would want native rulers for his slave population, but the gods needed worthy sacrifices. *Sunulok*'s priestess, Vaecta, was bloodthirsty on their behalf.

Perhaps this woman simply didn't want her people to know she'd changed loyalty. "Your villip will invert again now. Remember to care for it." Ending with the insult of extra words was an appropriate way to chastise her.

The villip spoke again, though. "Wait, Warmaster Lah. I have new information."

He waited.

"It concerns my SELCORE operation at Duro. I learned today there is a Jedi at one settlement who has sworn off using his abilities. Maybe you can make use of him."

This matched what he'd heard from Nom Anor and other agents. The young one had allegedly abandoned his comrades in arms. Tsavong Lah could hardly imagine such treachery. Though such an individual did not deserve the dignity of having his name reported, he might prove useful if dissected.

"Have you learned anything else you should report?"

The villip remained silent for several seconds. Eventually, she said, "I dislike delivering individuals, but as I told your agent Pedric Cuf, I am a businesswoman."

That was not additional information. Tsavong Lah laid a hand over his villip, silencing it.

CHAPTER TWELVE

Jacen woke up clenching his hands so tightly they hurt.

He rolled away from the sleeping hut's wall and peered toward his dad's comm unit, on a stack of mud blocks at the foot of his cot. Something had been flung over the chrono, and he could see only a pale-red glow.

The night felt old, though. Old and deadly.

He sat upright, shut his eyes, and tried measuring the feeling. Under his uncle's tutelage, he'd worked on developing his danger sense. It had saved him in several tight situations. If those had been flickers, this was a full-fledged conflagration. It occurred to him that he didn't hesitate to use the Force this way, not in the least.

I'm just listening. There's nothing aggressive about it. He threw on the nearest clothes and slipped outside. Along the dusty lane, he eyed the next hut for those mysterious worms. Several days earlier, the youngsters had stopped bringing them in. They couldn't find any more. At least that was one less thing to worry about.

He found Jaina several huts down. Nothing was obviously threatening her, so he scratched that danger off his mental list. Silently, he opened her door and peered in.

The grizzled Ryn woman's snore had a high whine, like the *Falcon* halfway through its warm-up. Jaina slept on her back—normal sleep, not a healing trance. He could barely see her by the dim light of outdoor security lamps. Her hair had just enough curl to stick straight up in the front, like his often did when he woke up.

He tiptoed over to her cot and dropped his hand onto her shoulder. "Jaina," he whispered.

Her eyes fluttered open, and she turned her head. "Jace? What is it?"

"Sorry to wake you," he whispered. "Come outside so we can talk."

He led the way into the lane between huts. The big overhead lights gleamed faintly, giving the illusion of a necklace of moons under the gray dome. He caught the faint odor of Ryn and a whiff of phraig-bedjie stew.

Jaina stood beside him. In the dimness, her vision mask looked like a military night-sight.

"You don't have to tell me," she said brusquely. "Something's wrong."

"You feel it, too?" He glanced around. Blue-roofed huts, hydroponics tanks ... the control shed's inner corner, jutting into the dome. Nothing looked amiss.

She nodded. "Danger. To the whole colony." Jaina shut her eyes and leaned against the hut's exterior, frowning hard.

Look at her, Jacen's inner voice taunted. *You'll rely on somebody else's casual Force use. What kind of hypocrite are you?*

I just don't dare to stumble, he answered the voice. *I'm the one who was warned, not Jaina.*

She shook her head and tucked a strand of hair back up under her mask. "I can't find anything wrong," she said. "Sithspawn, I hope we don't have Vong on the way."

"One way to find out." He led toward the control shed.

Randa lay wedged along the back wall, snoring softly. Jaina told the night tech about their sensation. "We don't know what it is," she said, "but we're both getting it. Keep a tight watch."

"Yes, ma'am." The young human tossed off a casual salute.

Back outside, Jaina paused at an intersection of two lanes. "Okay, brother. You're the one with the functioning eyesight. Get a good look." She reached toward an illumination control.

Jacen almost stopped her. If she turned on the daylamps, she'd wake up the whole colony, maybe for nothing.

This didn't feel like nothing, though. He ducked back into the shed and seized a pair of macrobinoculars off the supply wall. Clutching them against his chest, he climbed a set of rungs up the shed's exterior wall as the big lights came on. Then he peered out over the colony.

Nothing, nothing, and nothing. No skulkers, no lurkers. No obvious breaches or . . .

Wait.

A flock of large moths, or maybe small birds, gathered around one of the daylamps. Adjusting the macrobinocs' resolution control, he got a closer look. More moth than bird, he decided, though the black wings didn't divide quite right. They had horns instead of antennae, and large, white imitation eyespots on their black backs.

He zoomed out again, swept the binocs back and forth, and spotted a larger group of them, seemingly plastered against the dome's underside, up near the top.

"What is it?" Jaina called up at him.

"I'm not sure. Looks like—huh. Almost looks like young mynocks, or . . ."

Spotting movement at the corner of his peripheral vision, he sighted the binocs down and left. Close at hand, one of the creatures fluttered up from under a hut's blue eaves.

He clambered down. Telling Jaina, "I'll be right back," he sprinted up the lane to the hut where the creature had taken flight. He looked up and down and around and . . . there. Under the eaves, something papery dangled from the synthplas roof panel. He flicked it free, then examined it on his hand.

"What?" Jaina's voice demanded behind him.

His mind flashed back to Yavin 4, a menagerie he'd kept in his room—and a collection of pupa cases, where his peggelars had overwintered, to emerge in the spring as exquisite rosewings.

His insides congealed. "Wake Dad up," he said. "Fast. I'll activate the ERD-LL droids."

The infestation had vanished because the worms had pupated. Now they were emerging as airborne adults. Whatever *they* ate, Jacen was willing to bet that up out of everyone's reach, they were laying eggs for a second cycle of destruction. Settlement Thirty-two might have a few weeks to find and destroy the eggs, but his danger sense said otherwise. They were feeding *now*, in numbers that all the dome's emergency repair droids wouldn't be able to stop.

He armed the ERD-LLs—hybridized binary loadlifters with long, telescoping waists—with the only tools he could find, batter beaters from the open-air kitchen booth. Two sleepy Ryn staggered out of the nearest shelter, leaning against each other. One squinted while the other pointed at the near ERD-LL. It swung a batter beater, knocking loose a flurry of the seemingly white-eyed creatures. Fluttering along behind its swath, the white-eyes settled back against the dome's underside.

Jacen switched on his comlink and pressed in an ID sequence.

"Yo," a Ryn voice growled. "Did somebody lose track of the day cycle?"

"Romany," Jacen said. "I need you. Emergency."

Jaina came back at a quick walk. "Dad's coming."

"Good. Go wake up the Vors and get a rebreather count." For the Vors, a breach could be deadly. That winged race was superbly adapted for its own atmosphere, but off Vortex, Vors' lungs were notoriously twitchy.

Jaina headed up the lane.

Next he called Mezza. He met her and Romany, who brought his lieutenant R'vanna, at the open area at the center of the Ryn group's wedge of huts. By this time, Han had arrived.

"Quietly," Han said, "without panicking anybody, get your people suiting up. Just in case."

Jacen broke in. "At the moment I'm more afraid of a stampede than a breach, but we haven't done a breach drill in too long. Call it a drill, if anyone will believe you."

Mezza honked scornfully and jogged away. Romany slipped into the nearest hut.

"Okay, kid. This way." Han led Jacen to the dome's center, where he pulled out a large blue tank with hose and nozzle. "I told SELCORE this was useless, that we wouldn't be cleaning the ceiling. Guess I was wrong."

Jacen helped him haul the tank to the hydroponics area, where one of the ERD-LL droids was uselessly brushing white-eyes aside.

"Down," Han barked. "Retract."

The droid telescoped downward. Han secured the tank on one metal arm, then grabbed the droid's other hand.

"Gimme a boost," he grunted.

Jacen was reaching forward when a large furry object catapulted between himself and his father.

"I can do that," Droma announced. He clambered up nimbly.

"About time you got here, wire-hair." Han brushed dust off his sleeves. "Think you can figure out—"

"Up," Droma honked. The ERD-LL elevated again. The nimble Ryn gripped a metal loop on the droid's large flat hand, locking his feet, ankles, and prehensile tail around a rigid extension arm.

"What's in the tank?" Jacen demanded. It was about to come showering down on everyone's heads.

"Don't know," Han admitted. "Supposed to be non-toxic, even to Vors."

Six minutes later, they knew it wouldn't harm the white-eyes, either. They kept fluttering up from under eaves. Ryn roamed the settlement, crushing intact pupae, but for every white-eye they found, ten more flew up to the dome and started chowing down.

Jaina sprinted back. "The Vors need thirty-eight more rebreathers, Dad."

Han fixed Jacen with a stare. "Think you can talk thirty-eight Ryn or humans out of their breath masks?"

Jacen gulped. "I guess—"

"Look at this," Droma shouted. He slid down the ERD-LL's midsection, holding something in one hand.

Jacen, Han, and Jaina circled him. Droma held up a clear spray-nozzle. Trapped inside, a white-eye attacked the synthplas nozzle with relish. Viewed from below, its mouthparts looked like twin rasps. They ground against the clear surface and then rotated inward, swallowing the dust.

"Worse than mynocks," Han grunted. "That's it. Jacen, get on the horn to Gateway. I'll get a few Vors into landspeeders. We're getting out."

Jacen sprinted back to the control shed, counting days in his mind. Gateway should've had a comm-line crew out late yesterday, if they were on schedule. If the lines were down, though, Thirty-two's only hope was to load up the caravan ships and hunker, praying their air scrubbers functioned long enough for rescue to arrive—or else to lift off on repulsors and head for another settlement. Some of those ships barely had made it here—and some refugees were dropped by ships that traveled on.

Randa sat up. Slowly blinking his huge eyes, he belched.

Jacen ignored him and strode to the comm tech. "I need Gateway. Intercolony assistance."

The tech punched panels. To Jacen's relief, a crisp voice came back instantly. "Gateway."

"Gateway, this is Thirty-two. We've got a breach pending, a big one. We need the evacuation crawlers."

"On their way. What kind of breach? Can it be mended?"

"I don't know. We've got some kind of an infestation."

"Copy that. We'll have the crawlers to you in about . . ." Pause. "Twenty-six minutes. Meanwhile, keep your people calm. Get them in rebreathers and chem suits if you can, and aboard whatever crawlers you have on hand."

"We have one small crawler, Gateway." They used it to move ships off the landing crater and under shelter.

"Affirmative, one crawler. Load it." Jacen faintly heard another voice, evidently someone else near the person who'd greeted him. "Thirty-two," the voice came back, "what kind of infestation?"

Jacen hesitated. "We're, ah, already suiting them up. Thanks, Gateway."

"Thirty-two," the voice repeated firmly. "Describe infestation."

Jacen admitted, "Nothing I've seen before. I'll save you a sample."

A different voice spoke over the link. "Make sure it's tightly contained, Thirty-two."

"Will do." Jacen turned around to see Randa rising on his long, strong tail.

"What is this?" the Hutt demanded.

"We're evacuating the dome," Jacen told him. "Those little worm creatures have metamorphosed into something like moths. They're all over the dome's underside, eating it."

"Use the Force," Randa demanded. "Crush them, choke them!"

Jacen tried to imagine seizing hundreds of tiny creatures, throttling the life out of them . . . "No," he said. "Too many of them."

"You haven't tried." Randa slithered forward.

"Listen, Randa." Jacen didn't need this. "You can get in the way or you can help. Get your breath mask and help keep order. We're about to take twelve hundred scared people through one gate."

"You ask me to direct traffic?" Randa puffed out his chest. "Me, Randa Besadii Diori, you ask—"

Jacen pushed past the Hutt toward the shed's door. "All right, then. Just stay out of the way. Stay in here," he added, turning around. "As soon as Gateway's crawlers call in, ready to load, comlink me."

This quarter of the dome teemed with refugees, some of them masked, a few chem-suited. A family of Vuvrians staggered past, bobbing their huge heads to point first one eye, then another, then another, up at the dome's underside. Their faces reminded Jacen of deflated balloons, with perpetually puckered mouths and knobbed, drooping tentacles.

Right in front of him, a Ryn pointed a blaster at the dome. Jacen rushed forward, shouting, "Put that away!" He was about to stretch out with the Force when the Ryn fired a blue stun burst. The energy dissipated before it reached the growing moth colony.

"Good try," Jacen said grimly, "but we've got a no-blaster policy." He grabbed the Ryn's weapon and tucked it into his belt.

Atop the other ERD-LL's outstretched arms, two Ryn clung and swatted white-eyes with long-handled kitchen tools. A few mangled moths fell to the ground. Others fluttered around the Ryn. One Ryn dropped his spatula and got busy swatting moths off the other—and himself.

The winged Vors would've been incredibly helpful in a larger dome, but Thirty-two was too small for them to maneuver—and one whiff of Duro-stink might kill them. They shuffled along on the ground, huddled around their young.

Jacen comlinked Han. "Twenty-two minutes," he said. "They want us in rebreathers and chem suits."

"Tell Mezza and Romany. I've got a droid freezing up."

Jacen spotted Randa, pushing out through the assembled crowd toward the hydroponics area.

He sprinted to intercept the Hutt. "What are you doing?" he demanded softly. "Get back to the gate and stay put!"

"I will lock down the food supply, against our return."

"Dad's got a Vuvrian crew working on that. Go on, get back."

"If you try to give me orders, young Jedi, you will regret it."

Jacen shifted his approach. "Not orders, Randa. We need you. Please do it our way. Help keep those people from wandering away from the gate. If they do, we'll have a stampede when the crawlers get here."

Muttering a retort, the Hutt turned tail and slithered back toward the gate.

Jacen took a deep breath and looked over the Ryn area. Other than Randa, the alert was going well, with the last families donning gear and proceeding toward the gate area—except for the swat team, still hard at work atop its ERD-LL droid. Close to the Vor quarter, a dribble of gray haze started flowing from the area thickest with moths. The colony's breach siren sounded, a low electronic moan. The hindmost Vors, still emerging from their huts, shrieked and erupted forward, a mass of slender limbs and long faces. Jacen sprinted toward them.

The forefront of the charging contingent hit him and spun him against a rough mud-brick surface. Winded, he took a few deep breaths. Then he spotted a Vor without a breath mask. "Here!" he shouted, tossing his own.

The delicate-looking creature jammed the mask over his pointed face and pushed on.

Then he spotted another gray dribble. Moths skittered away from the second breached spot, settled closer to a strut, and started chewing again.

Jacen hoped Duro's atmosphere would kill the creatures. He grabbed his comlink. "Dad?"

"Gateway's here, Junior. Bring 'em on."

"Copy that."

Jacen thumbed off the link and pressed away from the wall. One of the Vors staggered and fell. A Ryn bounded up and gathered the slender female into his arms.

Two Vors turned around, shouted something, and grabbed their kinswoman back from the Ryn.

"Thanks." Jacen clapped the Ryn on one shoulder. "Go on, go ahead. I'll bring up the rear." He scrambled up onto a roof and got one good look.

The entire colony had streamed out onto the lanes, pressing toward the gate like fizzbrew against a bottle cap. Some stragglers were spinning around, pointing up at the two—now three—breached spots, ducking and cowering like ten-year-olds with a crystal snake loose in their quarters. A gray cloud boiled down over the Vors' huts. Jacen caught a whiff of Duro's ghastly odor, the concentrated stench of thousands of abandoned Imperial war factories. He held a fold of his vest over his mouth while he strode toward the gate.

A Ryn met him, wearing a full chem suit and mask. "What else do you need?" it wheezed in Romany's voice.

"Has anyone checked your people's shelters? If we leave anyone behind, asleep, they might miss the ride out."

Romany pulled two hefty adults out of line to assist him, then demanded the chem suits of a less muscular pair. "We're going back," he explained. "We could be here for a while. Go on, get on board!"

The others protested. Jacen left them to their argument and pressed back into the control shed.

Randa and the comm tech were gone. Jacen peered out the viewbubble. Outside, five enormous idling vehicles reminded him of hydroponics tanks laid side to side and joined over three axles, each of their knobby tires bigger than five refugee huts. Flexible cofferdams had been extended to three of them. Colonists wearing full suits streamed away from the boarding tubes through Duro's perpetual fog, toward the farthest vehicle, directed by similarly suited SELCORE personnel.

He pushed out of the shed, into the mob.

More SELCORE crewers had taken control of the boarding area, directing refugees forward. To Jacen's dismay, Randa slithered forward, knocking down Ryn and humans in his rush to reach the gate.

"Hey!" Han's voice rose. Jacen spotted him standing on a stack of crates. "Back off, Randa! Push like that and you'll be the last one on board!"

The Hutt drove on, parting the wave of refugees like one of Lando's cruise ships at full throttle.

Han drew a blaster. "Hold it right there, Randa. If I let you do this, there's no stopping anyone."

Randa halted, glaring back over his shoulder. Refugees paused to help up the ones Randa had bowled over, then streamed around him.

Jacen spotted a young mountain of belongings alongside the gate, and an officious-looking Twi'lek in a SELCORE chem suit directing refugees to drop their bundles before he let them pass.

Jacen sidled alongside the SELCORE man. "Look," he murmured, "these people have hardly got anything left to call their own. Don't beggar them all over again—"

The Twi'lek spread his pale hands. "We will send back for your belongings. For now, saving life is our priority—wait! What's that?"

An elderly human woman clutched one hand to her chest and supported her husband with her other arm. Something black and furry stuck up out of the woman's bunched coat. The Twi'lek seized the coat and fingered it open. A furry bundle clung to the woman, splaying four scrawny limbs against her tunic. Jacen recognized a young whisperkit, betrayed by one quivering ear.

"Sorry," the Twi'lek grunted. "Don't know how you got a pet this far, but it can't come aboard."

The woman's blue-gray eyes thickened. "Sir, we're keeping it safe for our grandson. He's with the Fifth Fleet, and we promised—"

Saving life. Priority. The galaxy, teetering on a balance point the size of one frightened whisperkit.

Jacen shoved forward and tugged the Twi'lek's fingers off the woman's coat. "If we don't see it, it isn't here." He turned around and glared at the SELCORE official. "How much," he muttered, "does a whisperkit eat or breathe, compared with what leaving it here would do to morale?"

The Twi'lek set his knobby jaw. "What whisperkit?"

Jacen backed away. The Duro-stink grew stronger with every breath. The last mixed mob of Ryn and Vuvrians pressed forward, dropping bundles in their haste to reach the cofferdams. The final refugees trampled the bundles.

Droma flicked Han a salute. "That's everybody, Solo."

Han lowered his blaster. "Go on, Randa. Jacen? Stun him if he gives you trouble, but don't leave him here."

Jacen followed the fuming Hutt up the near crawler's boarding ramp as Han sprinted past. Randa halted just inside the hatch, blocking Jacen's way.

Three SELCORE crewers loped up behind Jacen. "Come on," one urged. "We're moving out."

"Randa," Jacen shouted. "Farther in!"

The Hutt turned his head, rumbling angrily. "Your father said I would be the last one on board. So this crawler is full."

Something pushed Jacen from behind. He fell over Randa's surprisingly solid body. The Hutt's muscular tail whipped around, flinging several Ryn against other refugees. One fell senseless.

Jacen thumb-checked the stun setting on his confiscated blaster, leveled it at the Hutt, and fired. Randa drooped. Hoots, whistles, and muffled applause broke out on board.

Something dug into Jacen's ribs. "Nice going," Jaina growled.

He exhaled. "Glad you're aboard."

"What was that about not being aggressive?"

"He was hurting people." Jacen returned the blaster to his belt. "And I wasn't using the Force."

"And the Yuuzhan Vong aren't hurting people? So they shouldn't be stopped with everything we've got?"

Ignoring her sarcasm, Jacen braced himself against the hatch. The crawler started to vibrate.

"Everybody get steady," he shouted. "This road's a little rough."

CHAPTER THIRTEEN

As the crawler lurched along, the warmth and odor of several hundred none-too-clean bodies—compounded by nervous sweat—made Jacen wrinkle his nose. He felt lucky to be next to a hatch. He'd be one of the first off.

"Lovely," Jaina murmured. "Where's my breath mask?"

At the far end of the hold, someone started singing. Singly and in groups, Ryn joined the melody, some whistling harmonies through their perforated beaks. Jacen didn't need words to recognize a traveling song. The perennial outcasts were moving on to their next adventure.

His comlink chirruped. "Excuse me," he said to the Ryn he elbowed while raising it to his mouth. "Sorry," he told the one he shoved while trying to steady himself. "Jacen Solo," he said.

"Crew deck here. You're the one who called over?"

"Affirmative."

"Tell me again what caused the breach. All I've got is a report that sounds like miniature mynocks."

"Didn't someone get you a sample?"

"Not if you don't have one."

"I don't." Jacen explained as little as possible. When he got to the point about the moth creatures pupating on the outside of sleeping huts, there was a long silence.

He flicked the comlink. "Crew deck, did you get that? They're singing in here, and—"

"Copy," a voice that hadn't spoken before said. "We're calling ahead, about decontamination."

The refugees close enough to hear Jacen's comlink turned their heads.

"Believe me," Jacen said, "nobody brought a pupa."

"Not deliberately," the comlink voice said, "but one egg, stuck to one hairy Ryn, will restart the cycle—and our dome's taller than yours. Put a flock of moths up there out of reach, and you'll bring down the whole operation."

Jacen clutched the link, leaning against Jaina and swaying with the crawler's motion. Other than Randa, most of the other passengers at this end of the cavernous hold seemed to be Ryn. If Jacen couldn't have told that by looking, he could've figured it out by the odor. If it bothered him, it must be driving the Ryn out of their minds. Several of them had raised their arms and were rotating in place, actually dancing.

Jacen murmured into the comlink, "Ryn are almost compulsively clean. There won't be white-eye eggs or anything else on them."

"Maybe you're convinced," the crewer said. "A furred species is tricky to decontaminate. We've got a sealable refugee processing area inside Gateway dome. Only problem is, we don't have any UniFumi stockpiled— SELCORE usually ships their decontam chemicals with every boatload of refugees. High-energy irradiation would work, but it could cause skin damage. And low-energy lamps won't get through fur. So they're going to have two choices. We can strip-and-dip everybody in med-lab disinfectant, but I can't guarantee that won't make them sick. Or we can shave and irradiate."

The Ryn next to Jacen honked softly. He turned aside and muttered to three others.

"Isn't there something else?" Jacen asked, uncomfortably aware that he was surrounded by several hundred sleep-deprived Ryn, who'd just left all their belongings behind—again.

"We can separate out the Vuvrians and Vors," the voice continued. "Hairless folks can zip through a fast irradiation, and we'll send them on their way."

Jacen curled against the hatch. "Why are you asking me? Where's Captain Solo?"

"He seems to have lost his comlink. You're next in charge."

Jacen thumbed off the comlink, hoping SELCORE's administration would come up with a better idea. The engine thrummed rhythmically under his feet. Some of the Ryn were now stamping out that rhythm as others sang. Jacen flexed his knees, swaying against Jaina.

"That doesn't sound good," she muttered.

The comlink chirped again. "Solo?"

He raised it. "Here."

"We've got word from someone named Mezza. They're refusing to be dunked in med-lab juice, not that I blame them."

"Me, neither," Jacen said. "And don't discriminate against Ryn. Whatever goes for them, goes for Vors and Vuvrians and humans. And the Hutt," he added, glancing down. Randa had curled up in a bulbous spiral.

The song ended. Someone started a new one. Two verses later, Jacen got another announcement via comlink.

"Finally found the other Solo. He says fair's fair, same treatment for everybody."

Well done, Dad. Jacen murmured to Jaina, "I don't care if they shave me."

"Me, neither. I've seen buzz-cut female pilots."

When the shaking and thrumming died away, something clanged against the hatch. Jacen tried to move back. The mob behind him pushed in the opposite direction. He braced against a bulkhead. Fortunately, the crew had moved a ramp up to the hatch, so when it opened, he didn't fall headlong. Crewers called commands, directing the debarking refugees to fan out and keep moving. Ryn streamed around the prone Hutt.

The crawlers had been driven inside a mammoth metal room, larger than many docking bays and sealed off from the rest of the dome. A chem-suited crewer waved Jacen and Jaina aside, so they headed for an elevated platform—and spotted their father on his way to the same spot, trading shoves with Droma. Other Gateway crewers directed the new refugees toward a fenced area, where still others scurried around, laying something out on the ground. The noise level rose steadily, Vors and humans and Vuvrians and Ryn all talking at once.

Through a bay door that resealed instantly, there whirred a small ground-effect vehicle marked ADMINISTRATION. Four figures sat inside, wearing brilliant orange chem suits and full helmeted masks. Jacen appreciated their situation. Like the crewers, anybody who joined them in quarantine would face decontamination. But why hadn't they just set up a holoprojector?

Then he got a feeling about that vehicle.

Incredulous, he nudged Jaina. She'd been right here. Here, all along. At Gateway!

Jaina nudged him back. They turned toward one another so each one could watch their father with side vision.

The second-smallest of the three orange-suited figures jumped out of the vehicle. Her face was shrouded, but her determined gait was unmistakable, and Jacen felt her through the Force. Her smaller shadow had to be one of the Noghri.

Han and Droma strode up. Han looked half-ready to send Droma flying. "No, they don't have repulsor combs. We're just going to have to do this—"

"The hard way?" Droma interrupted. "What do you care, if they take off that little patch of fur on top of your empty head? Do you have any idea how *cold*—"

The orange-suited figure reached them.

"Hello," Han said, hastily setting his dirt-streaked face to a slight smile. "Thanks for sending the crawlers, but we've got a slight problem. One of your crewers just found something he thought was an egg. We've got to find out where those bugs came from, but my people here deserve a little respect."

"We'll do our best."

Jacen strained his ears. The voice sounded husky, but right.

"Equal treatment for everyone. SELCORE is enormously grateful for refugee sponsors."

Han extended a hand. "Glad you understand. Han Solo."

Instead of taking his hand, the administrator reached up for her mask's clasps.

"Hey, wait," Han exclaimed. "You'll end up in decontamination."

She pulled off her mask one-handed. A long coil of dark-brown hair tumbled loose. "That's all right," she said somberly.

Leia stared at Han's weary face—his gaping hazel eyes, his slack jaw stubbled with gray. Luke and Mara must have known Han was here, and assumed she did, too. How many people made that assumption—and so they just didn't tell her?

Now, she knew she might have only a moment to reach him, before he remembered the last time she spoke to him. Angrily. "If your people have to be decontaminated," she told Droma, "I'll show them Gateway and SELCORE are with them, not against them." For the moment, her aide Abbela could manage Gateway's day-to-day business. Before Han's eyes went hard and empty again, she had to reach him. She stepped closer. "Besides, I had no idea you were here. I should've known, but . . . I don't think you ever sent over a roster."

"We, ah, didn't." A lopsided grin appeared. "I suspect SELCORE's been too busy administering Gateway to notice."

She glanced over her shoulder. Olmahk stayed close, on watch, as C-3PO assisted the newcomers. *Where* would she put them all? She'd hoped to bring those poor Thirty-two people inside her more permanent dome eventually, and send workers back in week-long shifts. Gateway had plenty of space, but construction equipment was booked for weeks ahead, her new apartments filled before she built them. There *were* tents, carefully struck when her first charges moved into sturdier huts—and there was the decontamination issue . . .

Later! She had four-fifths of her family in plain sight, everyone but Anakin. This hadn't happened in months!

She flung her arms around Han. His body remained stiff, but he laid an arm on her shoulders.

She backed away from him.

"Hello, Mom." Jacen opened his arms, then hesitated.

Leia set down her droopy fabric helmet. Since she was committed to quarantine now, she yanked off her chem suit and then flung her arms around Jacen. "By the Force, you're as big as your father."

Then she spotted Jaina, hanging back. "What are you doing here?"

Jaina dangled a pair of fancy goggles from one hand. "Sick leave. We tried to find you."

Leia's stomach took a dive. "Were you injured?"

"Temporary partial blindness. Nothing serious." Jaina lowered her voice. "Get it straight with Dad, Mom. That's first." She turned and strolled back toward the Ryn mob.

Smiling ruefully, Jacen placed both hands on Leia's shoulders. He gently turned her toward Han, who had thrust his hands back into his pockets. "First," Jacen murmured.

Hesitantly, Leia caressed both twins through the Force. Jacen glowed with the pleasure of being reunited; in Jaina, there was a repressed bitterness that she'd obviously have to face—later.

"Guess it's time I found something to do." Droma replaced the soft cap he'd doffed. "Good to see you again, Princess Leia." He followed Jaina.

Leia linked one arm through her husband's. "Let me show you the whole quarantine area," she said lightly.

In a converted repair dock, families clung to each other, shuffling forward. She mustn't look at them. She had to settle things with Han. Her fault, his fault— didn't matter. Beneath her strength and independence, she really was happiest with someone to help carry her burdens.

On the other hand, that meant she had to help carry *his*.

"Yes," she admitted, "SELCORE and Gateway have been taking care of themselves. And trying to reclaim the planet. Remember Honoghr, where we couldn't do much of anything? Here, it's in reach. And the Yuuzhan Vong don't want it. This could be a haven for millions."

"I don't think you've paid much attention to the Duros." He frowned. "They're—"

"Barely tolerating us," she admitted. "But we haven't given much back, yet. This world is the key to a new future, where all peoples can live side by side. Wait until you see what our scientists are starting to accomplish."

"Where's old Goldenrod?" Han rubbed his rough chin. "I could've used him. All they gave us was a pair of beat-up modified loadlifters. I had to scam a medical droid."

Leia half smiled. "Threepio? Just what you needed. Someone to *really* irritate you." Han must be utterly distracted, she thought, not to recognize C-3PO in a vermin-proof chem suit.

Han's eyes narrowed. "Has Isolder shown up?"

She pulled away, feeling blindsided. "What?"

"At least ten people played me that HoloNet bite of you and His Gorgeousness stepping off that Hapan ship together on *Yald*. You looked pretty cozy."

Leia got a good breath. "You, who wants everybody to trust you—can't you trust me? The nets have used that as a publicity stunt. I couldn't back out without losing the Hapans' support. We needed those ships."

His expression softened. "Yeah. We did need them. Too bad, how that turned out."

One crisis resolved! On to the next. "How's Jacen?" she asked. "I heard he was taking it all pretty hard."

"Still chewing on it, I guess." He grabbed her hand. "You accused me of having a fling with my past. Well, look at these people. Does *this* look like a fling—"

"No," she said. "Han, I'm sorry. It's been tough, lately. Really hard."

"Yeah. Well." He firmed his lips, swallowed, then glanced up again. "You probably won't forget some things, but I was hoping you'd forgive them."

Leia threw her arms around him again. This time, he

returned the embrace. His arms gripped her, his breath had the sweetness of . . .

Well, of a wet Wookiee.

She held her breath while she kissed him.

Then there was no more time for reconciliation. They walked toward the repair dock, which was rapidly filling with strangers of several species. Leia had ordered it furnished with sleeping pads.

Han frowned. "Looks good, but I hope you don't care if the Ryn reshuffle their area every evening."

"Why?"

He stood loose-limbed, looking out on the mob. "They have some interesting taboos. One of them is against sleeping twice in the same place."

"I don't care if they sleep on top of each other. I'm more concerned about feeding them."

"Just give them whatever you would've shipped to Thirty-two. I'm more worried about water."

"We've got a well started, under the admin building."

For ten minutes, they talked about supplying refugees with basic needs. Really, for someone who didn't do administration, he'd managed fabulously. She told him so.

"Sometimes," he drawled, "I still amaze myself. But Droma thought through a lot of it. Him and the clan heads, Mezza and Romany. And Jacen has been trying to keep the peace. Me, I'm the hope-of-rescue guy."

She slid her arm around his waist. They'd climbed onto the top of a controller's cubicle. Olmahk followed at a discreet distance. Among the milling Ryn, she spotted Jaina with a group of grizzled females, once again wearing her mask.

"How badly was she hurt, Han?"

"She ended up EV."

The thought of her daughter drifting in frigid vacuum,

in the middle of a battle, made Leia's stomach churn again.

"We've got a decent medical facility. I could process her through decontamination quickly—"

"No," Han said. "Only time will fix this. No special treatment for humans, and especially not our family. These Ryn have been kicked around for centuries. They're not a big group, but they're loyal to people who treat them decently."

A pair of stretcher bearers stalked past, pushing a float cart loaded down with a young-looking Hutt.

"What's he doing here?" Leia demanded.

Han shone that lopsided grin again. She felt she would never get enough of it. "He claimed that he wanted to defect, and hit the Vong where it hurts. But did you ever know a Hutt who could cooperate under pressure?"

Leia thought hard. "I'll tell you if I remember any. I have an idea, Han. How many sick and injured have you got?"

He pursed his lips and stared out over the mob. She eyed his profile, cataloging features she'd loved half her life. Had he broken his nose again?

"Other than Jaina, mostly just scrapes and bruises from trying to kill the moth things. Why?"

"We'll process the sick and injured as priority. Then we can include Jaina, unless she'd rather stay in quarantine indefinitely than get her head shaved. She's at that age, you know. Young men are looking."

He reached out and fingered the long coil of hair that hung forward over her blue uniform. "Can the old guys look, too?"

She touched his hand. "I . . . guess it'll have to come off, Han."

He shrugged. "It'll grow. It'll just take a while."

"Will you stick around while it does?" She tried not to plead, but she wanted to.

He ran a hand over his unruly hair. "Hey, someday I might lose mine for good. We'll call it a dry run."

Then he winked, and she melted inside.

She led back down into the controllers' cubicle. At the loudspeaking station, she punched in a sharp tone that silenced the roar of outside conversations.

"Attention, please," she said. "This is Gateway administration. Welcome. We will try to settle you and meet your needs as quickly as possible. Stand by for a message from your own administrator."

She pushed the comlink at him.

"What?" he demanded.

"Sick and wounded, back to the debarking area," she muttered. *Nerf herder!*

He nodded and echoed the announcement.

Fifteen minutes later, Leia's health administrator—fully suited—was explaining priority decontamination to a cluster of Ryn and Vors and five elderly humans.

Leia stepped back. She didn't see Jaina. Han had gone out among the Ryn. Frowning, she climbed back up to the lookout perch. It took longer than she anticipated to spot Jaina along the south wall.

She clambered back down and made her way over. The odd odor of Ryn came from everywhere. She made another mental note: *Plain-water baths.* And something warm for all those poor Ryn to slip on, after the decontamination crew took their fur.

Fortunately, the supply ship carrying her mining laser had gotten through. She'd put the new laser to work, deepening the well under her admin building. Fresh, reliable water would be essential, with Pit Thirty-two potentially lost.

Jaina stood leaning against the south wall.

"Didn't you hear the announcement?" Leia asked. "We're processing anyone sick or wounded first, so we can get them into our medical facility. I'll walk you through."

"Thanks," Jaina said, "but if Coruscant's med center couldn't do anything for me, I doubt yours can."

"I can use you," Leia said, "personally. I'm swamped out there. I have an aide, but by the time everyone here gets out of quarantine, I'll be so far behind that—"

Something hard tapped her shoulder. She turned her head and looked up into the blank mask of a chem suit. "What is it, Threepio?"

"Excuse me, but there is a priority transmission from Bburru waiting on line six," he told her. "And the report you requested from Dr. Cree'Ar—"

"That'll keep," she told him. "Say hello to Jaina."

"Hello, Mistress Jai—"

"Good to see you, Threepio." Jaina turned aside and said bluntly, "You'll never catch up. Not with my help, not with a dozen assistants. That's because you take on everyone else's problems. Well, you weren't there for mine. Not even the military could find you, Mother. I thought you'd finally been caught by some unreconstructed Imperial terrorist, or that the Yuuzhan Vong dropped a moon on you. Jacen and I tried to find you from Thirty-two. What a joke. First we couldn't get an outsystem connection. When we finally reached SEL-CORE, we got Viqi Shesh. That was another joke."

"I haven't signed my reports, but if she wanted to find me, she could." Jaina's words stung, but Leia thought it would be best to let her vent. Senator Shesh *had* done very little toward easing supply problems.

"I don't care," Jaina said. "I don't want special treatment. I want to help these people. What about the old ones? There's no treatment that will cure their aches and pains. Before, at least they had their ways, their traditional meds. Now they've got nothing. Are you going to process all of them through first, too?"

"Yes," Leia told her. "Immediately after the—"

"*Shaved*, Mother? The old people?"

"Mistress Jaina," C-3PO butted in, "you will be pleased by our relatively fine medical facil—"

Leia felt warmth spread up her neck, toward her face. "Jaina, I'm trying to help them—and you."

"Maybe," Jaina said through her teeth, "I just don't want help anymore. You showed me I had to learn to do without you. So I did." She stalked away.

Leia gave chase. "You seem to have missed something," she said. "I'll be decontaminating out of here, the same as you, the same as anyone. Think about it."

Jaina stared at the long coil of hair. "You're kidding," she said quietly. "Mother, if you . . . how long did it take to grow it that long?"

"That's not even slightly important. *You* are. I suppose we won't ever find it easy to live in the same place, again. We're too much alike."

Jaina's grin showed teeth. "Bullheaded, obstinate, perfectionist . . . me? How could you accuse me of—"

"Heredity," Leia answered. "And environment. You were doomed. At least you've got your father's luck."

Jaina's smile faded. "Before I forget, Mom, you need to talk to Jacen. You know how well he reads people."

"And?" Leia prompted, confused again.

"While we were looking for you, he got a look at your Senator Shesh. He had a real strong reaction. Negative."

Leia thought back to her own dealings with Shesh, on Coruscant. Publicly, the senator had staunchly supported SELCORE—and the Jedi, despite their PR problems—

and yet there'd been unexplained shortages, communication problems, defense shortfalls. If Leia wanted to suspect Senator Viqi Shesh of duplicity, it wouldn't be hard.

"I'd better talk to him," she said.

CHAPTER FOURTEEN

"So." Droma waggled his mustachios. "She could've married royalty, and she took you instead?"

Han backhanded his friend with a spoon full of synthetic stew, driving Droma backwards off his stool.

Jacen could barely stay awake. It had been an incredibly long day. Most of the Ryn were laying out their sleeping pads.

"Randa was the first one out of quarantine, after the sick list," he interrupted.

Han stirred his stew and gave Droma the look Jacen and Jaina had always called "the stare." "And Leia's people locked him up already."

"Now what?" Droma asked.

"The usual. Tried to get outside the dome, just to look at the ships. *Just* looking," Han repeated, as Droma clambered back onto his stool.

Droma eyed his own bowl and spoon. Jacen, suspecting the Ryn was calculating range and elevation, slid his stool back.

Jaina and Leia had processed through, too. Han had convinced Jaina he would need an outside liaison with the people who processed through, and someone to keep an eye on Randa. At that, Leia decided she'd cover her own job better outside than in here. She'd left Olmahk in quarantine, to assist with security.

Jacen took the news philosophically. He'd hoped his parents would spend a little more time together, after so long.

"Twenty-three Ryn followed Jaina out," Han was saying. "Leia found them flight suits, so at least they'll stay warm until the fuzz grows back. I thought they looked pretty good."

"*You* would." Droma bristled. "You're getting nearsighted."

"Your mouth looks just as big as ever."

Now Jacen spotted the soft light in Han's eyes and a self-satisfied grin. Maybe his parents *had* found a few moments alone. In his opinion, they'd both made convenient use of their circumstances to keep from reuniting. There was something splendid about the universe when your mother and father loved each other.

"Someone ought to go back over to Thirty-two," he said, "and get our belongings."

The Ryn smoothed his mustachios. "Possessions? They're just something to lose. I'm more interested in whether there are still spaceworthy ships over there."

"Yeah," Han said. "Figure out how to get them here, while you're at it. If we leave Gateway in a hurry, it won't be by crawler."

Jacen clenched his fists at the sight of Thirty-two's ruins. Synthplas scraps drooped between struts that arched like the ribs of a beast picked clean by carrion crawlers. Through those ribs, from a vantage near the remains of the entry gate, Jacen could see rows of blue-roofed huts through what used to be the protective dome.

Gateway's driver had donned a chem suit before bringing still-quarantined refugees on board. He shook his head. "Good thing you weren't in there when it started to breach." His voice came filtered through the transparent faceplate.

"Actually, we were," Jacen muttered.

He stepped into the overalls of his own rebreather-equipped chem suit. Over them went an orange jacket, gloves attached. He worked his fingers down into the gloves, which didn't hamper his touch when he attached his soft helmet and anchored the clasps. SELCORE must've gotten the suits from a military source, he reflected.

"Ready?" he asked his team.

Droma had slid into his orange suit. Mezza, older and bulkier, struggled to bring hers over her head. Six other suited figures moved toward the crawler's hatch.

"Scanning for life-forms," the driver's assistant said. He worked a few controls. "Negative in this line of sight, but be careful."

Jacen hooked his lightsaber on the outside of his suit. Mutant fefze beetles were the only creatures known to have survived the collapse of Duro's ecosystems.

He led down the crawler's ramp. Each pair of the others pushed a repulsor cart. Their mission was simple: gather as many belongings as possible and get back before dark. Jacen, nominally in charge, would help wherever he was needed, then bring the *Falcon* over to Gateway while Droma followed in Thirty-two's battered I-7 Howlrunner.

He moved out with a pair of tall, thin Vors who had volunteered for a duty that was much more dangerous for them, with their twitchy lungs. They also had their pride—but they looked almost skeletal in orange chem suits, except for the arms, plumped unnaturally by bunching their leathery wings into the sleeves.

His insulated boots crunched on dead moths as he strode up the first lane. Evidently Duro's atmosphere *did* kill them. They wouldn't spread overland to other domes.

Grateful for one small blessing, he escorted the Vors to the first hut in their sector. They ducked inside while Jacen stood guard, vaguely uneasy. Within minutes, the Vors emerged carrying armloads of clothing and other belongings. Jacen helped bundle that load together, and then the Vors quietly pushed on to the next hut. Saving their breath, Jacen guessed.

They'd cleared several huts when Jacen's comlink squealed. "Solo," Mezza's voice barked. "Get over here!"

He sprinted back up the lane, searching the Ryn section. Finally, he spotted a tethered repulsor cart. He shifted direction and headed toward it, gripping his lightsaber with his right hand so it wouldn't bounce against his hipbone.

He plunged into the shelter. Two orange-suited forms had backed against its inside wall. Closer to Jacen was an insect he'd seen only in holos and nightmares. Fefze beetles, loosed on the planet's surface during the Duros' early days of space travel, had the odd quirk of both internal and external skeletons, so the mutant strain had been able to grow to enormous size. This one was well over a meter long, with segmented antennae waving toward him, sniffing through the Duro-stench. Evidently it had taken this hut as a nest, because the crumpled wings of hundreds of white-eyes lay along one half-eaten cot. Under iridescent wing covers, the beetle's soft abdomen was grossly distended. It had evidently gorged on white-eyes and the Ryn's pitiful possessions. It was getting ready to lay eggs.

Unfortunately, Mezza and her partner had gotten past it before spotting it. They crouched against an interior wall, brandishing a cast-off shirt and a pair of leggings.

Whenever the beetle's antennae twitched, they flapped the clothing.

Jacen drew and ignited his lightsaber. The beetle turned, working the air with two of its armored, pincer-footed legs. Green, blue, and purple light reflected off the iridescent grooves of its body, and its mouthparts—easily wide enough to grip a Ryn leg—clicked ominously.

"Load your pile and get out," Jacen said.

"Kill it!" Mezza's voice hooted out of the nearer, bulkier chem suit.

Jacen didn't turn his head. "Why? There are thousands of them, all over the surface—"

"Kill it," she shrieked. "One beetle dead is a hundred less next season. It's going to lay eggs."

Jacen saw the sense in that, but the creature had no evil intent. It had found an excellent nesting spot, complete with food source, and he didn't want to kill needlessly.

"Just load up the cart and move on," he told Mezza. "I don't think she'll come after you."

"She?" Mezza demanded. "So now it's a *she?*"

"Do males lay eggs?"

"Solo!" the comlink in his pocket shrieked. "We have trouble!"

He fingered it on as he raised it. "On my way," he said. Then, to Mezza, "Get your things and get out."

He positioned himself between Mezza and the clicking beetle until she'd cleared the hut, then he backed out after her. The beetle didn't follow.

Standing well out into the lane, he closed down his lightsaber and touched the comlink again. The cry, almost avian, had sounded like a Vor—or was that just the distortion of breath masks and fluctuating reception? "Where are you?"

"Over here. On a roof!" Grunting and whacking noises sounded over the link.

He scrambled up a nearby shelter and balanced on top.

About twenty meters away, two pudgy-armed orange figures—definitely Vors—stood on another blue roof, menaced from below by five iridescent beetles. Side by side, the orange figures flung someone else's heirlooms at the creatures. The huge insects ducked, then came on again, scrabbling against the rough wall, mouthparts clicking and sliding against each other like hand-length saws.

Jacen leapt down, not liking to think what would happen if the beetles climbed up and holed the Vors' chem suits. This time, he *did* have to kill. These creatures were attacking prey, not defending a nest.

Half stepping back into a fighting stance, he lit his lightsaber again. He'd never tried lightsaber fighting without using the Force. *But how hard could it be?* he asked himself, and he waded in Force-blind.

These beetles, swarming toward fresh food, weren't about to back down. Jacen swung the lightsaber through the nearest, slicing it between abdomen and thorax. It collapsed.

Jacen swung for another one's faceted eyes. Two more beetles pivoted and came for him, leaving the hut's other side safe for the Vors.

"Back to the crawler," Jacen shouted. "Signal the others—we're leaving!"

The Vors scrambled down. One tried to grab their cart's handles. Two beetles lunged for his loosely suited legs, snipping with their mouthparts. The Vor shrieked and ran after his partner.

Another half-dozen beetles clambered over the dead ones. Jacen swung the lightsaber wildly, keeping a circle clear around himself. Without drawing on the Force, his motions seemed jerky, disconnected—but he didn't stop. Another swarm reached him.

On Yavin 4, he recalled, certain crushed or wounded insects gave off pheromones that called in more of their species. Whether or not this was the case here, something was drawing them toward him. Five more scuttled closer, up another lane.

Then an orange-suited form pelted into view.

"Get back," Jacen shouted.

The form waved a vibroblade. "I'll clear you a path." That was Droma's voice.

The Ryn came on, slicing for the beetles' undersides, dancing out of the way of claws and mouthparts. They didn't seem nearly as interested in Droma as they were in Jacen.

The thought hit them both at the same instant. As Jacen shouted, "They're drawn to the light—" Droma's voice echoed, and then finished, "—saber!"

Now what? Jacen sliced, backstepped, turned, and sliced again. The mindless creatures kept coming, waving their antennae. The comlink in his pocket whistled, then a voice said, "Solo, everyone but you and Droma has gotten to the crawler. Run for it!"

"Shut off that glow light, Solo," Droma shouted. "You're as crazy as your father."

Shut down his lightsaber? Backstep. Swing. Beetles boiled over each other, some stopping to chew on the ones he'd killed. The biggest one yet, black antennae as thick as a Twi'lek's lekku, sailed in over the others' backs. Jacen sidestepped and sliced it in two, but as he did, something sharp closed on his left ankle.

"Get to the Howlrunner!" he shouted at Droma.

Droma vaulted an iridescent abdomen and landed beside Jacen. Breathing hard, now—harder than a Jedi should, for lightsaber work—Jacen jabbed at the beetle who'd seized his ankle. As it fell away, he spotted a tiny tear in his orange pants leg.

"Throw the lightsaber." Droma crouched, brandishing his vibroblade. "I'll cut us a way out. Then you can levitate it to you."

"You *know* I'm trying not to use the Force." Swing. Sidestep. Jab.

"Fine—then leave it here. But throw it, or I will!"

Jacen locked his lightsaber on, flicked his wrist, and let go. As the lightsaber flew, he had another flashback to his vision—of a lightsaber, sailing off into the distance.

"Go!" Droma grunted.

The pack of beetles scuttled off after the glimmering lightsaber. Jacen headed for the hydroponics tank, jumping over a beetle with every other step. Now the ominous Duro-scent reached his nostrils. They'd breached his suit, all right.

Droma slashed the antennae off one bug that got too close. They broke free of the swarm.

"This way." Jacen led toward a long breach in the synthplas wall, instead of the gate. "I left the I-7 close to the *Falcon*."

"Right behind you," Droma called.

Jacen pulled out his comlink. "Crawler, this is Solo. Stick around till we can get airborne."

Then he turned to look back. The mass of beetles boiled, an iridescent tumble of black antennae and wing covers. Somewhere in there was his lightsaber.

If he left it behind, that would be like leaving a leg or a hand—but if he used the Force to call it to his hand, he'd break his own resolve again. Either way, he would be miserable. He had to decide—soon—whether to abandon the Force altogether or plunge back into its flow. This constant weighing and evaluating endangered others.

He shut his eyes, willed the tiniest wisp of energy, and called the lightsaber. It rose out of the battling beetles in a low, shining arc to land solidly in his palm.

He shut it down with a sigh.

Droma stood staring at him. "Hurts to watch you," he said.

"Because you know what I'm going through, I suppose," Jacen answered. "If I use it, I'm miserable. If I don't, I'm sunk."

The Ryn nodded, then stepped out over the tattered remains of the dome. "Come on, kid. Move."

Jacen processed through decontamination the next afternoon and reported to the admin building. According to Leia's aide, Jaina was outdoors in Gateway's ship lot, helping an inspection team. Leia sat at the big SELCORE desk, ignoring an undertone of conversation between C-3PO and someone on the other end of a comlink— something about spiro grass, marshlands, and weather modification.

Leia straightened her white head wrap. "I'm glad you're here, Jacen. A CorDuro freighter we just off-loaded is missing a third of its cargo. Think you could get anywhere with CorDuro's administration?"

Jacen gaped. "I haven't got much experience with negotiating."

Leia shook her head. "No, but you're a Solo, and that ought to impress them. I haven't got time to fly up to Bburru, and your dad says you're trying to get more in-volved in non-Jedi activities. I can sympathize with that." Her left cheek twitched. "More than you know."

"I guess you probably can," Jacen admitted. His mom would understand that not everyone who showed Jedi talent was destined to follow that path. She'd shown him that not every life had enough time for Jedi disciplines.

He'd tried to tell his dad about his vision, and how it confirmed his decision to hold back. Han had turned away, shaking his head, confused.

"Want to try something new?" Leia asked.

Jacen ran a hand over his strangely smooth head. "Droma just brought Thirty-two's Howlrunner over. I could take it up to Bburru, see what I can do."

"I'd appreciate that. Be careful, Jacen."

"Always, Mom."

"May the Force be with you—anyway."

"You, too."

Randa Besadii Diori propelled himself up Gateway's main street, relieved to put the admin building—with its rough, dry detention cell and glaring lights—behind him. He'd tried to explain to Jedi Jaina Solo that he only wanted to evaluate Gateway's ships, but she was as self-righteous as her brother.

So far, he'd evaded their mother.

He passed a pair of shaved-down Ryn, standing outside their tent wearing snug blue flight suits. Their vests and culottes hung limp over lumpy blue leggings.

Even after he'd served his detention—which he had every intention of protesting, after the fact—he had been temporarily excluded from the communication area, the one place where he finally could hope for decent transmission equipment! He *must* contact Borga. He *would* find a way to get off this drab, impoverished world and rejoin her.

He wet his lips. He needed a pilot, of course. He still might convince the young Solo female. As his people said, *Where persuasion fails, bribery prevails.* His kaji-dic had wealth on worlds the Yuuzhan Vong hadn't touched. The young Jedi must have a weakness—jewels, shimmersilk—better yet, a ship of her own.

Encouraged by his thoughts, he hurried up the sandy lane to the SELCORE shelter he'd been issued, a miserable blue tent in Gateway's Tayana ruins district. He could hear the continual grinding of Gateway's rock chewers underfoot.

Pausing inside his door flap, he caught an odd odor. He clenched his little hands, furious at the intrusion. He snuffled, following the scent to his sleeping mat. He had used his flimsy bedcovers as additional padding. Beneath them, he spotted an unfamiliar lump.

Reaching around with his tail, he flicked off the covers.

A leathery ball—not quite the size and shape of a human head—lay on the sleeping mat.

It was a Yuuzhan Vong villip, like the ones he'd seen on board the clustership. Borga had come through for him quickly.

Then he trembled from head to tail tip. Too quickly, actually. For this villip to show up in his dwelling so soon, the Yuuzhan Vong must have an agent inside the Gateway dome, masquerading as human. An agent who now knew where to find him.

Undaunted, Randa picked up the leathery creature and sank onto his rumpled mat. His plan, to lure key Yuuzhan Vong personnel here where the New Republic could trap them, still seemed ill-formed—but he had promised Borga he'd try to bargain. One Jedi for the world of Tatooine? The idea created an inner sensation he didn't quite understand, since he'd never experienced it before: a twinge of vague pain, as if this might not be an appropriate use of someone who wouldn't do this to him. Maybe this was what humans called *guilt*.

He dismissed it. His loyalty was to Borga. Even if Jacen wasn't using the Force, he wouldn't be taken easily.

Randa stroked the villip, then set it down, wondering who would answer. While he waited, he sealed his door flaps. Gateway was too bright for his taste. Thinking of Nal Hutta, and the painstaking planetary development that the Yuuzhan Vong were even now destroying, made his eyes feel thick and pleasantly moist.

Features appeared on the villip—a prominent brow ridge, splayed nubs of nose, cheeks with deep sacs under the eyes. "Randa Besadii Diori," it said. "Finally, you report."

Randa didn't recognize the face's fiercely chiseled features or the imperious baritone voice. He tipped his head respectfully toward the villip. "You have an advantage of knowledge on me, my lord."

"I am Warmaster Tsavong Lah. Can you truly offer a Jedi?"

"I can," he answered. *Warmaster?* His feelers had brought in a prize catch! Now, to lure him to Duro, for the New Republic to snatch. "His name is—"

"Useless Hutt," the warmaster said, "your parent told me what you want in return. Know this. The Hutts betrayed us. Only exemplary service will win back our trust."

"I know and respect your caution, Warmaster. I remember, though, your kinsman's fascination with Wurth Skidder, on board the slave ship with which I traveled too briefly. I would be pleased to deliver this Jedi to you— to you personally, Warmaster. As for my request . . . what use to you is Tatooine? A forsaken world, barely able to sustain life—"

The villip's rendition of the warmaster's eyes looked like unfathomable black holes. "Why," he demanded, "should I value your sense of honor enough to come personally to Duro?"

This, Randa admitted, was the gaping hole in his net. "You would honor me deeply," he began, "and be honored in return—"

"You," the warmaster said, "are not worthy of honor. Nevertheless, I will take this Jedi. Arrange to deliver him, and I will consider your request. Fail to deliver, or offer the slightest deceit, and I shall flay the hide from your body with my coufee."

The villip softened, its features retracted, and Randa was left to wonder what he had done. The aliens' agent here in Gateway could grab Jacen—or stab Randa in his sleep. Had he just made a terrible mistake?

Was there really any way he could hand Jacen over? Surely the young Jedi would come to his senses, sweep out his lightsaber, and fight back.

What Randa really needed, then, was an extra layer of defense. Duro was protected by one cruiser, a few snub-fighters, and the orbital cities' planetary shields, which also protected whatever was immediately below them on the surface. If the New Republic brought an additional battle group closer to Duro, Randa would be defended— the bargain would have to be canceled—

He burst out of his shelter, headed back to the admin building. There, he found two communication techs—a human and a small, toothy Tynnan—talking to a half-size holo of a magnificent, dark-haired woman.

Elated by his good fortune, he muscled the furry Tynnan aside. "Senator Shesh," he gasped, "I have discovered a traitor on Duro! The Yuuzhan Vong have planted an agent here, surely a scout for a future invasion. You must double our defenses, or all these refugees surely will die. You are in a position to send help from the military. Send it quickly!"

Senator Viqi Shesh turned her head slightly away. "Haven't we spoken once before, sir?"

He bowed deeply. "I am Randa Besadii Diori, and—"

"You say you have unmasked a Yuuzhan Vong agent inside the Gateway dome?"

"Not unmasked," he said boldly, "but discovered irrefutable evidence of his presence."

"Then we thank you, Randa Besadii Diori. Deliver your evidence to Gateway's administrator, Ambassador Organa Solo. I have just been apprised of her presence. Her security force will investigate."

"I thank you for your time and attention, Senator. Here again are the people with whom you were conversing." Randa swaggered out of the building. He would do just as the senator suggested: give Leia Organa Solo the villip and let *her* deal with it. His prompt action—realizing he'd made a mistake—had just saved him, and maybe Gateway itself, from a grim fate.

How clever he was.

Senator Viqi Shesh of Kuat shut down the holoprojector and reached for her maggot-textured villip.

This would not wait. Business, like diplomacy, required making concessions, and she had no qualms about reporting one young Hutt's treachery.

She stroked the repulsive alien object, detaching her attention from her right hand by eyeing the curtained wall across from her private office's comm unit. Her servants swept those curtains three times daily for listening devices. Sometimes, they neglected to straighten the folds when they finished. She needed to speak with them—again.

Viqi Shesh had no doubt that the Yuuzhan Vong would soon wrest this galaxy away from the New Republic, just as the New Republic had won it from the

Empire. Rapid change created opportunities. There would be a thousand worlds to govern, and Kuat might be treated better if a Kuati held a high position under the Yuuzhan Vong governors. Certainly *she* would fare better.

The warmaster reacted predictably to her report. "But he has not identified anyone as this operative?"

"Not according to his report, sir."

The villip's alien face pulled its scalloped lips to one side in a sneer. "Our experience with Hutts has shown us nothing but treachery," it said. "We will deal with Randa and his clan. You were correct in reporting him."

Viqi bowed her head silently. For an instant, she considered mentioning the news about Centerpoint.

No. As soon as the Yuuzhan Vong knew Centerpoint was malfunctioning again, they might strike Coruscant. She had too much to accomplish before that day arrived.

CHAPTER FIFTEEN

It was unusual for Kubaz to visit Bburru, the largest orbital city in the Duro system. But nowadays, Bburru's docks were so crowded with offworld construction workers, shippers, and camp followers that the dark, short-trunked trio who arrived—trailed by a bronze astromech droid—attracted little attention in the off-loading area.

The Bburru Docking Authority agent eyed their credentials. According to the datapad, these weren't typical refugees from Kubindi's recent invasion. This family had holdings in the Core Worlds, and they were looking for trade. That explained the fine yacht they'd docked in Slip 18-L.

"Everrrything seems to be in order, gentles." The tall Duros official momentarily mated their datapad with one of his own, programming a map from Port Duggan to CorDuro Shipping's main office at Duggan Station.

Oddly, a minute after they had passed from sight, he had no memory of their arrival.

Mara found the hooded cloak, trunked mask, and goggles stifling, but she took advantage of the disguise to observe Duros' reactions as Port Duggan's long rideway carried them up the dockyard arm to Duggan Station. She caught red-eyed glares, lowered brows, and stares; and if Duros had noses, she didn't doubt they would've wrinkled in distaste. Tresina Lobi had hinted that the Duros, like other species on worlds the Yuuzhan Vong hadn't reached, resented the refugee influx. On Duro, that might be complicated by general nervousness about the political tensions at Corellia.

They'd arrived from Coruscant in Mara's newly modified ship, a yacht Lando had picked up for a song—so he claimed—as soon as he realized how easily its broad aft cargo bay could be modified to carry an X-wing. Other hands had shaped this ship, too. Lando's wife, Tendra, just back from an extended visit to her Saccorian kin, named it *Jade Shadow* after admiring its nonreflective gray hull. Talon Karrde and his connections had found the retractable laser cannons, camouflaged torp launchers, and shields to make *Shadow* almost a match for the *Jade's Fire* that Mara had sacrificed at Nirauan.

Carrying Luke's fighter in the bay, and escorted by Anakin in his own X-wing, she brought the *Shadow* over Duro's south pole, using one of Ghent's universal transponder codes. Groundside, they locked down Anakin's X-wing, and R2-D2 rerouted Anakin's shields to draw on a stack of spare power supplies, setting them to pull just enough power to protect the X-wing from Duro's atmosphere. Then they all boarded *Shadow* again. Flying with Luke as copilot, Mara made a microjump outsystem, changed transponder codes, and they arrived at Duro as a well-heeled Kubaz family.

Drall and Selonian refugees, leaving Corellia while they still were considered first-class citizens, mingled with dockworkers of half a dozen other species retooling the civilian shipyards for military use. A horned Devaronian shouldered past three gray-skinned, long-faced Duros natives. A massive silver-tipped Wookiee plodded in the other direction. Mara caught a whiff of exotic perfume and spotted a comely Trianii swaggering up the corridor, drawing stares with her feline grace.

Mara still hadn't felt anything unbalanced or unhealthy about the cluster of cells dividing, differentiating, digging ever more tightly into her body—none of the gut-wrenching signs of abnormality she'd felt in so many diseased cells. She was determined to take every day without ominous developments as a gift, and not worry how many more she might be given.

There'd been nightmares, though.

She eyed Anakin's slightly slumped posture as he stood to one side of the rideway. She'd coached him in the characteristic Kubaz whirring accent, their cultured speaking style, and their gait, after nixing Luke's idea of disguising themselves as Duros. It was always hard to pass for a native.

The rideway decanted them in a broad open area that their datapad labeled Duggan Station.

"Straight across," Luke whirred at her, steering an elegant old luggage float.

At the other side of the open area, a Duros stood on a knee-high platform. She spoke through a powerful amplifier, addressing a crowd of fifty or sixty: almost exclusively Duros, but Mara spotted a Bith and two turquoise-skinned Sunesi.

Luke, walking point, halted and turned his face—what Mara could see of it—toward the speaker. "Listen to this," he murmured, standing just a little closer than he usually did. Another woman might not have noticed, but Mara was exquisitely aware of her personal space.

The Duros on the platform spoke loudly, waving a knobby hand. "Independence is virrrtue," she shouted. "In dangerrrous times, depending on an outside force for sustenance or defense could kill us all. If you cannot feed yourrr family group, you fail them. If you cannot protect yourrr own, you kill them. Arrre you murderers . . . or prrroviders?"

"Anakin," Mara muttered, "go with Artoo, but stay in visual contact. Get a feel for the crowd. If you sense danger, get back over here."

"Right," he said. "Mom."

Right in character.

"Symbiosis," the Duros called, "has been prrreached since time immemorrrial. Has it made us frrree? Does it make us safe? They say we depend on each otherrr." Now she took on a simpering tone. "That we need each otherrr. Hutt slime!"

Several Duros cheered.

"We, we must be strrrong. We, ourselves. Whoever needs help will fall. Each—one—of—us," she cried, punctuating each word with a grunt, "must be strrrong enough to take what he wants. Or all will die. All!"

On Mara's left side, a few Duros turned toward her, then moved aside, whispering. She didn't catch any intent to attack, and her danger sense lay still, but she kept one hand near her lightsaber, under the dark cloak.

The speaker raised her arm, reaching toward a bank of lights that gave Duggan Station the appearance of yellowish daylight. "We are independent of the worrrld below."

"Yes!" someone from the crowd cried.

"We are independent of the worrrlds at great distance."

The answering "Yes!" picked up volume.

"Symbiosis," she cried, "interrrdependence. They are for the weak. The weak must stand togetherrr to stand at all!"

The Duros cheered.

She crouched down, pressing her palms together. "Like the point of a duha spear, like the blade of a knife, strrrength lies where metal comes to a point. Where worrrlds stand alone, with no need to wait for other fleets to defend them, there is trrrue might. Each of us," she concluded, sweeping an arm out over the crowd, "must be strrrong. Strong enough to take what she wants . . . and defend it!"

Loud cheers.

Mara backed up against Luke and turned her masked head slightly. "This kind of talk could finish what's left of the New Republic."

She caught just a shade of Force energy spinning around him, extended to protect her. Evidently he wasn't trusting completely to their disguises, but taking a basic defensive stance, blurring the orator's view of their faces.

"I've heard enough," he said.

Anakin hadn't gone far. R2-D2 couldn't roll sideways in a crowd, so when Mara caught Anakin's attention and flicked a gloved finger, he nodded and backed away from the podium in a straight line. R2-D2 rolled beside him, wearing a new coat of copper-hued glaze.

The avenue inbound from Duggan Station was lined with planters that served the obvious dual purpose of aesthetics and air-scrubbing. Most local traffic seemed to travel on one- or two-passenger hoverbikes or enclosed hoverpods.

They found an inexpensive hostel, where Luke took a two-room unit. It had three basic cot-over-storage units and a refresher. One wall was programmable to several flatscreen images, including—according to its instruction panel—an exterior view of Bburru City, hanging majestically in space over the dull-brown planet below; Coruscant's night side, with or without an overlay of auroral displays; or shipping traffic entering and exiting hyperspace near Yag'Dhul, at the intersection of the Corellian Trade Spine and the Rimma Trade Route. Mara left it blank.

R2-D2 rolled straight to a data station and plugged himself in. Mara peeled out of her goggles, mask, gloves, and dark robe, emerging in a comfortable flight suit.

By then, Anakin's disguise lay strewn all over his cot. He sat down, stretching and flexing his fingers. "After all the New Republic has done for them, how could they think that way?"

"That's just one troublemaker," Mara said. "But sometimes, it only takes one. Remember Rhommamool, and that firebrand Nom Anor."

"Fortunately," Anakin said, "I didn't meet him."

For Mara, Rhommamool had been a second encounter. Serving as a minor diplomat's bodyguard to festivities on Monor II, she'd endured Anor's rhetoric until even the gentle native Sunesi couldn't tolerate him. They'd asked him to leave.

"Anor fanned an intrasystem resentment into open warfare at Rhommamool. Got most of his own people killed . . . and himself, too. But one troublemaker can sometimes be reached."

Luke nodded. "Reasoned with. I hope that's what we've got here—"

R2-D2 bleeped urgently.

Luke paused halfway through pulling off one boot. "What is it, Artoo?"

Mara couldn't follow the stream of toots and whistles. Evidently Luke couldn't either. "Hold on, hold on." He pushed up off his cot and crossed to the readout over R2-D2's data port. Mara felt a sudden, somber change in his mood.

"Nothing serious," he told her, "everyone's all right. But Han and Jacen's dome just got evacuated into Leia's. Some kind of infestation."

"Jacen's probably collecting again," Anakin said.

"Not funny," Mara muttered. "I don't think Duro supports much life."

Luke's eyes unfocused for a moment. "They're all fine," he said. "And Jacen just arrived up here on Bburru."

"Great," Anakin muttered.

"Anakin," Luke said softly, "Jacen has to find his own path. It's part of hitting maturity. Sometimes that takes a while."

Anakin sniffed. Mara wondered if she'd ever had a sibling, and if they would've gotten along.

"All right," she said. "We'll bump into him sooner or later. But for now, our priorities are to find Tresina's missing apprentice and figure out Duro's political situation. Number one's probably dependent on number two."

"Right," Luke said. "I'll talk to CorDuro Shipping. Unless I'm wrong, that's where Jacen has headed."

"Do that." An idea was forming at the back of Mara's mind. She'd brought along other disguises. Other people could have come to Duro fishing for well-formulated reasons not to open their worlds to refugees. The Kuati senator Viqi Shesh certainly hadn't established SEL-CORE's main camp anywhere near Kuat. Maybe Mara could scare up some information on who *else* here had antirefugee leanings.

She hauled one of her duffels into the refresher.

When she stepped out half an hour later, Anakin grabbed his cot's edge with both hands. His eyebrows rose so far that they almost vanished under his dark hair.

Laughing inwardly, she tilted up her chin and stared down at him. "You may kiss our palm," she said in a languid Kuati accent.

"Wow," he choked.

Luke folded his arms and leaned against the blank

view-wall, grinning. He'd seen her in many guises, but this one *was* spectacular. She'd tinted her red-gold mane a deep reddish brown and pulled it back severely into a tail at the crown of her head, securing it with a circlet of false émeraudes. Bits of masking putty raised the bridge of her nose; shadowing gel gave her cheeks a prominent hollow. More émeraudes rimmed her ears and dangled halfway down her neck. The amethyst-colored tunic, belted in what would pass for gold, had a spatter of green gems on one shoulder, and the cutout beneath the high collar plunged drastically. Her elevated shoes were tapered to give the illusion that the extra height was all her own, but the heels could be kicked off if she needed to make a fast getaway.

She cuffed Anakin's shoulder. "Don't drool on the carpet," she said. "I'm surprised you're still here."

"We won't be for long." Luke pushed off the wall.

Mara smiled ruefully, sensing that he'd like her to stick around for another hour or so. Actually, that sounded good to her, too—but after putting on all this gear, she wanted to keep it unrumpled.

"We have an appointment," Luke said. "That is, two Kubaz have an appointment."

Anakin frowned, still massaging life back into his face from wearing the rubbery mask.

"I'm just going to nose around," Mara said. "See what I can get from that crowd down at Port Duggan, where the performance is going on."

She read *Be careful* in his eyes. Respecting his restraint, she didn't promise that she would. She simply nodded.

His lips twitched.

She enjoyed that—communicating without words *or* the Force. "I'll send Artoo a message if I end up elsewhere," she promised.

Then she realized that she wanted to say, *You two take care*—simply as a parting nicety. She was getting soft.

She offered Luke her palm. He seized her hand, touched it with his lips, then tugged her close enough to whisper, "Come back soon."

CHAPTER SIXTEEN

An aide ushered Luke into CorDuro Vice-Director Durgard Brarun's sumptuous office. Lit by crisscrossed strips on the ceiling and walls, its focal point was a decorative air-circulation grille. Other black grilles reached from floor to ceiling in freeform designs. At the room's front was a narrow counter, like something out of a tapcaf. A lone Duros sat behind it. The triangular CorDuro insignia on his right breast had a gold edging. Gray-green skin hung in folds under his chin. Over his ears, his hairless scalp was turning pale.

He stood to greet the pair of imitation Kubaz. "Gentles, how may I serrrve you?"

Luke wasn't sure what information might be available. He meant to convince Vice-Director Brarun that he and Anakin were harmless, trying to bluff their way into dangerous circles.

It mattered more than ever that he succeed. Everything mattered more, now. He was helping to shape the future in which his child would grow up.

In his best Kubaz whirr-overlaid Basic, he said, "Many of our people are homeless. We have set up a colony on Yag'Dhul, but we need supplies. I was told there were basic goods to be bought here, for a price."

The Duros reached toward his countertop. "The price could be more than you wish to pay, gentles," he said.

Two large humans appeared from behind a brown wall screen. Luke recognized the determination in their eyes, then the hopelessness behind it. He'd seen that mixture before—in Peace Brigade collaborators, humans who were already convinced the Yuuzhan Vong would win this war.

That was an unwelcome complication. Had CorDuro been corrupted? Or had Thrynni Vae vanished because she detected collaboration on an even wider scope?

A second thought hit him like an ion cannon blast, disrupting his other thoughts. Were the Yuuzhan Vong already targeting Duro, and were these their advance agents?

He scrambled to regain his composure. "We are prepared," he whirred, "to offer New Republic credits, Kubindi bonds redeemable offworld, or—"

A tone sounded through the room, and their host straightened. "One moment, gentles."

Brarun touched something in front of him, eyed a readout, and half smiled. Luke sensed an urge to send the strangers away. He countered it subtly, suggesting that Brarun perceive his Kubindi guests as neutral witnesses. After all, their world was already gone.

Brarun appeared to consider the new thought, then said, "Gentles, please lingerrr for a few minutes. I am reminded of a guest that my staff has kept waiting, so that he will know his place. I shall admit him now. Keep still, or your escorrrts will have to see you out."

"Gladly," Luke whirred, "for my people's sake."

He gestured Anakin back toward the brown wall screen. As they backed away, Luke evaluated the big human guards again: commanding in size, but not devastatingly brilliant. They shouldn't present two Jedi much challenge if this came down to blows—which it shouldn't.

Luke sensed Jacen as he walked in, wearing a soft blue cap and a brown flight suit. To his deep concern, Jacen neither probed nor reached out with the Force. In fact, Luke sensed a deliberate damping of the Force all around his elder apprentice, worse than before.

He'd told Anakin that Jacen must find his own path. He knew it with all his heart and mind, but seeing Jacen like this hurt badly. Luke had made mistakes. He knew how painful the consequences might be.

Especially here and now.

He stretched out and nudged Jacen.

Jacen had spent most of the last hour in an anteroom, waiting for the vice-director to admit him. He'd tried to sit patiently and reflect on his vision. It hadn't exactly called him to diplomacy, but this didn't seem like a wrong path.

Now, like an echo out of his vision, he sensed his uncle—there, one of the two Kubaz in the corner, between muscular bodyguard types.

The other Kubaz was Anakin.

From his uncle, he thought he sensed a nudge to get the Duros talking.

Straightening, he faced Vice-Director Brarun. What an opportunity! He could show his uncle *and* his brother the direction his vision and conscience and experiences were taking him.

"Jedi Jacen Solo." The vice-director, like other Cor-Duro employees, wore a red-trimmed brown flight suit. "This is unexpected."

"Thank you for—" Jacen stepped toward the desk.

"Stop," the Duros said. "That's close enough."

Jacen halted. Did Brarun want him standing on this exact spot? Testing, he edged sideways. The vice-director didn't object.

He deduced that the Duros wasn't trying to stand him over or under a Greenie-trap, but was simply frightened of Jedi and trying to protect himself.

"Sir, I'm here on behalf of some very needy people. The refugees inside my mother's dome—"

"She is Leia Organa Solo. Corrrect?"

Jacen's ear for accents and languages had almost adjusted to the Duros' tendency to gargle their *R*s. "Yes, sir. Those refugees are living under unbelievably primitive conditions. They—"

"Where are your Jedi robes, Jacen Solo? Are you here as an infiltrator?"

"No." Jacen spread his hands. "Not at all."

The Duros pointed a long, knobby hand down at Jacen. "Your supply problems are not our concern. Perhaps SELCORE is shorting you."

"Why would SELCORE do that?"

The Duros shrugged eloquently. "Why not? SEL-CORE decided for us that we wanted our planet reclaimed." He raised a hand before Jacen could answer. "We were consulted, but only nominally."

"Why is this a problem?" Jacen asked. "Don't you want it habitable, down there?"

"We," the vice-director said, "are content with our roots pulled free. That sphere of stone once anchored us. Its factories became places to send malcontents and gutter-grubbers. Now those citizens are returning to our well-run cities, upsetting our social balances." He tilted his long head. "And if you restore a habitable planet, the Yuuzhan Vong could choose to move in. If they do, the blame will rest solely on SELCORE." He shot a glance toward the Kubaz.

Jacen shifted his feet on a deep, soft carpet. "Sir, if our supply shuttles don't get through, people will start to go hungry. We need your help. It's urgent."

The Duros reached for the edge of his counter. A high tone sounded. The door behind Jacen swished open. Two armed Duros stalked in.

What was this? Jacen kept his hands lowered. "Sir, I'm just asking for the chemicals we need to grow food. I have no intention of threatening you."

"No?" the vice-director asked. "Your enabling of Centerpoint Station, our near neighbor, changed the power balance in our region. Jedi make me nervous. Especially young ones who use words like *urrrgent*. Often they don't have the maturity to know when to back down."

Thank you, Kyp Durron, Jacen muttered to himself. He hoped Anakin was paying attention. "Sir, it was no Jedi who fired Centerpoint Station."

"A new sentiment is spreading through the New Republic. Surely," Brarun said, "you have heard the Jedi philosophy challenged."

"I have," Jacen admitted. "Most recently, down at Port Duggan. When I arrived."

"Ah," he said. "You met my sister, Ducilla."

"An eloquent speaker," Jacen said, though the woman's philosophy might have come straight from the Yuuzhan Vong's propaganda offices. On second thought, they probably never bothered with subterfuge.

Still, if Master Luke wanted information, this was going well. Now he needed to state his position. "You have nothing to fear from me, Vice-Director. You asked where I left my Jedi robes. At the moment, I have stood down from my status as a Jedi in training."

The Duros bowed his long head and laughed bitterly. "Any Jedi whose mother is a Skywalker cannot stand down. Ever." His red eyes glimmered. "It's time you learned that."

Jacen clenched his hands at his sides. "I'm learning to be my own man. Not just my mother's son."

This time, the four guards laughed, too.

"All right . . . man," the vice-director said. "What is it you want to offer CorDuro Shipping in exchange for this missing cargo?"

"You don't understand," Jacen insisted. "Those supplies belong to us. They were sent by Coruscant."

"So really," Brarun said, "you have come here to accuse my people of robbery."

Again, at the back of his mind, Jacen saw the galaxy tip toward darkness. He spread his hands and backtracked. "I have little to offer," he admitted.

The Duros folded long, knobby hands on the bar-desk's surface. "Well said, Jedi Solo. Now let me tell you some things.

"I am old enough to remember Emperor Palpatine. There was a human who could keep order. Maybe he carried some programs too far, such as trying to wipe out your kind, but I doubt that the Yuuzhan Vong would've stuck a tattooed toe into this galaxy if they arrived while he was in power."

Jacen stood silently, wondering what else the Duros meant to tell him.

Brarun seemed to have forgotten the two Kubaz. "Some of our orbital cities retain drive units," he said, "from the days when our ancestors first steered them into place. Our homes aren't locked to Duro. We could leave and take home with us."

In that case, Jacen wouldn't put it past them to divert and stockpile refugee supplies, though they could not admit that publicly. "In the face of a possible invasion," he said softly, "you do have to consider your own people first."

The Duros raised his head, then cocked it in surprise.

"Exactly. What use would the Yuuzhan Vong have for mechanical habitats?"

Jacen straightened. At last, the Duros was listening—because instead of pushing his demands, Jacen had sympathized. "I agree," he said. "But they destroy what they despise. There are things you don't know about the Yuuzhan Vong. I've even been their prisoner. I've—"

"How did you get away?" Brarun demanded.

Jacen exhaled heavily. He looked down at the floor, then raised only his eyes. "My uncle came for me." It had been spectacular. Since Master Luke was undoubtedly tracking his feelings, he sent a pulse of gratitude.

"There, you see?" Brarun drew up taller. "Anyone whose mother is a Skywalker cannot stand down from being a Jedi."

"I'm trying," Jacen said. "I am seriously trying to find out what I am, apart from all that."

Brarun rubbed his gray-green thumbs together over his folded hands.

"I've seen terrible things," Jacen continued. He related some of them: the slave-taking, the preoccupation with pain. "And death," he finished. "We've seen them sacrifice whole shiploads of prisoners. We know it's sacrifice, not simply elimination. I've spoken with a woman who was also their prisoner." Danni Quee's sad face flitted through his mind. He hoped she was safe, back on Coruscant. "I don't think you'd be safe, even if you took these habitats to another world. They'd shoot to destroy your technology."

"Is that a threat, Jedi?"

"No," Jacen exclaimed. "I'm trying to help you, Vice-Director. To warn you, not threaten you. We have to stand together."

"The old symbiosis dogma. Did you know that even

as your water-treatment settlement tried to become symbiotic with the Gateway dome, Gateway was trying to develop more-dependable water sources of its own and become independent of you? That was in your mother's weekly report." He tilted his head triumphantly. "She, a Skywalker, was not working toward symbiosis at all."

"We *are* interdependent," Jacen insisted. "Every settlement's work will contribute to making the surface habitable again." A bizarre idea drifted into his head. He wasn't authorized to do this . . . but . . . "Vice-Director, if we settlers, the first people of a new Duro, offered to pay a tariff, a percent of all future goods, would that help ensure delivery? Say . . . two percent?" That seemed plenty generous.

The Duros stared over his clasped hands. Jacen held his breath. They both knew Jacen wasn't authorized to offer this. If other settlements called this a betrayal, they'd come braying for Jacen's blood, not the vice-director's.

"Twenty." Brarun waved one hand. Out one corner of his eye, Jacen saw those big human security guards relax.

"Too much." Jacen felt increasingly awkward. His mother had authorized him to try diplomacy, but did that include giving away goods? "SELCORE negotiated with CorDuro for delivery of supplies," Jacen insisted. "Your people are already being paid."

"And you," the vice-director said, "have been sent to me as a negotiator. Fascinating." He raised a finger, beckoning one bulky aide away from the two inoffensive Kubaz. "Jedi Solo, I would like to continue these negotiations. Please consider yourself my guest, for the time being. Until I can contact your mother, and Coruscant."

Did the Duros mean to hold him for ransom, or as a hostage? Or would Brarun really negotiate? Jacen was glad there'd been witnesses in here, though no one could call them impartial. He couldn't wait to tell Master Sky-walker about his vision, too. Finally, he might get some help settling his mind.

"I'll ask one condition, though."

Brarun's brow ridge rose. "I do not believe you are in a position to set conditions."

"Wait. Listen. Deliver all the supplies you contracted to take groundside, as long as I'm your . . . guest." His uncle would like that, even if Anakin was too young to understand.

"You have no way of checking that, Jedi."

"Don't I?" Jacen looked hard into the Duros' large eyes. In fact, he didn't. But Brarun didn't know that. "You must help us hold back the Yuuzhan Vong. If we can't maintain a strong front against them, they'll pick us off, one system at a time. They're already doing it."

"We've heard that story," the Duros said, but he waved the second guard forward. "Escort young Solo to my guest room," he said. "Stay with him—outside, in the hallway. I will speak with him later."

Jacen glanced toward the brown wall screen on his way out. *Hope you got what you wanted, Uncle Luke,* he thought, knowing his uncle would recognize only an unspoken query.

One Kubaz barely nodded. The other turned away.

Mara dropped her datapad on a console as she re-entered the rental unit. A quick check of both rooms confirmed that they were empty, and her practiced eye saw no sign that anyone else had entered.

Sporting her new disguise around Bburru, she'd had no trouble finding a Duros willing to talk, especially when she explained that she was afraid she'd wake up one morning to find Kuat pocked with refugee camps.

The Duros merchant talked freely, sensing a potential

convert. She recorded his philosophy on her datapad, pressing harder and deeper for clarification on doctrinal points. Finally, convinced by her eagerness, he promised to forward her the very latest "word of wisdom," which should arrive in two days.

At that point, her ear for intelligence pricked. How, she asked casually, could he know so exactly?

He shrugged. That was always the day it arrived.

Mara thanked him regally, departing with more information than he knew he'd given out.

Without bothering to lose her costume, she sat down at the rental room's data port and plugged in her pad. Minutes later, thanks to codes Ghent developed years ago for Talon Karrde, she was deep into Bburru's communications bureau.

Dozens of broadcasts "always" arrived on that day of the week. Out of those, she narrowed her possibilities to three that came from outsystem and one that arrived from the surface, an official report from SELCORE's Gateway dome, where research was conducted. SEL-CORE in its wisdom still tried to keep the Duros duly impressed with the detoxification process.

That source, she could check quickly. She keyed up the most recent broadcast. On the surface, it was nothing more than a series of progress reports: two toxic swamps seeded with reclamation organisms. Three enclosures drained and plowed for planting. Small mammals loosed on the grass prairie; that experiment hadn't turned out so well—half died, and the other half showed no eagerness to nest and breed.

She carried one of Ghent's decoding programs in her datapad. It was the matter of a minute to copy the transmission and run the program. She waited while it applied various codes to the program, coming up with only gibberish . . .

Until it hit pay dirt. Her hair tail fell over her face as she leaned into the datapad. One of the dirtdown scientists had used an old Rhommamoolian military code.

Mara remembered the passionate, even illogical antagonism of the Rhommamoolians' slain spiritual leader, Nom Anor. Toward the end of this text, she even spotted some of the exact phrases that Duros orator had used at Duggan Station.

She pushed away, tilting her chin to let the hair tail settle behind her head. Someone down at Gateway—a Duros, or someone else with reason to make trouble in the Duro system—had connections to Rhommamool, where she'd already heard this kind of rhetoric.

The *Jade Shadow* had belonged to a spice merchant before Lando's refit droids installed its camouflaged armament. It would pass as a noblewoman's runner. As Kuati nobility, she ought to have at least one servant, but she couldn't always get what she wanted.

She left Luke a message with R2-D2.

Han's head and shoulders glimmered over a holoprojector in one of the Gateway admin building's offices. "Sounds exactly like Randa, crashing the comm office that way," he said. "Threaten him if you have to. He respects you."

"He used to," Jaina said, "for a while." She shook her head. Now she just wished the Hutt would leave her alone.

"Guess we shouldn't have let him sleep in our control shed. I shouldn't've even brought him along."

Jaina shrugged. "No, you did the right thing."

"Well, go warn him he's headed for permanent lockup, and then keep an eye on him. Keep him out of Leia's way. Somebody tried to sabotage her mining laser last night."

"Then I'll stay out of her way, too." Jaina pulled her soft, SELCORE-blue cap low, warmly covering her ears, and went out.

She found Randa's tent quickly. Blubbering noises filtered through its blue walls.

She pulled open the flap. Randa sat on his sleeping mat, holding a leathery ball in one little hand. He twitched that hand, as if to hide it—then thrust it forward, more forcefully. His blubbering and moaning shut off.

"Take it," he ordered. "I expected Ambassador Organa Solo, or her security people."

Jaina recognized the villip. Her stomach wrenched. Randa, a spy? No wonder he'd been hanging out in the communication centers!

"How long have you been working for them?" she demanded, holding herself ready to fend off an attack.

"I am *not*," the Hutt growled. "I asked to speak with them, hoping to negotiate on behalf of my people. They rebuffed me—"

"When?" Jaina took another step forward. "When did you contact them?"

"Yesterday."

"Only once?"

"I swear it by my—"

"Oh. Right, I believe you," she said, loading her voice with sarcasm. "So that's why you tried to warn Senator Shesh there were Yuuzhan Vong on the way. Because you somehow found a villip, somewhere inside Gateway dome."

"The senator assured me that reinforcements will arrive shortly."

Jaina worked the tip of her thumb with one fingernail. If Jacen was right, if Shesh wasn't to be trusted, then the woman would *not* lobby to send reinforcements. She might even report Randa to the Yuuzhan Vong.

"I made an error," the Hutt assured her. "Truly I did. But I have repaired it, now—"

"Do you think anyone will believe that? Give me that."

Jaina snatched the leathery villip. That brought her momentarily chest-to-belly with the Hutt, close enough to catch a whiff of his fetid body odor. Clutching the stiff villip under one arm, she stalked out of the shelter and hustled toward the gray admin building.

CHAPTER SEVENTEEN

Mara was ordered not to land at Gateway's main gate. "The decontam area just inside's under quarantine," they told her—doubtless from the evacuation of infested Settlement Thirty-two. A young voice directed her northeast, to a smaller, blasted-out landing area that was actually bordered by green plant growth. The scientists really had made progress here. The world was coming back to life. Whether or not it survived could depend on what she found out.

A fringe of slender boarding tubes clustered from the northeast gate. Mara waited shipboard until Gateway's crew connected one to *Shadow*'s starboard access hatch, then threw a thin cloak over her finery and hurried up the synthplas tube.

Inside the huge Gateway dome, to the southwest, she spotted a gray building, two stories tall, ringed with lower constructs. Steam boiled out of one of the outbuildings. In an open area to her left, sandy soil had been raked into short rows that suggested settlers' private gardens. To the right, behind a powder-blue city of tents, low ruins bit into the skyline. A distant rumble pulsed, some kind of digging or mining apparatus.

Not bad, for a refugee city. She pulled a deep breath. It even had good air, when most refugee settlements were stinking mudholes.

Sympathetic administration.

She decided to speak with Leia before she poked around. If her mysterious contact gave her trouble, she might have to leave in a hurry.

The admin building's lower story was centered on a staircase instead of lift tubes, its duracrete blocks crumbly in spots. She climbed the stairs, found a door marked ORGANA SOLO, and strode in.

A familiar protocol droid stood inside. "Good morning," he greeted her. "I am See-Threepio, human-cyborg relations—"

"So I see." Remaining in character, she dropped her cloak on a metal-frame chair and looked haughtily around the room. Large desk, cot, focus cooker, storage lockers—one room for all functions. But no Leia. "I am Baroness Muehling of Kuat. I wish to speak with the administrator."

The droid spread his arms. "I am terribly sorry, Baroness. Administrator Organa Solo is engaged at present. We have had a series of rather vexing shipping problems. Perhaps I could deliver a message."

Mara shook her head, letting the masquerade lapse. "You certainly can, Threepio. Tell Leia her sister-in-law wants two minutes."

C-3PO swiveled his head. She almost laughed at his perpetually puzzled expression, and just how appropriate it looked at the moment.

"I . . . shall attempt to break her free . . . Baroness?" His voice sounded dubious. "Wait here, please."

"I'm not going anywhere."

C-3PO swish-whirred out the door. He needed lubrication. If Leia was missing little details like oiling C-3PO, she *was* busy.

The door opened again forty seconds later, and Leia

hustled in. She'd swathed her head in a white scarf, and her cheeks looked a little hollower, her eyes darker, than Mara had seen before. She looked long and hard at Mara.

"It is you," she finally pronounced.

She leaned forward and embraced Mara—cautiously, as one overdressed diplomat would greet another. C-3PO backed away, shaking his head.

Mara bent down to squeeze Leia's shoulders. "I've got to talk with you."

"I didn't know you were insystem."

"Just arrived."

"Is Luke with you?"

"And Anakin."

"Sit down. I could stand to sit a few minutes."

Mara took the metal-frame chair, facing the large window. Steam from the outbuilding created a sort of exterior curtain.

Leia sank into a similar chair behind the massive desk. SELCORE had probably shipped it. Opposite the cot and cooking area, Mara spotted a pair of incongruously ornate wall sconces, crafted of dark iron in fantastic shapes.

"Can I get you something?" Leia asked. "We have the basics."

"Just a glass of water."

Leia sent C-3PO to the cooking area. While he clattered and poured, Mara caught Leia up to date on the military situation at Coruscant. She said nothing about the Force-warm spot under her belt line. Instead, she related what she'd heard at Bburru—and what else she'd found.

"A Rhommamoolian code?" Leia's eyebrows rose toward her white turban. "I hope we don't end up with Red Knights of Life here." She tapped the edge of her desk with a writing stylus, and her voice turned bitter. "From ten to thirty percent of our supplies aren't getting through. I just sent Jacen to check on that."

Mara raised an eyebrow.

Leia chuckled. "Always in character, aren't you?"

"It's a survival instinct."

"Don't change it for me."

C-3PO brought over a pitcher and two glasses. Mara drank deeply as Leia finished cataloging her recent troubles. The water tasted musty, and one admission obviously came hard: Leia had been twenty klicks from Han, and neither one knew it.

"We've put it behind us," she insisted, "but it'll take me a long time to live it down. For all they knew, I was back on Coruscant. I wasn't there for Jaina."

"Jaina's grown up, Leia."

"So she reminds me. You know, daughters are tricky. They're your closest friend and your worst competitor, all rolled up in a package that reminds you how *you* used to look."

Mara almost told her.

Instead, she asked, "Who made last week's SELCORE report about seeding the toxic swamps?"

"Dr. Cree'Ar." Leia turned to the master board on her desktop, touched a few panels, and nodded. "My head researcher. He's a miracle worker. Why?"

That wasn't what Mara expected. "What do you think of him—personally?"

Leia shrugged. "I'm sure Threepio tried to chase you off by telling you how busy I am? Well, it's true. And I haven't met Dr. Cree'Ar. He's—"

The door slid open. Jaina strode in, wearing a gray flight suit, a narrow-rimmed cap pulled low, and a peculiar face mask. Mara felt a whisper of energy brush against her.

"Aunt Mara," Jaina exclaimed.

"Very good. I needed an introduction to get through to your mother."

Jaina's smile faded. "Before you ask what's wrong, I was too close to a ship that blew. I should have perfect vision again in a couple of weeks. So whatever that fancy blur is you're wearing, it didn't even register."

Mara laughed.

Jaina swept off her cap to display a faint brown stubble. "Decontamination. Quite a mark of status, in here."

Mara eyed Leia's white scarf. "Was this necessary?"

"Maybe not," Leia said, "but the gesture was appreciated. A lot of refugees forget that my world was destroyed twenty-five years ago. They like seeing this. It reminds them I'm a refugee, too. We're already having minor problems with the Ryn."

"What are they doing?"

"Nothing. The problem is other people. They've grown up thinking Ryn are baby-snatchers and compulsive thieves. They're shunned. It's amazing how stoically they take that."

"Mm," Mara said. Her mind had shifted back to another subject. "I need to speak with your Dr. Cree'Ar, but I won't ask for an introduction, since you haven't met."

"I'll go with you," Jaina said. "I'm not doing anything important at the moment."

"Can you see well enough?" Mara demanded. "If this Duros is somehow connected to Rhommamool, he might not be much of a host. Remember our reception there?"

Jaina laughed shortly. "Don't worry, I can use the Force to amplify what I can't see—and don't tell me that isn't a justified use."

"It is," Mara murmured. "And I can use you. A real Kuati wouldn't travel without at least one servant. I've got some things back at the *Shadow* to dress you up." She shot a glance at Leia. "If you don't mind my borrowing your assistant for a few hours."

Leia flicked her hand. "She isn't at my beck and call, Mara. Even if your children ever come home, they really aren't yours anymore."

The research building was a showpiece—banks of scientific instruments and devices, all manufactured on Core worlds—smooth, sterile white walls and acoustically textured ceilings. Its main floor was divided into six laboratories, looking exactly like labs on any other world, thanks to SELCORE. In each one, some experiment or another was humming.

Mara found Dr. Cree'Ar's lab and walked in. Two aides sat at a long lab bench. One supervised what looked like a titration experiment, involving a six-by-ten array of transparent tubes. Another poured dollops of viscous liquid out of a flask into flat dishes.

She waved Jaina forward.

"Good morning," Jaina said imperiously. "Is the doctor about?"

The near tech, a hefty young man with a red mustache, set down a flask of cloudy liquid. "He's gone out. Said he'd be in Sector Seven."

Mara looked around at the scientific setup. According to the file she'd just studied, Dr. Cree'Ar had produced plants and protozoans that were creating an arable zone, gleefully chowing down on soil toxins that would've killed everything but fefze beetles.

"Very well." Mara laid a hand on Jaina's shoulder.

Jaina, dressed in the carpet-textured gown of a Kuati

servant, clasped her opposite wrists inside her long, draped sleeves. Mara had found her a braided wig.

"We can wait," Mara said.

Two hours later, Mara leaned one arm against a laboratory counter and fixed a still-imperious stare on one of Dr. Dassid Cree'Ar's human and Sullustan aides. Unlike Leia, Mara did have the time to hunt down Dr. Cree'Ar, and as she'd told his technicians several times, she was perfectly willing to wait out the day. She amused herself striding around the laboratory, lifting flasks and examining culture gels, making the techs nervous.

Finally, another aide—who'd been trying to center a row of tiny glass tubules under an array of slender nozzles—rocked back on his stool. He brushed hair away from his face.

"Baroness," he said wearily, "why don't you and your servant get a couple of breath masks out of the first-floor storage bin, go down through the tunnel, and see if you can find Dr. Cree'Ar outside in the swamps?"

Now we're getting somewhere. "You can see I am not dressed for swamp travel."

"The ground's dry around them. I'm sure he'd be willing to talk with a distinguished visitor."

Mara raised an eyebrow. "If he returns in my absence," she said firmly, "direct him to follow the . . . tunnel, you say?"

"Down the stairs, turn right. Last door on your right is storage, and be sure to get those breath masks. Right outside this building, you'll see a covered stair. Admin let us dig our own route to the research fields, since the north gate's so far out of our way. We're in the soft-rock zone. It only took a couple days."

"Very well." Mara overlaid her voice with a measure of irritation. "Emlee, come along."

Jaina bowed slightly. "Yes, Baroness."

Mara led the way downstairs, found the breath masks where the harried tech described, and headed straight for the tunnel entry. It dropped quickly at first, then more slowly, scantily lit by occasional overhead glow rods.

Mara slowed enough to murmur, "You're all right with this?"

Jaina shrugged. "I've gotten used to feeling my way in the dark."

"All right. Back into character, then. And stay in character unless I make it obvious that we're through playacting."

"Right," Jaina whispered.

Mara led on. The tunnel gradually curved right—headed, she guessed, through the soft-rock cliffs toward the flatland she'd seen on approach.

"Wait," she murmured.

She backstepped several meters. She'd heard a faint change in their footsteps' echo.

At the darkest point between two glow rods, a side passage had been cut. A sheet of stiff fabric, roughly the shade of the surrounding stone, covered the passageway.

"Ah," Mara said, slipping back into character. She peeled the fabric away from the stone's edge and found a faint glow, illuminating a narrower passage. "This way, I think."

She marched five meters to a ninety-degree bend in the passage, turned left, and found a sizable chamber. Standing beside a lab bench was a tall, slender Duros, holding two flasks of opaque brown liquid.

"Dr. Cree'Ar." Mara raised her chin. "You are difficult to find. I hope you will make this journey worthwhile."

The Duros scientist set down his flasks. "Madame,"

he said sternly, "this is my prrrivate research area. State your business."

The chamber's walls, floors, and ceiling were bare stone. Mara spotted a sleeping pad against an inner wall and several elevated . . . were those reagent tanks? The petcock assemblies looked organic. In a compartment along one wall, she recognized an open water-bath incubator, warmed by a flame from below. It looked like a storage facility.

Jaina shuffled forward, keeping her hands inside the drape of her sleeves. "Doctor," she said, "this is Baroness Muehling of Kuat. She has come to you with a grave concern."

Mara spotted a backless chair that had the look of a cutout shipping crate. She strode toward it and seated herself.

Finally, Cree'Ar stepped toward her. His large red eyes seemed to glow. "Why have you honored me with a visit, Baroness?"

"Even on other worlds," she said, "word has reached us of your fine work, your dedication. Indeed, Administrator Organa Solo calls you a miracle worker."

He spread his hands modestly.

"Duro," she said, "has obviously been made a dumping ground for other species. My people may face a similar fate. Contacts whom I met up in Bburru City say that you are a close disciple of someone who is trying to turn that tide, on behalf of your own people." In the baroness role, she usually got further by piling flattery on a subject than by bullying.

She piled it deeper.

From the moment they entered the chamber, Jaina had sensed something odd. She hadn't encountered any Duros here—her med runner had been cleared directly to ground, without stopping in orbit—but she didn't like this guy.

Hesitantly, she reached out with a flicker of the Force. How hostile was he, really?

She felt nothing. She couldn't even find him.

She kept her eyes lowered with an effort. She hadn't heard of Yuuzhan Vong masquerading as Duros, but if they could breed creatures that made them look convincingly human, this would be only a small step further. The only way she'd know for sure would be to unmask him.

One problem. The masquers' activating spot was alongside the nose, and Duros had no noses.

Cree'Ar's face was only a blur, anyway. Jaina hesitantly directed a flicker of the Force toward it. She stroked the spot on his face where she thought his nose would be, if he were human.

Nothing happened.

She tried stroking another spot, slightly left, away from the blur's center.

Still nothing. Meanwhile, her mind raced. What if she needed to draw her lightsaber? She could hardly see the guy!

He batted his face distractedly, the way a nerf herder might flick away summergnats.

But she'd practiced endlessly against remotes, sometimes blindfolded. Remotes had no more Force presence than a Yuuzhan Vong.

She pressed outward again.

Mara sat stiff-backed on Cree'Ar's shipping crate, as if it were a baronial throne. Dr. Cree'Ar had finally consented to explain some of his philosophy.

" . . . undermine local jurisdictions, and . . . ai!"

He flung up both knobby hands, but not before Mara saw something horribly familiar. Just below one of the dark folds that crossed his face, his gray hide rippled. A corner peeled back, exposing pale skin and the edge of a black tattoo.

She sprang to her feet, seized her lightsaber out of her amethyst-colored tunic's folds, and activated it. Instantly, Jaina jumped back, whipping her own lightsaber from her dark, heavy sleeve.

Blue-gray skin kept shrinking, revealing a skeletal face with bluish eye sacs. As if his hide had turned to liquid, the loose flap melted down inside his laboratory coat.

Cree'Ar stood his ground, laughing. For all Mara could see, he was unarmed.

"Don't move," she warned him. "You're not wearing armor, and you're vulnerable."

Cree'Ar's laughter died, and his pale lip curled. "Mara Jade Skywalker, is it? Why aren't you dead?"

Caught off guard, Mara demanded, "Have we met?"

The Yuuzhan Vong tossed back his hideous head. "No wonder the New Republic can't hold on to a galaxy. Even its so-called heroes are stupid. Yes, we have met. I've nearly killed you."

Jaina took one step closer. "I know that voice," she muttered.

"You should," the alien growled. "Let me give you a hint—"

"Rhommamool." Jaina held her lightsaber low. "You're Nom Anor! You tricked people into believing you were human, then you tricked them into thinking you were killed."

He inclined his head. "You, at least, approach worthiness. But you are not worthy yet."

Mara gripped her lightsaber, thinking back to another meeting with Nom Anor, at Monor II. The native Sunesi had invited several hundred diplomats to the accession of their tenth priest-prince, Agapos the Tenth. Some trigger-poppy splinter group had threatened a minor diplomat from Coruscant, so Mara went along as a bodyguard. She'd also wanted to see Monor II's glittering, cirrifog-laden atmosphere.

"You wore a black mask and black robes," Jaina said. "What happened to your slave, that mousy little man?"

The creature's lips peeled back in a sneer. "Shok Tinoktin was well rewarded for faithful service."

Mara glanced around the laboratory. Even if Anor had biological weapons in plain sight, she might not recognize them—but she would love to catch him alive. She'd made a science of stomping on massive egos, of throwing people off guard and probing for their weaknesses.

"So the petty troublemaker is making petty trouble again," she said, raising one eyebrow.

"Petty?" He reached toward the lab bench.

"Freeze," she ordered. "Pick anything up and you're dead."

His fingers twitched toward the flask, the one he had been holding when she entered the room. "You couldn't reach me before I threw this. It's full of coomb spores, Jade Skywalker. The spores I painted on a hundred abominable breath masks, before that outdoor ceremony."

Mara's stomach lurched. "They didn't all sicken right away," she recalled. She'd fallen ill two months later. "The epidemiologists eventually concluded multiple causes." But that occasion *had* been fingered as the single time all those sick people were in one place.

He laughed. "They were meant to conclude that. The coomb spore's sheath dissolves at different rates in different species. This is your worst fear, Jedi." His fingers twitched again. "Relapse. Weakness. Death. A much higher dose than before, and that was fatal in all other cases. All species."

In that instant, she realized how vulnerable she was. If

she got sick now, her child could be destroyed—if he wasn't already doomed.

Anor could infect Jaina, too. Jaina had other senses than eyesight, but she was in no shape for hand-to-hand combat against someone who couldn't be sensed through the Force—and whose weapon was suspended in a liquid.

"You never answered my question," he called. "Why are you still alive?"

"You're the last one I'd tell." Vergere was still out there—somewhere. "Get back, Jaina."

Then Mara lunged, slicing low with her lightsaber. Only a feint, but instead of returning her attack, he turned and fled—not up the passage where they'd come, but beyond the lab counter, toward a smaller door.

He left the flask on the countertop.

Her impulse was to chase him down. *Trap!* her instincts shrieked. *Don't follow!*

Then her danger sense went off like a siren. She hesitated as Jaina sprinted around the laboratory bench. She had to make the right call. Three lives were at stake, and only one was in fighting trim.

"Blast," she muttered, kicking the elevated heels off her fancy shoes. "Jaina, this way!" She spun toward the passage where they'd come in.

Three retorts like ricocheting projectile shots sounded overhead. Startled, she glanced up. A crack opened in the stony ceiling. It branched, branched again, and again.

She waved Jaina toward the tunnel, crying, "Run!" A chunk of stone hit the floor beside her.

Jaina reached the doorway. All around them—ceiling, walls—soft rock crumbled. Mara pushed Jaina ahead of her, reaching deep inside herself, trying to divert each stone as it fell. She split a dozen with her lightsaber.

But they fell too thickly. As rock dust choked off the

light ahead and behind her, she pushed Jaina down, fell on her, and pushed out with the Force. She kept the presence of mind to extinguish her lightsaber.

The noise went on, like a powerful waterfall, for several age-long seconds.

Jaina rolled out from under her. She'd killed her lightsaber, too. In utter darkness, Mara couldn't see what Jaina was doing, but she did hear a plaintive "Ow!"

"Hit your head?" Mara asked quietly.

"Slightly." Momentary silence. "You're keeping that up with the Force?"

"No. Just my radiant personality." She softened her voice. "Do you still have the rebreathers?"

"Yes. Here."

"Keep mine for now."

Mara rose to a crouch, planted her hands against hard stone, and tried pushing up harder with the Force. If only a small stone-fall surrounded them, it ought to move. Or shift, at least.

It didn't.

"Ten to one," she grumbled, "he brought his own kind of rock chewers here to Duro. He dug out his own side tunnel—and while he did, he set traps for Leia's security people."

Jaina's voice sounded sour. "You retreated because of me, didn't you? We could've taken him. We could've killed him, right there."

"I'll get that creature if it's the last thing I do." Mara hadn't hated anyone this desperately since . . .

Well, since Luke Skywalker. A lifetime ago.

Luke? She stretched out and felt his concern. *I'm all right,* she assured him, *for now. Don't drop what you're doing just yet.* He wouldn't catch words, only sensation—but he would catch a lot of that.

Jaina said, "There's a good chance the rockfall's shorter, back the way he went."

"Point," Mara said. "And that it's also the way he wanted us to go." Her instincts had warned her, and she would face a hundred other horrors before she let that Sithspawn expose her child to his deadly spores.

Maybe the flask held something else, this time, but she'd heard truth in his boast. He *had* infected her.

The same instincts were finally blaring, loud and clear, that it was no Yuuzhan Vong bioweapon deep inside her body. It was a normal, defenseless child. A Skycrawler, as Leia had teased optimistically, shortly after her wedding.

She thumbed her comlink, though she didn't have much hope. "Leia? Do you copy?"

Silence.

"Hello, Gateway. This is an emergency. Does anyone read me?"

Nothing. The stone was too thick.

"I think the air smells strange, Aunt Mara."

"Put your rebreather on." Had that flask on the counter-top shattered? "We're not getting any dust through this Force bubble. I don't honestly know what else might get through, but probably not microbes." Then she said, "I need you to join with me, so I can nudge the bubble higher in the direction we want to go. I'll try to slide rocks off the back of the bubble while I lift other rocks ahead of us, and I'll fill in those gaps before the ceiling collapses any lower. Do you see what I've got in mind?"

"Do you think it'll work?" Jaina sounded dubious.

Mara frowned. "I'd love to hear your better plan."

After several seconds, Jaina answered glumly. "Can you picture what it is you want to do?"

"I'm working on it." Visualizing this wrong would flatten their bubble of safety. She needed to move about a hundred rocks simultaneously, up, over, and behind them. Then another hundred, and another. It could take hours. "Open to me, Jaina. The way you used to do in training."

She was glad they'd grabbed the masks.

CHAPTER EIGHTEEN

Still wearing his Kubaz disguise, Luke paused in a tall residential tower's hallway, where Jacen had been escorted. Another sudden crisis had caught Mara unawares. Again, adrenaline gusted through him. Again, he had to fight the urge to drop everything, dash to the docks, and go to her. Instead, he reached deep and listened.

Details didn't reach him. Her alert level dropped rapidly to her usual deadly calm under fire. He couldn't make out much else.

Anakin hurried back toward him. "What?" he demanded.

"Your aunt."

Luke shut his eyes, alert for details. Earlier, he'd caught the sense of danger, then anger, then a moment of painful decision, of shoving aside her considerable pride. It was harder to flee than to stand and fight. Didn't he know it . . .

Now he plainly caught her flicker of assurance, focused toward him. Unbeaten, she was exerting herself powerfully. He caught the image of darkness, and thousands of stones, and the daunting job of repositioning them.

He formed a query. It would take him hours to reach her. He wouldn't hesitate to get to his X-wing, though.

He'd barely shaped the thought when he felt Jaina's presence alongside Mara's. With Jaina's help, she felt confident that she had her situation under control.

And his child's!

He sensed her gratitude, though. That fortified him like few things he'd ever felt. Reluctantly, he turned to follow Anakin through the twisting halls of the massive residential complex's twelfth story. As he did, he tried threading some of his own strength—love, and calm power—into the bond that joined him with Mara. He had no idea if that would give her more energy, but he sensed she was drawing something. She could need everything Jaina had, and more. It comforted him to try, even if he had no assurance this would work—no assurance but his faith in Mara, and in the Force itself.

Concluding his business with Vice-Director Brarun hadn't taken long. Brarun had nothing to sell, and that seemed to confirm the theory that some of the Duros were stockpiling goods, hoping to take one of their orbital cities and leave Duro entirely.

Luke could see them doing that only if they'd sold out the rest of the system, particularly the refugees dirtside, laboring to build a new world. He'd sent R2-D2, plugged in back at the hostel, another message: Search CorDuro records for anything that smacked of Peace Brigade involvement with CorDuro or SELCORE itself. He hadn't forgotten Karrde's warning that there were suspicions that the Intelligence division, maybe even the Advisory Council itself, had been infiltrated. Maybe SELCORE had, too. Unfortunately, he hadn't had the opportunity to evaluate the different councilors during that last meeting.

He glanced at the tiny heads-up display inside his goggles. If R2-D2 found anything, he could send an alert, then a message that would repeat until Luke signaled him by comlink.

First, though, he had to find Jacen. Luke had seen clearly, in Brarun's office, that Jacen stood at a major junction on his journey. Forsaking the Force might not be as deadly as turning to the dark side, but that wasn't the future Luke wanted for his nephew.

Evening had arrived, and Bburru City's big lights dimmed outside the hallway viewbubbles. Two tall Duros in CorDuro uniforms waited on either side of an unmarked door around the next bend.

"Take the near one," Luke murmured.

Gently, almost tenderly, Luke pushed the farther guard down into a deep sleep. The Duros sagged against the synthplas-mosaic wall. The other guard followed him down.

"Good," he told Anakin. "Stay out here. If anyone else shows up, put them down the same way. I shouldn't be long."

Jacen's host had left him in a bedroom with a large, round transparisteel window and two hallway guards. Standing beside the window, he'd watched the big lights fade on Bburru's central plaza. The open space was almost large enough to create the illusion of a living planet, with diagonal bracing struts that ran from street level to the faintly blue artificial ceiling. As in the avenues, raised planters supported massive trees that were layered with vines. It was a far cry from the jungles of Yavin 4, but Jacen was starting to understand why the Duros would rather live here than down in the murk.

Now he lay on a soft bed in semidarkness, wondering if he'd done the right thing after all. Brarun didn't seem to be in any hurry to finish negotiating tariffs.

The hall door opened silently.

Jacen slid his hand under his pillow and got a grip on his lightsaber. A dark form slipped through. Jacen saw the short trunk and goggles of a Kubaz, then heard as the door slid shut, "Jacen, it's me."

Jacen knew the voice. He would've sensed the presence, if he'd been alert to the Force. He let go of his lightsaber, but he didn't wave on a light.

"Master Skywalker, there could be listening devices—"

"Not at the moment." Luke sank onto his bed's foot, moving as silently as a shadow. He pulled off his trunked mask and laid it on the bed beside him. "What is it you're trying to accomplish, Jacen? How can I help?"

Jacen didn't need any further encouragement. He poured out his vision, relating every detail he could remember. When he got to the parts about Luke in shining white robes, a magnificent warrior of the light, his uncle's cheek twitched and he looked away, seemingly embarrassed. Most vivid of all was the voice, though— and the command to stand firm.

"I didn't," Jacen said. "I slipped. I fell, barely on the dark side of . . . of the balance point. Everything started to slide. Everything." He shuddered, remembering the stars turning dark. "Do we have the right," he asked, "to use this . . . magnificent, terrifying light . . . as if we were in charge of the universe?"

Faintly lit through the window, Luke frowned. "Jacen, the Force is our heritage. Unless we use it, we have no better way to safeguard peace and justice than any police group."

"Many Jedi are misusing their powers."

"Not all," Luke answered softly.

"I want to reach them," Jacen said. "I've finally had time to think this through. I'm marginally famous, just because of you and Mom and Dad . . . and Anakin," he admitted, "and Jaina. If I go out on a limb, if I refuse to channel the Force in aggressive ways, other Jedi would have to pay attention."

"It's a noble cause." Luke's weight shifted on the bed. "But are you ready to stake your life on it?"

Jacen had thought about just that. "Yes," he said. "Even if I died, my death might wake up the rest of the Jedi. It might prick their consciences into realizing they can't just blast around with all the power at their disposal, without suffering consequences."

"But it's you," Luke said gently, "who would suffer the consequences. Not any of the others."

"I can't do anything about them. I can only offer myself."

He felt his uncle's scrutiny. "Never forget that it's one thing to lay down your life when you have to. But to choose death when you could've escaped—that diminishes us all."

Jacen frowned. He didn't want to overestimate his importance, or the other Jedi's willingness to pay attention. "We're developing bad patterns," he insisted. "We're slipping past everyone else's laws, and those laws are the foundations of society and security. We're leading the charge back into the dark times, into the survival of the meanest. We'll be ruled by bullies if this goes on."

"That is an excellent point," Luke said. "Be careful, though. If you feel this wrong about using the Force aggressively, then you can't simply cut back. You don't feel confident about deciding what use is aggressive. You're afraid to act, afraid that your actions will have repercussions beyond imagining."

"Yes," Jacen exclaimed, "yes, that's it!"

"In that frame of mind," Luke said, "to direct the Force at all is wrong."

"At all?" Jacen pulled himself upright. That put his

head and shoulders out of the bed's heat field, giving him a faint chill.

"Every act that doesn't come out of absolute faith can lead to fear and darkness," Luke said sternly.

Jacen's memory fled back to his uncle's academy, to the praxeum, to countless conversations. "I have been imagining terrible consequences of making mistakes," he admitted. "Don't you see? This is why I've hoped that you wouldn't reestablish the Jedi Council. We must be answerable to the Force itself, not a group of fallible individuals. If we can understand it well enough to use it, we ought to be able to use it rightly. Or else decide not to use it at all."

His uncle looked puzzled. "Does that follow," he asked, "from all you've been telling me?"

"It has to," Jacen mumbled. "Somehow, it all has to fit together."

"Be careful your pride doesn't destroy you, Jacen."

Jacen gripped the bed's thin privacy cover. "Pride? You told us that power, driven by vengeance, led to pride—and the dark side."

"There's a more subtle pride," Luke explained. "You're claiming to be too humble to use the Force, aren't you?"

Jacen thought hard. Was he?

"Maybe you're the only Jedi who's perceptive enough to realize that what we *all* do is wrong—"

"No," Jacen interrupted. "I'm the one who was warned. You're not doing anything wrong—"

"But if it's wrong for you," Luke said calmly, "shouldn't you be warning the rest of us?"

Jacen slumped against the wall. "That's what I was trying to tell you. That's exactly what I'm trying to do."

"They're not listening," Luke said softly.

Jacen felt as if he'd been kicked.

The silhouette laid a hand on his shoulder. "You're

dealing with the very heart of what it means to be a Jedi. Be careful about sacrificing your gifts, to help others see the truth as you perceive it. That's too close to the kind of sacrifices the Yuuzhan Vong practice. They serve extinction."

Jacen shivered. "I don't want to even get close to that."

"You see your heritage as a grave responsibility. You've caught my attention, Jacen. You've shown me that we should make much more of the ethics of using our powers, when training our apprentices. Thank you."

Jacen's cheeks twitched. He couldn't help grinning. What an honor!

"Do you have any leading?" Luke asked. "Where your destiny could be taking you next? You don't have to fulfill it all today, you know. I never dreamed, at your age, where mine would lead me. What's your next small step?"

"I think," Jacen said slowly, still stunned by his Master's show of confidence, "that if I can, I should convince the Duros to support the New Republic by keeping their promises."

"That could be," Luke said gravely. "But there could be treachery in high places. You can't negotiate that away."

Jacen's stomach tightened. "Is that what brought you and Anakin to Duro?"

Luke nodded. "An apprentice vanished here. Now we find CorDuro isn't making deliveries. And I just met two humans who remind me very much of Peace Brigaders. Artoo's seeing what he can get off Bburru's mainframe."

If Brarun had Peace Brigade connections, this "house arrest" wasn't safe. "Thanks for warning me."

"You have to choose. Use the Force, as you've been

trained to do—or leave it alone. You can't just cut back."

"All right, then," Jacen said. "I'll leave it alone."

He saw his uncle's slack-faced astonishment, but only for an instant, and he barricaded himself against the sensation. He had to prove—to Luke, to himself—that he was utterly serious about his commitment.

"This will put you in harm's way, Jacen. People will assume you can get out of situations that you can't handle anymore."

"Just tell them why, Uncle Luke." Not *Master Skywalker*, this time. Not if he really meant to go through with this.

"Do you have a comlink?" Luke asked somberly. Even without using the Force, Jacen heard regret and concern in his voice.

Jacen shook his head.

Luke tossed something onto the bed between them. "Keep it hidden. If we find out anything, we'll call. Maybe Brarun's not corrupted. If you want to stay here and try to talk sense into him, that might help. But be ready to get out quickly."

"I will."

"And get some rest. Don't try to save the whole galaxy yourself. Believe me, it doesn't work." His uncle rose off the bedside, smiling faintly. "I have to warn you about one more thing. If you choose not to do what you can do, you will endanger the ones you love most."

Jacen shivered again. "Have you seen the future?"

Luke shook his head. "It's just a . . . a feeling," he said. "May the Force be with you, Jacen." He slipped his mask back on, and then his goggles. Immediately, he drew out a second comlink. "Got it, Artoo," he said.

"What?" Jacen asked.

"We might have a break in our disappearance case . . . finally."

With that, Luke left the room—headed out, Jacen knew, to try to get justice for one person. Not the whole galaxy, at all. Just one person, one situation, one at a time. Just as he'd always taught his students.

Jacen rolled over. Could he really stop using the Force? Trying to silence it felt like putting on a blindfold or plugging his ears. He would have to live that way, for the rest of his life.

Jaina had learned to adapt to diminished vision.

But Jaina was getting her vision back.

And when he shut his eyes, he still saw a galaxy sliding into darkness.

As *Sunulok*'s crew prepared her to depart Rodia, Tsavong Lah's aides called him out of a briefing. In his communication chamber, his Nom Anor villip sat on a stand, waiting. The moment he slipped into the chamber, the villip spoke.

"Warmaster, I have excellent news. My naotebe wingling organisms successfully brought down Settlement Thirty-two, and now, the young Jedi coward has been detained by one of my contacts, on board the abomination they call Bburru City."

Tsavong Lah did not speak. That news was not worth interrupting his briefing. He knew full well that the master shapers who provided Nom Anor with detoxification organisms had also created the winglings.

"Even better," Anor continued, "I have just sent two other Jedi, members of his family, to the gods. His sister, and their aunt—the notorious Mara Jade Skywalker."

Tsavong Lah crossed his arms, irked. His shipboard coven of priests had finally decreed that the portents for his ultimate success would improve with every *Jeedai* that he, personally, sacrificed.

"You saw them die?"

The executor hesitated. "They tripped a stone-fall trap they cannot escape. Without vonduun crab armor, even our bodies would not survive that."

Tsavong Lah's fighting nails twitched. "We have seen *Jeedai* call on supernatural abilities."

"I set this trap with Jedi in mind—set it, actually, for Ambassador Organa Solo, in case she intruded in my private place. Even if they survived the initial crushing, they will die slowly now. I am confident that such mass cannot be cleared aside. Organa Solo and her investigators still have no clue that the stone-fall is anything but a natural collapse."

And Nom Anor, the Trickster's disciple, remained under orders not to tip his hand. If the women were dead, the gods would not be displeased. Tsavong Lah nodded.

"Can your Bburru agent's *Jeedai* prisoner be sedated for breaking and study? We still must develop ways to kill them easily." He would not insult Yun-Yammka by offering a known coward in sacrifice.

"I have suggested that my contact hold him, pending your arrival. Meanwhile . . ." Nom Anor's cheek pouches crinkled with pleasure. "I have arranged for riots."

Nom Anor's field of expertise. "Those will focus the Duro system's attention on Bburru until we bypass them."

"You repeat my thoughts. I will time the outbreak to honor your approach."

Tsavong clicked his finger claws against each other. Riots would create new martyrs for Nom Anor's latest imitation religion, sending the gods another round of sacrifices. No wonder Yun-Harla, the Trickster goddess, favored Nom Anor. Even mighty Yun-Yammka sometimes bowed to her pranks.

"Are your agents prepared to deal with the planetary shields?"

"Whenever you order it."

Yes, maybe this interruption was worthwhile after all. "And the young Hutt?" the warmaster demanded. "Have you disciplined him?"

"Again, I await your order."

"Again, do not insult the Great Ones by offering him. Hutts are beasts and gluttons. Save him for the nutrient staff. Our new slaves will commemorate our arrival with a rich feast."

Anor's villip head inclined.

"You promised the Duros we will leave them their abominable habitats, if they lay down their weapons?"

"As ordered."

Tsavong Lah smiled slowly. Nom Anor's promises weren't worth the breath that delivered them.

Yun-Harla surely loved that.

Creeping forward over gouged stone, Mara breathed shallowly through her borrowed mask. The Force bubble overhead lost precious millimeters with each group of stones she conveyed over the top. She felt Luke's distant touch again, and a pulse of strength with it. *Thanks, Skywalker,* she shot back at him, feeling a little limp. There was a time for gratitude.

She did wish she'd gone for Nom Anor, though.

Sure. Then we'd all three be dead. But if he'd caused her disease, though, maybe he would know how to make sure she was cured. She'd like to figure out how to get that information from him. Preferably just before she showed him what justice meant.

Jaina's body felt warm alongside her own. So did Jaina's anger.

"Don't worry," Mara muttered through her rebreather. "I'll get him. Just not this trip."

"By the time we get out," Jaina muttered back, "he'll be five worlds away."

"Explains plenty, though." Another dozen rocks clicked down into place behind them, and Mara slithered forward a centimeter. When she raised her head, even slightly, she bumped rock. "About Rhommamool."

"Finally," Jaina agreed. "He's just been stirring up trouble, not caring who gets killed."

"Distracting us all from their real invasion vector."

It was better to keep talking than think about the slowly flattening bubble. She hated to admit it, but Luke might have called this one right when she assured him she didn't need help. If they ran out of space, she would have Jaina slip into a hibernation trance, and then she'd call Luke—and hope he could get here before her air ran out, because she couldn't do hibernation herself, not if she hoped to keep the unknown weight of rock from smashing them. She had to stay conscious.

"And the droid burnings," Mara said. "Remember that?"

"D'you think that flask really was . . ."

Mara had given that more thought. "No." He hadn't known she was coming. "But I'm sure he has more of the stuff." Coomb spores, whatever that meant.

"You don't think he was lying, then?"

"Not this time," Mara muttered. She had felt the weird weakness again, in his presence—faint, but strong enough to confirm his claim.

"Hey, I caught a whiff of good air." Jaina's voice came through clearly. She must have pulled off the breath mask.

Mara kept her own mask on. Another group of rocks

lifted. She caught a glimmer of light through the space beyond them. "Almost," she grunted.

It was hard to keep stones moving slowly, now. The mental image of dying within half a meter of freedom kept her focused. Moving the last stones took over an hour.

"Okay," she said at last. "Roll forward. I want you right up here." She pushed Jaina against the bubble's fore edge. She gathered her legs and arms underneath her, knees and elbows bent, and took a deep gulp of the strength flowing in from the distance. *Ready, Luke?* She formed the words in her mind, wryly recognizing a secret double meaning. *Push!*

"Now!" She shoved Jaina clear. Then she rolled free, ignited her lightsaber, and deflected the last falling stones. They fell glowing along their cut surfaces.

Jaina's scalp bled from a cut near her right ear. She whipped out her comlink. "Gateway Security, this is an emergency. I need Administrator Organa Solo on the line—now!"

There was no answer.

"Back up the tunnel," Mara ordered.

CHAPTER NINETEEN

"Okay, Mara, what is this?" Over *Shadow*'s comm unit, Leia's voice had a deadly edge. "How did you find him out?"

Mara still wore the remains of her Kuati costume. She'd blasted off without waiting for clearance, once she understood that things were about to break in Bburru. Jaina sat next to her, wearing a brown flight suit from one of Mara's lockers.

"Simple," Mara answered. "He wasn't there through the Force. That's why he avoided you. Jaina found the masquer disengage spot. When he started to ripple, we went for our lightsabers."

"How long did he think he could stay out of my way?" Leia's voice muttered in Mara's headset.

Mara didn't like the obvious conclusion: He hadn't thought he would need to avoid Leia much longer. "Grab him. Don't let him out of Gateway."

Leia's voice sounded weary. "The dome's too crowded for sensors or scanners to pinpoint one person. By now, he could be out in the swamps—or even underwater, from what Danni told us about their breathing devices. And now we know he's got his own way of tunneling. He might even be in the old mines."

"Can't always have what we want," Jaina muttered.

Mara shook her head.

"We cert . . . derstand Rhommamool better, d . . . we?" Interference ate into the transmission as they soared through Duro's atmosphere.

"Losing you," Mara came back. "I'll send what I can from Bburru."

Mara cut the transmitter, leaned back in her chair, and checked her readouts. Then finally, she let herself relax enough to check the spot between her hipbones. It was still an almost imperceptible tingle. *You've got a good grip,* she complimented . . . him? *Keep hanging on. The ride could get a little bumpy.*

"Didn't ask about me, did she?" Jaina raised her head to stare at Bburru, growing on the fore screen.

"I would've told her if you'd been hurt."

"Some women shouldn't have children."

Mara drew up straight, and a back muscle twanged. She must've overstretched it, scrabbling along on the stony ground. "I can't believe you said that."

When Jaina pursed her lips, she looked a very young seventeen. "To her, I'm an inconvenience. 'Winter, take Jaina for a walk.' 'Threepio, tell Anakin a story.' 'Here, Chewbacca, watch the twins.' "

"And how many mothers gave up a seat on a shuttle headed for safety this year? Put their kids on board and stayed behind, to die or be enslaved? Sometimes staying with your child isn't possible."

"Then mothers who are too important to raise their kids should just sign them over and go off to work."

Mara, who had only vague mental images of her parents, dropped her voice to an icy alto. "For such a mature young woman, you are being surprisingly childish."

Jaina ran a hand over her bare head. It was starting to show a faint brown shadow of regrowth. "I'm also being honest. Mara, I nearly died at Kalarba. I lost an awfully good friend at Ithor. She gave up everything, to give families a chance to survive somewhere else."

"And your mother is giving those survivors somewhere to live. This planet is hope, literally and symbolically."

Jaina sighed heavily. "Poor Mom. She's got a half-blind, stubborn daughter who can't fight anymore and a son who's afraid to be a Jedi. Good thing Anakin came along."

"You've got a temporary weakness. File this away for your future, Jaina Solo. It's all right to take risks for yourself. But never, never commit someone else to hand-to-hand combat if they've had their fighting edge blunted. Do we understand each other?"

Stars appeared as they broke through Duro's opaque atmosphere. Mara switched *Jade Shadow*'s comm unit to her private frequency. "Luke," she called.

He answered. "Mara. On your way?"

Of course, he felt her getting closer. "We met an old friend," she said grimly.

They docked the *Shadow* at Port Duggan. Mara threw on a hooded cloak over the remains of her costume and led Jaina back to the cheap rental unit. As she slipped through the door, she felt a hesitant touch—Luke's, making sure she was all right. She ran the same check herself, just to keep everything in perspective, as he embraced her.

Anakin sat on the near cot with his eyes shut, passing his lightsaber grip from hand to hand behind his back—a very young Jedi's equivalent of fidgeting. A strand of dark-brown hair drooped into his face.

Jaina dropped onto the near cot and frowned at him, then over at Luke. "Did you tell him?" Jaina asked. "Anakin, Nom Anor didn't die on Rhommamool after all. He's here, and he's a Yuuzhan Vong agent."

"One more tidbit," Mara said, staring straight at her husband's eyes. "He claims he infected me with this disease. At Monor II."

She hadn't wanted to transmit that over the link because she wanted to see his reaction, and he didn't disappoint her. He raised his head, eyes wide, radiating a depth of fury she rarely saw in him. He controlled it instantly, of course.

"What do you think?" he asked, once again projecting that Jedi Master calm.

Mara had crossed her forearms. She clenched her opposite elbows. "He might know how to tell if I'm really cured. I would love to go back for him."

Luke's cheek twitched—again, the reaction so subtle that Jaina and Anakin missed it entirely. "So would I," he said, "but if you've confirmed a Yuuzhan Vong agent downside, that fits what we've been finding."

He gave her a sketchy report, implicating CorDuro Shipping in the downside colonies' shortfalls—and his own suspicions. By digging back through layers of encryption in altered shipping records, R2-D2 had discovered that the Port Duggan branch of CorDuro Shipping was in fact diverting SELCORE and other supplies to another Duros habitat—but recording the supplies as sold offworld, in case SELCORE enforcers got suspicious.

"We also checked every lead Tresina Lobi gave me, and Artoo's been searching the port authority's records."

Mara glanced at the little droid, who stood at a data port. "Comparing arrivals with departures?"

Luke nodded. "And tracing them both back. We're trying to verify a connection with the Peace Brigade. And possibly a link to SELCORE itself."

If Karrde's suspicion proved correct, and SELCORE or other high-level councils had been infiltrated, the New Republic was in worse trouble than anyone suspected.

No wonder Luke seemed agitated: the small, jerky hand movements, the set to his chin, and most of all, the ediness that was getting through to her on the Force.

"Thrynni Vae vanished in a seedy area of Port Duggan," he continued. "No surprise, really. Anakin and I just looked it over. The tapcafs are quiet. Almost too quiet."

R2-D2 squealed softly.

Luke straightened. "Got something more?" He leaned toward the readout over R2-D2's data port, and Mara bent close.

Letters appeared, scrolling rapidly. It started with a list of entries that had been deleted or altered in some way: recent hires at Port Duggan, arrivals back half a year, visitors logged into Vice-Director Brarun's office. Several names reappeared.

Under that list, R2-D2 had tracked the frequently mentioned names' travel backward and forward. For several, the trail vanished after three hops. Two, though, had traveled to Ylesia and back—several times. Those entries were flagged.

Next appeared a security file from Duro's communication repeaters. Very few droids in the New Republic carried the programming it would take to slice into that log. The links between here and Ylesia showed multiple hits.

"What's there?" Anakin asked, peering around Mara's shoulder. "That's clear out in Hutt space."

"The Hutts used to run a slave-snaring scam there," Mara murmured. "And your dad claims it's a Peace Brigade hot spot." She turned to Luke. "So maybe Thrynni was abducted there?"

Luke hesitated for several seconds. "It's the best lead we've had, but I hate to send anyone on a wild yunax chase."

"I'd guess Vice-Director Brarun is in this up to his big

round eyes," Mara said. "Add this to the diverted goods ending up at Urrdorf, and an influx of Duros there—"

She caught a gust of concern out of Luke.

Jaina spoke up from beside the window. "Let me guess. All their brightest and best, suddenly taking vacations at lovely Urrdorf."

Luke turned away from the readout.

"What?" Mara demanded.

"Jacen's with Brarun. He could be in danger."

Jaina pushed away from the window.

Luke raised a hand. "Not for a while, though, I think."

"Brarun's being cagey?" Mara demanded.

Luke nodded. "We're all seeing the same pattern. Someone is about to sell out the SELCORE refugees and make a run for it. For the moment, Jacen wants to stay where he is."

Mara shook her head.

"We've got to call for another downside evacuation, and somehow do it without tipping off the Peace Brigade. I'd guess they've promised the Yuuzhan Vong several thousand prisoners for sacrifice." Luke rubbed his chin. "Unless . . ." He trailed off.

Mara cleared her throat.

"Unless it's not the refugees they mean to sacrifice, but the Duros in orbit. They could use the refugees as slaves. We've seen that before. And think about this. If the Yuuzhan Vong occupied Duro, they could hit the Core from here."

Mara firmed her lips. Worse and worse.

"Mara, Jaina, did you get any kind of information on SELCORE while you were down there?"

Mara frowned. "What do you mean?"

"They may have been infiltrated," he said.

"Let me think." Mara shut her eyes. "Nothing obvious so far. Just what seems to be a normal set of bureaucratic problems."

Luke laid a hand on R2-D2's dome. "Artoo, you can break into the outsystem military net, can't you?"

The droid warbled in a major key, sounding confident.

Luke pulled a comlink out of one pocket and handed it to Anakin. "And I want you to connect this with Artoo's manipulator arm."

Whistling cheerily, R2-D2 plugged himself back in. Mara watched her husband. In Lando's terms, ten to one he was going to try to contact the military on Coruscant without alerting SELCORE.

She wrapped her hand around his arm, squeezed tightly, and headed for the refresher to clean up and wash the tint out of her hair.

When she came out again, Luke was sitting close to R2-D2's temporarily modified manipulator arm.

"Hamner," Luke said urgently. "Kenth, are you there? This is Skywalker."

A sleepy groan came out of the comlink. Luke smiled ruefully up at Mara, then turned back to R2-D2.

"I'm sorry," he said. "Kenth, we're getting indications that the Yuuzhan Vong could be getting ready to hit Duro, and it's too vital a system to lose. If millions of lives weren't reason enough, it's actually inside the Core. From here, they could block trade on the Spine, too."

"I know, I know," the sleepy voice muttered.

"Is there any way you can get a battle group sent?"

She heard another groan. "Try SELCORE—"

"There's a good chance," Luke said, "that SELCORE is part of the problem. I know, the forces are already spread thin. Do what you can, Kenth. May the Force be with you."

"Right." Hamner's voice was heavy with static. "You, too."

Luke thumbed off the comlink. "Good," he grunted, straightening his legs to stand slowly. "Well done, Anakin. You, too, Artoo."

The droid trilled. Anakin took back the comlink and sat down on the bed, fiddling with its components.

Luke slumped against the wall, bowing his head, rubbing his eyes.

"What's wrong?" Mara asked. "You got off a warning."

He shot Jaina a glance. "Jacen," he said simply. Then he crossed his arms. "And I'm not looking forward to flying escort to another retreat under fire."

"I don't even have a ship here," Jaina complained.

"I've got *Shadow*, and I'll need a copilot," Mara reminded her. "Stick with me."

Jaina nodded somberly.

Anakin snapped the cover back onto the comlink and handed it up to Luke. "Before things get wild," Anakin said, "we ought to try to find Thrynni Vae again. We didn't accomplish much by going out in disguise."

Looking amused, Luke pocketed the comlink. "Do you think we'd do better, declaring ourselves?"

Anakin squared his shoulders. "I don't like to skulk."

Mara laughed shortly. "You need the practice. But it isn't always necessary. Jaina and I could use a rest," she added. It'd been a long day.

"All right." Luke pointed across the room. "Artoo?"

The little droid gave a rising chirp.

"How many security people are on duty at SEL-CORE's transshipping dock, in the next hour?"

R2-D2's interface slid back into place and rotated. He made contented chuckling noises. Then he peeped a short, cheerful signal.

"Five," Luke told Anakin.

Anakin straightened his tunic. "We can do that."

"Without making enemies," Luke emphasized. "We're going to be civilized."

"In other words," Anakin said, "we're going to act like Jedi Knights."

Durgard Brarun embraced his wife, then handed her the controls to their hovercart and said, "I'll join you as soon as I can." He hated to lie, but she never would've left Bburru for Urrdorf without that comforting falsehood.

She followed their son and daughter-in-law up the ramp, onto the regularly scheduled shuttle.

Now everything was in place. When Brarun had heard SELCORE was looking for a place to locate millions of refugees, he'd had the same reaction as most Duros: Not on my planet! A second reaction formed slowly. If the Yuuzhan Vong ever started looking in this direction for an advance base—and he'd never doubted that day would come—then thousands or millions of refugee lives would make excellent bargaining material.

To his mind, they were doomed anyway. They'd just managed to delay their fate for a month, maybe a year.

So he grabbed the SELCORE contract and bought off a few votes in the Duros High House. He encouraged Ducilla's theatrics, knowing other Duros didn't want the refugees here. Someday, his people would thank him. His Peace Brigade connections assured him that the Yuuzhan Vong admiral, or warmaster, probably would spare all twenty orbital cities in exchange for those refugee lives.

Just in case, though, he'd arranged a family vacation on Urrdorf.

The servant who brought Jacen's next meal wore a CorDuro uniform, but his flattened skull was a brilliant shade of turquoise. Silvery brow ridges tapered into prominent bulges on both sides of his forehead.

A Sunesi?

"Just set it there." Jacen turned away from the round window and motioned toward a long table alongside his bed. "Who are you? Do you want something?"

The Sunesi set down the covered meal pouch. "My name is Gnosos, though I don't expect you to remember that. More important, I have a gift." He held out a turquoise hand.

Jacen gingerly took a data card from the brightly colored alien. "And this is—?" he asked.

"It contains my voiceprint, which will key a hoverpod in slip thirty, in the second-floor garage. I think it likely you will need to leave Vice-Director Brarun's hospitality in a hurry."

Startled, Jacen touched his lips with one finger and gestured toward the listening devices he'd found—but hadn't deactivated.

The Sunesi spread his hands. "My people can overlay our speech or another's with ultrahigh-frequency noise. That disrupts such devices as the ones that concern you."

Intrigued, Jacen slipped the data card into a pocket. He tried, without using the Force, to get a read on . . . Gnosos. The Sunesi carried an air of serenity Jacen hadn't seen in anyone, even his uncle, since the first reports of Yuuzhan Vong intruders.

"Why?" he asked. As he spoke, Gnosos's mouth opened slightly, but Jacen picked up no sound in his own range of hearing. "I mean, thank you," Jacen continued, "but—"

"As the Maker gave me, I give to you."

"Maker?" Now Jacen remembered. The monotheistic Sunesi went through a dangerous metamorphosis between their juvenile and adult stages. Supposedly, surviving that change predisposed them to believe in life after death.

"Maker and Giver." The Sunesi spread his hands. "To my people, the universe's endless variety implies a master Maker, one with a fine and glorious creativity and affection. And a sense of humor, as well."

Lumpheads, the Imperials had called the Sunesi, for those prominent cranial bulges. Jacen patted the data card in his breast pocket. "Maybe this time, the joke will be on CorDuro Shipping."

His visitor spread long, smooth hands. "An excellent thought." He hurried out.

And what eerie timing, Jacen reflected. If his guest's theology had anything to do with reality, then the Force not only refused to be abandoned, but something or someone was taking a firm hand in showing Jacen the next logical step.

"Thank you," Jacen mouthed the words silently.

Luke swiped his ID past a reader at the hoverbike stall just outside the hostel, rented two units, and straddled one. Driving conservatively, he and Anakin stepped off at Duggan Station ten minutes later. For the moment, people ignored them. Workers of several species, followed by droids in all states of repair, crowded the dock area and its rideways.

So many worlds were endangered. He had just a few months to find a safe place for one small child—and, wishfully thinking, her mother. He knew better than to go beyond wishing to hoping, though. Mara wouldn't take their child into danger, but she wouldn't avoid an enemy that must be fought, especially now that she'd seen the enemy's face.

He strode beside Anakin. Tresina had come back here once, after Thrynni vanished. By then, their contact had vanished, too. As Luke and Anakin approached the area R2-D2 had targeted, Luke noticed less foot traffic. A few heavy loaders passed by, motors laboring, cargo-bay doors shut.

Around the second bend in this corridor, his danger sense started its odd, subtle vibration at the back of his mind. Just ahead, a chest-high barricade blocked the corridor. Patrolling the narrow gap, three hulking Gamorreans and a Rodian stood in CorDuro-brown flight suits. The Gamorreans' uniforms bulged on them like overloaded shipping sacks. The Rodian's looked half-empty.

Five, R2-D2 had told him. The security team's supervisor was keeping out of sight.

Softly, Luke reminded Anakin, "Don't antagonize. But cover me." Then he picked up his pace, to arrive several meters ahead of his apprentice.

The Rodian moved forward—a thin one, who looked as if he'd always been ill. "Restricted area," he wheezed. "Unless you got authorization, this isn't your street."

Luke reached into a breast pocket. Simultaneously, he stretched out with the Force, gently brushing up against the guard's memory. "I'm looking for a missing person. My group on Coruscant would appreciate your help." He handed the guard a small holocube.

It was too easy, really. Like Gamorreans, Rodians were notoriously weak minded, their reactions simple and violent. As the guard clenched the cube, the image of the Jedi apprentice's bloodied body, dumped out a side airlock, hit Luke like a blast of pain. From her wounds, he knew her death hadn't come easily.

May the Force be with you, Thrynni Vae! He struggled momentarily to regain his own balance. In reviving the Jedi, he'd put out the call that Thrynni followed—to die for someone else's freedom.

He didn't look forward to telling Tresina Lobi.

He made himself concentrate on the refugee crisis, and the possibility of imminent attack. "Thank you for helping. I'm sure you'd like me to leave, now." Luke backstepped, then started to walk away.

Anakin hung back about four meters, balancing his weight on both feet, keeping his hands loose at his sides. A good covering stance, if a little obvious.

"Just a minute," a deep voice gargled behind Luke.

Luke turned slowly.

The security team's fifth member had arrived: a male Duros, unusually tall, dressed in red-trimmed brown coveralls with the triangular CorDuro Shipping insignia on his right breast. Luke heard more foot-shuffling behind his back—even behind Anakin, judging from faint echoes. Several more minds suddenly nudged his awareness.

Luke kept his hands limp at his sides, but he reached out in all directions, getting a grip on the Force between himself, the deck, the bulkheads—and the CorDuro employees. Ten of them, now. He took a split instant to make sure none of them was a masqued Yuuzhan Vong.

Then he made the slightest bow to the supervisor. "One of my people went missing several weeks ago. I've been inquiring into her whereabouts. We've spoken with Vice-Director Brarun about this." Literally true, but his conscience twinged at implying Brarun authorized this investigation. Even after all these years, he despised shielding a lie behind "a certain point of view."

"Would you care to come with me while I check that?" The security super phrased it like a question, but his body language offered no quarter.

"No, I would not," Luke said softly. "I am sorry to have inconvenienced your staff."

He turned away a second time. He took two steps toward Anakin.

His left foot was touching down when Anakin's lightsaber cleared the pocket where he'd hidden it. It ignited with a *snap-hiss* recognizable anywhere in the New Republic. Beyond Anakin, a startled Rodian in CorDuro brown-and-red backed away.

Displaying his empty hands, Luke kept walking.

"Take them," the supervisor growled.

Luke spun around, activating his lightsaber. Two Gamorreans headed toward him, two toward Anakin. The rest of the CorDuro people hung back. Anakin's eyes gleamed, his chin set with satisfaction. The guards brandished local-made blasters, offering the Jedi little challenge.

But Luke didn't want to make enemies. Now he would see how well he'd trained Anakin. He calculated the oncoming guards' angle and then reached out with one hand, beckoning subtly. All four converged on him.

He somersaulted out of their midst, leaving them to pile up together, while he landed lightly between Anakin and the supervisor.

"We're not going to hurt them," Luke said, "but you can't hold us."

To his satisfaction, Anakin held his ground, ready to strike—but only if necessary.

"Skywalker," the supervisor muttered, "so it is you. A word of advice, then."

Luke raised his head.

"Get out of Bburru. Your kind isn't wanted here."

Luke spread his hands. "We will, as soon as we finish our business. One of your employees, there, remembers the woman I'm looking for."

"So you want to talk with him?"

"He remembers seeing her dead."

The supervisor's lips pulled back in a humorless smile. "Then kill him. Fair's fair."

Luke shook his head. "I expect you to discipline your own staff. I will check back."

Again he turned on one heel and walked away. He felt Anakin follow, disappointed but alert.

Anakin was young. He wanted to make a stand, just as Jacen wanted to make a difference.

The image of Thrynni Vae's bloodied body thrust itself back into his mind, and for one moment, Luke wondered how he ever would face his sister if any of her Jedi children met that fate.

CHAPTER TWENTY

Leia had barely stopped moving, or giving orders, since Mara had transmitted the information that Dassid Cree'Ar was actually Nom Anor, the unmasked firebrand from Rhommamool—and a Yuuzhan Vong. Breathless from running to the research building and back, she sank into a chair in her communication center, near the main gate and quarantine area. C-3PO stood at another terminal, running duplicate analyses of every lab result Cree'Ar had ever reported. How much of the reclamation had he sabotaged? she wondered. All that work, that sense of accomplishment—a future for exiled refugees! Had he planted destructive organisms out there? And—

"There's the source for our white-eyes," Han's voice said over the comlink. He'd hidden the *Millennium Falcon* in plain sight, on a nearby bluff. SELCORE had left a pile of anthracite out there for emergency fuel, and the *Falcon*—now matte black—all but vanished from view. According to the best current reports, the Yuuzhan Vong did not seem to have sensors that would detect it.

"And we've still got over a thousand people in quarantine. You know," she said, "the simple fact that Nom Anor's *here* makes this world look more like a target than a haven."

"Don't get excited yet, sweetheart—"

"The Yuuzhan Vong didn't invade Rhommamool," Randa insisted.

The Hutt pressed himself against a wall, cringing and flexing his little hands. She'd thought about locking him up permanently. It didn't feel right, though. The Hutts were also refugees. She would never trust him again, but she wanted him where she could watch him. She was determined to accord him the same sympathy and respect she'd give, say, a Ranat. So she allowed him limited freedom, and an escort: Basbakhan.

Han must've overheard. "They didn't have to. They just stood back and watched the locals burn it to a cinder. And look how far he's gotten with the Duros."

C-3PO bent over his console, silent—as ordered. He'd recited the odds of annihilation until she finally threatened to shut him down.

"Going to talk to the Duros High House?" Han asked.

"Soon as I can get a clear transmission to Coruscant. And after I make sure our people down *here* haven't been talked into murdering each other. Last night I had three reports of Ryn out skulking."

"What kind of reports?"

"Conflicting. I put out that they're probably just rumors, somebody trying to start trouble." She hesitated. "Where is Droma, anyway?"

"He's around."

Skulking, Leia concluded, and this time she was glad. "Han, we do need contingency plans for evacuation. We're warehousing half a dozen ships that SELCORE didn't want to risk taking up again. I don't think Jaina finished checking them out. Tell Droma—"

"If SELCORE mothballed ships here, they're ours now."

C-3PO's head swiveled. He pantomimed frantically with both hands.

"It's all right," Leia told him sternly. "Good, Han. We're down to saving as many lives as possible . . . already. Start putting people on board. Especially the Vors."

"And all the droids we can find," he said. "If the Vong get here, they're scrap. That includes Goldenrod. Get him over here. In pieces, if you have to."

Leia turned down the comlink. "Go on, Threepio," she said gently. "Get shipboard before the Yuuzhan Vong show up. We need you."

He was already shuffling out the door.

"So Admiral Wuht has a soft spot for injured military personnel?" Mara asked softly.

"Seems to."

Jaina sounded fully awake again, lying on one of the hostel's other cots. The moment Luke and Anakin had gone out on their reconnoiter, Jaina had fallen instantly and blissfully asleep. Fighter pilot's habit.

Mara got up off her cot, feeling considerably less chipper, thinking about things she should've done before she rested. At that rate, of course, she never would lie down.

"Artoo, get me a link to Admiral Wuht's office."

R2-D2 whistled a smart salute. Shortly, an aide's image appeared over the in-room holoboard.

"You have a situation developing, Major." Mara sketched out a warning.

The military aide answered gruffly. "You may think our people are guilty of complicity with the Peace Brigade," he said. "That is not true. We disliked being told to open our doors to refugees, but we would never conspire to sell their lives. We will call for a prompt investigation of CorDuro Shipping."

"There might not be time for that," Mara said. "Get your battle group on alert."

Luke and Anakin returned shortly with the bad news about Thrynni Vae, and the quickly changing mood of Bburru City.

And dinner. Mara dug in. "Then we'd better get Jacen and go for Anakin's X-wing."

"Good." Anakin said, half a nutrient bar muffling the word.

Mara eyed Luke over a half-eaten kroyie drumstick. "Jaina and I can fire up the *Shadow* while you and Anakin spring Jacen."

Luke shook his head slowly. "They're watching for me now, but they don't know Jaina and Anakin quite so well."

Mara frowned. "What are you saying?"

"You and I can create a diversion. There've been demonstrators outside Brarun's home, down at the plaza. We'll go talk with them . . . openly. While we do, Jaina and Anakin can slip in and pick up Jacen. We'll rendezvous at the dock."

R2-D2 bleeped.

"Okay," Luke said, "we won't leave you alone. You're with Mara and me. Whatever happens," he added softly, "no Duros are to be hurt unless it's life and death for us. Anakin, Jaina—understand? You'll follow about ten minutes behind us"

They nodded.

After washing up, Luke and Mara descended the lift.

"How's Jacen's mental state?" Mara murmured. "Have you contacted him, since . . ." She let her voice trail off.

"He didn't answer when I comlinked half an hour ago. Brarun's people might've taken it away."

And he wasn't going to intrude on Jacen's emotions from the distance? Mara nodded. All along, she'd advised Luke to use the Force cautiously. She'd never dreamed Jacen would take it this far.

Again, they rode hoverbikes. Luke rented one with a sidecar. He helped R2-D2 wriggle into place before he climbed aboard.

Mara rented a second bike, a two-seater with room to carry Jacen. "Ready," she said, settling on the narrow forward saddle.

She stayed half a length behind Luke, slightly to his right, flowing with inward traffic on the avenue.

Under a bank of lights so high overhead that the illusion of daylight almost convinced Mara, Bburru's central plaza was dominated by four tall housing stacks. The buildings rose as high as the diagonal braces, set up at midplaza like four long spokes of a wheel. A green park surrounded them. Along one building, a crowd had formed around a platform that was considerably taller than the one Mara saw at Port Duggan. From several directions, Duros were hurrying in on foot and by hoverbike.

Luke swooped toward a parking stall near a pair of trees that drooped from their weight of dangling moss and vines. Mara left him to scout the situation and found another stall some distance away.

She hoped her guesses were wrong. If the Yuuzhan Vong struck here, these Duros were probably just as dead as the refugees.

Luke strolled to meet her. The wind had disheveled his hair and put color in his cheeks. She liked the effect, and she let her stare linger just long enough to make sure he got the message. An answering warmth blossomed up from the Luke-place at the back of her mind.

"Jacen's up there, I take it?" She turned and eyed the building nearest the demonstrators. Obviously, their show was for his benefit.

Now she recognized the Duros onstage: Brarun's sister, Ducilla. "One, alone, is strength. One, alone, is unity." Her voice, clearly audible as they walked out onto the plaza, fell silent. Duros backed out of Luke and Mara's way, nodding their long heads and creating a path. Mara knew full well that she and Luke were letting themselves be surrounded, but she didn't sense danger yet.

They approached the chest-high platform. Two larger, heavier Duros stood behind Ducilla, sporting brand-new Merr-Sonn blasters.

No wonder Duros were backing away from her. Amused, Mara kept several paces' distance from Luke. They might both need room to swing lightsabers.

Close by, Duros made shushing noises as Luke stepped into an open space below the platform.

"An individual, alone, can be strong," he called back, and Mara was surprised by how well his voice carried. Ducilla must've set up a transmission field so she could work the crowd. "But how much stronger are two," Luke asked, "who can watch out for each other?"

Ducilla's lipless smile broadened. "The Jedi," she said, mocking him with a singsong. "The ultimate disciples of interdependence. You are weak because of your diversity. You pull in too many directions."

Mara would've challenged that statement, but Luke used it as a launch point. "There are people all over the New Republic, diverse people, who desperately need help. Won't you set aside your frustrations for a little while, and lend a hand to people weaker than yourself?"

Behind Mara, there was a chorus of shouts. "SEL-

CORE had no business—" "Refugees in our system make us bait for a Yuuzhan Vong strike—"

"If you've come to Duro hoping to bring us back in line," Ducilla said, spreading her hands, "I think you can see you made a mistake."

"No mistake," Luke insisted. "SELCORE has offered your home planet back, in exchange for your help shuttling goods down to its surface ... for which your brother's shipping concern is being well compensated."

Her gray cheeks flushed darker.

Luke went on. "SELCORE is too thinly spread to set up its own shuttle ships. It's easier to bring in big freighters, and count on your distribution network—"

The Duros whistled him down.

Mara glanced up at the housing stack, trying to sense Jacen's presence behind any of the large round windows. He was there, all right, but she couldn't pinpoint the spot. R2-D2 stood where Luke had left him, between the sidecar bike and a blocky automated street cleaning unit, its massive sweeper arms folded up alongside the bulky digester. Jaina and Anakin were just arriving from separate directions. Jaina parked her bike and disappeared into the housing stack. Anakin slipped into the crowd and started pressing forward.

Mara frowned. Those were not his orders.

Ducilla raised her head. "Jedi," she called, "have preached their philosophy of light and darkness, of knowledge and wisdom, and what have they given us? Violence and fear!"

Murmurs surrounded Mara.

"Domination, suppression."

The murmurs grew louder.

Luke's glance flickered sideways. He undoubtedly sensed Anakin coming, and that odd, elated determination the boy was broadcasting. Luke's chin firmed, making him look irritated—but just for a moment. Then his lips twitched.

"How many of the New Republic's problems—right now—could be traced to the Jedi?" Ducilla called.

And how much of what you're saying, Mara wondered, *could be traced to Nom Anor?*

Anakin reached the platform, set both hands on its edge, and vaulted into a Force-boosted somersault. He came down between Ducilla's bodyguards, who reached for their blasters. Almost casually, Anakin swept one of the Duros off balance with his left foot. The other guard fired, but Anakin's lightsaber was already out. He diverted the shot, then swept in and sliced the blaster in two.

Stang the kid, anyway! What was he trying?

Luke vaulted onto the platform, shouting, "That's not what we came here to do."

To Mara's utter shock, Anakin spun around and dropped into a dueler's crouch. "That's right," he shouted. "*This* is what we came to do."

As Luke drew his lightsaber, Anakin smiled sardonically. Mara backstepped. They were both out of their minds!

Luke stepped in, sweeping his lightsaber in a wide arc, slow and flashy. Anakin parried gracefully, locked blades, and held the pose.

Then she understood. Anakin was challenging Luke to stage a demonstration, taking advantage of people's fascination with lightsabers. She tended to forget that most citizens of the New Republic went their lifetime without seeing even one—let alone two at once, expertly handled. As Luke's green blade crossed Anakin's faint purple, she half smiled. Duros all around her pushed toward the platform.

She wondered if Luke would make a speech while he

had their full attention. As Luke lightly pushed Anakin away, a Duros woman standing near Mara nudged her companion, smiled, and then turned back to watch. Mara sent out a Force flicker herself, launching the second guard's Merr-Sonn out of his hands into a vine-draped tree. She ached to join them on the platform, but that would be pointless. She could accomplish more here as a sentry.

Luke and Anakin moved through a half-dozen basic drills in order, trading the lead, dropping in and out of deep stances, rising into dramatic blocks. The upstaged Duros orator and her bodyguards backed away. One guard pulled out a comlink and turned his back. Mara didn't like that.

Abruptly, Luke broke out of the classic sequence. Making a surprise rush, he swung low. To parry in place would send Anakin off balance.

Instead, Anakin hopped back, locked blades, and stayed on his feet.

Mara saw pride and praise in Luke's slight, somber nod.

Anakin pressed the unchoreographed attack, following slashes with short, chopping strikes. Mara was struck by the intensity, the balance, the sheer accuracy of Anakin's use of the Force to anticipate Luke, pressing his attack beyond obvious blocks and parries. When Luke mounted a wild, sparkling offense, pushing Anakin past anything the young Jedi had faced before, Mara knew he, too, was impressed.

She'd worried about the Solo brothers' rivalry. Now she saw that practicing against Jacen—so similar in style, so different in execution—had matured Anakin tremendously.

Only one problem. The crowd was growing, and as Ducilla's bodyguard returned his comlink to his belt,

Mara guessed Luke's audience wouldn't remain unarmed for long.

Jacen was watching the crowd watch the practice duel when a faint tapping caught his attention.

He pushed away from the transparisteel window. He'd never deactivated the listening devices in here, but now he had a hunch—not the Force, just a hunch—that with Luke, Anakin, and Mara in plain sight, twelve floors down, this could be Jaina.

He made a fast circuit, gathering the snoops before he touched the door's interior opening panel.

It slid open, and his sister slipped through. "Hey," she said.

He poked his head out the door, glanced left and right, and spotted his guards, slumped comfortably against the wall. Shaking his head, he tossed the snoops onto one guard's lap, then stepped back into his room and sent the door shut.

"Hey," he answered. "Nice of you to visit."

She'd thrown on a vest over her brown flight suit and black utility belt. He also noticed the close-fitting cap.

"Great hair."

She glared at him. He'd left his own cap on the bedside. "Speak for yourself. What are you doing here, waiting for Hoth to melt?"

"Vice-Director Brarun did send down a message that Uncle Luke had been spotted, out at the docks. He wants to talk with us all. Want some cold kroyie?"

"You've got to be kidding." Jaina strode across to his window. Instead of looking out, she stood alongside it and cautiously peered up, down, and to both sides.

"The only guards are in the hall. Were in the hall," he corrected himself. "Doesn't look like they gave you any trouble."

"As guards go, they weren't real impressive."

"I think," he confessed, "that their only real job is to let Brarun know if I decide to leave."

Jaina pointed down at the platform. He could plainly see the green and amethyst spark and flash of lightsabers engaging. "See that?" she demanded. "That's going on in your honor—a distraction, so I can get you out. We're headed back down to Gateway."

"Is it necessary? I'm waiting to talk to the Vice-Director—"

She whirled around. "Are you even marginally aware of what's going on around you?"

"How about you?" he asked softly. "How's the vision coming back?"

"Well, for one thing, I'd forgotten how big your nose and chin are getting."

He snorted softly. His features *had* matured, this year. Hers had looked womanlike for three or four years—one of the temporary injustices of having a female twin.

"Listen," she said. "Aunt Mara and I just exposed a Yuuzhan Vong agent down at Gateway, and he nearly killed us both." She snatched off her cap to reveal a synthflesh strip above her right ear. "And Uncle Luke just found connections between your precious vice-director and the Peace Brigade."

Jacen felt his insides shrink. "That's why Brarun's anxious to get a Jedi in custody? Because the Peace Brigade has figured out that the Yuuzhan Vong want to neutralize us?"

"Give the boy a medal. And meanwhile, you're just sitting here, blind to it all. Aren't you listening to the Force at all? Can't you tell? Something's about to happen. Again."

He thrust both hands into his pockets, feeling guilty. "Actually, I . . . decided to stop using it. Completely.

Uncle Luke challenged me, and I . . . I'm tired, Jaina. If I can't fight darkness with darkness, then maybe I can't fight violence with violence. I just feel like I'm . . . waiting for something to happen."

Her eyebrows rose. "What's going to happen is another invasion, Jacen. And you're coming with me, whether you want to or not." She flipped back her vest and laid one hand on a holstered blaster.

Startled, he sat down on the bed. "You'd make me come with you?"

Jaina drew the blaster, and he saw that she'd set it for stun. "You may want to set yourself up as a tragic hero," she said, "but it isn't going to happen. Yes, idiot brother. I would make you come."

He half smiled, almost relieved. The universe had been knocked out from under him, and his vision beckoned him to a destiny he didn't understand, but Jaina hadn't changed. She'd just matured.

"I'll come," he said, reaching out one hand.

"Going to shoot back, if somebody shoots at us?"

"I guess I'll have to. But maybe nobody will." He pulled out Gnosos's data card. "We've been offered the use of a hoverpod."

"Whose?" Jaina's eyes narrowed.

"A Sunesi."

"One of those strange preachers?"

Jacen shrugged. "I've never heard of one of them going to the dark side."

Frowning, Jaina flipped her hand on the blaster's handgrip and gave it to him—then reached across and pulled a second blaster from her utility belt's cross-draw holster.

Then she peered out the window again. Her frown slackened. "Uh-oh," she said. "Maybe we aren't going anywhere."

* * *

If Luke had hoped to make a speech, it was too late. Mara heard someone behind her fire a weapon—a little BlasTech DW-5, by the sound of it. Luke swept in and deflected the bolt.

Mara spun around. Spotting the Duros gunman, she plunged through the crowd. Leaning her weight into his balance was easy. She threw him gently to the ground and disarmed him.

Then she heard someone fire a deeper-pitched weapon. A shout went up, inarticulate, plainly hostile. Mara didn't need to check her danger sense. Newly arrived agitators had turned a harmless crowd of fascinated spectators into a sharp-toothed beast of a mob. Duros who'd looked friendly almost knocked each other down, hurrying out of the middle of it.

Someone grabbed her left arm. She stepped sideways and used his momentum to toss him almost casually against another Duros, who went down. Two more, from behind: she crossed her arms through the leader's, ducked, and felt him slide over her back into his partner's face.

She flexed her hands. She was sick of watching Luke and Anakin have all the fun, anyway. It felt unconscionably good to cut loose—and with so many Duros close around her, they couldn't fire weapons without hitting each other. So it was hand-to-hand, and Mara could do that in her sleep. A high roundhouse kick, fueled by her fury over having to retreat from Nom Anor, sent another holdout blaster up onto the tree limb.

If she fell, though, her child could get hurt. She focused quickly and surely as each threat presented itself. Blaster after blaster flew into the vine-draped tree. A half-dozen Duros rushed her. She let them get close enough to grab—then leapt clear, aiming herself toward the street-sweeping machinery and R2-D2. Not far behind her back, she sensed another knot of closely controlled violence: Luke and Anakin, likewise headed out of the mob's center.

Another crowd of Duros bore down on R2-D2. His domed head spun left, then right. He let out a frightened squeal.

Mara took the offensive, using the Force to toss Duros aside. One of R2-D2's attackers made a grab. Mara saw the flash of an electric discharge, and the Duros jumped back. Another Duros tried to grab him, and R2-D2 shocked that one, too.

Then a group of them clambered up the street-sweeping machine, and it roared to life.

Jacen and Jaina avoided the lift and tiptoed down the emergency stairs. With only two flights to go, Jacen heard rustling noises below. He backed into Jaina, who'd donned her enhancement mask. The footsteps plainly were coming up toward them.

Then the sound stopped.

Jacen pressed against the exterior wall, close to his twin. He double-checked the unfamiliar blaster, making extra sure it was set for stun.

By the time he lowered it, Jaina was pushing away from the wall. She placed two hands on the banister, leapt gracefully, and vanished.

Jacen pounded down the next flight after her. He heard a blaster below his feet, and less than a second later, he spotted three Duros in CorDuro Shipping uniforms—two sprawled in the stairwell, one dashing for a door. Jacen stunned that one. Jaina had already fallen past this level, leaping out of the stairwell's core, headed for a side door.

Jacen followed, not liking what they'd done—not at all. This wasn't fair! He was Jedi, trained to fight to protect others. *And* himself.

"This way!" He waved Jaina toward a service garage, then pressed the data card into a wall slot.

A two-seat hoverpod in the nearest row rose on its repulsors.

The street-sweeper swung out a long metal arm, aimed at R2-D2. Mara couldn't get there in time to stop it. R2-D2 flew into the air, and an angry cheer erupted.

Behind R2-D2, Mara spotted a pod soaring off the housing complex's second floor. She confirmed Jacen and Jaina on board, then stretched out to nudge Luke. He and Anakin were holding their own, keeping the Duros distracted, laying them limp on the pavement, if necessary.

Mara vaulted onto one of the hefty diagonal braces that rose up from street level. She made sure she had a good grip, then reached out with the Force toward R2-D2.

He changed course in midair, swooping around like a blunt silver missile.

Duros scattered out of his line of fall. The mob surrounding Luke and Anakin stampeded aside.

Luke broke into a sprint, headed away from Jacen and Jaina's escape route, toward the hoverbike Mara had parked. Anakin followed, still gripping an ignited lightsaber. Mara guided R2-D2 toward them, then carefully set him down, facing in their direction. Instantly, he extended his third tread and rolled forward.

She exhaled heavily. The key to "size matters not" was realizing *she* hadn't lifted him at all. The Force had energy to spare—but directing its flow still tired her. She dropped lightly onto her feet and then pounded after

Luke. Right in front of her, Anakin deflected a dirt clod with his lightsaber.

"Get Artoo hidden," she ordered him. "We'll draw them off."

Luke climbed onto the hoverbike and fired it up. Mara sprang onto the second seat. Luke took off so fast she had to grab him with both arms.

"Not exactly—the distraction—we had in mind," she puffed, setting her chin on his shoulder.

"Anakin changed things a little. Not badly, though. Just a little hazy on the escape plan."

He circled back, buzzed the crowd chasing Anakin and R2-D2, then headed up the nearest boulevard, toward a shopping strip. Mara craned her neck to look back. Anakin ducked around a building, out of her line of sight. The crowd came on, following Luke.

"How are we going to get to the *Shadow*?" Keeping one arm around Luke's waist, she corralled as much as possible of her streaming hair with the other hand.

"I'll think of something."

"Think fast, Skywalker." She knew how much he was enjoying this—but she was tired.

She still couldn't say it, though.

CHAPTER
TWENTY-ONE

Jacen leaned into an inadequate flight harness as Jaina piloted the borrowed hoverpod up a boulevard lined with manufacturers' offices. She *claimed* she could see all right.

As she rounded one corner, three pods marked with CorDuro's triangular insignia swooped after them. "Don't slow down," Jacen told her, "but—"

"What makes you think I'd slow down?"

"But we just picked up three more shadows," he said. "They've got CorDuro markings."

"Meaning what?" Jaina accelerated toward the approach ramp for the public pod-driver bound for Port Duggan. Fortunately, there was little early evening traffic.

"Meaning don't go that way!" he exclaimed. "Get us to a private dock. We won't be able to get anywhere close to main shipping."

"That's where Mara docked the *Shadow*," she growled, but she changed course without hesitating, blasting along at second-story level, scattering gray-skinned pedestrians. "Just tell me if I'm about to hit anything small."

Glancing at her enhancement mask, he gritted his teeth. "Right," he said. "Okay, what was it you found out about Thrynni Vae and CorDuro?"

"And the Peace Brigade, we think."

She related a sketchy story, constantly interrupting herself to swerve, jink, and dodge traffic. From her flying, he had to conclude that she *could* see. Mostly.

"All I can say," she finished, "is that Thrynni's dead, Brarun's on somebody's payroll—not SELCORE's—and Mom's scrambling refugees onto evac ships. Again."

"We'd better find one uncorrupted government official, report Brarun, and—"

"Oh, sure," she said. "There's time for that."

Jacen glanced back. "They're still with us."

"Got any ideas? Or do we just wait for the speed police to get a bead on us?"

"Give me your comlink," he said. "I'll see if I can get Uncle Luke or Aunt Mara."

As the comlink chirped, Mara pressed into a doorway and turned her face toward the deepening shadow. Luke's warm back pressed up against hers. For the moment, they'd eluded attention.

"Mara here," she said softly.

"We're on our way," Jacen's voice said, "but we can't get to the *Shadow*. We'll take something else and meet you down at Gateway. Are you all right?"

"Well." Mara curled her fingers around the comlink. "We've been . . ." Screamed at, she recalled—taunted, vilified. She'd felt Luke's anguish. These were people he wanted to help. "Busy," was all she said. "If we make any public move, the rioters are likely to turn violent. We're trying to get invisible again."

"See you downside, then."

Bburru's daylights were fading. Mara could barely make out R2-D2's domed top. Anakin stood sentinel over him, in a planter. They'd finally lost their last pursuer in this residential corridor.

Mara pocketed the comlink.

"Okay." Luke held his deactivated lightsaber in his right hand. "Let's see what Artoo can find us."

The little droid had alerted them that their hostel room had been entered, snoops and homing devices planted in their belongings. Not a major concern, but a nuisance. This route was closer to the *Shadow*, anyway. They would just have to do without disguises.

A little farther up the avenue was another public terminal. Mara took the sentry post this time, while Luke covered R2-D2's unauthorized breach. Only a few seconds later, he waved her down out of the musty bushes and strode off with R2-D2. She followed about four meters back, and she felt Anakin follow at a similar distance. A group of Duros passed on the corridor's other side. She felt Luke using the Force to cloak their side in darkness.

R2-D2 had found a vacant apartment with an outside door, where they could lie low, grab a snack, and wait for Bburru to cool down a little more before heading on toward the *Shadow*.

As they paused in the entry, Anakin looked disappointed. "Go on ahead, then," she told him. "Make sure it's not being watched."

Looking pleased, he grabbed a handful of concentrates and headed out.

Mara sank down in a narrow, built-in dining booth.

"Move," Luke said gently, sitting down on the bench's edge. "Please."

She scooted aside and rested her head on his shoulder. She would *not* fall asleep. There wasn't time.

"Feels strange, doesn't it?" she asked.

Luke slipped his arm around her shoulder. "Something wrong?"

"No," she said wryly. "It's just disconcerting."

"Oh. To stand back and let these young people take up the torch."

Mara nodded. "We've still got so much to teach them. They're not ready."

Luke tightened his hand on her shoulder for an instant. "I wasn't ready," he said flatly. "At least you were well trained. I can't believe the trust Obi-Wan must've had, when he let Vader . . . Father . . . strike him down, on the first Death Star."

"Trust in you," Mara said.

"And in the Force." Luke rested his head against hers. "You're right, this isn't easy. But that's why I'm not as worried about Jacen . . . as Jaina is."

"As I am," she admitted.

"The Force is strong in him. We want to show him the right path, and we'll do our best to influence his choice, but in the end . . ."

"It's his life." She fought back a yawn. *Stang,* she was tired! "And Anakin's, and Jaina's. I hope you haven't been trying to read their future."

Luke shook his head. "I tried once, about a week ago. The future has always been in motion, but now it's spinning so fast that everything contradicts everything else. And only one future will actually play out."

"Uncanny, isn't it?"

Luke nodded. "Mara, you're exhausted. Would you let me refresh you? With the Force, I mean."

"I knew what you meant." *Farmboy,* she wanted to add, amused but touched. *Always the innocent, even after almost seven years of marriage.*

And even after that long, she still hated giving in, to him or anyone, but she'd taught the Solo kids that teamwork meant helping each other. The hardest part about giving in to Luke was taking the first step.

So she usually reached out to him first.

"Yes," she said, and it came out like a sigh. "Please."

It came at the edge of her spirit, like a touch of white-hot light. It spread strength, and unwavering approval, and a love as deep and as strong as a Mon Calamari tide. She plunged into it, inhaled it, bathed in it. She reveled in the surge of renewal, and then she splashed it back at Luke as hard as she could.

When she opened her eyes, she was lying beside him, twining her arms and her body with his, and his lips were pressed tightly to hers.

She shut her eyes and drew him closer yet.

Jacen braced himself as Jaina jinked past commercial buildings. This part of the city's layout just wasn't complex enough for shaking off pursuers, and the hoverpod's engine had no guts at all.

What did he expect a preacher to own? "Try to get out of their line of sight," Jacen suggested. "Then put it on autopilot landing cycle, and we'll bail."

"Oh, great idea. Stellar."

"Got a better one?"

She rounded a corner into a straightaway, poured on speed for several seconds, then ducked up a side alley.

"Nope," she said, flicking levers. "Out."

She popped the hatch on the pod, which was still streaking up the alley at an impressive speed, pushed one raised button, and jumped.

He followed, falling hard without his Jedi skills. At least he'd been trained to roll gracefully, absorbing most of the impact.

"This way," he called.

Jaina pressed to her feet and followed him into a gap between buildings.

"Are you okay?" he demanded.

"I'm not the idiot who's refusing to use the Force."

They waited several minutes, but pursuit didn't come.

He tried phrasing it differently. "How well can you really see?"

She straightened her mask. "I flew, didn't I?"

"Yeah, you did. Pretty well."

"All right," Jaina said. "We're going to be Duros for a while."

She must've blurred their faces, because they had no trouble getting to a private dock, where she slid a hand across an ID reader, and they left on a small private shuttle.

Jacen buckled in. His conscience jabbed him. Besides piggybacking on Jaina's Force use, this was stealing.

But he didn't want to go the long way around, to get to the rattletrap shuttle he'd brought up from Gateway dome.

Jaina set a course that was little more than a braked fall from geosynchronous orbit.

"Look out below," he murmured.

They were on final approach when the comm unit hissed. "Shuttle on approach vector," a male voice said, "decelerate and identify yourself. This dome is on alert."

"This is, um, NM-KO two eight," Jacen said, frowning at Jaina as he read off an ID plate. "Decelerating now." Then he added, "Is Administrator Organa Solo available? Mom, are you there?"

The next voice was his mother's. "Jacen," she exclaimed. "Are Jaina and Anakin with you?"

"Just Jaina."

"I take it she's flying," Leia said. "Slow it down just a little more, Jaina. How many passengers could you squeeze into that shuttle? Is it hyperspace-capable?"

That sounded ominous, after what Jaina had told him. "Looks like . . ." Jacen eyed the control panel, then peered back over the seats. "Room for four or five, and there is a hyperdrive."

"Good. Park it . . ." Leia gave landing instructions. To Jacen's surprise, they were to head for the main entry. Gateway must've canceled the quarantine.

Jaina slipped the little craft under the edge of a fog-shrouded landing bay next to a blast crater. Figures in orange chem suits swarmed several freighters and haulers, cleaning Duro-crud off rectennae and viewports, scrambling in and out of access hatches. Jacen took one last breath of good air, then followed Jaina toward the nearest boarding tube.

At its inside end, he heard his mother give a curt order. He turned left, toward that voice. Inside a duracrete-block room that'd been off-limits during quarantine, three sloping consoles with holographic displays clustered under a small screen representing local space. The room smelled like someone had eaten a late dinner in here. His mom bent over one comm unit, wearing a white scarf wrapped around and around her head—and her lightsaber, dangling over her SELCORE-blue coveralls.

Too bad about her hair. If she'd waited a few days, she might've kept it—with the quarantine canceled.

She spun around. "Jacen, Jaina, good. Load up that shuttle and get offworld. I don't think we've got long."

"There's room for you on board." Jaina pushed forward. "You, Olmahk . . ." She glanced toward the room's inner corner and the ever-present gray shadow. "And maybe two others."

"I can't leave yet. Get away now, before the Yuuzhan Vong get here."

"They might not be coming."

Recognizing the new voice, Jacen turned around. "Hello, Randa," he groaned.

The other Noghri, Basbakhan, stood beside Randa.

Leia shrugged. "He's staying out of the way. Take him with you. As a favor to me."

"I'm staying," Jaina said flatly, "if you're staying."

"Please, you two," Leia said. "Before—"

She never got to finish that sentence. At the far edge of the small local-space screen, a wave of unidentified ships appeared. Until the DDF's threat analyst painted them friend or foe, they shone white, but Jacen had little doubt that the enemy had arrived.

"Too late," Jaina mumbled.

On-screen, blue grids that represented the planetary shields sprang up around one after another of the orbital cities. Off to Jacen's right, another comm unit—evidently Gateway's ground-orbit link to Bburru—emitted a staccato buzz, followed by a curt feminine voice.

"Attention, all downside residents. This is Duro Defense Force. Take emerrrgency shelters. Do not attempt space flight. This system is under attack."

Leia spun back to the other console, swatted a control, and leaned down. "Attention, Gateway dome. This is Administrator Organa Solo. If you have boarding orders, report to your transport immediately. If you have not been assigned to a transport, get to your assigned emergency shelter. Do not stop for belongings.

"And here we go again," she muttered aside.

Jacen pushed forward. "What can I do?"

Dark circles looked like they would swallow his mother's eyes. "Find your dad," she said. "He's not answering the comlink. Jaina, how are your eyes? Can you run a comm unit?"

"Fine. Yes." Jaina dropped onto the chair Leia vacated. "Um . . . Mother?"

Her tone of voice made Jacen turn around, too.

"What?" Leia demanded.

"The planetary shields are up around every habitat, now—except three. Bburru, and the city on either side of it."

Jacen eyed the display. Blue gridlines surrounded orbital cities and the domes directly beneath them, in a ring around Duro's equator—except for the zone over Gateway.

He intercepted his sister's stare. "Sabotage," Jaina exclaimed. "Mom, we're ground zero."

"Go, Jacen. Get out of here," Leia exclaimed. "Tell your dad."

Jacen dashed out the door. Mixed-species knots of people hustled shoulder to shoulder, traveling against him toward the main gate. He stopped to hoist a frightened Chadra-Fan child onto his shoulders and help her find her family. In the midst of a group of humans, a white-haired man carried the black whisperkit over one shoulder. Three children followed closely. The smallest child laughed at the small creature's quizzical face. The two older children had wide, haunted eyes.

So the kit hadn't been shaved, either. That made Jacen almost irrationally glad.

In the Tayana district, Ryn congregated around one of the larger ruins, where a jagged, two-story wall still stood mostly intact. The ground shuddered underfoot. Jacen broke into a run again.

On top of a growing pile of reddish-brown rock rubble stood his dad—wearing an ancient gornt-hide racing helmet, although wisps of hair stuck out at front and back. This had to be another solidarity gesture.

More rocks spewed up from behind the pile.

Jacen ran up. "What can I do?" he shouted.

The roar from below was almost deafening. It had to be the tunneling equipment, digging a hiding place.

"Good, you're back." Han wiped a grimy sleeve

across one cheek, then shouted again. "Somebody stepped on my comlink. Whoever can't get into ships or crawlers, send them this way. Romany's people started a tunnel three days ago. *Skulking*," he growled. "If we can't get these people off Duro, we'll at least hide 'em in the mine complex. Come on up, lend a hand."

From her post in the comm center, Jaina called takeoff orders. Two freighters lifted simultaneously, loaded past capacity with frightened refugees. At the same time, three crawlers lumbered off toward Thirty-two and the Ryn caravan ships. She half heard Jacen's voice over Leia's comm station, announcing he'd found their dad. Between transmissions, she fiddled with the small local-space screen.

She raised her mask, experimenting. When she squinted just right, she could focus the glowing pips. As expected, the incoming swarm suddenly painted itself red. It swept in, an offset-wing formation. A swarm of blue dots— Duro Defense Force—deployed into combat flights just off Bburru habitat. And Anakin had shown her a trick, once.

The screen blanked. "What are you doing?" Randa demanded.

Then the screen blinked on again, displaying twice the field of space it'd shown before. Randa's howl became a cry of admiration.

Jaina straightened her cap, watching one arm of the red arc split off and double back. One of the unshielded Duros cities, Orr-Om, had drifted off its geosync point. She wondered if its stabilizers had been sabotaged, besides its shields. Green speckles flew off its docking bays, civilians trying to evacuate. Around them swarmed red bogeys that had to be skips. The speckles vanished almost as quickly as they appeared.

She felt less guilty about swiping that shuttle. It would've been vaped if any Duros launched it now.

She clenched both fists anyway. In her mind, she was grabbing stick and throttle, coaxing everything she could wring out of her X-wing's sublight engine. She couldn't stand this!

But she couldn't look away, either. One of the larger bogeys doubled back toward the drifting habitat. Disbelieving, Jaina watched the bogey ram directly through its outer docks.

She gaped. What kind of beasts had the Yuuzhan Vong brought this time?

Half a dozen blue dots went after the big red bogey. The others hung back, defending Bburru and its shipyards. From the planet's other side, the Mon Cal light cruiser *Poesy* accelerated toward this quadrant. Jaina had looked up its tech specs. With fourteen turbolasers, eighteen ion cannons, half a dozen heavy tractor beam projectors, and fabulous shields, it ought to make a difference.

Then a bizarre, heavily accented voice thundered over several comm channels. "Return to your cities and settlements," it said. "We offer you peace. Return, and we will speak with you. Attack or try to flee, and you will be destroyed."

Leia pushed back from her transceiver. "They've learned to transmit on our channels," she exclaimed. "If that means they can listen in, too, we haven't got a chance."

Jaina stared at the screen. Several freighters had popped up toward orbit, some from Gateway and some from the other unshielded refugee settlements. Those closest to the approaching *Poesy* went unchallenged. Two that had barely made orbit, departing Gateway, were surrounded by red coralskippers. One turned back.

"Coming back in," a voice said out of Jaina's link box. "If we keep running, they'll blast us, too."

"Copy," Jaina answered. "Landing crater two is clear for you."

If she'd been in command of that ship, though, she would've kept running. She'd rather die in space, trying to get somewhere, than wait here for the Yuuzhan Vong to make her a slave.

Most of the red swarm came on, virtually unchallenged. It wasn't a big group, but Duro wasn't mounting any defense of the refugee settlements, only the orbital cities. Kenth Hamner's reinforcements, if they came, would arrive too late to help Gateway. The enemy force had a target lock on this dome.

She'd bet anything this was Nom Anor's doing.

A wheezing Mon Cal voice made her receiver buzz. "Administrator Organa Solo, this is Commodore Mabettye. *Poesy* has been ordered by Admiral Wuht to stand down and withdraw to our previous station. I am sorry. We will support you as we can."

Jaina couldn't believe it. Had the Vong bought off Admiral Dizzlewit, too?

On the other hand, *Poesy* couldn't have reached Gateway's quadrant before the Yuuzhan Vong did, or launch its fighters in time. By holding that point in orbit, it could still defend several evacuating settlements.

The enemy's main force seemed to be shapes that the sensors represented as bigger than skips, but smaller than cruisers. Landing craft? she guessed.

"All evacuation ships," Leia called into her pickup, "you're on your own. If you think you can make hyperspace, go! If not, do whatever you can to save lives." She flicked a tile on the console. "Gateway to all crawlers. Don't turn back. Get to Thirty-two. We're ground zero."

She turned on Jaina. "Where did you park your shuttle?"

"I just sent it off," Jaina admitted.

Leia hesitated only a second. "Good girl," she said. "I can't get through to SELCORE now. We're going underground."

"And we aren't quite alone," Jaina exclaimed. "Look!"

On the local-space screen, a single white "unidentified" craft blasted down from Bburru City, headed toward Duro's south pole.

"Got to be Aunt Mara," Jaina said. "They dropped off Anakin's X-wing down there."

Leia smiled grimly. "Two X-wings and Mara's *Shadow*? I'm glad they're here, but we could use Rogue Squadron. I'd even take Kyp's Dozen if they showed up."

Ten yorik-trema landing craft dropped in formation toward Duro's surface, each captain keeping the other flattened ovals in view as they decelerated through hideous mists. The ultrasensitive eyes of each living yorik-trema moved constantly, tracking the wedges of deadly coralskipper fighters flying escort. In this atmosphere, it was almost a blind fall.

Tsavong Lah stood behind his pilot in the small forward compartment of the lead lander. Beside him, cradled in a blastula, was a specialized villip. A second creature gripped it, surrounding it like a husk that dangled a long straight tail. A metal-rich diet had deposited conductive material in the oggzil's vertebrae, creating a living antenna, a means to send villip-speech over frequencies that the infidels used, just as Tsavong had been promised. A master shaper waited back at the *Sunulok* for his praise—if it worked—or else his reduction in caste. There were many former shapers among the Shamed Ones.

Tsavong stroked the villip, careful not to dislodge its oggzil companion. He already wore a tizowyrm in one ear.

"Citizens of Duro," he addressed the villip, "we have no interest in your mechanical cities, only the planet's unwanted surface. The ychna, our servant in orbit, will destroy any of your other monstrosities that threaten us. Stand ready to send down a delegation to consummate your surrender, with your . . . in your . . . in persons." The tizowyrm had some trouble with that phrase. He gave the villip a sharp pat, and it shrank again.

Once they'd passed through the worst mists, he stared out the mica-scale viewing panel between the yorik-trema's ablative, regenerative ventral surfaces. He'd ordered his coralskipper pilots to make a symbolic sweep, a first step toward cleansing the planet that would be his next staging point. The coralskipper fighters swooped down, launching deadly accurate plasma streams at monuments too huge to have been crafted by hand tools. Black and gray stone shattered into shards. A massive, flat-topped ruin fell beneath their deadly fire-flow. Three small dome shelters collapsed. In the distance, a trio of slow-moving mechanical vehicles, undoubtedly full of infidels, crawled away from the target dome. The coralskippers attacked. Yellow-green flame erupted from the crawling vehicles.

"To you," Tsavong Lah murmured. "Yun-Yammka, accept those lives. In return for that gift, grant us success."

His yorik-trema shuddered as its landing claws seized the ground. Ignoring the settlement's artificial boarding tubes, he ordered molleung worms extended from the yorik-tremas' sides.

One of his lieutenants gave his cadre of landing troops—young warriors in unscarred armor—final orders. One group, assigned outdoor duties, already wore gnullith breathing aides.

"Destroy only those who threaten violence," the lieutenant ordered. "Gather any who lay down their weapons into a holding and purification area." He looked up to Tsavong Lah.

The warmaster raised his armored arms in benediction. "Go with the gods," he said. "All glory to you."

He turned to a villip-choir view of local space. The native defenders were settling back into their landing bays on board their abominations. The crippled mechanical city drifted. His native agent there would meet the gods escorted by an entire city, once gravity caught it.

Satisfied, Tsavong Lah turned to a display table of small, dedicated villips. He stroked one.

"Off-load Tu-Scart and Sgauru," he ordered, "and release them."

CHAPTER
TWENTY-TWO

Even without a copilot, Mara could call on most of *Jade Shadow*'s capabilities. Lando's techs had installed pilot-controlled AG-1G lasers—nearly as powerful as the AG-2Gs he'd put on the *Millennium Falcon*, years ago—plus a full KDY shielding suite. Shada had shown up with a gift from Talon Karrde, two Dymex HM-8 torp launchers. Mara hadn't asked the former Mistryl Shadow Guard where they came from; she'd simply specified that they, too, had to be pilot-accessible. Now, just so long as nothing went wrong with life-support—which she would need a third arm to reach—she was almost as single-handedly capable as Luke and Anakin in their XJ X-wings.

She'd dropped Anakin at his ship, down near the pole. Now she keyed her heads-up display to paint him and Luke silver-blue. In the distance, beyond Orr-Om's death throes, Luke turned tightly to take one more strafing run at the monster coiled around it.

Sharply tapered forward from its tandem power core and drive unit, *Shadow* flew almost as smoothly as *Jade's Fire*, if not quite as nimbly as the X-wings. Mara clenched stick and throttle, diving into atmosphere again. Down in the opaque goop, her port and starboard visual scanners were useless. Long-range sensors, mounted just below her heads-up, showed a trio of mismatched but aerodynamic craft rising to meet her.

Duro Defense Force already had been driven back to defend the other orbital cities, and their few B-wings had flown straight into the enemy's attack wing and been shot to pieces. Nimbler DDF E-wings and local Dagger-D police ships harried the landing force's coral-skipper escorts, but plainly, this small Yuuzhan Vong force meant only to establish a beachhead—too quickly for Gateway to evacuate. Now the dome dwellers were hostages.

As Mara closed with the skips, she eyed her long-range scanners. About thirty degrees across Duro's surface, a convoy of three freighters and a dozen smaller craft popped free of the toxic clouds and dashed for open space. A tetra formation of coralskippers blasted toward it.

"I'm there," Anakin announced.

One of the silver-blue pips on her screen headed toward the convoy.

Her own trio of skips came straight at her, firing molten projectiles and streams of blinding plasma. Lando's new service droids had fitted *Shadow* with a stutter trigger, and Mara targeted the lead craft as they came on, weakening its dovin basal defense as well as she could.

"Luke?" she called, pulling back on her stick and setting an evasive roll as she pulled for black space. Twin ion drives responded smoothly. "Want to lend a hand here?"

"On my way," he came back.

She had time for only a fast glance at her long-range scanner. The silver-blue pip streaked away from Orr-Om, headed straight for her.

The *Shadow* shivered slightly with unevenly absorbed

energy. Mara juked into a rising reversal, then snap-turned to port and was rewarded with a broadside shot at one coralskipper. Again she pounded its shielding, decelerating and rotating simultaneously, keeping that one skip dead in her sights. Her brackets went live around it, a dead lock-on, but she wouldn't waste a torp until . . . until . . .

Not this pass! The enemy pilot's friends were headed back, almost in range. High behind them, where they couldn't see him, Luke swooped into position.

She knew exactly what he wanted from her. Playing her etheric rudder, she set a spinning dive. The coralskippers followed like hungry mynocks.

One hard turn to starboard put them squarely in Luke's sights. His X-wing pounded the lead skip. The second broke off. Mara jinked hard, came back, and put the torp right where she wanted it. Multicolored coral sprayed in all directions.

Luke had taken up position on another skip's tail. The coralskipper decelerated hard, a maneuver guaranteed to make an inexperienced pilot overshoot, putting him precisely in the enemy's sights.

That X-wing pilot was anything but inexperienced. "Cut speed, Artoo," Mara heard on the private frequency, and the X-wing came to a relative standstill, still in killing position behind the coralskipper. His lasers showered it with deadly firepower.

Mara vaped it with a second missile.

At that instant, her threat board went red. Coralskippers' weapons didn't set off torpedo-lock alarms, so she had only a moment's warning. She slammed the throttle forward, pushed down on her stick, and danced on the rudders.

"Got him," Luke announced.

And Mara came about as the last coralskipper was jetting off toward open space.

"How'd you do that?" she demanded.

"He must've been chasing you on full power. That would distract a dovin basal just as badly as projecting full shields. I think," he added. "Where did they come from?"

"I was headed for Gateway. Hoping to give Leia time to get some more evac ships headed out."

"Leia's gone into hiding," Luke told her. "We can't do her any more good, here . . . yet. She needs time to get people on board."

"Ask her if it'd help if we keep the landing party looking up, instead of searching for her."

While she waited, another voice gargled out of her comm unit. "All forces, this is Admiral Wuht. You have been ordered to disengage and withdraw. Noncompliance will result in immediate disciplinary action."

She'd set her transceiver to listen broadband, even though she was transmitting only on private frequency. That order confirmed what Duros squadron leaders had been calling.

"They're out of their minds," she growled.

"No," Luke came back. "I mean, yes, you're right. But Leia wants us to hold back a little longer. She thinks she's got a better chance of getting her refugees away if the Yuuzhan Vong don't know we're still hanging around."

"All that through the Force, Luke?" she challenged him.

"Not with words, exactly. I'm interpreting a little."

"Still sounds reasonable."

Their furball with the coralskippers had set her on a vector toward Orr-Om. The monstrous Yuuzhan Vong creature had attached itself to one docking area. As Mara watched, it appeared to break off another vast hunk of superstructure with its wedge-shaped head. It shook that vigorously, let go, and then darted back and forth, gobbling up whatever it had flung into space.

She keyed her sensors for a tight-beam view. "Looks like the creature's got some kind of pouch clinging to its dorsal area," she said. "Maybe life-support, over a blowhole."

"All forces," the static-charged voice repeated, "stand down. We have been threatened with a second strike if we do not disengage."

"*Stang,*" Mara whispered.

Luke murmured back, "Wuht swallowed it—the threat of further attack, the promise that they only want the planet. He's going to settle for a stalemate. I'm reading a deactivation order on everything that gets docked."

Mara felt her eyes widen. Full deactivation would drain off the ships' power and send their pilots and even their crews home. "They're not even going to try to help Gateway evacuate, and now our people are prisoners down there." She pushed the *Shadow*'s sharp nose back down.

Then she changed her mind. Gateway's fragile dome protected several thousand refugees from corrosive atmosphere, and she'd seen the invaders' biotechnical breathing apparatuses. One ill-planned attack—even by three Jedi, coordinating their strike through the Force— and the refugees would suffer, while their captors were only inconvenienced.

She'd had a run of unbreakable situations lately! She'd never been so frustrated.

And . . .

"They've got their beachhead," Luke echoed her thoughts, "but that's the low ground. We're still holding the height."

"Which makes sense," Mara pointed out, "only if they think they've got an even better vantage."

"If they've got more ships coming in."

"Exactly."

"Leia'd better hurry." His words, her thoughts. "Maybe Hamner will get us reinforcements here in time."

"Luke," she muttered, "with Fey'lya in charge, it could take another week."

On her heads-up display, one dark-blue blip slowly shrank in the distance. It had been one of Leia's freighters, loaded with refugees. Her scanners showed six breaches along its port side. It spun slowly as atmosphere and debris vented into space.

Leia would need the Duros' full support, the moment she got her other evac ships loaded, and before the Yuuzhan Vong's second force arrived. *Before* their groundside force figured out what Leia was up to, and smashed the last evac ships.

Mara wondered if she could talk sense into Admiral Darez Wuht. If she didn't feel any duplicity in him, she could tell him—quietly, without tipping off the traitors!—that he had reinforcements on the way.

If she docked the *Shadow*, though, she ran the risk that some bantha-brained idiot would power it down.

In the distance, Anakin picked off a second coralskipper as the convoy accelerated toward hyperspace.

"X-wing, stand down," Mara's comm unit growled.

She slapped it off.

Luke came alongside her, setting a slow arc toward Bburru. "CorDuro and the Peace Brigade have Wuht in a tight spot."

"Wuht can't honestly believe they only want the planet, can he? Either he's a traitor, too, or . . . well, somebody's got to get that stand-down canceled. I'll try, on Jaina's behalf. She said he'd shown her some sympathy. But I don't want to get marooned."

"I could dock in your hold again."

"Then stay aboard, in-dock?" Mara asked. "Take off if you have to, come back to fly cover for me if you can?"

"I don't like that much, either." But they had to do something.

"I'll talk to him," she decided. "If they feel threatened by Jedi, you're the ultimate threat. But I'll tell him not to give up. That reinforcements are coming."

"We haven't heard back from Hamner."

"So we don't know if he's been turned down," she pointed out.

She vectored away from Bburru, putting the widest possible angle between any hostile eyes and her *Shadow*. They didn't know she could carry an X-wing, and she wanted to keep that little secret.

Luke tight-docked the fighter, off-loaded R2-D2, then made his way to the triangular cockpit. By then, she had Bburru on visual.

"Port Duggan," she transmitted, "request permission to dock."

"Any further discussion?" Borsk Fey'lya's violet eyes shone vindictively. No one else at the table spoke. "Your vote, then."

Kenth Hamner remained at attention, but he had less hope than ever. Senator Shesh of Kuat had spoken persuasively, regretfully, citing excellent reasons not to pull a single fighter off any of the other shipyard systems. Councilor Pwoe of Mon Calamari reminded the council that others, notably the Hutt Randa Besadii Diori, had recently called in false alerts from Duro.

As he feared, the vote went against him.

He kept his shoulders at a dignified brace. "I will

notify Master Skywalker," he said, "but you'd better remember this day, all of you. If Coruscant falls to Yuuzhan Vong forces based on Duro, you will regret this decision."

He pivoted on one heel and left the chamber.

"This way," Jacen shouted.

"Get to the admin building," Leia called behind him.

He shouted back over his shoulder, "No! Dad's got a tunnel started."

Jaina pounded along beside him. Evening had fallen, but the overhead lamps stayed on—probably an emergency measure. Leia followed with Olmahk and several others, up a lane in the deserted Tayana district. As they approached the tallest ruin, Jacen glanced back. Dark figures swarmed in through the main gate.

"This way." Jacen led to the far side of the rubble pile.

Inside the tumbledown building, Droma's furry, mustachioed face peered out, his blue and red cap still perched at a rakish angle. He waved a bristly arm. Jacen dashed forward, glad that Droma had held out until the quarantine was canceled. His next thought: He hoped all that shaving and isolation really had been pointless, and that no one would carry the white-eyes offplanet on an evacuation ship.

At the rubble pile's edge, Jaina tripped and went down, scraping her hands and knees. Jacen helped her back to her feet.

"I'm all right," she insisted. She scrambled inside.

Jacen stood in the roofless entry, momentarily at a loss.

Then he heard scrambling and puffing noises from his left. He spun in that direction, following Jaina, who'd heard them first.

Two fallen duracrete slabs lay on the floor. He saw a

gap between them, wide enough to squeeze through. The scrambling sounds were coming from down there.

"Jacen," his mother's voice called. "Jaina?"

"Coming." Jaina dropped to hands and knees beside the gap, slipped in feetfirst, then vanished.

Jacen followed, dropping into darkness. He almost pitched forward, but someone caught him.

"Thanks," he puffed.

His mom's voice answered. "Go. Hurry."

Jaina shuffled forward. He imitated her gait to keep from tripping on fallen stones. The passage dropped steadily, toward a dim glow on rough-cut rock.

Jaina rounded the corner first. Jacen followed. He thought he heard Leia behind them.

In a sizable room at the T junction of two tunnels twenty Ryn huddled. Some wore blue SELCORE flight suits under their culottes and vests, their faces almost humorously stubble-covered. A pair of glow lamps threw faint shadows on the rocky walls. Up the right branch, he heard muffled voices and saw a longer lineup of faces—many shapes, shades, and sizes—disappearing in a dark distance.

The digging noises came from up the T's other branch. At the junction, Han stood next to another Ryn in SEL-CORE blue draped with culottes.

"Romany?" Jacen murmured, not quite sure.

"Hey, baldy." Yep. Romany's voice.

Han stepped to Leia's side. The flap of his battered leather helmet dangled alongside his chin. "End of the line, for the moment."

Leia pulled away, glowering at Jacen. "There's a tunnel punched through to the old mines, from the admin building—"

Han raised a hand. "This one's almost through, and the Vong are more likely headed there. I'm in charge of this group. They've been running chewers down here day and night. Only about four meters to go, but if we run machinery now, we'll bring sacrifice hunters down on our heads."

Leia glanced up the tunnel. "Yes, but *we* were using the mining laser. It's on a repulsorsled. And I've got a GOCU transmitter set up over there, patched through to a surface antenna. We could've transmitted out, over there."

So that was why she'd kept it guarded. "Want me to go back for the laser?" Jacen offered.

"No," said Leia—and Han.

"Now it's pick work." Han jerked his head up the left branch. "We're taking shifts. We'll be through in an hour, maybe two."

She sank onto a rock pile. "I can't sit and wait that long," she muttered. "Did you hear, Han? They got the crawlers. All three."

"I heard." Han looked away. Jacen thought he'd seen a furry ghost peer out through his eyes.

"But Luke and Mara are topside," Leia reported, "with Anakin. They'll give us an escort outsystem if we can get these people to ships. And I need someone on that GOCU link."

Jacen nodded. Along one wall of this stone chamber, the Ryn had piled water containers and crates labeled TRAVEL BISCUITS. Among the refugees—mostly shaved, but some as hairy as ever—he spotted two human families. A huddle of Vors, too. As usual, the mothers held their children close, away from the Ryn—but this time, they'd trusted the Ryn with their lives.

Abruptly he missed someone. "Where's Randa?"

"He didn't follow us?" Leia asked. "Frankly, I wasn't watching him. Basbakhan will keep an eye on him."

"I don't even care," Jaina said, and no one contradicted her.

Jacen edged toward Han and Droma, who were talking with Mezza.

"From the other end," Mezza said, "we've traced a route to the SELCORE ship lot. The minute we break through this rock, there are people on the other end who can get us to a transport, thanks to Leia's map."

"Map?" Jacen asked.

"Of the mines. From the Duros' archives." Leia raised a datapad. "Listen, Han. Out below the bluffs, just out of the marshy area, we did some camouflaging ourselves, weeks ago. We've still got one of the five big haulers that brought in almost everything for our original building site. It's ungainly, but it made hyperspace getting here. It'd hold about two thousand, according to my figures."

Han sat down on the floor beside her. "What's wrong with it? Why didn't SELCORE take it back? Why didn't it take off already?"

Jacen watched his mom squint, frown, and shake her head. "I don't remember. I'm sorry. Threepio would know."

"He's on the *Falcon*," Han said.

"Can we comlink him?"

"You can try," Han said, "but I've got him running preflight. I'll check out the hauler. What did you do, bury it?"

Leia nodded. "Piled harvest debris on top. Our scanners would find it in a heartbeat, but the Yuuzhan Vong might not have thought to look down there by the bluffs. And we know they don't have the technology."

"They've got technology, sweetheart. They just build it in different ways."

"Maybe," she said with exaggerated patience, "they won't have found it yet. I don't know. But it'd be a lot

faster to get there aboveground than by following this."
She brandished her datapad map of the mines.

"Skulking! Our specialty," Droma put in.

Han broke a lopsided smile. "Not to mention ship repair. Okay, Mezza—Romany. Droma and I are going to
go check out a hauler. As soon as the pick people break
through, start people moving through the mines toward
the bluffs, and station someone at Leia's transmitter—
but watch those side tunnels."

"Right," Jaina put in. "Nom Anor could still be down
here. And if he is, he could Greenie-trap more ceilings."

A few refugees stared up at the stone overhead.

All expression faded from Leia's face. "A couple more
hours, you said, till they're through?"

Mezza nodded.

Leia stood up and brushed rock dust from the seat of
her SELCORE coveralls. "Almost midnight," she said.
"There's some time."

"For what?" Han demanded. "Hey, Leia. Stay right
here. I just found you. I want to find you again, when I
get back."

Leia compressed her lips. "Thanks," she said. "Really,
Han. Thank you—but you're right. You're in charge of
this group, and I left something important over at
admin."

Han scowled.

Nom Anor led Tsavong Lah toward the laboratory
built-thing, taking such obvious pleasure in walking unmasked that the warmaster briefly wondered what it
would be like to live most of his life in an infidel's guise,
and pitied him.

They strode up the sandy main road between hideously
ugly constructs, past a three-sided built-thing filled with
monstrous machinery. Sgauru and Tu-Scart, the huge

Beater and Biter creatures he'd ordered released, attacked the nearest wall. This symbiotic pair could destroy artificial constructs within minutes. As soon as his own energy-creating creatures nested down and started to feed, he would put Tu-Scart and Sgauru to work on whatever abomination the infidels used to fuel the overhead lamps.

Tsavong Lah turned to an aide. "Dig the pit here," he ordered.

A contingent of warrior escorts fell out of the group.

Near the dome's north edge, Nom Anor led him into a construct shaped like one of their ugly bricks. In the main hall, he heard sloshing and clanking noises.

"My coworkers," Nom Anor said proudly. "When I unmasked, I told them that those whom you found at work, helping remove poisons from the planet, would be specially honored."

"All accepted?"

Nom Anor blinked his genuine eye. "Two refused to work any further," he admitted. "Even when I offered them full honor, and . . . amnesty."

"Amnesty." The tizowyrm in Tsavong Lah's ear didn't translate anything he could comprehend. "What is this?"

Anor smiled. "A word like *peace*, with two meanings. They define it in a way we do not. Something like . . . *mercy*."

The tizowyrm didn't translate that, either. "Explain *mercy*."

Nom Anor paused at the entry to a room built around a long table. Tsavong Lah saw two infidels seated inside, wearing spotted white gowns.

"To the infidels," Nom Anor answered, "it seems generous to let them escape destiny."

"It is not possible to escape destiny. Death is inevitable. How it is faced . . . that is all-important."

"Incredible though that may seem, they do not understand."

Tsavong Lah shook his head. "Then we will give your coworkers better than they deserve, as thanks for their tireless efforts."

"You speak my thoughts," Nom Anor said.

"Perhaps some will volunteer to assist with *our* research?" There were never enough volunteers for that noble work, but his staff had brought the requisite planters and coral seeds.

"I offered that option. Sadly, all declined. Perhaps having directed research makes them reluctant to contribute as participants."

Tsavong Lah shrugged. "Then we shall consecrate this built-thing for your future use." He turned to his black-robed priestess. "Vaecta?"

The hunched, older woman had followed them, leading her ritual musicians. She stepped forward, carrying a translucent bivalve shell against her robes.

Tsavong Lah reached inside, wriggling his fingers, calling one of the tkun creatures to his hand. He felt the delicate touch of a furless nose, then the warmth of furry coils wrapping around his wrist.

He drew out his arm with the crimson tkun coiled around it. Master shapers had recently created the species, responding to the need for quick, efficient—but spiritually significant—individual sacrifices.

From another aide, the priestess took a wad of tishwii leaves. She arranged them in a water basin, then held a flint spark against them and dropped them into the basin to smolder.

"Bring the first researcher," Tsavong Lah said.

CHAPTER
TWENTY-THREE

Han wrapped an arm around Leia's shoulders and pulled her close, momentarily resting his chin on her white turban. "Take care of yourself, then."

"You, too."

Jacen's parents kissed each other—barely a peck at first, and then Han leaned into it. Leia went up on her tiptoes. Jacen lowered his eyes, caught Jaina's glance, and half smiled.

She nodded.

But Han's expression was grim as he and Droma headed back up the entry. Jacen watched until they disappeared. His memory fled back to Belkadan and a marsh full of villips, and he wondered what the Yuuzhan Vong would do with the Thirty-two reclamation project. Maybe they had creatures who could live in poisoned water.

Leia stared at her feet, grimacing.

"Mom," Jacen said gently. "You don't look real diplomatic."

She raised her head. "You don't think you three get all your grit from your father, do you?"

"Whatever you're going to try," Jaina said, "I'm with you."

Leia's smile reflected Jaina's. For three seconds, all the

gaps and irritations between them fell away. They looked like conspirators. Sisters.

And since they thought Jacen had gone soft, he said, "So am I."

Leia wrapped a hand around his forearm and one around Jaina's, and squeezed. "First . . ." She raised her voice. "Mezza, Romany, we did drill out some other bolt-holes, and I have three maps. I need someone to get to that transmitter and someone else to pull people out of those holes. Either to here or to the admin building, and from there to the haulers. We'll have to ask for volunteers—"

A Sullustan girl rocked forward and stood up. Her mother—or grandmother?—opened her mouth, then plainly decided against objecting. Then several others volunteered.

Leia distributed her datapads, keeping one back for Mezza and Romany. Close by, the rhythmic *tick-clink* of picks went on as the volunteers headed out.

Then Leia crouched beside Jaina and Jacen again.

"I've got an idea," Jaina said softly. "We could do a lot of damage with that mining laser, if the Yuuzhan Vong haven't found it."

Leia nodded, then glanced up at Jacen.

"Is that too violent for you?" Jaina demanded.

"It's rescue," he said. "It's defense. As long as I'm not manipulating the Force—"

"If the repulsor cart hasn't been sabotaged, you won't have to." Leia peered up the side tunnel, at the refugees packed inside.

To Jacen's surprise, Leia's sinuous gray shadow-guard slipped forward. "Think about this," Olmahk said in a low, mewling voice. "If the laser is fired, that will bring the Yuuzhan Vong down on us. That post should be mine. I claim it as my due, Lady Vader."

Leia's frown twisted sideways. "You're probably right," she said, but Jacen guessed she had every intention of firing it herself.

His memory served up a vivid image of the galaxy, tipping toward darkness. "Look," he murmured, "I know you all think I'm crazy. But are you sure there's no chance of negotiating? Mom, you're a professional—"

"So I know when it won't work," Leia said wearily. "When your contact parties don't come back alive, the enemy won't talk. You don't waste more contact parties."

Still, maybe he could . . .

"Don't even try it," his mother added darkly.

Maybe she wasn't a fully trained Jedi, but she had no trouble reading him.

She pushed up to stand again, then beckoned the Ryn clan leaders closer. "Mezza, Romany, you've done an excellent job of gathering people. If I don't see you again, thank you. You're in charge. May the Force be with you.

"Jaina, you're with me. Jacen, you follow."

Olmahk came alongside Jacen. They hurried back to the slabs that concealed their entryway.

Han listened carefully from under the fallen duracrete slab for two minutes before deciding to poke his head out. When he did, it was with a blaster alongside his ear.

Under the big emergency lights, nothing moved.

He knew exactly what Leia wanted to do: sabotage the Yuuzhan Vong operation herself, no matter what it cost her—or him. Call him selfish, but he wanted her alive. Not a dead hero. With or without that gorgeous hair, she had the spark that lit a fire in him.

He looked all around, then clambered out. He eyed all corners of the ruined building while Droma pulled himself out of the bolt-hole.

Then he edged close to the door and glanced out. The dome that had previously been a hive of activity was almost still. He heard clanking and crashing noises from some distance away, but the hum of voices had ended. He didn't see any motion close by, either. He would have given a lot for a life-forms sensor.

And while he was wishing, a turbolaser would be nice.

Droma came up alongside him.

"It'd be shorter to cut close to the admin building," Han murmured, "but . . ." He didn't bother finishing the sentence. By now, he just expected Droma to do that.

"Safer along the dome's edge." Droma holstered his blaster.

Han did the same. The Yuuzhan Vong were probably wearing battle armor anyway. One shot, and they'd hear him—and all come down on him.

He paused, shocked by his own thoughts. Where was the old Han Solo who would've charged right in?

Maybe he had died with Chewbacca. "Right," he said. "Keep me in sight, but if they get me, tell Leia . . ."

Droma didn't finish that one.

"Nah," Han said.

Bending low, he sprinted to the next ruin, then slipped inside. One room was dusty; the other, cluttered with someone's abandoned possessions. At least it had a back door. He emerged on the other side.

This time he spotted a massive, muscular-looking figure in black armor sauntering past, carrying an armload of survival gear—looked like two lamps and a small cooker. Han ducked back inside, spotted Droma slipping in through the front door, and caught his glance with a head shake.

He waited until the looter passed, then hustled on.

They made their way to the end of ruined Tayana, then

stealthily through the tent city. At one point, hearing footsteps, he flattened himself on the ground and peered out a tear in one tent's wall. A line of prisoners shuffled past, heads down. Someone was crying. Three Yuuzhan Vong followed the column—armored, unfortunately. Han clenched both fists, longing for the good old days, for Imperial stormtroopers with known weak spots in their armor—and for Chewie.

He'd lost half himself, but he still had his luck. They made it to within sight of the dome's northwest entry. The last good cover was a power station, *luckily* still standing.

As Droma eased into its shadow behind him, Han observed, "They must not be knocking out everything technical until they can bring in their own power source—"

"Whatever that is." Droma nodded.

From this point, they had a clear view toward the research and construction area. A crowd milled in the open street. Han spotted humans, Ryn, Vors, a few Sullustans, and a family of horned Gotals. Several black-armored aliens came into view, dragging a brick-loading machine. Han gaped at their strength. As they drew even with the milling crowd, their leader slipped out of position and got behind it, pushing with the others. Abruptly it vanished. Two seconds later, there was another loud crash.

"Not everything," he muttered, "but they're getting a good start."

He turned back toward the gate. Three humans lay sprawled on the ground, looking to Han as if they'd been shot from behind, trying to reach the gate.

Had the Vong posted a sniper, or were these bodies left from the enemy's arrival?

"May they dance the stars in joy," Droma murmured.

Dance the stars? That was a new one. Han knew Droma's people were a bunch of romantics—

Then he saw the creatures. Coiled around Gateway's construction shed was something like a gigantic snake, darting its head from side to side, feeding. A second creature clung to its top coil with powerful rear pincers. Like a stretched-out Hutt with armored white segments, it reared up, flailing stubby front legs against the construction shed, and then it lowered its huge head to crash against the duracrete shed. Debris tumbled down on both of them. Out of the upright creature's mouth lashed dozens of tentacles. It looked for all the thousand worlds like an everted Sarlacc as it gobbled up the shattered duracrete.

"Sithspawn!" Droma whispered.

If Han had been even remotely tempted to go in that direction, he wasn't now. Turning back toward the northwest gate, he picked up a stone and chucked it out into the open area.

Nothing happened.

"I think," Droma said, "we're better off to run for it."

Han clasped Droma's forearm, wordlessly closing his hand on the bristles. Then he sprinted for the arched tunnel where gray dome met sandy ground, pausing only to scoop up the environment hood that one fallen human clutched in a stiffening hand. He flung it on as he ran.

He'd nearly reached the gate when something whizzed past his ear. Panting, Droma plunged into the cramped airlock alongside him. He too wore a hood. Han slapped the cycling control, seating his air mask.

A palm-sized creature zoomed past his ear, sprang off the lock's rear wall, ricocheted off the front, then whizzed toward him again. It grazed his hood as he swung his blaster like a club.

Got it! It fell to the floor, hissing and sizzling as it spun. Its edges looked like sharpened steel. He patted his head and came away with a hank of hair, cut through with the hood and helmet. If he hadn't dug out this ridiculous helmet, he'd be bleeding like a stuck gornt.

He stomped the creature as the gate's outer door slid aside and Duro's ugly gray fog swirled in.

Droma gingerly picked up the biggest remaining piece. "Might need a knife. This'll do."

Then they were running for the bluff's edge. From behind came weird, watery-sounding cries.

Han turned, aimed, fired. He caught the lead warrior guard square in the face, at the very center of a star-shaped thing that looked like a growth on its face. The alien jerked and tumbled backwards.

Another weak spot! His luck was holding. Encouraged, he sighted on the next one in line, fired, dropped that one, too.

At that point, he expected the rest to turn tail and run. Instead, they rushed him.

Hey, this isn't fair! Han shot the breath creatures one at a time. If these people wanted to die, he didn't mind obliging them. He just didn't intend to let them return the favor.

He followed Droma down the bluff, bearing east over tumbled rocks. He hadn't seen Leia's big marshes before. From this slightly elevated vantage, they looked like a double line of square and triangular curbs that enclosed raised ponds. The nearest ones were green, the farthest ones toxic orange or eerily glowing brown, and between them he could see all shades in the process of changing. Alongside those marshes, he spotted a pale-green pile of mowed grasses.

The cargo hauler should be underneath. Droma

reached the pile and burrowed in without hesitating. Han followed, depending on his breath mask to keep out hay dust. Within moments, he was buried so thickly that his worst fear was suffocation. He flailed deeper, then even deeper. *It'd better be here!*

His left hand hit something hard. On a hunch, he ducked down and crawled forward, pushing hay away in front of him, kicking it out behind him. It reminded him of swimming.

Moments later, the debris thinned out. He emerged into a square, metal-roofed cavern.

"Droma!" he shouted. Down here, his voice took on a slight metallic twang. He could see the Ryn's silhouette, a darker smudge against grass-filtered light. "Get down here!"

The air actually smelled good through his mask. In such a toxic environment, there probably weren't many bacteria of the right kind to rot clippings.

"Come on!" he called again. "Move your fuzzy tail!"

Finally the Ryn flailed down into the low cavern. He crab-crawled sideways to where Han lay. By then, Han had taken a good look.

"If I've got my guess," he said, "it's an old TaggeCo WQ 445. A big box-shaped scow. Sitting flink."

"Not my first choice for a getaway ship," Droma said.

"Mine either. But it's all they've got." Han frowned. Leia hadn't said whether she had anyone to fly this bucket, and he was itching to get to the *Falcon*. "The engine ought to be about there," he said, pointing past his left foot. "And the service hatch should be . . ." He scooted three meters to the right. "Not much farther this way."

It took Droma a few moment's deft work, using the dead razorbug, to pry open the access hatch. After that,

Han was in his element. He found an emergency cache next to the hatch, pulled out a pair of pocket lights, tossed one down to Droma, then started for the cockpit. First things first: Run the diagnostics, see if this beast really could be trusted with a couple thousand lives.

Remembering the captive mob outside the research building, and the pit into which machinery was being flung, and the monsters at the construction shed, he swallowed hard. There wouldn't be many lives to save if he didn't hurry. "Come on, Bristle-face. Move."

A rasping Duros voice guided Mara to dock the *Jade Shadow* in slip 16-F, back on Bburru's familiar Port Duggan arm. The same voice instructed her to power down all onboard systems.

"If they're scanning for life-forms, you might be in trouble," she said quietly.

Luke crouched beside R2-D2, finishing a few final programming details. Normally, *Shadow*'s onboard computer handled security. With the ship powered down, R2-D2 would fill that gap.

"I don't think so," Luke murmured, straightening. "Just hurry back."

"You don't need to say that twice." She hesitated, getting a good look into his eyes, checking his emotional state.

He raised one eyebrow. "Take care . . ." he began.

She frowned.

". . . of the little one."

Her mouth quirked sideways. "I'll accept that as a polite way of saying, 'Get here on the double, mother-of-my-child.' "

Luke touched her shoulder with one hand. She also felt a more subtle caress. She returned it.

Then she hustled out through the hatch, slapped the

external hatch control for the sake of Bburru's visual monitors, and strode up the Port Duggan arm.

No more figures in CorDuro brown patrolled. She saw only a Rodian, hurrying inbound like herself. Then she passed a security post, manned by two of the CorDuro guards that Luke and Anakin had encountered.

"Where you docked?" the skinny Rodian demanded.

"Sixteen F," Mara said sharply.

Another guard slipped out of the post, headed back the way she'd come.

She smiled grimly. That hatch release had peculiar camouflage. They could go at it with a laser torch and still not get on board.

When she stepped off the shipyard corridor's rideway, the big open area was also deserted. Even Ducilla's podium stood empty.

She turned around and spotted a transparent lift tube. R2-D2 had shown her a readout of Duro Defense Force's command post, located on a superstructure over Duggan Station. She stared up the lift tube—way up—to a small platform just under the habitat's main structural supports. Two tall, gray guards stood outside the tube's base.

"I need to speak with Admiral Wuht," she said.

"He is not available," the near guard answered.

"So I assumed." Mara glanced upward again. Too far to jump—maybe Luke could make this one, but she couldn't.

"Listen," she said quietly. "I only want to talk with him. I'm not going to harm him, but if you insist on getting in my way, I can promise you I *will* hurt you." She added an overlay of Force energy. Too much was at stake, too many lives on the line, to hold back. "Let me through," she said firmly, barely raising her hand to gesture.

One guard touched the lift control, opening the door. The other pulled out a comlink and turned aside.

Mara tossed her head, marched onto the lift, and punched for the command level.

CHAPTER
TWENTY-FOUR

Leia slid into the upright gap between the number-one hydroponics complex and her administration building. Here, the duracrete walls were less than half a meter apart, just close enough that a reasonably agile person could climb them chimney-style.

She holstered her blaster, then pushed one foot and one hand against the right wall, one foot and one hand against the left wall, and started up.

Though the duracrete was rough enough for hand- and foot-holds, chimneying meant holding her wrists and ankles at angles that brought on a dull, throbbing ache. Using Jedi techniques to ignore that pain, she kept climbing. Finally, she stretched out prone on the roof and peered north, toward the construction barns.

Motion caught her eye almost directly below. A pair of Yuuzhan Vong hauled a travoislike cart down the admin building's main steps. Her breath caught as she recognized Abbela Oldsong's pale-blue shoulder wrap, bunched around one limp form that lay on the travois. Leia leveled her blaster at the nearer alien's neck, at the joint in its armor, then lowered her weapon. Abbela wasn't breathing. Something like a crimson snake had wrapped tightly around her neck.

Leia grimaced, glad that the woman lay facedown. Other limbs, human and nonhuman, stuck out beneath

Abbela's body. Leia wondered if they'd been sacrificed to some horrible, so-called god.

She was barely aware of Olmahk creeping forward to lie beside her, his lean gray face coming level with hers.

"Keep your head down, Lady Vader."

"I am."

Then she saw one of her block-stacking machines jerking forward, being dragged and shoved instead of running under its own power. Ahead of it, between the construction shed and garden plots, lay a deep new pit. Yuuzhan Vong swarmed its edges, deepening and enlarging it with what looked like picks and staffs, but were probably creature-tools. West of the pit, hundreds of refugees sat close together. Although the evening was slipping toward midnight, no one lay down. As Leia watched, another group joined them. Yuuzhan Vong on lizardlike beasts patrolled the area, and near the construction shed, something moved.

Then she saw the upper creature's tentacled head, attacking the wall in a frenzy.

She clenched a fist. Where was SELCORE now? Senator Shesh sat on Coruscant while Leia lay here, watching alien biocreations shatter SELCORE's haven.

Not alone, though. She heard more soft scuffling behind her, then Jaina crept up on her stomach.

"Remind you of anything?" Jaina asked, adjusting her mask one-handed.

Leia nodded. "Rhommamool, and a pit full of droids. We've got to get those people out of there."

"With what?" Jaina asked bitterly.

"Just help me get the mining laser up here," Leia said. "They still haven't shut down the main power plant."

"What about lifting something out of that pit," Jaina suggested, "using the Force? And just dropping it on them? They wouldn't have a clue where we are."

"We could smash them," Leia said, "or we could try to get some prisoners released."

"How's that?"

As Leia explained her sketchy plan, Jacen scrambled up alongside his sister.

"We need you," Leia said bluntly, hoping he had finally settled his mind. She explained what they wanted to do.

Jacen stared out over the scene. His eyebrows lifted, and he looked bitterly unhappy. "Mom, I . . . I can't," he murmured. "Jaina, you know size doesn't matter. You can do it. Draw on my strength, if you want to. But this is it. The vortex, the critical moment. I can feel it. I don't . . . dare . . . misstep."

"Either help us or get out of the way." Jaina's brown eyes blazed. "Deserter."

"Olmahk can't use the Force, and he's no deserter."

Leia frowned, hearing the frustration in Jacen's voice. She'd never refused to use the Force this way. Still, she hadn't kept up her training. She'd obviously set Jacen a lousy example, and he was taking it one step further.

Jaina crept forward another half meter, almost to the roof's edge. One earlobe poked out from underneath her sky-blue cap.

"Okay, Mom. Just lean into the Force, then lean into me. You can do that."

Leia's frustration eased a bit. Jaina had figured out how to take charge, even how to give her mother orders without rubbing Leia's nose in her relative ineptitude.

Leia pushed down inside herself, toward the sensation of pure life that always was there—not a nothingness at all, but a spot that teemed with power and life. Even with hope, she sensed, as she reached out from that spot toward her daughter. For once, their similarity worked for them instead of dividing them. Jaina seemed to wield Leia's Force energy easily. Slitting one eye open, determined to watch—though she didn't dare to stop concentrating—Leia saw an ore-smashing droid rise out of the construction shop.

Yuuzhan Vong on that side of the pit scattered. The monsters snapped at it but missed. On the other side of the pit, refugees jumped to their feet. Their guards stomped toward them, turning their backs on the disaster that sailed through the air.

Leia went cold as the Force stopped flowing. The machine smashed to ground, catching at least five Yuuzhan Vong warriors underneath it. Other aliens dashed into nearby garden huts, pitiful shelter.

A Vuvrian leapt to his feet and shouted, "Run! Scatter!"

The throng seemed to explode. People dashed in all directions. Aliens riding their saddled creatures brought some down, but others sprinted, singly and in groups, out of the herders' range.

Leia hoped some would find the bolt-holes. Deeply satisfied, she exhaled and eyed her daughter. Jaina had rolled onto her back, panting.

"Well done," Leia murmured.

Jaina smiled crookedly at her, then eyed her brother. "Thanks so much, Jacen."

He lay prone, staring down his blaster sights, biting his lip.

"All right," Leia said. "The admin building's main shaft goes straight down three levels, below ground. The laser should be under guard on the second level."

"Should be," Jaina muttered. "What do you bet Nom Anor sabotaged it?"

"Maybe not," Jacen insisted. "Olmahk and I will cover you."

Good—except for one more thing Leia had to say.

"Listen," she muttered. "I'm point on this mission, and I'm coming back up here. With Olmahk," she added, staring down her scowling bodyguard. "If anything happens, get away. Before we move the laser, I'll show you the way out. You're my hope for our future. Both of you, and Anakin, and your whole generation of young Jedi. If you carry it on, I can—well, just don't fail the people who are counting on you."

"Come on," Jaina snapped. "We've got work to do."

Exactly the right touch. Jaina was right: No more time for the overture. On with the show.

Leia jumped from the hydroponics plant's rooftop to a window ledge on the admin building. From there, it was a quick scramble into a vacant office.

Abbela's.

Fortunately, the Yuuzhan Vong seemed to be congregating at the pit. The office was empty. She considered unhooking her lightsaber, then decided she'd leave lightsaber work to Jacen and Jaina. Drawing her blaster, she started down the dark stairs as silently as possible.

One flight below ground, Leia paused with Olmahk and waited for her twins to catch up.

"Laser," she murmured, pointing toward a side chamber.

Two blurred smudges marked the dust beside it, and she knew Abbela's guards had met their mistress's fate. Between those smudges, not quite so close to the laser, a broad swath had been swept in the dust, as if an even larger corpse had been dragged away.

Randa? she wondered. Where was Basbakhan?

"But I'm going to show you the way out first," she said.

Jaina shook her head. "I'm going up to the roof with you."

"No." Holding her blaster at the ready, Leia silently pushed the next door.

A storeroom filled with storage crates—nitrates, potassium compounds, micronutrients—was dimly lit by a glow lamp near the exit. Leia saw no sign of intruders. Even the dust had a spackled, untrodden look.

Leia stepped through, toward a hatch that looked like one more permastone panel. She tugged it slightly open and jerked her head aside.

"Tunnel. To the mines," she murmured.

Jaina rolled her eyes. Jacen frowned at his twin, crinkling his lips.

Leia led the way back out. From a canister beside the metal-sheathed power conduit, she took a handful of sand and strewed it out onto the floor, masking their footprints.

Olmahk lingered at the door. As Leia opened it again, she heard harsh voices from the main level and heavy footsteps going up the steps. She held still and waited. In a minute or so, the voices stopped.

But were they really gone? She'd gotten used to being able to sense living presences through the Force. Around Yuuzhan Vong, she felt half-blind.

She glanced aside at her daughter, wearing her mask, then at her son, with his cap pulled down snugly. She pushed the door the rest of the way open.

No one challenged her.

She led across the open area, headed toward the laser. She'd almost reached it when a harsh shout spun her around. A Yuuzhan Vong warrior in black armor stood on the stairs, sweeping something off a bandolier.

"Go!" she shouted. "Back!"

She fired off a shot, but her blaster bolt only glanced off his armor. She aimed under his arms, at the known weak spot.

A gray streak vaulted past her. Olmahk plunged toward the Yuuzhan Vong's throat.

A second alien vaulted over the balcony, hit the ground running, and came at her. Leia fell against the duracrete door, slamming it shut with her children on the other side. She didn't stop firing until the alien's hands closed on her shoulders, wrenched her away from the door, and then drove her against it.

She crumpled into darkness.

Jacen pounded down the laser-straight tunnel, chasing Jaina. She ran as if she had an assassin droid at her heels.

"Do you have any idea what direction we're going?" he demanded.

"North. When we hit the main mines, bear to the right, toward the transmitter."

The main mines. Was Nom Anor still down here?

Jacen grabbed her hand. Jaina almost yanked it free.

"What?" she demanded.

"We've got to go back," he said. This made no sense, but at the back of his mind, something huge and white was spinning. "We can't leave her."

"What? Hello. Duro to Jacen. She sent us away. She's getting real good at that."

"This doesn't feel right." Jacen listened hard, to the place inside himself where he used to find wisdom. It lay silenced. *Help,* he begged. *What do I do?*

"This doesn't feel right," he repeated. "Go ahead, get to the freighter. Warn Dad what's going on, call Luke and Mara. Tell them I'm going back."

In the distance, there was a throbbing head.

Leia didn't want to get anywhere near it, but something kept pushing her closer, until finally she went inside.

Then she realized she was lying on her back, eyes tightly closed.

Memory returned in pieces. She didn't move, barely dared to breathe, waiting for some hint, some clue, of where she lay. She didn't feel any bonds, any shock cuffs, any binders—anything amiss except that horrible headache, centered behind her left ear.

She did know enough about using the Force to turn that down a few notches.

Then she listened hard.

"Get up, Administrator Organa Solo."

The voice seemed to echo, and she recognized it. She lay still a moment longer, reaching out with her other senses. All other humans must have fled the building. Most vitally, she couldn't feel Jacen or Jaina close by. Either they'd escaped, or . . .

No. The Yuuzhan Vong had *not* killed them.

"We are aware," the familiar voice said, "of when you regained consciousness. Get up. Show the courage that proves you worthy."

Then she knew the voice. She'd heard it over her comlink, but never in person.

She opened her eyes. They showed a gray, weirdly slanted duracrete ceiling.

Stairwell. She'd been felled outside the storeroom. At the edge of her vision, duracrete spiraled up into the distance.

A Yuuzhan Vong stood between her and the nearest gray wall. He was smaller than many, with most of his head covered by tattoos. What little hair he had grew in a black tuft at the back. He wore a khaki-colored tunic over a thinner-looking version of the black body armor. But his face . . .

The nose was barely present, like two dark holes opening directly into his skull. The right eye was pale blue, with the eerie stripe of a feline pupil. The thing in his left socket was no eye. It looked leathery, except at the center, where a vertical slit split it like another pupil.

The creature held her lightsaber in one hand.

"Dr. Cree'Ar, I presume," she said. "Or should I say, Nom Anor?"

"We have met," he said, stretching his lips in a parody of a smile.

She sat up, rested her back against a rough wall, and straightened her head wrap. Now she saw three more of the alien warriors, one standing guard on the next landing up, two more behind her ersatz researcher.

"So you solved our problems," she said, "using Yuuzhan Vong biotechnology."

"In part," he said. "I have dabbled in the kind of alchemy that can change your more useless microbes into powerful tools."

"You made Mara sick. But here, you were only stalling. Distracting us."

"You learn wisdom."

"I suppose," she said, also stalling—in the hope that her children would be far away before the aliens realized she hadn't come alone.

Alone? What about Olmahk?

For her to be here, they must have killed him.

Chewie, Elegos, Abbela, and now Olmahk. Again, they made this war personal.

"I suppose," she went on, "you actually have everything you'll need to clean up Duro yourselves."

"That is nothing to you. If the warmaster chooses to do so, he will."

Warmaster? "Who is that?"

The alien's lips drew back, exposing even more of his teeth. "Get up," he said, "and I'll show you."

Her legs moved stiffly. Nom Anor and his muscular

cronies walked her up the stairs, into her own office-quarters.

The alien who waited between her equipment lockers and her desk was half a head taller than even his tallest guard. Large, rust-colored armor scales covered his body from neck to knees. His lips had multiple slits, his elongated head was tattooed, and a channel-like groove crossed the top of his head, almost from one ear to the other. She didn't want to guess how he'd gotten it.

A smaller alien, with painful-looking black burn scars crossing her cheeks, offered the warmaster something on a tray. As he picked it up, pinching it delicately between claws that extended from each fingertip and knuckle, she saw that it looked like a worm.

She glanced aside. She'd left her bunk rumpled, rising in a hurry. The remains of her breakfast still sat on a plate beside the focus cooker. On her desk's other side, near the tall alien, her equipment lockers hung open. Most of their contents lay on the duracrete floor, smashed into a tangle of ruined components.

The big alien tilted his head slightly and let the worm slide into his left ear.

Leia shuddered and planted her feet a shoulder's width apart. She needed to stall him long enough for Luke and Mara to get back with reinforcements. Long enough for the refugees to escape.

"Warmaster," she said, "your seizure of this dome, this planet, is utterly illegal. You may not—"

"Silence," he ordered.

Over his left shoulder, one of the dark iron sconces still hung on her wall. Something about the intruder's presence seemed to turn its abstract form into a misshapen, multihorned head.

Leia had faced down Borsk Fey'lya. She'd defied Grand Moff Tarkin and a dozen other petty tyrants, but this creature lived by utterly different standards of respect and behavior. She *must* get through to him. To stop the killing, once and for all.

"Sir," she said, "we are both leaders. Our people respect us, and we have many things to say to each other. My name is Leia Organa Solo."

"I know who and what you are. I have vowed to my gods to sacrifice you and your kind. You will merely be the first, and surely one of the most famous *Jeedai* I give them."

Leia's stomach churned. "I am not Jedi," she said. "Not really."

"Our reports say otherwise."

"Your reports are wrong. I have a little training, but that's all. In this galaxy, we have learned to live alongside each other. Surely, you—"

"We do not live side by side with impurity," he said. "Your civilization is built on abominations. Your galaxy is polluted. We have come to cleanse it, so that others besides our warrior caste may occupy it and live cleanly here. It is our destiny, according to Supreme Overlord Shimrra and the priests."

Destiny? She shuddered. "Like this world," she insisted, sweeping a hand aside, "pollution can be cleansed without killing everyone who lives in it."

"It will be cleansed," he answered. "All that mocks life is an abomination. Do you not understand that, *Jeedai* Organa Solo? Your machines mock life. They are abominable. An affront to life. An insult to the gods, who created all that exists by sacrificing parts of themselves."

Understanding flashed through her. These people believed that their own creators had mutilated themselves. Naturally, they tried to follow that example.

"We admire your creature-servants," she said cautiously. "We are deeply impressed by your biotechnology. May I suggest that you, too, have much to learn from us?"

"We are learning," he said somberly. "We have seen that you deny the all-transcendent reality. Instead of learning the most worthy way to meet it, you forestall it, or pretend it does not ultimately own you . . . forever."

"We have also developed creature-servants capable of healing," she said, rising to the argument. "We call them bacta. Other creature-servants help us make food, and—"

"And still you mock death and try to evade its servant, pain. Death, Leia Organa Solo, is the highest truth of the universe."

"No," she said. "Life is the highest truth."

"Death ends life."

"There can be no death where there has been no life. Life binds the galaxy together. Life—"

"Silence, blasphemer!"

The force of his shout drove her back half a step, but Leia was in her element now. "Sir," she said, determined to try angle after angle until she forced his vision open a hair, just a hair. "You and I can speak because we are alive. Your gods—" Yes, he'd definitely mentioned gods, plural. "Your gods can only be served by the living, not the dead."

"You know nothing."

He turned slightly aside and said something in a strange, guttural language. Behind her, one of her guards laughed horribly, and she realized she must've said something that seemed unutterably stupid from their point of view.

"What is it you want, here at Duro?" she asked.

"You," he said, "who mock death, will meet it very soon. Then, for Yun-Yammka—the true master of war—

we will purify this world of the abominable machines in their orbits."

The Duros' cities, she realized with a sinking sensation. Millions of lives.

"We will preserve the people you call refugees, though. Their labor is needed for the task of cleansing this world." He nodded at Nom Anor. "Finally, Duro will become our platform to take other worlds. The ones you call the Core."

Leia's head felt light, as if it were floating over her shoulders. They meant to take everything—and she no longer doubted that they could.

"Sir," she said, "even the gods can't want you to remove all other life from the—"

"You do not speak for the gods! But soon, you will speak *to* them. Tell my master, Yun-Yammka, that more of your kind—more *Jeedai*, our most powerful enemies in this galaxy—will crawl into his presence. Give him that message when you meet him, Ambassador."

CHAPTER
TWENTY-FIVE

One of Leia's captors stalked closer, brandishing a creature with a tiny body and long, outward-curving claws. Did they mean to sacrifice her here and now? Leia backstepped.

"Wait," she exclaimed. "I want to know more about these gods of yours."

The warmaster's laugh was a horrible bass rumble. "That is wisdom speaking. There will be time."

The other alien seized her left arm. The creature he held took her wrist between one pair of claws, then grabbed her other arm, holding her as effectively as a pair of stun cuffs.

The warmaster said something in that other language, and one of her guards grasped her left elbow. The last she saw of the warmaster, he was delicately pulling the long worm back out of his ear.

Her guards took her to a storeroom, shoved her in, then spun her around. One took hold of the creature that held her hands together and plucked it off. Then he gave her another shove and shut her into darkness.

She let herself stand motionless, unthinking, for one moment. She couldn't escape the sensation that she'd evaded death by micrometers.

Then something moved in the shadows to her left. Something huge.

She shrank away.

"It's only myself," a blubbering voice rumbled. "Your fellow prisoner."

"Randa?" she demanded. "I suppose you went to them, offering to ship prisoners—and they threw you back."

"No, no, I swear by my kajidic! I tried to reach your mining laser. I meant to sacrifice myself, and kill as many of these despicable creatures as I could."

"Oh, certainly," Leia said. She'd known too many Hutts to believe this. "You meant to sacrifice yourself."

"But it is true," he moaned. "I deserve nothing better. My repentance is sincere, my mortification utter and complete. I—"

"Mortification?" Leia tried giving the door a shove. Nothing happened. "Where's Basbakhan?"

"They took him," Randa moaned.

"He's dead, then."

"No, no."

They took a Noghri alive? She'd thought that couldn't be done. She wiped a sheen of sweat off her forehead.

"What were you doing with that villip? Answer me, answer honestly, and maybe I'll believe you. Maybe."

He gave a low moan. Then he mumbled, "I tried to bargain. I tried to get them to promise my people a safe world. Would you not try to do the same?"

Was there anything, she wondered, that might buy a world's safety? "In exchange for what?" she asked curtly.

Her eyes were adjusting. Now she could see a long, bulbous tan-colored shape, pressing up against the storage closet's other corner. She couldn't tell if he'd been hurt, and she didn't much care.

He licked his lips with his fat, pointed tongue. "They

want Jedi," he said. "They know nothing about the Force. They want to find out what makes you powerful."

"So you tried to sell me to them? Is that what you're telling me?" How utterly appropriate, then, that they'd locked him up with her.

He flattened himself on the floor. She'd never even imagined what a Hutt might look like in abject misery.

"No," he said. "Not you. Jacen."

Her son? This . . . Hutt . . . had offered her son to the enemy? Her hands flexed, her spine straightened. She would've crossed the closet and tried to take him with her bare hands, but it'd taken a chain to kill Jabba and a lightsaber to finish Beldorian.

Randa probably didn't know about Beldorian, but it was common knowledge she'd killed Jabba. "How dare you," she said through clenched teeth.

He pulled himself even farther away. "Now you understand," he said, "why I tried to sacrifice myself. Not that you believe me." His voice fell dismally into the bass range. "Not that you ever trusted me, or you will ever believe me again. I wish, oh, I wish I could convince you how sincere my repentance—"

"No," she said, "I don't, and I won't, and you can't." On the other hand, she had seen tracks that looked as if Randa had been dragged out of the laser's storeroom. "But go ahead, tell me another lie to pass the time. How did they catch you?"

"I was bending over the laser, trying to activate the repulsorsled—"

"Which you couldn't do," she interrupted. "I coded it to my voiceprint."

"Ah-h." He made it a long, sobbing sigh. "I am glad," he said, "to have been able to tell you this. If no one else ever knows, and we go to our death together, at least I—"

"Oh, shut up," she muttered.

She leaned back against the stone wall. Her left shoulder hit a power-cable conduit, and she shifted to get comfortable.

She couldn't. The warmaster had told her he would destroy all the Duros' cities, then drive on to Coruscant. Only one conclusion was possible: he had more forces on the way.

Bburru, and CorDuro Shipping, had consistently cheated the refugees they'd been contracted to aid. Evidently, though, it wasn't the refugee population in imminent danger of being slaughtered, after all—but the Duros themselves!

She shut her eyes and reached out for her children.

She sensed Jaina's subtle resonance at some distance. Jacen's might be farther away, or closer—damped down. In the mines? she wondered. Or still in her secret tunnel?

She scratched her shoulder absently against the power conduit—then spun around, grasping it in one hand. It ran from the closet's floor to its ceiling. She thought back, imagining the admin building in her mind: which rooms lay above her, which ones below. This conduit ran through the storeroom that opened into her tunnel.

She bent down and swept the floor with both hands.

"Is there some way I might help?" Randa asked.

"I want a pebble," she snapped. "There are always pebbles falling out of our duracrete. The factory never quite got the formula right—"

"Here, Administrator."

Something fell almost into her lap. She groped toward the noise it made, found the pebble, and seized it in one hand.

"Thanks," she murmured.

She tapped out a distress signal in the old Mon Cal blink code. Naturally, no one answered.

She stood up, flattened her palms against the closet door, and gave it another push. It still didn't budge.

"I tried that, too," Randa offered. "But if you think my weight, added to yours, might—"

"No," she said. Maybe he *was* sincerely repentant. For the moment.

Or just suitably scared of her.

She sat down again.

She had only one thing left to try, but she hesitated. If she called Jaina or Jacen back through the Force, they might endanger themselves.

Oh, right, her inner voice mocked. *As if Luke doesn't already know I'm in trouble.* She'd sent Jacen and Jaina away, though—insisting they save themselves—and she'd meant it.

But if Luke already knew . . .

She sat down and relaxed deeply. *Luke,* she cried silently to her own twin. *Luke, hear me . . .*

She sensed no answer. Maybe he was in hiding, too.

Curled up on *Jade Shadow*'s pilot's chair, Luke felt a tendril of energy brush against him. Alert for scanners from off-ship, he ducked down into the Force and let the probe pass over. As it faded, he touched it cautiously to confirm its electronic, impersonal nature.

Instead, he caught the faint sense of Leia, and danger, and warning.

Chagrined, he reached toward her. He instantly recognized the sensation of being trapped—and this time, she was in urgent peril. She wanted to make him understand even more, but the rest of it came through garbled. Battles—a warmaster—a threat to Coruscant.

He jumped off the chair and strode aft, toward his X-wing.

Halfway to the hold, he halted. Save his sister? Or stay on station, for the sake of his wife and child? Mara had told him to take off, if he had to.

He tried to get some guidance from the Force. Surprisingly, his clearest impression was that this wasn't Leia's moment at all. Her destiny was established, but within the next hour, Jacen must stand firm . . . or fall utterly.

Drawing down deep into the Force, Luke stretched out toward Jacen, and then to Leia. Was she doomed? He couldn't tell. Jacen remained closed off to him, walled inside his own barricades. Luke's shoulders slumped.

Jaina responded instantly, though. He even felt the assurance that Jaina was already returning to try to help her mother. Linked with her, now, circumventing the irritation Jaina usually showed toward Leia, Luke sensed her love for the woman who was so much like herself. Her first friend, her role model.

Maybe Jaina could get through to Jacen, too.

He reached for Leia again. If she were deliberately opening herself to him, he might be able to catch some memory, some image, that he might relay to Jaina. He had to save her, and Jacen.

The only clear image in her mind showed her tapping against a conduit with a pebble, and a location. He sent that to Jaina—

Then he caught a whistle from *Shadow*'s comm board. He hustled back to the pilot's chair.

"Skywalker," he answered.

"Luke, it's Hamner. I'm sorry, but it isn't good news."

"No reinforcements?"

"None. Sounds like you'd better evacuate, if you can."

"Good try, Kenth."

Luke sensed a shipyard crew approaching in the

corridor outside. He pulled back into hiding, closing his hand on his comlink. He had to get Hamner's word to Mara.

Wasn't there some way to help Jacen and Leia?

Jacen pulled himself into the smallest possible shape and waited for heavy footsteps to pass by in the stairwell. Five minutes ago, sick of slinking and wondering, he'd reentered the admin building. He'd found the smashed bits of a U2C1 housekeeping droid, plastic legs and shredded tubing scattered in the stairwell. Then this empty cubicle, exactly large enough to hold such a droid. Something nibbled at the back of his mind. Once again, something enormous was trying to break through, something out of the infinite. A warring urge tempted him to simply spring out of the cubicle and have done with all his struggles.

Wait. The sensation came through plainly.

Anguished—almost angry, now—he dug his finger-nails into his ankles. *Wait for what?* he screamed back.

Han leaned against a stone wall. Returning toward the underground gathering place from Gateway's last hidden hauler, he'd found Leia's GOCU antenna. He promptly patched in his comlink. He got no answer from Leia or Jaina, but C-3PO picked up.

"No sign of 'em, Threepio?"

In his mind he saw the protocol droid, perched in the *Falcon*'s offset cockpit, standing watch out on that bluff.

"No more of the alien ships have appeared, Captain Solo—"

"Check the sensors. What's on approach?"

Brief pause. Behind him, Han heard the soft shuffling of hundreds of feet, refugees making their way past him, up the tunnel toward Droma.

"Nothing, Captain. For the moment, it still appears as if the enemy has deployed only the small task force—"

"Good enough, Goldenrod. Be ready to fire it up the second I get there."

He tried Leia once more, then flicked off the comlink and stuck it deep in a pocket. He didn't like her silence.

One of the shaved-down Ryn paused alongside him. "Get through?" Han recognized Romany's voice.

"Yeah. Doing all right?" Han murmured.

Romany's blue jumpsuit sagged on his arms. He brandished his own comlink. "R'vanna says the last ones have gotten down into the tunnel."

"Good enough."

"Where are your children?"

"Probably with their mother." *I hope.* Han peered ahead. Just beyond this point, they were entering the most dangerous section, where the ancient mining tunnel joined Leia's scientists' recent dig, connecting their lab with the marshes. Here, if anywhere, there could be a trap—

As if on cue, he heard a soft *crack* overhead. Then a *crackle* that seemed to go on for a full minute. Gravel sprinkled his leather helmet.

"Don't panic," he muttered to Romany. "Not yet, anyway . . ."

Unbelievably, no one cried out. Far behind, a section of ceiling dumped itself on refugee heads. He heard gasping noises, saw and felt a press of bodies surge toward him. But even the children stayed quiet.

"What'd you do to them, Romany?" he demanded.

The Ryn shrugged. "They know if they're heard, we're all dead. They've been running so long they're starting to get good at it."

Mentally Han cursed the Yuuzhan Vong. He turned and moved on.

At tunnel's end, daylight shone faintly. Droma had scavenged an old cargo-stacking frame off the hauler and painstakingly pushed it along the cliff's base toward the tunnel. As he moved it, he—and a growing number of refugees—kept stacking hay over it, creating a tunnel. Han was able to move this largest group yet onto the hauler without being seen from outdoors.

As they streamed past—human, Vor, Vuvrian, here and there a Gotal and a Snivvian—he ducked against the hay frame with Droma. Now that it was time to say good-bye, he didn't want to do it.

Neither did Droma, evidently. "If we can break orbit, I'm going to head out the Trade Spine. Senex-Juvex might still be taking refugees."

"You've changed," Han said bluntly. "What happened to the loudmouth I met back at Ord Mantell?"

"Guess he died," the Ryn said somberly. He pulled off his red and blue cap, knocked straw out of it, and replaced it at the usual angle. "With about half of his clan."

"If I find any stragglers, I'll put 'em on the *Falcon*."

"Right," Droma said. "You know," he said wistfully, "I really wanted to meet Luke Skywalker."

Han laughed shortly. "You did. On board the *Queen of Empire*—"

"Not to *talk* with him."

Han shrugged. "I'll send him along someday." He backhanded the Ryn's bristly upper arm. "Keep your scanners up."

"You know, Solo, for such a mouthy human you've got a good heart."

The line's end passed them by. Droma fell in with the stragglers, hustling them along. They'd agreed he would wait for Han to signal when the *Falcon* was ready to run for open space. Han would escort him to the jump point, then head in his own direction—with Leia and the kids. He thumbed the comlink, but once again, none of them answered.

He was turning toward the tunnel when Droma came dashing back. "Comm unit's dead," he puffed. "Transmitter seems to be functioning, it's just the voice pickup. Let me patch in your comlink."

Han hesitated, then decided he could talk to the kids from the *Falcon*—and it was high time he got there. He handed Droma the link. "We were even on that running rescue total," he said. "I think you owe me, now."

"Put it on my account," Droma said.

Leia's prison door opened wide enough for a clawed hand to reach down, leaving a pitcher of water and a bowl full of something that squirmed. Randa snored softly in his corner. She sniffed the water. It seemed all right. She took a cautious taste, rolling the sip over her tongue, listening hard for the infant danger sense that protected Luke and Mara so effectively. She sensed no warning, so she drank thirstily. Then she considered the bowl. No matter how hungry she got, she couldn't face *that*.

She nudged Randa's midsection with her foot. "Hey," she said. "Dinner."

He came awake quickly, blinking his huge black eyes.

"It's something you'd like." She shoved the bowl into his small hands.

"Oh," he exclaimed. "It's been so long."

She turned away, repulsed by his appetites.

A faint pinging that had gone on for several seconds finally caught her attention. It seemed to be coming from the conduit.

She pressed closer. In blink code, she heard letters

formed by long and short groups of pings. R-M-E. Pause. C-A-N-Y-O-U-H-E-A-R-M-E. Pause.

By this time, she'd found her pebble again. She pinged back, "W-H-O-I-S-T-H-I-S."

"Jaina," the answer came. "What floor you on?"

Exultant, Leia stretched out through the Force. There, indeed, was her daughter. From Jaina's mind came images of Luke hiding shipboard, docked at Bburru, and of Mara speaking with the Duros military command—but nothing from Han. For secrecy's sake, Jaina had switched off her comlink.

Laboriously, Leia spelled out the warmaster's threefold threat as she formed explanatory images in her mind. The others *must* know about the incredible danger to the Duros cities, word for word, exactly as the warmaster threatened. Also the impending enslavement of refugees, and the promised strike on the Core.

"Warn Mara," she concluded, sliding back into signaling mode. "Use GOCU transmitter. Hurry, then come back. Randa prisoner also."

Jaina pinged back, "Get you first."

"No. No. Warn Mara first. Get Han, come back," Leia answered.

Silence. The warm echo at the back of her mind faded, cooled, vanished. She counted off almost a minute. Then, "OK," Jaina pinged back.

Leia sank back down, dropped the pebble, and rested her elbows on her knees.

Four armed Duros waited for Mara at the top of the lift.

"Charming," she said. "A welcoming committee. I need to speak with the admiral."

"You're under arrest," the Duro wearing the most stripes on his collar snapped.

"On what charge?" Mara demanded.

"Trespassing on military property, to starrrt."

"Mm." Mara flexed her hands, holding them close to her blaster and lightsaber. "Tell you what. You can try to lock me up, in which case either you'll end up on the floor or else as Yuuzhan Vong sacrifice bait . . . or you can take me to see Admiral Wuht first. If he still wants me locked up, I'll go peacefully. Think you could handle that?"

The lead Duros' eyes blinked once. "This way," he ordered.

She followed him, ready to make a break the moment he took a wrong turn. But less than a minute later, the escorts marched her into a private dining room, where a Duros sat next to two burly humans. The Duros' charcoal-gray uniform had filigreed epaulettes, white shoulder cords, and a row of stars around his collar.

"Admiral," Mara said. "My name is Mara Jade Skywalker. I urgently need to speak with you."

Admiral Wuht cocked his long head to one side. He glanced at his human guests. "Interesting," he said. "These gentlebeings just predicted that you, or one of your kind, would force your way in to see me within the hour. And here you are."

Mara got a good look at the humans. The nearer one wore close-cropped hair and sat with his shoulders slumped. The other had a bizarre, distant look in one eye, probably a malfunctioning prosthetic. They openly wore the clasped-hand Peace Brigade insignia, one hand recognizably human, the other hand completely tattooed.

They always left off the claws.

"Good," she said. She leaned both hands on the back of the nearest repulsor chair. "Admiral, I don't know what you've been told about the chances of a second

Yuuzhan Vong attack on this system, a final one, but we have reason to believe it's imminent."

"They are coming to take possession of the planet's surface," the slump-shouldered human said. "They have no interest in the Duros' cities, and there is no reason we cannot coexist peacefully with them."

Mara glared. "So you sold them what, half a million refugees to be sacrificed?"

He spread his hands. His bad-eyed friend slipped both hands under the tabletop.

Mara got a grip on her lightsaber, beneath her long tunic. "I know you've been told to believe they have no use for your orbital cities, and that they'll leave them alone," she told the admiral. "I assume you struggled with the decision to let them take hundreds of thousands of lives, down there, once *this* slime got to you. But your own people are your priority, and this is war. Am I close?"

The slumped one crossed his arms. "I think it's time you left, Green Eyes."

Mara shook her head. "We transmitted back to Coruscant," she said. "We requested reinforcements. They turned us down."

Again, the admiral's glance flitted sideways. His large eyes narrowed, then he looked at her again. "Please make your point, Jedi Jade Skywalker."

"I'm surprised you haven't already seen it," she said. "Have you heard how they destroy technology? Did you see that creature out there, chewing on Orr-Om? Don't you realize they consider technology—all technology— to be an abomination, an offense against their gods? Can you really believe they would leave you your cities?"

"We have been given those assurances," he answered. "It is as you say. My responsibility is to my people. Sadly, I cannot help evacuate your downside settlements. We did try to warn SELCORE against colonizing that surface. Duro swallows everything that touches it."

"So get out of here," Bad-eye said.

"I'll leave when it's time to go." Mara watched his shoulders. If they twitched, she was ready. "First—"

The comlink on her belt toned, and from a distance she felt Jaina's urgent concern. The girl's timing was execrable.

"My apprentice is trying to rescue Ambassador Organa Solo, who has been taken prisoner down there," she explained, raising the comlink left-handed. "Mara here," she said. "I'm with Admiral Wuht."

The instant she confirmed Jaina's voice, she flicked the comlink, turning up the gain.

"Admiral, this is Jaina Solo. Gateway dome still has a GOCU link in the tunnels, and Mom's people hooked it to an external rectenna array. Mom's being held in the admin building, by a Yuuzhan Vong they're calling warmaster. He has told her they're going to destroy the Duros' cities. All of them. She said it was urgent to warn you."

Mara glared at Bad-eye, whose good eye had widened considerably.

"He said that verbatim, Jaina?" Mara asked. "Or was that just an inference? This is extremely important." Mara held the comlink at arm's length, making sure everyone in the room could hear Jaina's reply.

"She took the time to quote him. He told her, 'We will purify this world of the abominable machines in their orbits,' " Jaina confirmed. "And from here, they mean to take the Core. If Admiral Wuht can't hear me, tell him one more thing. We found evidence that CorDuro Shipping has been working with the Peace Brigade for a long time, probably in exchange for a warning to get one city prepped to leave orbit. Sir, if you want to protect the

Duros people, evacuate them to that habitat. Start building its momentum now, because you won't get much time. There aren't many of us who can help you insystem, but we'll help the DDF fly cover for its getaway—" Static interrupted the transmission for several seconds.

"Go again, Jaina. We missed that last part."

"Mom says to hit Gateway dome as soon as her people are out. This guy is high in their ranks. You've got to take him, kill him."

"Can you get back to Leia?" Mara asked.

"Excuse me, Admiral. I've got to get personal." Jaina's voice sounded strained. "She ran me off, Mara. I went back for her, but—"

"She had to get us that message." Mara stared at Bad-eye. His left shoulder was drawing back, just slightly.

"Jacen's . . ."

Bad-eye's blaster cleared the table. Mara used her lightsaber to deflect the bolt. She tried to aim it back at him, but missed by several centimeters.

He toppled anyway.

She backstepped, nearly bumping her escorts, and spotted a holdout blaster in Admiral Wuht's right palm. Now he held it trained on Slump-shoulder.

"You, sir," Wuht said, "are under arrest. Guards, deal with him. I need to speak with Jedi Jade Skywalker."

To Mara's deep satisfaction, two Duros from her escort squad carried Bad-eye out of the dining room. The other two escorted Slump-shoulder.

Mara fingered her comlink. "Jaina?"

No response. Jaina must have left the GOCU station.

Admiral Wuht clasped his knobby hands. "You were right," he told Mara. "We have been betrayed. Somehow, we must cancel the stand-down without alerting the traitors."

"And hurry your people to that other city."

He nodded. "Urrdorf. My forces are shorthanded. How many Jedi have fighter ships insystem?"

Luke on the *Shadow*, shortly to be in an X-wing. Anakin, out on patrol. And herself. "Only three," she admitted. "But Captain Solo has the *Millennium Falcon* planetside, and that's quite a ship."

Admiral Wuht's eyes didn't brighten much. "Then at least we might delay them," he murmured, "and evacuate a few more of your people and mine."

Anakin watched his sensors with half his attention, listening to the Force with the other half. He knew where his mother was, and Jaina, and his aunt and uncle. The Yuuzhan Vong battle group seemed to have lost interest in stray ships patrolling inside the roiling fringe of Duro's atmosphere. His job was to watch for a second wave of attackers. He'd set his astromech, Fiver, to scan space.

He'd picked up the early model R7 droid, most advanced of all the astromechs, on a hunch. R7 droids were notorious for working poorly with any fighter but an E-wing, and it had taken Anakin five attempts and two weeks of tinkering, but now his backseater was as sleek and dependable as his uncle's R2, but fully armored and capable of multitasking at blinding speed.

Anakin Solo would settle for nothing less.

His present course kept Orr-Om in view. The monstrous creature that coiled around it looked like a space slug, thick-hided for survival in vacuum, with a mouth easily eighty meters wide. A squadron of coralskippers escorted Orr-Om as it drifted lower in orbit. Anakin doubted he could do anything to help anyone still inside that habitat.

But if he could blast that creature off, he might keep it

from feeding again, on Bburru, or Rrudobar, or any of the other orbital cities.

On the tactical frequency, he could faintly hear transmissions between some officer on board the Mon Cal *Poesy*, on Duro's far side, and an E-wing patrol. They sounded just as frustrated by Admiral Wuht's standdown as he was.

They weren't Jedi. They had to follow orders.

So did he, supposedly—but he was out here, and they weren't. He had the Force and seven proton torpedoes. If he could neutralize the skips' dovin basals, he might be able to hit the monster.

On his scanners, he spotted the wrecked hulk of that refugee hauler, dipping down into atmosphere. That gave him an idea.

Gingerly, he pushed his throttle forward. "Fiver, give me a readout on that freighter's structural integrity."

Studying the visual display that appeared, he saw that the line of blast scars had elongated, leaving a slash along one side. Barely big enough to fly inside.

"Any life-forms on board?"

Fiver hesitated less than a second.

NEGATIVE.

Anakin's hands tightened. That was terrible news, but it gave him an enormous bulk to work with, without fear of harming any living bystander.

"How 'bout its main reactor? Did it melt down yet?"

NEGATIVE. REACTOR LIVE.

Even better! Flying by scanner and Solo luck and instinct, he closed down his S-foils and maneuvered through the breach into a cavernous central hold. Something had detonated inside, melting through decks and bulkheads.

"Fiver, set up a slingshot pass. I'm going to put our

nose up against an inner bulkhead and try to steer this thing."

His droid pasted a string of question marks on the visual screen.

"I want to pull g's around Duro and launch toward Orr-Om."

More question marks.

"Just do it," Anakin ordered. Even an R7 could be incredibly dense sometimes.

It took longer than he anticipated, first to calculate his course, then to pull down toward the roiling gas clouds and add every bit of acceleration Fiver could coax out of the X-wing's engines. He dialed his inertial compensator down to 95 percent, getting the best possible feel for his awkward hauler-shell.

His heads-up chrono finally started ticking off seconds. By this time, the freighter had picked up substantial momentum.

"All right," he said. "On my mark, decelerate."

The seconds melted down to zero.

"Now," he shouted.

He slipped down into the Force, letting it guide his hands on the control yoke, his feet on the etheric rudder. The X-wing's blunt aft end bumped only once as it slipped out the horrible tear in the freighter's side.

Obviously, the freighter didn't have enough momentum to hit Orr-Om in high geosync. Anakin had allowed for that. He armed one of his precious torpedoes, got a lock on the freighter's still-live reactor, and squeezed his right hand.

The torpedo arced away. Anakin waited for exactly the right moment, then maxed his shields. Facing directly into the inferno, his canopy went black for an instant. The Force guided his hand on the yoke, jinking back and forth, avoiding debris even while he accelerated, chasing a wave of destruction toward the doomed habitat's coralskipper escorts.

He charged them, still accelerating. Cued by the Force, he dumped a torpedo as his targeting reticle bracketed one skip—then a second. White-hot debris had overloaded their dovin basal shields. Each of them exploded into thousands of coral shards.

He caught a third skip with blasts from his lasers. A fourth with torpedoes. Time blurred. Vision no longer registered.

A toothy black maw opened in front of him, and a gullet big enough to drive a whole squadron of X-wings inside. Anakin dumped one more proton torpedo, then snap-rolled away. He pushed his throttle forward and dived toward Duro. Two of the surviving coralskippers gave chase.

On his aft screen, he saw one more explosion—and the monster's head vanished. The rest of it went limp, drifting off of Orr-Om.

Anakin smiled grimly. Now, he only had to deal with two coralskippers. He'd done that before.

CHAPTER TWENTY-SIX

Jacen heard weird, hypnotic music pass his hidden
compartment, playing a melody full of death and de-
spair. Several pairs of armored legs tramped up past
him. His cheekbone twinged.

He imagined himself as Kyp Durron, blasting out of
the compartment with his lightsaber blazing, destroying
everyone who got in his way. Utterly rejecting the idea,
he tried to imagine himself as his uncle, taking up the
lightsaber when necessary, sparing life whenever he
could. Then as Anakin, strong in the Force, unafraid to
use it, but not yet mature enough to see all facets of each
situation. As Jaina, a champion of her squadron, only
beginning her own rise to glory.

Who was *Jacen*?

Again he had the overwhelming sense that the Force
was about to shift. Something was ending, something beginning. He could crouch here until they found him, or
he could commit himself back to the Force—utterly.

But what do you want? he begged.

Again he saw the galaxy sliding toward darkness, and
this time, he realized that standing motionless at its center
wouldn't change the balance. Wouldn't save anyone, including himself.

What if he'd caught that lightsaber Luke flung in his
vision? He would be expected to strike, wouldn't he?

He could do that—on his own. Without the Force.

Or else he could give himself utterly to something he was too small to understand. As Uncle Luke said, there was no middle ground.

He unhooked his lightsaber. He thought back to the times he'd beaten Anakin, to the old familiar feeling of letting the Force flow through him, so that even a Force-dark Yuuzhan Vong's actions could be anticipated. It'd been like warm, living water flowing all around him. It was utterly tempting to go back.

No. He would not go back. He must go on.

Heavy footsteps approached. Leia backed away from the door.

Randa moaned, "This is the end. As night follows morning, as decay follows death—"

"Shut up," she said firmly.

A warrior in black armor appeared in the doorway. He held a snake-headed amphistaff across his body. He pointed out into the room and said something unintelligible.

Maybe they didn't have enough earworms to go around, not that it surprised her. She didn't expect them to want real communication.

Another guard emerged from behind the door, holding the clawed, wrist-grabbing creature.

"That's not necessary," she said. "You don't need to do this. I'm not going anywhere else."

She winced as the claws closed on her hands anyway. The guard turned next to Randa, brandishing a glob of yellow-green slime. He applied it to the Hutt's small hands, then pushed them against his globular sides and gave a guttural command. Randa wriggled his fingers. His hands stayed where the guard put them.

"*Guvvuk*," the guard ordered, shoving Leia's shoulder.

She obeyed, but she didn't hurry. He directed her across the circular landing, back to her office, shoving and poking with his amphistaff. More guards followed them.

The warmaster stood in front of her window, looking out toward the research buildings. To one side stood Nom Anor, again wearing his tunic over black armor.

On the warmaster's other side, a smaller, wrinkle-faced Yuuzhan Vong wore floor-length black robes and a hood that clung to her backswept skull. Flanking her, two lanky attendants held long-limbed crustaceans against their bare chests. Tattoos radiated upward and outward from their chests' centers, resembling explosions in shades of red and orange. A third attendant cradled an enormous, double-skinned drum against her tunic. As Leia stared at the drum, two protrusions near its top opened momentarily, revealing a pair of green eyes.

Leia's guards stopped at the door. Ignoring Randa, she resolutely walked forward.

"Good morning," she said.

The warmaster turned slightly, showing half his disfigured face. Leia thought she saw a smile on the fringed lips.

"Come here," he said.

She walked to the window. Between the research building and the construction barns, the new pit had been dug deeper. Down inside lay a jumble of machinery and construction droids.

"The gods give good portents today," the warmaster said, nodding toward the black-robed female. "It is a good day to burn sacrifices."

Leia gripped the window ledge with four fingers. "Wait! This is an enclosed dome. Open fires will deplete your own oxygen. You must—"

"Your expectations are false. The creatures who

cleanse our shipboard air will purify it inside your built monstrosity, as well. When waste gases increase, they simply multiply faster. Again, you see that technology is no match for life itself."

"I agree," she said firmly. "Life is vital. Living creatures are complex, matchless, and blessed with intelligence. So you must not—"

"All living creatures serve the Yuuzhan Vong," he said. "And we serve the gods." He nodded to the elderly priestess.

The priestess inclined her head, keeping her hands laced in front of her, both arms covered by long, full sleeves.

The warmaster turned back to the window. "Watch," he said. "You must begin to understand the destiny that approaches you all, star by star, breath by breath."

Several more warriors approached the pit, dragging another travois. Leia's priceless mining laser, already smashed beyond usefulness, lay on top of it. The warriors maneuvered the travois into place, raised its end, and pitched the laser into the pit.

Then another black-robed priest led a procession toward the pit, including a second travois. Something that looked like a large tank was balanced on this. As the second travois tipped, a bulbous creature with six stubby legs scrambled out to the pit's side. Leia had seen these fire breathers before. Big ones, at Gyndine.

This youngster trained its proboscis down into the pit and gushed out a stream of gelid flame. Leia glanced up and saw that the dome's synthplas underside glistened with spots and splotches of red and white. As smoke rose toward the splotches, the white ones slowly reddened.

"Your biotechnology is marvelous," she said dully.

"Do not call our servants *technology*," he growled. "We serve the gods, and other living things serve us. This

morning, we will return great honor to Yun-Yammka."
He stretched out one arm, pointing his clawed forefinger
toward the pit. "Witness this."

A line of Yuuzhan Vong guards circled around behind
the refugees. At a signal given by one standing at a
corner, each one let down an arm. Out of their sleeves
slithered long black ropes. In a single, coordinated motion, they bent down for the ropes and brought up stiff,
snake-headed amphistaffs. Then they drove refugees
toward the fire pit.

"No." As helpless as she'd been on the Death Star orbiting Alderaan, Leia turned to the warmaster. "No, you
can't do this. This is wrong."

"This," he answered, "will happen on all worlds. The
worthy ones were removed from the group while you
slept, Leia Organa Solo. Many agreed to serve us. In
other settlements on this world, they will *all* serve us."

Leia stared as the first line of refugees tumbled over the
brink, clawing at the dirt and each other. Grieving, she
looked away. She didn't have to watch them die. She felt
it through the Force, like blows hammering her gut. She
backed away from the window.

The warmaster raised both clawed hands, made fists,
and exclaimed something she couldn't understand. Then
he dropped his arms and turned toward her.

"Now, Leia Organa Solo," he said, "you, too, will
speak to the gods."

The black-robed priestess raised both arms. Her attendants swept out their red-limbed crustaceans. The creatures' long legs locked in an extended position, joined to
the bodies by tendons that now stretched taut, like
translucent harp strings.

The third attendant flicked her huge drum in a slow,
inexorable beat. The other two raised clawless hands

and plucked their creatures' taut tendons. An eerie, atonal music filled the room.

The priestess lowered her arms. Out of one sleeve slithered a black amphistaff. From the other sleeve, one of the furry, red coil creatures rolled down her other arm. It tightened around her wrist.

Leia had seen something exactly like it, looped like a garrote around Abbela Oldsong's throat. She pulled a deep breath, using the Force to stay calm.

"I would be glad to serve you as an interpreter," she insisted. "You need a translator for more than just language and words. Someone who understands idiom. Your earworms obviously can't—"

"Silence," he ordered. "You mistake my intention."

The priestess glanced at him sharply.

The warmaster stepped toward Leia. "My watchers tell us that someone is trying to enter this built-thing. One of your kind, a *Jeedai*."

Jaina? Leia thought frantically. *Jacen? Get out of here, get to the* Falcon!

Or could it possibly be Luke?

He nodded curtly toward the priestess. "We have seen how your people flock to the injured like carrion flies, hoping to feed your dreams of immortality by rescuing each other. You will be honored to serve the gods by suffering. Your screams should lure the other one to me."

"Stop," she said, backing away, refusing to understand. "Think about this. If you kill me, I can't help you any longer."

He stood between her and the window, but there was just a chance she could get past him. And jump. And use the Force to land softly. And lead them away from whoever else had gotten into the building. *It's a trap, Jaina!* She flung that thought out into the Force. *Get away!*

The warmaster stepped away from the window.

A massive tan object lashed at him. Randa's powerful tail, unrestrained by the guards or their creatures, whipped the amphistaffs out of two guards' hands, then lashed again toward the warmaster.

"Run, Ambassador!" he thundered. "I have my wish, after all!"

The gaunt priestess plucked the ropy red creature off her wrist and swung it over her head. Leia rushed Nom Anor, scrabbling with her fingertips for her lightsaber, still tucked in his belt. She wouldn't get far without that.

The priestess launched her rope. In flight, it stretched out to twice its former length. It struck the Hutt's neck and wrapped around like a whip. Randa lashed at the warmaster's guards with his mighty tail. They ducked out of range.

Leia drove Nom Anor against a wall, wrestling to unhook her lightsaber with her claw-contained hands. His nails raked her arms. She hit the activation stud, extending the ruby-red blade. It barely missed the Yuuzhan Vong's foot, burning a hole in the duracrete flooring.

Powerful hands wrenched her away, piercing her arms with knifelike claws. The warmaster's guards dragged her off her treacherous researcher.

In the middle of her office floor, Randa lashed and quivered, fighting the tightening cord with his neck muscles. "Leia," he gasped. "Betrayed you . . . it's . . . my nature . . . I'm . . . sorry . . ."

The priestess's drummer beat a crescendo. The garrote creature tightened again. Randa's huge eyes bulged.

Leia struggled uselessly against her guards. Those close to Randa now had dented and gouged battle armor.

The warmaster stepped around her massive desk, kicked the Hutt's motionless tail, then ordered his guards, "Take it to the kitchens."

Four of them dragged the huge body away. If Randa had been older and heftier, they probably couldn't have budged him, but their physical prowess was staggering.

Nom Anor fiddled with the handgrip of her deactivated lightsaber. "We will study this abomination," he told her, brandishing it. "We will take it down to small pieces and improve our defenses against it."

He thrust it back into his belt.

The remaining guard, the priestess, and her musicians formed a circle around Leia.

Get away, get away, get away. She thought it at the Yuuzhan Vong, at Jacen, at Jaina—at Han, hopefully in the *Falcon* by now. *Warn the Duros, warn the fleets. Get away.*

The priestess raised her left arm again. Another red garrote creature rolled down to her wrist.

Something else grabbed Leia from behind and flung her to the ground. Something heavy and sharp fell across her legs at the knees, blinding her with a double explosion of pain. She bit her tongue.

They struck again. And again . . .

A scream echoed down the stairwell. Jacen flung himself out his compartment's door.

Two alien warriors stood in the passage, one outside the office door where that scream had come from, one closer.

Jacen leapt up three stairs at the closer warrior. The armor itself could be killed, he reminded himself. The vulnerable point was under the warrior's arms.

But at the end of that arm, a black amphistaff coiled like a hook, narrowing its inner edge to bladelike hardness.

The Yuuzhan Vong attacked, taking advantage of his elevation. Jacen couldn't anticipate the warrior's strategy. He could only watch shoulder twitches, subtle shifts of feet. The other's first swing drove Jacen back down into a crouch. He sprang up quickly, stepping past his enemy with his lightsaber at shoulder height. Using his body as a fulcrum, he slashed for the armor's weak spot.

The warrior dodged as the door guard pounded downstairs. Off the bandolier on his chest whizzed three silvery creatures.

Jacen backswung, pushing his pommel toward the warrior's chin. The Yuuzhan Vong swung his amphistaff down, aiming for Jacen's neck. Jacen ducked aside and skewered the first thud bug with his glimmering, ice-green blade. The leering warrior spun on one foot, driving his amphistaff toward Jacen's midsection.

Jacen leapt aside, planting a kick as the amphistaff swept past. The warrior lost his balance and flew over the banister.

Jacen stood gasping for one second, then swung at the thud bugs, dimly aware that the other guard had vanished into Leia's quarters.

The second bug came at his chest. Now he missed the flow of the Force. He backstepped and swung, feeling half-blind. Somehow, he connected anyway. The bug skittered to the ground.

Its partner buzzed toward his head. He ducked, but not quite in time. He felt fire on his scalp as the creature slashed past, slitting his cap. He brought up his lightsaber, trying to stab it.

Without the Force, he just wasn't fast enough. He caught it on the backswing.

Ignoring his scalp wound, he dashed the rest of the way to the office. Panting, he burst in.

His mother lay sprawled on the floor. From her knees almost to her feet, her SELCORE-blue uniform was darkening rapidly with blood. She pushed up on her forearms, opened her eyes, then furrowed her forehead.

"Go," she groaned. "Get away!"

To his horror, three sluglike creatures rolled back and forth alongside her legs, cleaning up the visible red flow.

Beyond her stood the biggest Yuuzhan Vong he'd ever seen, and a small one all in black. Three musicians, covered with tattoos, and a midsize one—with his mother's lightsaber tucked into his belt—stood aside.

"You!" the middle-sized Yuuzhan Vong exclaimed. "The craven one! I thought you remained on Bburru."

Jacen gaped. The Yuuzhan Vong *knew* the Duros had detained him? CorDuro hadn't just sold out. It was collaborating!

Holding his lightsaber at the ready, Jacen stepped around Leia and said, "Let her go." A fully trained Jedi could've controlled blood flow to her own wounded extremities, letting enough through to oxygenate her nerves and muscles, but not enough to bleed to death. Obviously, Leia couldn't.

But Jacen could barely stand, he was so dizzy. The room spun and tilted around him.

"Craven still," the warmaster exulted. "You stand there looking, instead of trying to strike us down. Look, then. Look well."

The warmaster reached toward the small, black-robed individual and said something Jacen didn't understand. Her eyebrows lowered fiercely. She uncoiled something red from her left wrist and gave it to the warmaster.

He dangled it between two claws. "Ambassador Organa Solo, straighten your spine and compose your face. Meet destiny with courage, and inspire this young coward."

The black-robed one stretched out her arms. Her musicians started their ugly, throbbing tune again.

The room spun faster. *Stand firm, Jacen,* he heard.

He could not fight this darkness. Not without the light of the Force. And the darkness must be fought!

Jacen reached inward and outward for the devastating, ravishing energy that was too large to comprehend, too mighty to use without being changed forever. He balanced himself around his glimmering blade—and charged.

CHAPTER
TWENTY-SEVEN

Mara sprinted back up the crowded Port Duggan shipyard arm. Wuht had committed to scrambling the DDF, but plainly, something had gone terribly wrong planetside. Leia's agony made the Force ring, like gaffi sticks crushing Mara's knees and calves.

At the end of her own dock, a CorDuro group barred the way. Mara considered her blaster, unhooked her lightsaber instead, and tipped it up against her right wrist. A flick of her hand would drop it into her grip.

"Excuse me," she said, shouldering into the group of guards.

"Whoa, there," the nearest, a squint-eyed human, said. "This docking arm has been closed. Off limits."

"My ship is docked there," she said. "And I'm leaving." This time, she threaded her words with a hint of subliminal command. "Let me through."

"All ships on this arm have been co-opted by Duro Defense." A Duros stalked forward. "Sorry. You'll have to find another ride."

"You'll have to find another ship," Mara said blandly. "You're not having any luck getting mine open, are you?"

"Oh," the Duro said. "Slip 16-F? We just monitored an X-wing snubfighter launching out of your main bay."

"Right," Mara said. "And the hatch's lock is rather

unconventional, for good reason. If I'm going to claim diplomatic status, you probably want to see my papers." It was an old dodge, and she really didn't expect it to work.

The Duros extended a knobby hand.

"They're on board," Mara said. "Come with me."

He walked her up to the slip. Unfortunately, he brought his goons. Mara frowned. She didn't have time to make this a pleasant farewell.

She touched her in-port lock's corners in rapid order, then pressed her thumb to the center—but that was just for show. Luke had embedded a second locking mechanism under the plating, inaccessible to any non-Jedi. She levitated the hidden mechanical catch, and the hatch swung open.

A voice behind her said, "Now freeze."

Utterly unsurprised, Mara spun left. With one motion, she bent her knees slightly and dropped the lightsaber into her palm. Before the next heartbeat, she'd ignited it. "Don't make me—"

A uniformed Duros stood just behind the near human, pointing a blaster at her. Mara's left leg straightened, sweeping the human off balance. Her blue blade followed around as the Duros fired. Mara deflected the shot, leapt backward into the *Shadow*, and then shut the hatch.

Clanging noises reverberated from the outside. She dropped into her seat, secured herself, and signaled the docking cables to release.

They didn't, of course.

"If that's the way you want it," she muttered. She brought up the repulsors and hit the transmitter. "Docking authority," she said crisply, "this is *Jade Shadow* in 16-F. If you don't want your slip torn apart, I'd release the cables."

Someone babbled at her. By then, her engine lights had turned green. Keeping one hand on the braking lever, she twitched her throttle rods once, twice, in warning.

Then she cut the brake and roared out of dock, trailing the cables and a good-sized chunk of the dock's exterior bulkhead. Metal banged against her port-side hull, and she winced at every crash and crunch. Her external sensors confirmed electromagnetic locks on each of the three trailing cables. She couldn't do much to those.

Besides, an X-wing streaked skyward like a shining dart. "Anakin," she exclaimed, "I'm coming at you. Got some unwanted debris along my port side."

"I see it," her nephew's voice came. "Put your shields up, and I'll—"

"Shields are already up." She steered away from Bburru, into open space. "At minimum extension. Crease my ship and you're bantha fodder."

A blast of laserlight barely missed her port side. She checked her scanners as Anakin flashed past under the *Shadow*'s belly.

"Good try," she said, "but it's still there."

She couldn't fight coralskippers or go to lightspeed trailing that piece of garbage.

The she heard another welcome voice, sensed another strong presence in the Force. "Hold course, Mara. I'll get it."

She clenched both hands on the stick and throttle. From behind, a brilliant light shaft passed so close that the canopy's radiation shield momentarily darkened. Another XJ fighter followed the energy blast, S-foils deployed in combat configuration.

"About time you showed up, Skywalker," she murmured. "Thanks."

*   *   *

Jacen slipped deeper into the Force, committing himself utterly. Though the building seemed to be both spinning and tipping, his senses flooded with a reverent, joyous sense of thanksgiving and homecoming. Yes, he was small. Small people had to offer their hands, or else for all the Force's magnificence, it could do little. He longed to fall into that vortex. To serve the light, and transmit its grandeur.

Wait, he sensed again.

Ignoring his throbbing scalp wound, he slashed at the warmaster's arm as it dangled the red garrote creature over Leia. The big Yuuzhan Vong drew back and dropped it. Writhing, it curled up on the rough floor.

The warmaster whipped out a short, snake-headed baton and held it against his forearm. *"Do-ro'ik vong pratte!"* he shouted. He circled left, taking Jacen's measure.

This one's armor was different. Those scales grew out of his body, giving no clue where its weak spots might lie. Jacen still couldn't sense him in the Force, but now he felt a rippling of anticipation. He would know, microseconds ahead of the moment, where and when the muscular alien would attack.

He also knew that amphistaffs could spit venom. He backed out of range.

"Coward," the warmaster growled. "Unworthy."

Jacen sensed his mother's weakening presence. He buried his worry and used a light, slightly mocking tone to answer, "I'm just not stupid."

Sensing an odd flicker in the Force, he brought his lightsaber up to parry. In the next instant, the short black baton stretched its mouth wide, revealing four white fangs against a cottony membrane. A stream of venom sprayed at him. It boiled and hissed against his shining green blade.

That might be all the poison it could eject for several seconds. Jacen swept in, centering his lightsaber, then slashing wide and down.

The warmaster deflected his cut with the baton, whipping it away from his body, spinning and jerking. Jacen leapt back. At the corners of his vision, the priestess and her musicians edged toward the wall. The middle-sized Yuuzhan Vong had vanished, taking Leia's lightsaber. A door guard paced closer, holding something between hands that suddenly bristled with elongated claws.

Binding jelly? Jacen had time to wonder. *Extendable fighting claws?* "How many of you does it take to kill someone you call coward?" he taunted.

"You are beneath me," the warmaster said. "You are not worthy to die at my hand."

Now, a voice whispered at the back of Jacen's mind. *Fall in, and stand firm.*

Staring the warmaster fully in the face, Jacen dived into the magnificent depth. The galaxy spun and tipped around him.

Seemingly at the galaxy's very edge, the black-robed priestess raised her hands.

Jacen stepped over Leia and raised his own. Power flowed through him, around him, inside him.

A decorative iron sconce flew off the wall, piercing one crab-harp with a *spang*. A chair slid past the warmaster. The alien gave it only a glance, but it struck his door guard broadside, toppling him.

From another corner, several massive equipment lockers rose into the air. Leia's focus cooker floated, hovered a moment, and then joined the spinning vortex with Jacen and Leia at center.

Finally, Leia's massive desk started to slide. It struck the befuddled warmaster, knocking him toward the north window. Jacen half saw one musician fall, struck by the same sailing wall sconce that had pierced his compatriot's crab-harp.

Near the door, someone shouted, "Jacen!"

The warmaster sprang toward him.

He felt the Force bring the desk back around. He heard a satisfying *crunch* of armored scales. The warmaster tumbled out the window. The priestess and her remaining harper lay twitching on the stone floor, plainly stunned.

Jacen scooped up the furry red garrote creature. Jaina sprang through the doorway, lightsaber drawn and ready. She blinked as objects fell helter-skelter. Jacen arranged the red creature around Leia's legs, just above her knees. It hung limp. Struck by inspiration, he whacked the priestess's abandoned drum. The red creature tightened like a tourniquet.

"Wow," Jaina muttered. "I take it you're back to using the Force."

Jacen slid one arm around his mother's shoulders and slipped his other arm under her bloodied legs, already wondering if using the tourniquet was wise. If he cut off her circulation completely, for long enough, she could lose both lacerated legs.

It might come to a choice between saving her legs and saving her life. "You've got to run interference," he told Jaina. "If I use the Force to control her arterial blood flow, I can't concentrate much on where I'm going."

"And you're bleeding, too."

"Not serious," he insisted. "Not like—this."

Jaina raised her lightsaber again. "Follow me."

She led to the stairway, paused only a moment, and then vaulted over the railing. Jacen jumped next, slowing his landing as well as he could so not to jostle Leia. *Hurry,* he told himself. *Hurry.* In his mind, he saw

Anakin's haunted eyes, his dad's horrible grief for Chewbacca. Again he plunged deep into the Force.

Tsavong Lah struggled to his feet, then tumbled sideways. Besides the crushed armor scales along his side, his left foot would not hold his weight.

He made it up onto his knees.

Three warriors, on guard outside this built-thing, rushed up to him. Two averted their eyes, afraid to observe his humiliation. The third glanced up at the window, tightening his lips.

"You were attacked, Warmaster? We will avenge you. Take my life as offering, and make it certain."

Nodding at the perfectly appropriate offer, Tsavong swept out his baton. The warrior knelt, bowing his head. Tsavong swung, putting all of his fury into the gesture.

The underling collapsed lifeless.

"All glory to you, warrior." Tsavong wiped spittle from his fringed lips, then motioned for the two others to remove the fallen one's body to the burning pit.

Four more warriors arrived on the run. Deep, grinding pain jabbed up from Tsavong's wounded foot as they steadied him in a standing position.

"Bring Tu-Scart and Sgauru," he ordered, "and take down this built-thing." He ordered another, "Divert the outflow from the deep well underneath it. Flood the tunnels."

Nom Anor hurried up to his side. "They will not escape," he assured the warmaster.

Tsavong Lah glared at the executor, who had fled while the others fought. "Hope that Yun-Harla favors you today," he said through clenched teeth. "Your—"

"I was forced to retreat." Nom Anor interrupted before Tsavong Lah could lay the charge of cowardice. "The watchers still indicated another Jedi's approach."

Two massive shapes slithered up the street, driven by handlers with heavy amphistaffs, and Tsavong brushed Nom Anor aside. Serpentlike Tu-Scart looped the built-thing with his coils. Chitinous Sgauru attached herself to him, raised up, then let her powerful head fall against the windowless lower story.

Duracrete blocks crumpled like pveiz twigs. Sgauru's maw closed on a cascade of them, feeding with delirious joy. Then she took a second swing.

Han sank down on the *Falcon*'s captain's chair. "Get up here, Goldenrod," he shouted. "Move, move!"

The droid sashayed into the cockpit. "But, sir—"

"Sit," Han ordered, "or I'll replace you with a pair of clamps."

Han flipped a row of power switches. For once, the old bucket didn't whine and die.

"Buckle in," he muttered. "This won't be one of our smoother runs." Why had he sent Droma off on the refugee ship? C-3PO was the worst possible copilot!

He fired the repulsors. The freighter rose bare centimeters into the air.

"Sir, what *do* you want me to do?" C-3PO pleaded.

"Cover the comlink." Jaina had sent coordinates for the tunnel's nearest exit point. As soon as she signaled again, he'd have to move.

Jacen tried not to jolt Leia as he leapt one more fallen warrior. The physical world seemed foggy, less real to him than his invisible struggle to save his mother.

"This way." Jaina gripped her lightsaber in one hand. She led off the bottom flight of stairs into the storeroom and flung open the tunnel door.

A rush of foul-smelling water cascaded out. Jacen turned sideways and let the first flood wash past him, then waded forward. Leia's head slumped against his shoulder. She seemed unbelievably light.

Water would wash away any chance for blood clotting. He couldn't worry about saving her legs anymore. Only her life. With the Force still flowing through him, he virtually stopped the blood flow into her major arteries. The garrote creature, its masters' unintelligent servant, clung tightly, blocking surface bleeding.

He struggled past the gushing water source. At least the flood would push them and their scent downstream, so the Yuuzhan Vong couldn't send tracking creatures after them.

Ahead, Jaina's lightsaber gave off a soft violet glimmer.

Jaina eyed her datapad map. Where this tunnel joined the old mines, the map showed a major drain hole, a vertical shaft. They were traveling toward it with this flow. It would suck them down unless she established an anchor point.

"I'm going ahead," she told Jacen. "Watch for me."

Then she extinguished her lightsaber, hooked it to her belt, and plunged into foul, icy water. It tugged at her mask and made a sickening taste on her lips. She took strong strokes, barely sensing the walls that rushed by. Reaching ahead with the Force, she sensed the deadly tug from ahead as waters poured down the shaft.

She turned about and thrust her feet forward. Then she thrust them down, bouncing herself sideways, out of the strongest current. Each bounce took her just a little farther left. She couldn't see at all, but she'd learned to navigate half-blind. Her Force sense told her when she'd nearly reached the tunnel wall.

Giving one more powerful bounce, she flung herself up and almost out of the water. She scrabbled for a finger-hold on the rock, fell back into the water—and went under. Fear coiled around her, colder and deadlier than the flood.

She fought it aside, got her head up, gasped for air, then bounced herself clear again.

This time, she caught hold of a scratchy outcropping. She unhooked and lit her lightsaber, and saw that she'd missed the deadly shaft by only two meters. She jammed her lightsaber's pommel into a crack in the wall, like a lantern in a sconce, then yanked off the utility belt she'd scammed from the *Jade Shadow*.

Mara had taken *Shadow* on a long sweep out, watching for new hostiles, so she saw them first.

She slapped her transmitter. "*Jade Shadow* to Duro Defense Force," she called. "Big coral at four-five mark oh-six. Look out, *Poesy*."

A Yuuzhan Vong fighter-carrier had appeared at roughly forty-five degrees south, plainly targeting the Mon Cal cruiser. Waves of coralskippers flew off the big carrier's arms. Larger objects followed—maybe attack craft, maybe creatures—not that it mattered anymore.

Mara swooped back toward Bburru, searching her tactical display for Luke's and Anakin's X-wings. E-wings and Dagger-Ds poured back off Bburru and the other cities around Duro's inhabited ring. This time, shields went up on all the orbital cities except Orr-Om. Several explosions had shaken it while Mara patrolled. Its lights had gone dark. It had drifted down almost to blue-line. Or brown-line, in Duro's case.

She'd lost all sense of Leia.

Another Yuuzhan Vong battle group appeared out of hyperspace near Duro's north pole. This group split into four squadrons. Mara's sensors showed each squad with twenty or so coralskippers out front, followed by . . .

something bigger, unidentifiable ... and then more skips.

"Attention," the now-familiar alien voice thundered on her comm unit. "Defense forces, stand down. Go to ground at one of the onplanet settlements, and your lives will be spared. Resist and you will be destroyed. Settlement dwellers, remain where you are. Choose peace, not destruction."

A second voice, a Duros voice, spoke. "Evac ships, vectorrr south. Repeat, vectorrr south. The enemy is coming in from roughly north. Duro Defense Force ships will coverrr any escape shuttle we can."

Mara adjusted her headset and spoke on the private link. "Luke, where's Han? What's keeping him?"

"I'm not getting anything from him." Luke's voice sounded strained.

Another battle group appeared, diving toward a second sector of the orbiting arc. The first group's coralskippers skimmed the first habitat in their vector, blasting away at its defenses. Then the larger ship creature swooped in. It launched something at the city. Mara's sensors went berserk.

"Dovin basal," she exclaimed. "A monster."

Seconds later, that city's shields flickered out. A dovin basal with that kind of appetite could pull down the city, just like Sernpidal's moon.

Small craft popped off the other cities like flak-ants. The first wave of attack craft ignored them. A few evac ships winked out, vanishing into hyperspace. The Yuuzhan Vong's second attack wave caught the lag-behinds. Again, the voice ordered evacuees to go to ground.

Hardly any did.

With the second attack wave came corvette analogs that peppered the cities with asteroid-sized debris. Atmosphere jetted off into space. Here and there something exploded, lighting the city surfaces.

Orr-Om fell faster now, sinking visibly, starting to glow at its edges. Mara blinked. An entire city . . .

Coralskippers and defenders swarmed *Poesy*. Now and then its big lasers picked off a coral ship. Mon Cal cruisers' shields were legendary—almost invincible—but as one of the dovin basal launchers vectored in, and a flight of E-wings tried to divert, Mara guessed even *Poesy* wouldn't last long.

Then a third wave of attack ships appeared. If the warmaster meant to show the New Republic exactly how much force he could command, he was doing a fine job. The number of coral ships appalled her, assembling here for their strike at the Core.

And there'd be no help for Duro from Centerpoint or Coruscant.

Disk-shaped Urrdorf gathered momentum, driving obliquely out of orbit. Admiral Wuht had pulled most of his fighters in toward this quadrant, since Urrdorf was the only Duros city with any real chance of survival. Among its defenders, Mara spotted two X-wings.

"Party time," she muttered, vectoring in to join them.

Jacen heard Jaina calling as he fought the current, trying not to get sucked toward that thundering drain hole. Her presence drew him to the left. Then he saw her by pale violet light, crouching beside a stack of stones, dangling a utility belt's cable. She flung it. He grabbed it, hooked it to his waist, and braced himself against the current, helping her reel him in.

Then he sank onto the stones, chilled and exhausted, getting his strength back.

Jaina leaned toward Leia, touched her face. "She's alive," she murmured, "but barely. Can you go on?"

Jacen's legs ached as he pressed upright. "Go," he answered. "I'll be right behind you."

She paused to snatch her lightsaber off the wall and thumb her comlink. "Dad, can you read?" No answer. "This way, Jace. I'll get out where I can transmit."

Han held his position, waiting. He couldn't grab for orbit until he heard from—

"Dad!" Jaina's voice called out of the console. "I'm out, and Jacen's coming with Mom."

Han hit the main engines. The freighter soared out of concealment and swooped away from Gateway dome. Glancing down, he counted nine bristly landing ships, an infestation of gigantic seashells near the dome's north side.

"Go, Droma," he ordered over the comm. "All shuttles, vector south. We'll be right behind you."

Seconds later, the overloaded cargo ship blasted out of its haystack. Beyond the dome, one blocky hauler and a pair of YT-1300s clawed for space.

"There, Captain Solo!" C-3PO pointed at the sensors. Far below, a lone figure waved something like a glimmering violet candle.

"I see her." He feathered the main engines and swooped down.

"Oh, no," C-3PO moaned. "Those must be coralskippers, coming in at four—"

"I see 'em, I see 'em."

Han set the *Falcon* to hover and dropped the boarding ramp. To his satisfaction, a second figure followed Jaina, staggering out of the hillside tunnel entry.

Then he saw Leia in Jacen's arms, and the blood staining their legs.

CHAPTER
TWENTY-EIGHT

The planet was lost. Far below, its dirty brown clouds swallowed Orr-Om. A cruiser-sized, multicolored hunk of coral was closing fast with one of the unshielded cities. Oddly, it wasn't launching its fighters.

Mara realized it just as Luke cried out over the comm unit, "It's going to ram!" Mara vectored aside, keeping one eye on her sensors. The massive alien ship slammed into the top of the helpless city, which already was caught by the downward pull of the dovin basal launched into its heart.

The coral ship bounced away. Its smooth, lower surface showed no sign of stress, but the city lit it with a dazzling display of sparks and cascading gases. Mara's sensors also showed an ominous, downward vector shift.

Urrdorf was pulling away, but not fast enough. Another flight of coralskippers vectored in. There seemed to be thousands of them.

Luke veered off, and she followed. Yet another battle group had appeared out of hyperspace, and this time, it came from the south, springing the trap on refugee ships that had fled the initial phase of this attack. Three cruiser-sized vessels, their broad red and green arms already deploying showers of coralskippers, were escorted by a dozen or more midsize craft that looked like gunships.

Luke pushed his X-wing back toward the smaller flurry that was Urrdorf's remaining defense force. Mara couldn't help watching behind, though. Urrdorf still had its shields. Coralskippers soared in, splashing it with plasma.

A Yuuzhan Vong force circled Bburru. The city hadn't taken a dovin basal amidships yet, thanks to Admiral Wuht's defenders. Mara's practiced eye spotted another X-wing among them.

A gunship-sized object separated itself from the Vong attack force, coming in low, spraying the city with gouts of brilliant plasma.

"Breaking port," she called. "My sensors show a civilian shuttle launch off Bburru. I'll escort."

Luke soared off toward Anakin. Mara skimmed the city's surface, back toward the dock she'd left so unceremoniously. Someone had a lot of courage, launching this late in the show.

Three small shuttles took off simultaneously, holding together in a row.

"Shuttles," Mara transmitted, "this is *Jade Shadow*. I'll escort you to jump."

"Negative, jump," a voice crackled from her console. "We're headed planetside."

"That's suicide," Mara exclaimed. "They only want you for slaves, or sacrifices. Come around to—"

The shuttles' pilots held to their course. Then Mara saw the triangular CorDuro Shipping insignia on the shuttles' aft surfaces. It looked as if CorDuro, having done all it could to weaken Duro's defenses, was defecting to the Yuuzhan Vong en masse.

In that case, they deserved what they had coming. Mara vectored aside, found herself facing a flight of coralskippers, and went to work.

*   *   *

Jacen bent over the *Falcon*'s narrow first-aid bunk. Though the deck bucked and tilted, Jaina applied a pair of Sluissi grav-press bandage cuffs to Leia's legs, just above the knees, then connected them with the *Falcon*'s medical data bank.

"That should hold her until we can find a bacta tank. I don't know about her legs, though—"

Leia's eyes fluttered open. "Jaina," she murmured. "Heard your voice. Thanks."

Jaina tucked a thermal blanket around Leia's shivering shoulders, then uncoiled a fluid drip and applied it to her bared arm. "Jacen did the hard part," she said gruffly.

Jacen adjusted the bandage cuffs. Finely tuned micro-repulsor fields were already compressing the damaged arteries, even while they enhanced peripheral circulation to his mother's lower legs. Something just as invisible as the field, but warmer, flowed between his sister and mother. A deep understanding, a living connection.

"No. What you did," Leia managed. "Harder. Furious with me, but . . . came back."

Jaina made a wry face, then bent to kiss her mother's cheek. "Lie still. We'll get you out of here."

"But . . . Duro . . . Basbakhan . . ."

"We're evacuating," Jacen said. What *had* happened to her other Noghri? "Basbakhan?" he asked.

Leia's eyelids fell shut. Jacen looked up at Jaina, worried.

"There's a sedative in that drip," Jaina explained. "Otherwise she'd roll down, crawl to the quad guns, and bleed to death." In her voice, Jacen heard heartfelt respect.

"Right," he said. If Basbakhan was alive on Duro, he pitied the Yuuzhan Vong. "Then it's you and me for the guns."

"Take a quad," Jaina exclaimed, flinging herself

away from the bunk. "I'll join Dad. Coralskipper derby, three-way!"

"Mara, Luke? Duro Defense Force? This is the *Millennium Falcon*, escorting a big hauler. Last ship out of Gateway, coming up at you."

Mara eyed her sensors. Vectoring south, accelerating ponderously, came a big block of a hauler, a smaller freight ship, and three YT-1300s. The lead freighter, the one that reflected no light, wove back and forth in a very unfreighterly fashion.

Luke's voice: "Han, is she all right?"

Han sounded tense. "She's hurt bad."

No surprise there, either. If Mara had felt it through the Force, Luke must've, too.

"The kids are taking care of her, but—what?" Han's voice faded momentarily, then came back. "Can't talk. These haulers could use a few more escorts, though."

"On our way." Mara snapped off the comm and studied her sensors. Whether by skill or by Solo luck, Han had herded his charges onto the vector that was seeing the least action.

An enemy gunship appeared ahead of them, though. Almost instantly, the expected dovin basal anomaly appeared on Mara's sensors. She fired a storm of short bursts into it, loading it as heavily as possible. Not far to starboard, Luke's X-wing took a run at the gunship, his guns linked to fire dual bursts—two from above, then two below—then a solid quad burst.

The gunship swerved off course, ignoring the blocky transport to deal with its attackers. Mara pelted the singularity, keeping its shields busy, decelerating to keep from being drawn in.

As Luke set up for a second run, she spotted another X-wing coming in behind him—but also a tetrahedral flight of coralskippers. Stars spun as Mara jinked her ship, evading plasma bursts, still concentrating her fire on that gunship. Sensors showed another anomaly coming up toward her, projected by the coralskippers to devour her shields.

"Luke?" she called softly. "Anakin, this could be trouble."

"I've got the skips, Uncle Luke," she heard.

One X-wing altered course. Even from this distance, she sensed something flowing strong through the Force, as Anakin—without hesitating—reached down deep, with the utter calm of a warrior twice his age. His X-wing bucked and spun, firing constantly. He took two skips before the other two realigned their molten-projectile guns.

From another vector, Luke's X-wing dropped toward the gunship. She spotted the flare of a dual torp launch. The instant she knew the gunship couldn't swing its energy gullet into place and devour them, she broke off her attack, vectored high, and directed full power to her aft shields.

"Got 'im," Luke crowed. Then, more soberly, he called, "Cargo hauler, is that your maximum acceleration?"

She didn't recognize the voice that answered, but she knew awe when she heard it. "Skywalker? That's you, in the X-wing?"

"Right on you. Pour it on, hauler."

"Yes, *sir*."

Mara's sensors showed an infinitesimal acceleration, probably all the battered hauler could manage.

Not far off this vector, a similar hauler plunged back toward Duro's cloud cover, tumbling slowly. Bburru, too, was grappled in six places by objects that might be living ships, its shipyard arm already a web of twisted metal.

Another city, the one that had been rammed, now tilted—plainly falling toward a lower orbit. No more ships left its docks. A flotilla of Yuuzhan Vong followed alongside, and Mara's sensors told her they were using their own dovin basals to pull it farther down. All the Duros cities, except sluggish Urrdorf, were in ruins.

Mara clenched a fist. They were playing. Showing off. Not just overwhelming their victims, but taunting them.

She bit her lip, wanting to slam a fist against her control panel. She opened her hand with an effort and thrust anger away. Anger was poison. She'd had poison enough in her system, thanks to Nom Anor—and there was one small life she still could save. If she guarded that, then her own life counted more than she could have believed possible. *Hang on,* she said silently. *You picked a wild time to come into the galaxy.*

She crisscrossed Luke's path, presenting a confusing target. Now she understood why women willingly died for their children. One utterly helpless person depended on her for sustenance and safety. Silently, she promised that little one the fiercest defender he ever could need.

"She," a soft voice said in her ear.

Startled, Mara touched the earphone. No one else answered or asked Luke to clarify, so he was using the private channel. She touched a control, then muttered back, "Get out of my brain, Skywalker," but at the Luke-place at the edge of her mind, she let him feel how glad she was to know he'd survived this catastrophe, too.

Then, startled, she caught a new sensation—and she knew. "Nope," she exclaimed. "It's *he.*"

The boxy hauler winked out of sight.

Jacen squeezed the upper quad gun's firing control once more, and another coralskipper exploded into multicolored shards. The *Falcon* rocked back and forth, giving him a clear view of another coral shower, Jaina's work, from the cockpit. He could hear his dad's and sister's voices, pilot and copilot. The *Falcon* had never flown so wildly and well.

Urrdorf couldn't make hyperspace, the way Droma's hauler had done, but it accelerated steadily away from Duro's orbital plane, and the Yuuzhan Vong were no longer pursuing. Maybe it could lose itself in the darkness between systems.

"That's it," Han said. "We're breaking off. Good luck, Urrdorf."

"Thank you, *Falcon*," a distant voice said in Jacen's headset.

Then Han, again. "Jacen, Jaina, secure the guns. Get ready to jump. We're taking her home."

Jacen complied, then belted down in the engineering section near C-3PO. From the cockpit, he heard Jaina announce, "Anakin got another one."

"What's he up to? Eleven, twelve?" Han called.

"Don't know," Jaina said. "I'd better talk to Colonel Darklighter about that kid."

"Hey." Han's voice rose. "Luke, Mara, Anakin. You're the last force insystem. Get out while you can."

"Right." That was Uncle Luke. "Break it off, Anakin. Good job."

Count on Anakin to be the last human to get out of Duro space alive, Jacen reflected, but without jealousy. He'd found the balance between the Force's inner power and outward might. By giving himself—obedient, with no reservation—he became a walking, breathing, living sacrifice.

Maybe I caught that lightsaber after all, Uncle Luke.

He sensed Jaina, sitting beside the familiar glimmer that had always been their dad. Stretching out, he faintly touched his brother's incandescent brilliance. Then Uncle

Luke in his X-wing, alongside Aunt Mara in the *Jade Shadow*.

He paused there. Something was odd—different—about Aunt Mara. Not stale or fetid, the way she'd felt when her disease seemed terminal. At this new depth, he felt her shine like a binary star.

Then the *Falcon* hit hyperspace, extinguishing all those presences.

Jacen unbuckled and hurried down to check on his mother's wounds.

EPILOGUE

Tsavong Lah's left ankle throbbed, but Vaecta would no more have deadened that pain than cut off his unwounded foot without appropriate rituals. Tsavong had sacrificed body parts before, imitating his gods' work in creating the universe. Until higher priests arrived, he would stand on a simple artificial foot.

But he would petition the priest for a crafted enhancement. He'd lost that foot as a result of an honor duel. He didn't think the priests would refuse.

Step by painful step, he approached the delegation of Duros and humans who'd just landed, then had hurried here—to this temporary administrative center, pending the arrival of more-appropriate construction-craft materials. A cadre of infidels strode closer, wearing red-trimmed brown uniforms.

Through the reality of pain, he saw them clearly—not only infidels, but traitors. He would not waste time winnowing out worthy ones.

As soon as the delegation stood close enough, he held up a hand, signaling them to halt.

One scrawny Duros stepped forward. "Good sirrr," he said, "we must protest your extended offensive. I am Durgard Brarun, vice-director of—"

"I want information," Tsavong Lah said.

The Duros spread his knobby hands and spoke

rapidly. "Sirrr, we kept the bargain that your Peace Brigade brrrokered. Duro Defense Force stood down. Duro did not defend the planetary settlements or our shipyards. In return, you prrromised to spare all but one of our cities. We fully understood that you would need to make at least one example, but—"

"Tell your grievances to the gods." Tsavong set his weight on that throbbing ankle and false foot, then drew on the pain to focus his thoughts. "I require the name of the young *Jeedai* who escaped your custody." That craven young coward had proved worthy indeed. At the time of highest, best portents, he must be sacrificed to Yun-Yammka.

"I can explain," the Duros began. "He had outside help—"

"The name." Tsavong drowned out the sniveling infidel.

The Duros spread his hands again. "Jacen Solo, son of Ambassador Leia Organa Solo and—"

Tsavong signaled the dovin basal that lay buried nearby. A glimmering containment field quenched the unworthy one's voice.

Then he addressed the executor, who stood nearby. "Your penance here has ended, Nom Anor," he said. "Are the new slaves ready to transmit? Is the villip choir in place?"

Nom Anor dropped to one knee, visibly gloating—but his hands trembled. Plainly, he expected to receive his next promotion. "I will call the villip mistress."

Tsavong waited until Seef approached, leading a beast of burden that carried the largest villip they'd bred to date, still moist-skinned and larval white. At the suggestion of his human contact on Coruscant, the master shapers who had bred and nurtured it to this size had also delivered its stalk-partner to a deep-space beacon, protecting it from vacuum with additional dovin basals.

For this message, he would even use the abhorrent visual technology he found here, though only his new slaves would soil themselves by touching it. They were already defiled beyond cleansing.

The CorDuro officials, who would soon be digesting in Biter's belly, had proved again how easily his enemies could be turned on each other. They would destroy their own finest warriors, a tactic that should make Yun-Harla smile on him, too.

He assembled his victorious forces in a circle near the burning pit, where a savory aroma honored Yun-Yammka. Without activating the villip, he made a short speech to his on-site forces and slaves, declaring Nom Anor's penance complete—and that now, he would be sent elsewhere.

The executor folded his arms across his chest. One cheek twitched, betraying his confusion.

"Give me the woman's foul weapon," Tsavong ordered.

Nom Anor did not dare disobey. He took the light-cleaver from his belt and handed it over.

Tsavong Lah handled it firmly, knowing how thoroughly he would have to cleanse himself afterwards. After several attempts, he managed to make light shoot from one end—false light, a red mockery of natural luminescence.

Now Seef uncovered the giant villip and began stroking, using both arms. She also handed Tsavong Lah a tizowyrm. He slipped it into place. He would not have this speech mocked by infidels. Seef signaled the slaves with their sending apparatus.

He distributed his weight evenly on both feet, sending shooting pain up his left calf. "Citizens of the New Republic," he said slowly, "we speak from the surface of

Duro, a living planet that your forebears murdered, but which we and our new slaves will revive. In weeks to come, we will show you how the might of the Yuuzhan Vong addresses reconstruction—the rekindling of a world."

He drew another deep breath, imagining the infidels beckoning each other to abhorrent mechanical receivers, all the way from Duro to another technology-poisoned world—Coruscant.

"Until now," he said, "we have not declared our purpose. Now we do. We will end here, on Duro. We will suspend hostilities, and live alongside you . . . on one condition."

He drew a long, slow breath. After the judgment he had executed upon Duro, the cowards would want peace—with or without honor.

"Among you," he said, "live some who mock all gods by becoming small gods unto themselves, who abase the rest of you and *force* you to submit to them. We will content ourselves with Duro, if you will help us make one final sacrifice."

He paused again. He let them tremble, to wonder if their lives, their worlds, would be demanded.

Then he let them know they would live. All but . . .

"Give us your *Jeedai*," he demanded, brandishing the light-cleaver in front of him, pointing its blade at the dirt. "All of them, without exception. Any species, any age, any stage of training. Hold them back, hide them, and you see how your worlds will be treated. But I will reward—with special gifts!—the person who brings me the *Jeedai* with whom I especially wish to speak."

He poured hate and pain into his voice. He closed both hands on the light-cleaver and plunged it into the dirt. It sank to its pommel.

"Give me Jacen Solo," he roared, "alive. So that I may give him to the gods."

He nodded to Seef, who covered the villip. He wrenched the foul weapon out of the dirt.

The blade still glimmered, unsullied. Trembling with pain and anger, he flung it into the burning pit.

Luke Skywalker stood steady and straight before the gathered Jedi, his face composed and stronger than durasteel. The set of his shoulders, his precise gestures, the weight and timbre of each word he spoke all confirmed his confidence and control.

But Anakin Solo knew it was a lie. Anger and fear filled the chamber like a hundred atmospheres of pressure, and beneath that weight something in Master Skywalker crumpled. It felt like hope breaking. Anakin thought it was the worst thing he had ever felt, and he had felt some very bad things in his sixteen years.

The perception didn't last long. Nothing was broken, only bent, and whatever it was straightened, and Master Skywalker was again as strong and confident in the Force as to the eye. Anakin didn't think anyone else had noticed it.

But *he* had. The unshakable had shaken. It was something Anakin would never forget, another of the many things that had seemed eternal to him suddenly gone, another speeder zooming out from underneath his feet, leaving him flat on his back wondering what had happened. Hadn't he learned yet?

He forced himself to focus his ice-blue eyes on Master Skywalker, on that familiar age- and scar-roughened face. Beyond him, through a huge transparisteel window, flowed the never-ending light and life of Coruscant. Against those cyclopean buildings and streaming trails of light, the Master seemed somehow frail or distracted.

Anakin distanced himself from his heartsickness by concentrating on his uncle's words.

"Kyp," Master Skywalker was saying, "I understand how you feel."

Kyp Durron was more honest than Master Skywalker, in some ways. The anger in his heart was no stranger to the expression on his face. If the Jedi were a planet, Master Skywalker stood at one pole, radiating calm. Kyp Durron stood at the other, fists clenched in fury.

Somewhere near the equator the planet was starting to pull apart.

Kyp took a step forward, running his hand through dark hair shot with silver. "Master Skywalker," he said, "I submit that you do *not* know how I feel. If you did, I would sense it in the Force. We all could. Instead, you hide your feelings from us."

"I never said I *felt* as you do," Luke said gently, "only that I understand."

"Ah." Kyp nodded, raising one finger and shaking it at Skywalker as if suddenly comprehending his point. "You mean you understand *intellectually*, but not with your heart! The Jedi you trained and inspired are hunted and killed throughout the galaxy, and you 'understand' it the way you might an equation? Your blood doesn't burn to *do* something about it?"

"Of course I want to do something about it," Luke said. "That's why I've called this meeting. But anger is not the answer. Attack is not the answer, and retribution most certainly is not. We are Jedi. We defend, we support."

"Defend who? Support what? Defend those beings you rescued from the atrocities of Palpatine? Support the New Republic and its good people? Shield the ones we have all shed blood for, time and again in the cause of peace and the greater good? These same cowardly beings who now defame us, deride us, and sacrifice us to their new Yuuzhan Vong masters? No one *wants* our help. They want us dead and forgotten. I say it's time we defend ourselves. Jedi for the Jedi!"

Applause smacked around the chamber—not deafening, but not trivial either. Anakin had to admit, Kyp made a certain amount of sense. Who could the Jedi trust now? Only other Jedi, it seemed.

"What would you have us do, then, Kyp?" Luke asked mildly.

"I told you. Defend ourselves. Fight evil, in whatever guise it takes. And we don't let the fight come to us, to catch us in our homes, asleep, with our children. We go out and find the enemy. Offense against evil *is* defense."

"In other words, you would have us all emulate what you and your dozen have been doing."

"I would have us emulate *you*, Master Skywalker—when you were battling the Empire."

Luke sighed. "I was young, then," he pointed out. "There was much I did not understand. Aggression is the way of the dark side."

Kyp rubbed his jaw, then smiled briefly. "And who should know better, Master Skywalker, than one who *did* turn to the dark side."

"Exactly," Luke replied. "I fell, though I knew better. Like you, Kyp. We both, in our own way, thought we were wise enough and nimble enough to walk on the laser beam and not get burned. We were both wrong."

"And yet we returned."

"Barely. With much help and love."

"Granted. But there were others. Kam Solusar, for instance, not to forget your own father—"

"What are you saying, Kyp? That it is easy to return from the dark side, and that justifies the risk?"

Kyp shrugged. "I'm saying the line between dark and light isn't as sharp as you're trying to make it, or exactly where you want to put it." He steepled his fingers beneath his chin, then shook them with an air of contemplation. "Master Skywalker, if a man attacks me with a lightsaber, may I defend with my own blade, that he not take my head off? Is that too aggressive?"

"Of course you may."

"And after I defend, may I press my attack? May I return the blow? If not, why are we Jedi *taught* lightsaber battle techniques? Why don't we learn only how to defend, and back off until the enemy has us in a corner and our arms grow tired, until an attack finally slips through our guard? Master Skywalker, sometimes the only defense *is* an attack. You know this as well as anyone."

"That's true, Kyp. I do."

"But you back down from the fight, Master Skywalker. You block and defend and never return the blow. Meanwhile the blades directed against you multiply. And you have begun to lose, Master Skywalker. One opportunity lost! And there lies Daeshara'cor, dead. Another slip in your defense, and Corran Horn is slandered as the destroyer of Ithor and driven to seclusion. Again an attack is neglected, and Wurth Skidder joins Daeshara'cor in death. And now a flurry of failures as a million blades swing at you, and there go Dorsk 82, and Seyyerin Itoklo, and Swilja Fenn, and who can count those we do not know of yet, or who will die tomorrow? *When* will you attack, Master Skywalker?"

"This is ridiculous!" a female voice exploded half a meter from Anakin's ear. It was his sister, Jaina, her face gone red with internal heat. "Maybe you don't hear all the news, running around playing hero with your squadron, Kyp. Maybe you've started feeling so self-important that you think your way is the only way. While you've been out there blazing your guns, Master Skywalker has been working quietly and hard to make sure things don't fall apart."

"Yes, and see how well that's gone," Kyp said. "Duro, for instance. How many Jedi were involved there? Five? Six? And yet not one of you—Master Skywalker included—smelled the rank treachery of the situation until it was too late. Why didn't the Force guide you?" He paused and then smacked a fist into his palm for emphasis. "Because you were acting like *nursemaids*, not Jedi warriors! I've heard one of you even refused to use the Force." He looked significantly at Jaina's twin, who sat stone-faced halfway around the hall.

"You leave Jacen out of this," Jaina snarled.

"At least your brother was honest in his refusal to use his power," Kyp said. "Wrong, but honest, and in the end when he had to use it, he did. The rest of this group has no excuse for its ambivalence. If saving our galaxy from the Yuuzhan Vong is not a good enough cause to flex our true might, let self-preservation be!"

"Jedi for Jedi!" Octa Ramis shouted, still in the clutches of renewed grief over losing Daeshara'cor.

"It's both ourselves and the galaxy I'm trying to preserve," Luke said. "If we win the fight against the Yuuzhan Vong at the price of using dark-side powers, it will be no victory."

Kyp rolled his eyes and crossed his arms. "I knew it was a mistake to come here," he said. "Every second I waste talking with you is a torpedo I might be firing at the Yuuzhan Vong."

"If you knew that, why did you come?"

"Because I thought even you must see the pattern on the Huj mat by now, Master Skywalker. After months of doing nothing, of watching our numbers dwindle, of listening to the lies circulating about the Jedi from the Rim to the Core, I thought now, at last, you had decided it was time to act. I came, Master Skywalker, to hear you say enough is enough, to lead the Jedi, united, in a just cause. Instead I hear only the same vacillating I've grown tired of."

"On the contrary, Kyp. I called this meeting to make some real decisions about how we should face this crisis."

"This isn't a crisis," Kyp sputtered. "It's a massacre. And I already know what to do. I've been doing it."

"The people are frightened, Kyp. They're living in a nightmare, just as we are. They only want to wake up."

"Yes. And in hopes of waking up, they feed the dream monsters whatever they ask for. Droids. Cities. Planets. Refugees. Now Jedi. By refusing to act against this treachery, Master Skywalker, you come dangerously near condoning it."

"Bantha fodder!" Jacen snapped, finally breaking his silence. "Master Skywalker hasn't been complacent. None of us has. But the sort of naked aggression you condone is—"

"Effective?" Kyp sneered.

"Is it?" Jacen challenged. "What have you and your squadron really accomplished? Harried a few Yuuzhan Vong supply ships? Meanwhile we've saved tens of thousands—"

"Saved them for what? So they can flee from planet to planet until there's nowhere else to go? Jacen Solo, who denied the Force, are you lecturing *me* on what is and isn't effective?"

"What isn't effective is this argument," Luke interjected. "We need calm. We need to think rationally."

"I'm not sure that's what we need at all," Kyp shot back. "Look where your *rational* policies have gotten us. We're alone, now, don't you all see that? Everyone has turned against us."

"You're overstating."

Anakin switched his gaze to the new speaker, Cilghal. The Mon Calamari's fishlike head bobbed as her bulbous eyes searched around the chamber.

"We still have many allies," Cilghal said, "in the senate and among the peoples of the New Republic."

"If by allies you mean people without the guts to actually turn us in, yes," Kyp said. "But wait a bit. More Jedi will be killed or captured. Stay here, meditate, and wait for them. I won't. I know what the fight is and where it is." With that he turned on his heel and started from the chamber.

"No!" Jaina whispered to Anakin. "If Kyp leaves, he'll take too many with him."

"So?" Anakin said. "Are you so sure he's wrong?"

"Of course I—" She stopped, paused, started again. "It won't help any of us if the Jedi split. We have to try to help Uncle Luke. Come on."

Jaina followed Kyp from the chamber. After a second or two, Anakin followed. The debate began again behind them, in much more muted terms.

Kyp turned as they approached. "Anakin, Jaina. What do you want?"

"To talk some sense into you," Jaina said.

"I have plenty of sense," Kyp said. "You two ought to know better. When did either of you flinch from battle? It's not like you two to sit while others fight."

"I haven't been," Jaina flared. "Neither has Anakin, or Uncle Luke, or—"

"Spare me. Jaina, I have the greatest respect for Master Skywalker. But he is *wrong*. I can't see the Yuuzhan Vong in the Force any more than he can, but I don't need that to know they're evil. To know they have to be stopped."

"Couldn't you just hear Uncle Luke out?"

"I did. He didn't say anything I was interested in, and he wasn't going to." Kyp shook his head. "Your uncle has changed. Something happens to Jedi Masters as they grow older in the Force. Something that isn't going to happen to me. They become so concerned with light and dark they can't *act*, but can only be acted upon. Like Obi-Wan Kenobi—rather than act himself, he allowed himself to be struck down, become one with the Force, so Luke could then take all of the moral risks."

"That's not how Uncle Luke tells it."

"Your uncle is too close to it. And now he's *become* Kenobi."

"What are you saying, exactly?" Jaina said. "That Uncle Luke is a coward?"

Kyp shrugged and flashed a little smile. "When it comes to his life, no. But when it comes to the Force . . ." He gestured with the back of his hand. "Ask your brother Jacen—seems to me he's going gray early, in that respect. The whole galaxy is falling apart around him, and he's dithering over theoretical philosophy."

"He did use the Force, though, as you pointed out," Jaina retorted.

"To save his mother's life, from what I heard, and almost not then. How long was she in a bacta tank?"

"But he *did* save her, and me, too."

"Of course. But would he have called on the Force to save some Duros he didn't know? Given the fact that he had ample opportunity to do so before that, the answer is self-evidently no. So it wasn't some universal respect for preserving life or anything of that sort that led him to break his self-imposed ban, was it?"

"No," Anakin murmured.

"Anakin!" Jaina snapped.

"It's true," Anakin replied. "I'm glad he did it, and I'm glad he hurt the warmaster, even if he did call for the heads of all the Jedi, but Kyp's right. If you and Mom hadn't been there . . ."

"Jacen was going through a hard time," Jaina said.

"Like the rest of us aren't," Anakin returned.

"I've got to go," Kyp told them. "Any time either of you wants to fly with me, find me. Other than that, I sincerely hope Master Skywalker comes around. I just can't wait for it. May the Force be with you."

They watched him go.

"I wish I didn't more than half think he was right," Jaina whispered. "I feel like I'm somehow betraying Uncle Luke."

Anakin nodded. "I know what you mean. But Kyp *is* right, about one thing anyway. Whatever else we do, we're going to have to look out for our own."

"Jedi for Jedi?" Jaina snorted. "Uncle Luke knows that. I'm not sure where he sent Mom, Dad, Threepio, and Artoo, but it's got something to do with setting up a network to help Jedi escape before being turned over to the Yuuzhan Vong."

Anakin shook his head. "Fine, but that's what Kyp meant by only defending. We'll never win this war by being reactive. We have to be proactive. We need intelligence. We need to know which Jedi are at risk *before* they come for us."

"How can we know that?"

"Think logically. Any planet already taken by the Yuuzhan Vong is obviously dangerous. The planets near occupied space are the next most dangerous, because they're desperate to strike a deal."

"The warmaster said he would spare the rest of the galaxy, but only if they turn *all* of us over to them. That sort of spreads the desperation out, at least for people dumb enough to believe him. We saw what Yuuzhan Vong promises meant on Duro. Don't cooperate with them and they mow you down. If you do cooperate with them, they mow you down, laughing about how stupid you've been."

Anakin shrugged. "Obviously a lot of people would rather believe Yuuzhan Vong lies than take their chances. The point is—"

"The point is, what are you two doing out here rather than in the meeting?" Jacen Solo asked from the end of the corridor.

"We were trying to talk Kyp into staying," Anakin told his older brother.

"It'd be easier talking a siringana into a box."

"True," Jaina said, "but we had to try. I guess we ought to go back in now."

"Don't bother. A few minutes after Kyp walked out, Uncle Luke called a recess. Too much angst and confusion."

"It's not going well," Jaina said.

"No. Too many people think Kyp is right."

"What do you think?" Anakin asked.

"He's wrong," Jacen said without hesitation. "Answering naked aggression with naked aggression can't be the solution."

"No? If you hadn't used that particular solution, you, Mom, and Jaina would be dead right now. Would the universe be better off?"

"Anakin, I'm not proud of—" Jacen began.

Jaina cut him off. "Don't you two start again. Anakin and I were talking about something constructive when you joined us. Let's not degenerate into bickering, like the others. We're siblings, after all. If we can't talk through this without losing it, how can we expect anyone else to?"

Jacen held his gaze on Anakin for another few heartbeats, waiting to see who would flinch first.

It was Jacen.

"What *were* you discussing?" he asked softly.

Jaina looked relieved. "How to figure out where the worst hot spots are, which Jedi are in the most immediate danger," she said.

Jacen quirked his mouth as if tasting a Hutt appetizer. "With the Peace Brigade out there, that's an open question. They aren't tied to the interests of a single system. They'll hunt us from the Rim to the Core if they think it'll appease the Yuuzhan Vong."

"The Peace Brigade can't be everywhere at once. They can't follow every rumor they've heard about Jedi."

"The Peace Brigade has plenty of allies, and good intelligence," Jacen countered. "Given what they've managed already, they must have more than a few insiders, maybe even in the senate. They don't have to chase rumors. More often than not, from what I can tell, they don't even make half the captures they boast about. They're just the flesh merchants who turn Jedi over to the Yuuzhan Vong."

"I still have a bad feeling about the senator from Kuat, Viqi Shesh," Jaina muttered.

"My point is this," Anakin said. "It's hard to predict

which single Jedi might be next on their list. But if they could get a package deal, wouldn't they jump at it?"

Jaina's eyes widened. "You think they'll move against us while we're gathered here?"

Anakin drew a negative arc with his chin. "Things aren't that bad yet, and who would want to face all of the most powerful Jedi in the galaxy at once? That would be crazy—*us* they'll pick off one at a time. But—"

"The praxeum!" Jacen interrupted.

"Yes," Anakin agreed. "The Jedi academy!"

"But they're just kids!" Jaina said.

"Have you noticed that makes any difference to the Yuuzhan Vong, or to the Peace Brigade, for that matter?" Jacen asked. "Besides, Anakin's only sixteen, and he's killed more Yuuzhan Vong in hand-to-hand combat than any of us. The Yuuzhan Vong know that."

"What about the illusion the Jedi have been maintaining around Yavin Four? That's been keeping strangers away."

"Not since almost all of the Jedi Knights have left," Anakin said. "They've either come to Coruscant to this meeting, or gone off to try to help comrades who've disappeared. Last I heard, only the students Kam and Tionne are left, with maybe Streen, and Master Ikrit. They might not be strong enough. Where did Uncle Luke go? We should talk to him about this, right away. It may already be too late."

"That's a good call, Anakin," Jacen admitted.

"Thanks."

What Anakin didn't mention to his siblings was how he had awakened in the night, heart thrumming, gripped by a nameless dread. And though he couldn't remember the dream that had torn him from sleep, one image had remained with him: the blond hair and green eyes of Tahiri, his best friend.

And Tahiri was at the academy.